BOOTLEGGERS 2

BORROWED TIME

By

Paul Rudd

Bootleggers, Borrowed Time, by Paul Rudd

First Edition

Paperback published by Ravenous Roadkill

Cover designed by Southern Stiles Design.
Edited by Redwing Productions

Thanks go to my awesome cover artist, who always creates a classy cover.
To my editor, who never lets me down.
To every movie maker to have ever lived, without your industrious efforts, this book would not have been possible.

My dedication goes to one of my oldest friends Chris Jay, and his son Daniel.

Your support of the BLU has never waned.

Bootleggers 2 is for you.

Long live the BLU.

OPENING CRAWL ...

Somewhere, in the not-too-distant future,
in a REALITY not THAT far, far away,
but far enough away to not be considered close enough
...
ah, you get the picture ...

BOOTLEGGERS 2

BORROWED TIME

After ARCADIAN'S defeat, balance has been restored.
It leads to a long period of calm for our heroes,
TOMMY, MIKEY, KURT, AND THEODORE.

At least, that's what they think.

Until, in the year 2019, DAISY DREW whisks TOMMY
away from his PEACEFUL existence.

If DAISY fails in her mission to reveal the
TRUTH to our heroes, then peace will never return ...

NOW, FOR THE NEXT INSTALMENT OF

...

BOOTLEGGERS ...

Chapter 1

Where we're going, we won't need phones ...

EVIDENTLY, DAISY'S *fact* bombshell, to persuade the boy she loved to leave his perfect reality behind, made less of an impact than she had hoped for.

Stating the obvious.

A strategy that never failed.

Until today.

Tommy West reached straightaway for a handheld device. She recognized its similarities to one she had used not long ago. A futuristic communicator of some kind.

Her decision to throw it across the room went down pretty much how she expected it to go.

"What the hell did you do that for?" he bellowed.

Through the open visor of her racing helmet, her eyes appeared more intense than usual, like when they were young, which was why it made sense that she threw his phone across the living room.

"Did you hear what I just said?" she ranted.

"Yeah, the kids were taken."

"And your first instinct is to reach for your communicator."

"Duh, how else will we call the authorities?" Tommy reached down for the cell phone, only to see it kicked across the room.

"You're acting as if that thing is glued to your hand."

"Stop acting like you're still living in the eighties. Everybody has a cell phone nowadays."

"We've gotta go, Tommy."

"And before we go, I need my phone."

"Phones. Where we're going, we won't need phones."

Before he could pick up the cell phone, Daisy grabbed Tommy by the sleeve and dragged him towards the Trans Am.

Tommy wrestled himself free from her grasp. "Easy on the arm, Ronda Rousey."

"Are you coming or not?"

"I will on one condition."

"Which is?"

"You tell me who took our kids."

"I will. Not now. We're on borrowed time and the clock is ticking."

"I'm not leaving here until you blab."

Daisy's preference was to wait a little while before she had to shatter her boyfriend's soul. She also realized that their predicament left her with no choice but to let him decide the outcome for himself.

Daisy removed her racing helmet. His open-mouthed reaction was pretty much what she expected. "As you can see, I'm a teenager."

"I can see that."

"My hair is tied up in buns."

"I noticed that, too."

"Which means, we have no kids."

She already knew that the impact of just a few words could easily squash the fragile alliance built up over the last few minutes. Adding her younger appearance to the mix spilled the contents of the logic pool over the paneled flooring.

A teenager's first love formed the strongest of bonds. Seeing her true love struggle to come to terms with her comments showed that, worryingly, their bonds had already started to loosen.

"We have the twins, Starbuck and Apollo," he said.

"They're not real."

"What about Logan, young Tobias. I guess I just picked them out of a make-believe cookie jar?"

"Nothing about your adult life has been real."

"What a crock."

"It's true. Or is the car in the living room just a close encounter of the third kind."

Tommy dug in. "Come on. You mean this house, the carpet, the walls you destroyed. None of it is real."

"Uh-huh."

"Then why tell me that our kids were playing a game, and *he* took them. Who took them?"

"I said it to calm you down."

"Pop quiz. It didn't work. Did you even know that we had kids?"

"Technically, no."

"You guessed?"

"It was more of a hunch."

"You based all of this on a hunch."

Daisy shrugged. "In my defense, I had a fifty-fifty chance of being right."

"That's lucky for you then. Not so lucky for me."

"Fine. The pictures on the walls were a dead giveaway. Tommy, we don't have time to argue about rights and wrongs. And just because you're pretending to be an adult and I'm a teenager, doesn't mean you don't have to pay attention to me."

"Pretending!"

Following the outburst, the living room started to quake. Rows of shelved ornaments shattered on the floor, quickly followed by the television. Sparks erupted from the screen, which remained active despite being unplugged. Over the clamor, the voice that Tommy heard as he entered the room began to spout archaic nonsense.

"Get in the car, Tommy." Daisy slid onto the driver's seat and started the engine.

Tommy scrambled across the room through falling debris and retrieved a scenic photo from a busted frame. The photo showed Tommy, an older Daisy, and their four children as recently as six months ago outside of a tropical island Tiki bar.

"Will you haul ass!" she yelled.

Tommy boarded the passenger seat and jabbed the picture in her lap. "Here! Our kids, with you and I on the beach, this year. Who's lying now."

Daisy glanced briefly at the picture. "Look again, Hawkeye."

Tommy snatched the photo as both doors closed automatically, sealing them inside. The image had already faded.

"What did you do?" he asked.

"Nothing to the photo, but I did interrupt a reality timeline."

"A reality what now?"

"Everything before today is fading away. Your family never existed."

"You mean our family."

"No, your family."

"Mine, yours, ours, what the hell is going on?"

Rather than answer, Daisy focused on the modernized digital dashboard displaying the RPMs, MPH, fuel gauge, and Reality Jump Circuits.

MONTH - DAY HOUR - MIN
DEC 25 HOME SWEET HOME 08:12
PRESENT REALITY

MONTH- DAY HOUR - MIN
OCT 26 HILL VALLEY 01:22
LAST REALITY DEPARTED

The powerful engine forced Tommy to brace the dashboard with both hands. "When did you learn to drive?"

"After everything that's happened so far, that's your first question."

"Oh, there's more to come. Believe me."

Daisy punched in the co-ordinates on the Jump Circuits.

MONTH - DAY HOUR - MIN
JUNE 19 WISHVILLE 09:47
REALITY DESTINATION

"Why June 19th?" Tommy blurted.

"I'll explain when we get there."

The entire house bucked as a colossal wrecking ball barreled through the upstairs. Tommy watched in horror as his favorite furnishing, an $800 crystal light fitting, shattered on the bonnet of the Trans Am.

"Oh, man. I just bought that on credit."

"Buckle up, Buckaroo Banzai. Because home sweet home is about to go bye-bye."

As much as the surroundings tried to, crumbling walls and rupturing floorboards could not stop the duo's hectic escape. Daisy shifted the gearstick into reverse and swiftly maneuvered the Trans Am in a tight U-turn. Gunning the accelerator from zero to 88 mph, she guided the Trans Am towards the backyard and the blistering light of a reality tear breaking through the concrete patio.

A storm he had stirred once before now had Tommy in its clutches. He doubted a backdoor option to renege would be involved now that an ethereal glow beckoned them onwards from what used to be his garden.

With the fabric of reality peeling away, terror came hurtling back at him like a freight train.

"What have you dragged me into," he yelled as the wrecking ball crashed through the living room and bore down on them as if chasing Indiana Jones.

"Prepare for the temporal shift," Daisy warned as an incredible power hauled the Trans Am from the ground, flipped it over, as easily as a multi-axis trainer, and catapulted the car through a portal.

THE link between two realities could only be reached by jumping through one reality tear to another. As they traversed, everything Tommy knew blurred into one vision of the teenage boy that he used to be, now with a haunted expression.

The ghostly image reached out, snatching Tommy by the wrist, the slightest touch as cold as plunging his hand into a vat of cryogenic liquid helium.

"Who the hell was that?" Tommy yelled, expecting his arm to be in tatters.

"What did you see?" Daisy asked.

"Me, looking all dead and stuff."

"And?"

"I reached out and scalded my arm."

"It's one reality trying to stop you from reaching another."

"I knew I should've laid off the weed when I left high school."

"The same happened to me when I jumped to reach you. A phantom image of myself tried to turn me back."

"Guess what. Mine worked."

A world of hallucinogenic, bright colors sped by the car, making the nausea and brain tingling intensify.

"Turn back," he ordered.

"We can't," she replied.

"Turn back now."

"It's too late."

"Young Daisy, I'm telling you. If you don't turn back, I'll …"

Daisy held up a device no larger than a pen. Tommy was looking straight at it when she switched it on. He went into an immediate shutdown mode, his eyelids crashing down faster than two heavy duty Death Star blast doors.

Chapter 2

What's up Buck?

THE INTERIOR of Stranger 5's cockpit had to be seen to be believed. The spaceship's setup allowed the Astronaut access to hundreds of gadgets, switches, terminals, handsets, and thingamajigs, all from a central, padded flight seat.

Tommy West wore a flight suit and comfortable footwear. And yet, despite being the hero, he couldn't shake the feeling that he had all the gear and no idea.

A lackluster voice, over the headset, counted down to lift-off.

With the countdown at zero, the powerful flight engines of NASA's deep space probe vented beneath. Then came the release, and a young boy's wildest dream arrowed towards the stars in the wink of an eye.

Shortly after take-off, cosmic forces blew Stranger 5 and its pilot, Buckaroo Rogers, out of its trajectory towards a black hole.

The vessel's life support controls were quickly frozen by temperatures beyond imagination. This freak mishap ensured the pilot's survival as the craft was transported into a galaxy a thousand times vaster.

Reality and fantasy combined in a timeless dream as Buckaroo became enrolled as a pilot with the Earth Protection Board. Every day brought adventure in the form of huge space battles, within a galaxy brimming with bizarre alien beings and civilizations.

The entire galaxy swore to obey an obscene fashion sense, which would surely be followed by Earth's future generations. The choice of wardrobe allowed him to wear crisp uniforms and lavish attire.

Dinner parties were replete with his jokes that everybody laughed at. His friends consisted of small, humanoid robots made of silver and gold. They wobbled as they walked and used biddi-biddi-biddi noises as a language.

A brilliant mind of an Artificial Intelligence, stored in one of Rapper Flavor Flav's clock necklaces, became one of his closest confidantes. An infatuation with two women, one, a beautiful space pilot and her rival, a stunning alien princess, evolved into an angst-ridden love triangle.

His best friend resembled an alien Eagle who wore sharp clothes and thrived off his alluring demeanor. And the dream truly came alive once Buckaroo flew the greatest starship in the universe and became the hero of the galaxy.

Chapter 3

Truths

CITY OF WISHVILLE

TOMMY WEST had no recollection of the events leading up to him being face down in the dirt. He only knew that he had to stand up before the evil General's forces closed in on his position.

Buck, wait ... biddi-biddi-biddi ...

The open passenger door of the Trans Am clattered Tommy's forehead as he stood.

Buck ... duck ... biddi-biddi-biddi ...

Tommy's diminutive, robotic friend was nowhere to be seen. Had he really been a heroic space pilot exposed to a wealth of adventures?

Tommy's favorite eighties television theme song from the Buck Rogers TV show played on the car stereo. In the driver's seat, Daisy's motionless body was draped over the steering wheel, her helmet discarded somewhere in the backseat.

The same details Daisy entered before they jumped realities flickered on and off on the dashboard's Reality Jump Circuits.

MONTH - DAY		**HOUR - MIN**
JUNE 19	**WISHVILLE**	**09:47**
	REALITY DESTINATION	

The thread in his mind had been severed by reality's handbrake, releasing a flood of memories of his home, Rosewood Falls. A home he hadn't thought about, or visited, in what felt like decades. Maybe it was the sky full of green clouds, which Tommy misinterpreted as an aftereffect of the recent blow he took to the head. It left him feeling that a switch in his brain had just been turned back on to 'wake the hell up and smell the coffee'.

He glanced at the dashboard, his thoughts going no further than what was so important about Wishville.

What he knew for certain was that they found themselves beneath a highway. On route, somehow the Trans AM had evaded a maze of blazing oil drums and cardboard dens that made up a vagrant community. Most of the area was situated around a cluster of derelict warehouses. A flurry of sirens implied a major incident had occurred, not that he could see anything to back up his theory. Most of them sounded distant.

Tommy's reflection of his lower body in the passenger door window underlined his need to change from his dressing gown, bed shorts, and a pair of slippers. He looked again at the two slippers, occupied by his two feet. He remembered clearly, when he awoke, he had an artificial limb. One leg. One artificial. Somehow, he was now whole again.

How could that be?

"You're not dreaming," Daisy said, before turning her attention to her digital wristwatch and the countdown timer, which she set for forty-five minutes time.

Altering the settings was all she could manage due to the aftereffects from the temporal shift. She slumped back in the driver's seat, her hand massaging the back of her neck.

"What was that device you used on me?" he asked.

"Device! What device?"

"You know what device," Tommy said, mimicking clicking a pen.

"Oh, that device. We call it a SIPO," she replied.

"Never heard of it."

"It's a sleep induced process originator. A friend gave it to me."

"A friend, huh. Nice. Is that what people use in your reality to grow back limbs?"

"You're right. You slept so long; your limb grew back on its own."

"Really," he probed.

"C'mon, Tommy. Sense the sarcasm."

"Okay, hot shot. Why is it back?"

"Because it never left you."

"Oh, I think it did."

"You know what, you wouldn't believe me even if I told you."

"I've just had ten minutes of WTF moments, so lay it on me."

"WTF?"

"It means what the fuck."

"Why not just say it."

"Because we abbreviate everything in the future."

"Why?"

"I don't know. We just do."

"It's dumb, Tommy. And I put you to sleep to calm you down. You were giving yourself an aneurism. The ghost vision you saw, it was trying to stop you from entering this reality."

"It was working."

"Have you ever heard of the phrase the 'end is only the beginning'?"

"Once. In a fortune cookie." He hoped the comment would ease the tension a little.

Her warm smile melted his heart, as much as it used to when they were teenagers in love. The peculiar thing, without her helmet on, Daisy's drastic de-aging from a mid-forties married mum to a kickass teenager became more obvious.

The stereo switched to Phil Collins. Against All Odds.

'Take a look at me now ...'

Unlike the rest of his morning, the lyrics seemed to match his mood.

Daisy's hair had outgrown her mid-80s Wendy James fad and was now darker and tied off in two bunches like a goth. The sparkle that caught his eye from the first moment he knew what love meant, continued to twist his stomach in knots; just like he remembered.

"Those CGI guys must have worked overtime on your de-aging software," he said.

"I can only guess what that means, but take a long look in the wingmirror, babyface."

Tommy's paunchy cheeks and receding hairline had been replaced by a geeky teenager. The same teenager he had long forgotten about. He had to stroke his cheek just to make sure he wasn't hallucinating.

"I think the term you want to use is WTF," she said.

"How am I young?"

"Frankie would say relax."

"Frankie can kiss my ass. I've got like a ton of questions. The thing is, I don't really know where to start."

"Then don't."

"But if I do, you're not going to zap me again with that PINGO thing, are you?"

"SIPO. And no, we don't have time for a one to one."

"Just hear me out."

"Nope. Time, lack of. Just get dressed, Arthur Dent."

"Oh, you've got hitchhikers jokes."

"No jokes. Just supplies, in the boot. Go knock yourself out."

From a pile of clothes in the car boot, Tommy took out a grey striped t-shirt, then a green trench coat. His sweatpants fit just right. He found a pair of black, white, and silver Nike Vandal sneakers. Slipping his feet out of his comfy slippers, he measured the soles of the sneakers with the soles of his feet and found that they matched his size. He fastened them with the signature Velcro strap.

"Velcro, how I've missed thee," he said.

Daisy joined him at the rear of the car.

"Velcro, it's not really a thing in 2019," Tommy continued.

"I'll bear that in mind when I'm in my forties. There is an Ithaca 37 shotgun wrapped in plastic. You might want to keep it handy, for close encounters."

"Nothing like getting straight to the point."

"Time."

"I know, I know, and the lack of it." Tommy unwrapped the bundle. "It's already sawn off."

"I thought it might help conceal it beneath your coat. I also added a string sling. You can hook it over your shoulder. It'll make it easier to draw and fire."

"Why on earth would I do that?"

“Keep looking.”

Tommy moved some junk aside and came across an Uzi 9mm, and a plasma rifle with a 40-watt range. He hoisted the rifle and felt little weight. “It doesn’t weigh much.”

“It’s lightweight on purpose.”

“I’ve never seen a weapon like it. Only in the arcades when I was a kid. Huh, I am a kid. Still not sure how that works, or why. Maybe if we bump into Josh Baskin, we can ask him.”

“The weapon is not from our reality.”

“How many are there? Realities, not guns.”

“Probably more than we can count.”

Tommy lowered the weapon, his mouth agape.

She eased the plasma weapon from his grasp before he dropped it. With the brace located behind the trigger and handgrip, she nestled it against her shoulder. She aimed in the distance, her left hand bracing the barrel. “The rifle has improved maneuverability and is more streamlined than the original model. Hence the lack of weight. The action and magazine are located behind the trigger, so there is no wasted space. The caliber is plasma bolt and capable of unloading one hundred and fifty rounds.”

“Sounds impressive.”

“It’ll do for today.”

“Today. Today! Surely not any day for a weapon of this sort. Where the hell did you get it? Where the hell am I? And who the hell are you? You’re certainly not my Daisy.”

She lowered the gun and gestured for him to calm down. “Take a chill pill.”

“A chill pill. A damn pill is gonna sort this.”

“Believe me, there are worse ways to wake up from the dream state. You avoided the pill, so just relax, okay.”

“When was the last time you woke up in some warped reality and told yourself to calm down.”

“It’s funny you should ask that.” Daisy laughed out loud.

“Oh, it’s funny now,” he snapped.

“I wake up every day thinking WTF. Is that how you use it?”

“Yeah, but …”

“Does that help calm you in the slightest?”

“Not really. I’m not sure what will help right now.”

"Maybe this will." She dropped the gun in the boot and leaned in for a kiss, her tongue easing inside his mouth. The kiss lasted for a few seconds before Tommy peeled away.

"What the … right, erm." He turned away. His mind invaded with guilt.

"Damn, I've missed you, Tommy."

"I saw you last night."

"It wasn't me. You do remember we fell in love in 1987?"

"Of course I do. We talk about it all the time."

"We don't."

"We do. We even mentioned it on our marriage vows."

"Tommy, get this through your skull. You've been tricked into believing your adult life was real."

"Right, I keep forgetting my memories are fake It's kind of a mess up here," he said, pointing to his temple. He seemed to understand if massaging his temples and mumbling was anything to go by. "So let me get this straight," he said, clearly stressing beyond normal levels. "You're Daisy. Just not my Daisy."

"I'm your Daisy. The original. Not your fake wife Daisy."

"Cool. What's not to understand."

"Sarcasm doesn't help."

"Oh, it does. Trust me."

"Do you remember the cave. That squid thing?" she asked.

"How can I forget being crapped out of Arcadian's butthole."

"He crapped you out of … never mind."

"I told you about it."

"I definitely would've remembered that one."

"Right. Not you. I told my fake wife. Silly me. Well, the story goes like this …"

"You really don't have to tell me anything," Daisy glanced at her watch.

"But I am going to, if only to stop my head from exploding, like that dude on that Scanners movie. When you all left, I wore all five rings. The power unleashed was incredible. It allowed me to fly across a chasm, where I managed to get inside Arcadian's squid head. We battled a little, then a one-inch punch exploded his brain into mush. The gooey stuff needed to come out somewhere, right. And you're looking at me as if you want me to stop."

"You can stop at the mush."

"Are you sure?"

"Stopping is good."

"What do you remember?"

"The last time I saw you, Tommy, we were in the cave. After that, you never came home."

"I'm still grasping at how that can be possible. I returned to Rosewood Falls and we left when we were eighteen. We got married. We have four, beautiful kids."

"Here we go again. How best can I describe it? Everything you believe that happened to you since the cave, didn't. You didn't get married. You don't have kids. What you think is your life, is an accelerated lifeline. Created to make you believe it was real. Like a seed planted in the ground and grown with warp speed fertilizer."

"An accelerated lifeline."

"You know when you fast forward a VHS tape and the screen goes all fuzzy."

"Yeah."

"That's been your life."

"But none of it was fuzzy. I remember everything. Even more so when I awoke today."

"You remember on purpose. To make you believe it was real. Today, I interrupted your VHS. Like when the tape gets tangled, and the rest of the movie is ruined. That's why today you feel so alive. As if you're back to your old self."

"I can't argue with that. But, if I'm fortyish, why did you wait so long to find me?"

"You see the green vapor trail overhead?"

Tommy looked skywards. "That must be some big aircraft for the engine exhausts to leave a trail that long and wide."

"The discharge is from the reality condenser I used to open the shield protecting Arcadian's world. By invading his cave, we left reality footprints. Like a date stamp on a letter. The condenser was able to locate your exact co-ordinates, which allowed me to reality skip to you and then here. When we entered this reality, the condenser acted like a comet, punching through the atmosphere. Its green discharge from the plutonium fueling it entered the reality at the same time as us. As long as it stays, the atmosphere remains open and allows us to reach different realities. We now need to ditch the Trans Am and use something different to locate everyone else."

"Of course, reality skipping. Silly me. I watched a documentary on the discovery channel recently."

"Really?"

"No, course not. Shouldn't we be worried about radiation?"

"The only thing we need to worry about is if the trail starts to fade."

"Then what happens?"

"We see the plutonium trail for what it is, like a countdown for our mission. To everyone one else, it will appear that their worlds have been absorbed in the tail end of a rogue comet. The stronger the trail, the more the reality mashes together into one big cauldron of, well, I can't even think of a word to describe it all."

"A clusterfuck!"

"That works."

"We're trapped in a *clusterfuck* of epic proportions."

"The downside is that the adverse effects will make everything go nuts. Machines, weather, people, their narratives, reality, whatever. Everything under this atmosphere and others will be crazy. Some of it won't make sense, but we will be in full control of our actions. That perfect life you thought you knew, will be kindergarten compared to what comes next. And this clusterfuck ends when the comet goes bye-bye along with our chances of getting home."

"How long do we have?"

"I'm not sure yet. Five jumps, maybe a few more. What we need to worry about is, if we're not out of here by the time the comet fades, we'll be stuck in the clusterfuck forever. Which leads me nicely to …" Daisy tapped her wristwatch.

"You sure know a lot about this."

"Well, I've had time on my side."

"What would've happened when my lifeforce ended? Would I have died back there?" When Daisy didn't answer, Tommy slumped against the car. His gaze fixed on the flames spouting from a nearby oil drum. "I'll take that as a yes."

"I can't know for certain."

"I feel like I've woken up in the worst ever episode of the Twilight Zone."

"That's a little dramatic, don't you think."

"Is it?"

"Do I need to use the SIPO again?"

"You turn up in a Trans Am reality hopper … is that the right term? It's packed with futuristic plasma rifles, Velcro trainers and a reality condenser. Then, and this is the best bit, I experience the weirdest Buck Rogers dream, only to then wake up in the dirt and find out that my adult life was a dream which would have led me to dying at warp speed. And to top it all off, I have altered back to my teenage self and need to travel through a clusterfuck to try and get home to my real life. Do you know how much my teenage years sucked?"

"For the one hundredth time, you didn't change back to a teenager. You *are* a teenager. Adulthood never happened for you, Tommy."

"Now who's being dramatic."

"At least you have puberty to look forward to."

"Very funny."

"It's the truth."

"Screw the truth. Screw all this BS. Take me back."

"To die."

"Why not."

"Relax, Tommy. Preferably before you have a brain embolism."

"Answer me one question, Daisy."

"Didn't I do that already?"

"Fine, one last question. Why did Arcadian go to all these lengths to keep me occupied? Am I the star of his favorite reality series? *Hey everyone, it's time to watch Tommy and his pretend family. I'll tell you what a great episode would be. Send in Tommy's teenage girlfriend in a reality jumping Trans Am and let her flush his life down the shitter. Man, that would rock. Let's do that. The ratings will soar through the universe like a comet of bullshit, showering turds across the galaxy.* They'd call it Tommy's *shit show* just to mock me."

"Chill out."

"Could *you* relax? Be honest. If the roles were reversed, how would you feel right now?"

"I don't know."

"Try."

"What do you want me to say, Tommy?"

"The truth."

"You can't handle the truth."

"Try me."

"Fine."

"I'm waiting."

"Mr. Nobody, Arcadian, the squid thing, it needs to keep the game alive to survive. Players are the life source. It uses them like batteries. When your time is up, it's up. It moves on to the next victim. It doesn't care about you, me, or anyone else. We're just narrative to him."

"But I killed Arcadian."

"You didn't."

"I didn't get pooped out for nothing, Daisy."

"If I'm right, you didn't get pooped out at all. Maybe that's a good thing."

"How can you be so sure, if I'm not even sure myself."

"Being pooped out of a squid is hardly something to write home about."

"We changed the rules to beat him. It worked. Simple as that."

"Or were we playing the game?"

"We won, Daisy. End of discussion."

"At last!"

"Or did we?"

"And we're back in the room."

"Look, Daisy. Maybe I'm seeing things a little differently since you arrived back on the scene."

"Only a little. After a billion questions I was hoping we'd have reached at least third base by now."

"It's a start."

"My outlook is this, Tommy. If you changed the rules to win, it's an action nobody else has thought about trying. As a result, Arcadian moved the goalposts to accommodate us, to let us think we won. Or, maybe when you struck him down, he became more powerful than we could have possibly imagined."

"Perhaps that's a good thing. He might be vulnerable now."

"There you go, positive thinking for a change."

"Who am I kidding. Because of my actions, Squidwad continues to thrive elsewhere and is even more powerful. How is that positive."

"You were only doing what you thought was right."

"It certainly doesn't feel that way. All I ended up doing was making everything a hundred times worse. How could I be so naïve. I mean, come on. A geeky kid from Rosewood Falls defeats a powerful being with a one-inch punch. Then he marries the girl of his dreams and has the best life, ever. That kind of existence is only real in the movies."

To curb the onslaught of negativity, Tommy closed his eyes and nursed his forehead. His breathing had escalated towards what he knew to be a panic attack. Something he had experienced before, he thought, unless he hadn't. Maybe if his pounding heart exploded, he could wake up and include the last few minutes as an addition to his already overflowing personal vault of nightmares.

Ever since the game ended, Tommy's friends, the villain Arcadian, every incident from the game, no matter how small, had rarely crossed his thoughts and dreams. Meanwhile, in his actual reality, life continued to thrive, and without him being missed at all.

Except for the one person who was now looking concerned.

Tommy faced Daisy. "What happened back home?"

"The town was back to normal. I waited for you to return."

"And I never did. I can't imagine what that must have felt like."

"Oh, it wasn't just you. Mikey, Ted, Kurt, you all went somewhere else. It was like none of you ever existed. I had nobody to turn to, and I mean *nobody*."

"The guys have been here with me all along."

"That's not possible."

"Trust me. This, I'm certain of."

"Did you forget you were in a dreamscape?"

"Well, they were in the same dreamscape as me."

"That's not possible."

"We saw each other all the time."

"You were alone, trust me on that. You really need to wake up, Tommy. Whether you like it or not, you're still in the game. See it as a sequel."

"A sequel."

"If that's what makes it easier for you, then, yeah, a sequel."

"Sequels suck. Name one good sequel."

"…"

"See, you can't."

"Stop deflecting the inevitable and accept your circumstances."

"I'm getting there. Now name one good sequel."

"The Empire Strikes Back."

"Okay, apart from that one. Hold on, you've watched it. I didn't think you liked Star Wars."

"We don't have time for this, Tommy. "

"Time. I used to have lots of that to look forward to. Next, you'll be telling me I only need a pair of special sunglasses to show me who is good or bad."

"They would help. Do you have some on you?"

"No. Course not."

"Shame. They work. Look, forget that. My brother, your friends, they are out there, somewhere. We must find them before it's too late."

Daisy caressed his hands. He felt her trembling, as if she had put everything on the line and needed him to believe. Normally, he would do so in a heartbeat. She squeezed his hands as reassurance, and it seemed to shrink his tower of anxiety down to a cauldron of boiling fear.

It was a start.

Tommy had loved one form of Daisy, well, since forever ago and could read her expressions like a book. If this was the first time that she had seen him since that day in the cave, then he had to believe her.

"It's a tough ask for me to just drop everything," he said.

"You're dropping a dreamscape. Something you do every time you wake up."

"It's still tough to take."

"Not as tough as going up against Arcadian and getting our lives back on track."

"Perhaps not, but …"

"There are no buts. We've done it before. We can do it again."

"I watched those kids grow. I walked them to school …"

With so many memories to cope with, and his tears aching to break free, Tommy let go of her hands and walked away, if only to save himself the embarrassment of crying in front of the girl he loved.

Daisy's watch timer confirmed around ten minutes had already ticked away. From the moment she knew she had to find Tommy; she knew explaining the truth would be just as hard for her to accept as it would be for him. She just hoped he could gather his thoughts before it was too late.

She turned her attention back to the weapons cache in the car and removed the plasma rifle, Uzi 9mm and a Gloc handgun. She put them in a carryall and added a pair of hunting knives from the sheaths clipped to the lid of the boot. A stack of ammunition magazines she packed last.

Tommy ambled back, wiping the tears from his eyes. "Before we go anywhere, answer me one question."

"Yay, another question," she said jokingly, closing the boot.

"In theory, are my children alive? If I am being used by Arcadian, then perhaps they were being used as well. I don't mean as my own flesh and blood. I mean, these kids were tricked and used in my dreamscape, as part of the game."

"It's hard to say for certain."

"Humor me."

"I guess if Kurt, Ted, and Mikey are alive, then perhaps these kids are alive in some form or another. As other people probably are."

"There are others?"

"Probably."

"But if there is any chance that they are alive, I need to find them. If only to free them."

"We can't save everyone."

"Why not?"

"We don't have time."

"I can't just abandon those kids to die."

"If we go down this route, Tommy, you might not like how it ends. And I didn't go through all I have just to lose you again. You're my Tommy. The boy I love. The boy I gave everything to save."

It was Daisy's turn to well up with tears. She spun away from him, her shoulders heaving.

Tommy gave her a second to compose, before resting his hand on her shoulder. "It's not easy either turning my back on the ones that matter," he said.

"I understand that, Tommy. More than you realize."

"Then you know that I can't go anywhere. Not without knowing for certain."

She faced him and cupped his cheek. "I came back for you and my brother. Not a caravan of courage."

"If you really love me, help me."

"Even if there will be consequences for our actions?"

"If that's true, I'll pay for them. What else can he do to me that he hasn't already."

Her love for him had never been stronger than in this exact moment, but still the furnace of conflict raged inside her. She could feel his pain and anguish the longer she dallied.

"Do we find the kids? Yes, or no?" he fired off.

The most difficult question she had ever been asked needed answering, and quickly. She only hoped she would make the right choice.

Chapter 4

Wish upon a star!

"BEFORE I answer, you need to know one last nugget of information. We have one lifeline. If you die here, you die outright. That's as blunt as I can be," Daisy said.

"I'm fine with that. Let's do it." Tommy went in for an embrace.

His eagerness took her by surprise. She held him at arm's length, just to make sure that he understood. "One lifeline."

"Yeah, I heard you the first time."

"And the dying part?"

"Yeah, I heard that, too."

"Good. If you're happy, I'm happy."

"I am, can't you tell?" he said, smiling awkwardly.

"Ah, it'll do. Let's get going."

"You still haven't told my why here is so important."

"There is someone we need to visit."

"Are you going to give me a clue?"

"Is that another question?" she replied with a smile. "We're looking for the Wishgiver." She handed Tommy the carryall full of weapons.

"Normally you'd rub a lamp to make a wish, rather than threaten at gunpoint," Tommy added.

"The guns are for what stands between us and him."

"You make it sound like we're going up against an army."

"We are. Just not a real one."

"A dream army?"

"Nope. An army of the dead." Rather than answer the inevitable overload of questions that was bound to follow, Daisy led him towards the hobo townscape constructed from cardboard, blankets, and campfires.

ON the camp's east side, a forty-foot incline led up to a roadside lined with a mesh wire fence. From all over the city, sirens continued.

"Sounds like a warzone up there." Tommy shifted the bulky weapon bag to his other shoulder.

Daisy ignored the comment and started her ascent by climbing a thick rope tied to a stone pillar at the top of the slope. When she reached the top, she used a knife to cut a hole in the mesh wide enough so she could reach the other side.

Despite the added weight of the weapons, Tommy climbed as quickly as he could. When he reached the top, he pushed the bag through the opening and followed Daisy to the sidewalk of a sprawling metropolis.

The entire landscape was stifled by the condenser's trail that emerged at the same time the teenagers arrived in the Trans Am. Police helicopters buzzed the horizon like fireflies. Torrential rain showers were seemingly ineffective against the building fires running rampant through a host of skyscrapers.

Although the real dangers were still a few blocks away, Daisy knew that any further delays or questioning would almost certainly use up what remained of the forty-minute window she had allowed to reach their rendezvous.

She hurriedly led Tommy across the street to a row of shops. Metallic barricades were down on all but one of them. Adjacent to a Video Arcade, they entered Tin Can Alley. Posters glued to brickwork promoted the same videogame.

COME PLAY STAR CASTLE, THE LATEST GAME TO ROCK YOUR WORLD.

Intermittent spotlights secured to the brickwork showcased the grotty rear entrances. The lights ran in one direction, straight ahead, towards a dilapidated pyramid structure branded with the colossal initials O.C.P. One beacon of light at the peak of the pyramid appeared to meet with the sky, causing a ruddy atmosphere of dancing light.

It was not clear where the protective energy shield met the ground, but the teenagers were some way off from reaching it.

"No guesses where we're headed," Tommy remarked.

"I'll kiss you if you can name it."

"Now there's a challenge. I'd call it the pyramid of doom."

"I guess the kiss will have to wait. It's the Otherworld Colony Penitentiary. To get there we need to pass through the Spiral Zone. A radiation ridden area. If we spend too long inside, we'll start to lose our minds and join the clusterfuck."

"And you know that how?"

"I did my research."

"Course you did."

"Which is why I know that a percentage of the population has already turned. Hence the need for firepower."

Daisy unzipped the hold-all and reached inside for the Gloc and Uzi 9mm. After pocketing extra magazines, she handed Tommy the plasma rifle, an extra magazine and the second hunting knife.

"This Wishgiver," Tommy said.

"Before you ask, he's a Djinn. He grants wishes."

"I guessed the wish part. You do know that nothing good ever came from granted wishes."

"We don't really have a choice."

"I guess it worked for Aladdin."

"That was a Genie. This is a Djinn."

"What's the difference?"

"One is evil, one is good."

"Is that true?"

"I have no idea whatsoever."

Daisy made her way along the alleyway, keeping close to the back end of the buildings. Leaving behind the empty hold-all, Tommy followed her, keeping to the shadows.

"If this Djinn helps us reach Mikey, Kurt, and Ted, maybe he can help with my kids," Tommy suggested.

"If we have time."

"How are my real family?"

"You're asking me now?"

"Why not?"

"They're fine. Is that good enough?"

"But …"

"In all honesty, it was a nightmare. Like Tobias warned us. It was as if you, Kurt, Ted, and Mikey never existed. And yet I still remembered everything that happened. Life went back to normal for me. Your brother, your mom, life carried on without you, regardless."

"And my dad?"

She shook her head.

"It's not that I don't believe you, Daisy. It's just …"

"Listen to me, Tommy. The game never ended. Arcadian played you. He played all of us. Understand, thirty odd years for you was a blink and miss it moment for me. Now I need you to stop asking me questions, okay."

"There's still a big plot hole. Like, where the hell did you get a reality condenser."

"Let's just leave it in the with great difficulty category of events."

A human cried out from near the end of the alleyway they had just vacated. The cry was quickly muffled by a volley of terrifying screams.

Daisy dragged Tommy close to the wall and braced a hand across his chest to make certain he remained still. She glanced quickly at her wristwatch. Thirty-two minutes had passed. Time was eating away quicker than she realized. They had to keep going. Yet any false move could be catastrophic.

A crowd staggered to a halt at the entrance to the alleyway. The group leader wore a candy-apple-red jacket, with black strips, zips, and angular, rigid shoulder pads. He led them forwards for no more than ten feet. Their bodies swayed from side to side, their arms outstretched, heads tilting to the side, all in sync with a melody only they could hear.

"Don't move a muscle," Daisy whispered, whilst fearing her rapid heartbeat would give away her position.

The group remained in their zombie-like dance trance for no more than a minute, before they turned and left. To the teenagers, it felt more like an hour passed by.

"If I said Thriller right now, would that make sense to you?" Tommy said.

"Like I said, clusterfuck!"

With the coast clear, they carried on along the alleyway. They passed a fleet of abandoned garbage trucks, labelled *Zeke's Trash Garbage Removal*, and headed across the street. A shortcut then guided them through a convenience store car park, fenced off by a waist high brick wall, which they waited by.

To reach the O.C.P building the teenagers needed to cross a downtrodden basketball court leading to a neglected playground. Beyond the exit, a winding road of yellow bricks, lined by some bulky trash units. The route ran as far as the entrance to an underground parking garage that could be seen through the translucent energy barrier.

"No offence, but couldn't we have parked closer to the pyramid," Tommy said.

"I didn't tell the car where to stop."

"You mean it went bananas?"

"I guess so. I've not had it that long."

"Maybe you should start calling it Herbie."

Daisy scowled. "Maybe I should've left your ass where you were and forgotten about you."

"Where's the fun in that," he said, with the teenage glint returning to his smile.

Tommy glanced both ways to check the coast was clear, before vaulting over the wall leading to the basketball court. As he crept forward, he unintentionally kicked a metallic wheel trim and set off what sounded like unending screams from hordes of zombies.

"RUN!" Daisy ordered as she sprinted towards the playground.

From the moment the reality portal was breached by the comet, an ultraviolet radiation virus rampaged across the city. Thousands became infected within the space of a few hours. Zombies quickly evolved from brain sucking, ambling walkers, into mindless, blood thirsty pack hunters.

Behind Tommy and Daisy, two ravenous hordes of zombies collided at the entrance to the car park. Coming together did little more than expand the swell, forcing the frenzied wave of teeth and limbs to act out like plague-ridden locusts, overwhelming any structure it encountered. Parked cars, brick walls, no barricade could hold back their relentless pursuit for flesh and blood.

Daisy and Tommy ran neck and neck across the playground. The chasing pack's size was unfathomable. A tsunami of churning limbs, edging closer by the second.

"We need to slow them down. Got any grenades?" he asked.

"Sorry. I must have left my C4 in my other pants!"

Daisy unleashed a full magazine from the Uzi 9mm. The slugs hit the horde and had as much of an impact as a bug did hitting a windshield.

"Your turn," she ordered, whilst reloading.

Tommy had only ever fired a weapon as an avatar during Mr. Nobody's game, but nothing quite like the plasma rifle. To learn how to use the futuristic weapon, whilst running for his life, seemed as good a time as any to start practicing.

His first effort scorched the ground until his aim settled on the charging pack. Unloading one hundred and fifty rounds from the hardcore weaponry obliterated a quarter of the horde. Decaying flesh sizzled; limbs severed at the joints.

Tommy ran through the park's open gate behind Daisy, towards the yellow brick road leading to the pyramid facility.

"How do I reload this thing?" he asked eagerly.

Daisy barely broke stride as she snatched the weapon, loaded a fresh cartridge, and thrust the weapon into his midriff.

Tommy looked over his shoulder. The zombies had reached the park's entrance. A handful spilled through the gap. Most of them bottlenecked, forcing the others to pile up behind them. Stragglers climbed the fences and scampered across the top of the pile, as if escaping an ant hill. Tommy opened fire. Headshots made short work of the ones closest to him. Daisy's accuracy with the Uzi cut the bottlenecked zombies down, causing a blockage of corpses.

"They're still coming through," he said as his weapon ran out of ammunition.

"Forget the guns. Just run." She threw down the Uzi, knowing full well it would be no more use.

Ahead of them, the pyramid was protected by the translucent, fluctuating barrier. Separate packs of zombies now encroached from both sides, increasing Tommy's fear levels to panic stations. The adrenalin outbreak caused his knees and feet to go in opposite directions. He stumbled and fell, the plasma rifle sliding from his grasp.

Daisy grabbed him by the shoulders and hauled him a few feet across the pavement. He closed his eyes, fully expecting the grim reaper to greet his dismembered, eaten corpse at the door to hell, and then silence descended around him.

"Don't watch," he said, pulling Daisy down to the floor.

In the split second that followed, he wondered if this was how his end was supposed to go – being eaten alive by zombies and shielding his lover until the bitter end – heroism at its finest. Now if only she would stop punching and kicking him, he might appreciate his heroic deed a little more.

Chapter 5

Careful of what you wish for

LITTLE DID he know, but Tommy's visit to hell would have to wait a little longer. No more than six feet away from the two teenagers, a revolving doorway of decaying flesh collided with the protective forcefield. Bodies piled up like a stack of meat at a zombie BBQ. Only on a rare occasion did a body part manage to penetrate the shield, the severed limb left twitching on the pavement.

"Can you get the hell off me now?" Daisy demanded.

Tommy released his hold.

"I didn't need saving, Tommy. I had it under control." She stood and brushed some dirt from her trousers.

"How come we got through and they're zombie shish kebab?" he asked.

Daisy tapped her watch as it started beeping. "Like I said earlier. Time, the lack of it. The slightest change to being undead would've fried us upon impact."

"I presume the time limit was on a need-to-know basis."

"We had a short window. I didn't want to panic you. You've been a bit of a pussy today."

The O.C.P pyramid was not close enough for Tommy to observe any personnel on the ground. What he could make out were the exterior electrical power conduits that ran from the ground to the pyramid's highest point. From the peak came the power source for the electromagnetic shield, feeding off anything electrical nearby.

"Don't look so nervous," she said.

"That's easy for you to say."

"We're in the safe zone. We're okay here, as long as this shield remains active."

The forcefield's continual shaft of energy worryingly started to fluctuate and shattered what had been a welcome respite for the teenagers.

"You had to say something. Is this shield one of your tricks?" he asked.

"I was told it's a kind a magic." She winked as she helped him to stand.

The teenagers made their way towards the pyramid's first security checkpoint barrier. With no personnel on site to challenge their approach, they descended a steep ramp, towards a drop off point used for prisoner arrivals. A sizeable, dimly lit loading bay had been vacated in a hurry. Raised barriers and fire exits remained accessible.

On video monitors inside a row of security booths, rather than mentioning the comet, a headline blamed an ecoterrorist organization, designated Cobalt, for being responsible for the current national emergency. From the mugshots shown, Tommy recognized one person, the same person he was now following deep inside the facility. The name Louisa Marcus had been tagged underneath a photo of Daisy.

"I just spotted your mugshot on the screen. You care to tell me why they're calling you Louisa?"

"It's not what it looks like," she replied.

A second image attached to the footage showed an older man with wavy, grey hair, smartly dressed in a tuxedo, his identity listed as Connell McLeod.

"And who is this McLeod guy?" he asked.

"He's a friend. I really hope you don't grow up asking this many questions."

Their route across the loading bay led them beneath a row of enormous, mounted ceiling fans and towards a warehouse sized chamber. An invasion of damp ran as far as the host of maintenance elevators on the far side. All but one of them was tagged as out of order.

The teenagers stepped inside the only working elevator and closed the metallic door by pulling on a dangling leather cord. All the buttons on the keypad had been labelled with ancient symbols.

"What is this? Chinese or something, counting backwards," Tommy said.

"Not backwards. Downwards." Daisy pressed the bottom number and the floor jolted to signal the start of their descent.

"Any idea what you're going to say to this Djinn?"

"I thought a cool guy handshake would work."

"Seriously."

"Why not? It used to work for the dork brigade."

"You'll never nail the shake."

She faced him and crossed her arms. "And why not?"

"You're not cool enough."

Tommy associated Daisy's laugh with a simpler time of life. To hear it again after the few hours he just experienced felt like he'd taken a soul shower with the best antidote.

"I'm sorry about all the questions," he said.

"I get it."

"I'm not sure you do."

"You don't have to say anything."

"I do."

"You really don't."

"When all hell broke loose out there, all I could think about was what if this is the end. What if this is how we die?"

"There are worse ways to go than being chowed on by zombies. And we didn't die, Tommy."

"I know we didn't. It's just, I have so much more I need to say to you."

"Relax. We're still here, in one piece." Daisy squeezed his hand tightly. "Tommy. I know for certain, as we grow old together, no matter how many times we will say the words to each other, the bond of our love will never break. We will argue. Fall out. By all accounts, you are likely to ask so many questions I'll want to shoot you in the face, but that's okay. We will have the best times. Sad times. Life will break our spirits and hearts. But during all of it, we will be together. Always. And do you know why?"

"Am I supposed to answer, or …"

"One thing conquers all."

"Family. You were about to say family conquers all."

"I wasn't going to say that."

"Are you sure?"

"Uh-huh. The moment has kinda gone now but love, Tommy. Love. We both know, inside our hearts, our love will conquer all. Love conquers everything."

Tommy held Daisy close. A warmness spread through his body like it did the first time they kissed during the game with Arcadian. The memory felt poignant, like a lifeline back to reality.

She retained eye contact. This was her way of letting him know she felt the same way as he did. Yet something felt different, cold. Perhaps being alone might have taken its toll on her and she was still trying to adjust to being back in his company. The burden of being apart had to be hard to endure for any person, especially one cut off from her old life in such drastic circumstances.

"What does this guy ask for in return for wishes?" Tommy asked.

Daisy continued to hold his hand and rested her head on his shoulder. "Let's hope he takes an IOU, because I'm all out of bubble-gum."

"You mean you didn't pack any in your Sport Billy bag." Tommy glanced down as the elevator jolted to a halt. Water began to seep through the floorboards. It quickly reached their waists. "At least we know where we stand."

"Yeah, in deep sh–"

Engulfed by the water's rapid ascent, Daisy tugged on the leather cord and the doorway opened. Beyond them, the submerged belly of the pyramid ranged from somewhere between three to four Olympic sized swimming pools.

Light sources from above and below implied there were ways out of their predicament. They just had to choose the correct one and try not to drown in the process.

DAISY and Tommy swam inside for fifteen feet and surfaced in one of the lit areas. A central dome riddled with years' worth of damp and decay displayed artificial daylight and an oval power core secured just beneath the ceiling. The core flickered as the facility's electrical reserves drained of energy.

Tommy expected to see some evidence of the Wishgiver, and not to be stuck with no visible exits or flat terrain.

"Where is he?" he asked irritably, whilst spitting out water.

"He's below ground. We need to keep heading down."

"Aren't we below ground already?"

"We need to keep going."

"How far?"

"Until we can't go any further."

Her comment stung. Tommy guessed it had to do with his endless questioning.

Not much could be seen when they descended, except for the light source at the base of the pool. As they approached, they discovered a cover half made of glass panels and concrete.

Daisy motioned to Tommy to shoot the central glass panel with the shotgun concealed beneath his coat, something that he had clearly forgotten all about.

Being no expert with firearms, Tommy had no idea if firing off a couple of shots would work underwater or end up being a waste of time. Thankfully, he didn't have to wait long for the answer.

Two muffled blasts from his weapon shattered the panels, and wiped out the glass flooring, the resultant current snatching the weapon from his grasp.

WITH five lives at his disposal, Tommy had died and been resurrected, and still survived all the terrors Arcadian could muster during the game. In the split second the bullets ruptured the glass floor, he suddenly realized how vulnerable he had become with just the one life to spare.

Water surged through the ruptures to a chamber full of smooth, stone walls and rusted, iron drains. Sucked into a whirlpool, the teenagers became live bait for the cluster of huge meat hooks chained to the ceiling. Time and terror had no master at this point. Seconds, minutes, fear, pain, every emotion assembled into one wish, to end the deluge.

Finally, it did. The ceiling sealed off automatically, the water draining away.

Tommy lay face down on a smooth floor, feeling broken in half, and not daring to move an inch. All that he could do was let his lungs purge the water he had swallowed.

With his lungs cleared, Tommy gingerly rolled on his side. As he moved, a warm liquid from his busted nose seeped into the concrete and vanished. The very essence of his soul inadvertently started a chain reaction that would eventually alert the same prisoner they were looking for to their presence.

Across the chamber, Daisy lay in heap. Her shoulders heaved as she violently vomited sea water.

Tommy waited for her to stop heaving before he let his pain-wracked body start to adjust to his muscle movement. "Are you okay?"

Daisy lifted her arm and managed a thumbs up.

"That makes at least one of us," he said.

Daisy propped herself up on to her elbows and then her knees. "Maybe we should've chosen a different way down."

Tommy had watched enough horror movies to recognize that the meat hooks directly above the plethora of blood drains revealed they were in a kill room. Huge stone effigies in each corner resembled demons of an ancient underworld. The blend of horned and serpent like deities based on the horrific Cenobites from the Hellraiser movie franchise.

"I think we took a wrong turn," he warned her.

"And yet this is exactly where we need to be," she replied.

"Do you know who these statues represent?"

"Nope."

"Do you remember Hellraiser?"

"I never liked horror movies. I still don't."

"Well, if I'm right, these statues represent real nasty types that exist in an extra dimensional realm."

"Theoretically speaking, how evil are we talking?"

"The kind that like to rip your soul from your chest cavity and do a little dance on your remains."

"You should've led with that. What about the markings on the doorway?"

The outline of a fascinating puzzle box design on the only twin doors in the chamber had been tainted by the same blood spilt from Tommy's busted nose. On the box itself were some hieroglyphics. Just like the bootlegged Cenobites, Tommy recognized the box from the same movie franchise.

"If I had to make a guess. I'd say that's the puzzle which unleashes hell on Earth," he said.

"And the red stuff is blood, I imagine?"

Tommy wiped the blood away from his nose. "Yep, that could be mine. And he probably knows we're already here."

Without hesitating, Daisy wrapped her knuckles on the steel doorway.

Dud, dudda, dudda, dud dud, dud, dud.

"Did you not hear what I said?" Tommy asked.

"I did. I just chose not to listen."

"Then listen to Billy Ocean."

"Why would I do that?"

"Billy said red spells danger."

"I don't see Billy here. Do you? And how else will we get in if we don't knock?"

"We could slip a note under the door."

"Don't be a pussy, Tommy."

"I'm not. It's just, why else would a psycho demon from another reality be locked in a dungeon, beneath an ocean of water, if not for the exact reason we're both thinking."

"Which is?"

"He's not to be messed with. He's also locked behind a sealed door."

"A sealed door that is now stained with your blood."

"Okay, fine, it's my blood. It's also adorned with a symbol that implies certain death to anyone who enters. If it's not for everybody's safety, then why bother adding it at all."

"This is a reality prison, Tommy. All sorts of dimensional beings are kept here."

"I don't think you realize the dangers. Carbon copy statues of Cenobites. Hooked chains. Sacrificial human hors d'oeuvres."

"You remember we discussed a clusterfuck. Well, we're in the heart of it."

"None of these issues bother you."

"What bothers me most is the fact that in that dream reality, you got me to marry you. At least now I know not to make the same mistake twice."

"You'll still marry me."

"Not after this I won't."

"Yeah, you will."

"We're already over."

"As the legend, Richard P. Astley, once sang. *I'm never gonna give you up.*"

"I wish you would."

"Never gonna let you down."

"You're even more annoying than Ted used to be."

The hooked chains snapped to abrupt attention and soared in the teenagers' direction.

"Duck!" Daisy yelled, dropping to the floor.

For a change, Tommy was thankful for the warning before something hit him. Instead, the hooks imbedded in the doorway.

Firmly locked in place, the chains tightened, and the archaic hinges groaned with a century's worth of agony. The doors opened to reveal a humanoid form, complete with decaying flesh, and a black leather trench coat.

An hour ago, the teenagers began their search for an ancient Djinn with the moniker of Wishgiver. They had just found him.

Chapter 6

"Got a light?"

THE REAR of the circular prison cell showcased a colossal, horned skull, lined with jagged teeth. Waves of an unnerving mist streamed from the demonic eye sockets and nostrils, filling the upper reaches of the chamber. Beneath the skull, a stone plinth, with a central stairwell of white stone and a red stair runner, led up to a decaying concrete throne. A fitting abode for a sinister granter of wishes.

The inmate bore a resemblance to a zombie version of the Matrix's Neo and Barker's Pinhead. Tommy's nightmares lasted for weeks after watching Hellraiser in 1987. It made sense not to reveal the truth to his friends. On the other hand, his friends had been more forthcoming about their nightmares of the titular horror characters Freddy Krueger, Michael Myers, and Jason Vorhees, a group Tommy believed paled in comparison with Barker's creations.

The Djinn's twisted smile implied he held the trump cards in this game. He knelt and ran a fingertip along a groove in the concrete that was filled with Tommy's blood. As he licked his finger, the inmate's soulless, black eyes shifted in Tommy's direction. At the same time, the meat hooks released their hold on the doorway. Now under the Djinn's complete control, the hooks hovered inches in front of the boy's body, snapping back and forth like snakeheads, spitting venom.

"Not that I'm not grateful for you opening my cell, but you have five seconds to tell me why you are here, Tommy West." The powerful, dark, and terrifying voice echoed around the chamber.

All Tommy needed to do to answer was to overcome every single ounce of dread invading his nerve endings. "You got my name from tasting my blood?" Tommy reached for the wound on the bridge of his nose.

"Now answer me before my chains rip you apart," the Wishgiver demanded.

"We need your help."

With a wave of his hand, the Djinn released his control of the hooks and they returned to their dangling positions. He then studied the female teenager's tentative approach towards his cell.

"Why are you really here?" he asked.

"Isn't that obvious, Mr. …?" Daisy replied.

"Scrimm, Angus Scrimm. My help comes with a mortal price. A price that starts with you. I can smell your fear, Daisy Drew. Fear follows you around like a virus."

"Oh, he's not a virus," she said, jabbing a thumb at Tommy. "And he always smells like that. You know why I'm here, or have your wishes shriveled up as much as your skin?"

With a swish of his hand, Scrimm beckoned her inside and led the way towards the carpeted stairwell.

Tommy followed. No matter how hard he tried to keep up, Daisy was always five strides ahead, as if guided by a supernatural power. With every step, Tommy felt like Prince Charming in the Adam and the Ants video. Pride. Courage. Humor. Flair. Each one of the arm-crossing dance moves held meaning towards an element of Adam Ant's personality. Without even realizing, Tommy had been doing the dance all the way across the chamber.

"Are you okay?" Daisy said from halfway up the stairwell.

Tommy stopped abruptly. His cheeks flushed with embarrassment. "Is this normal behavior from someone suffering from concussion during a clusterfuck?"

An invisible barrier stopped Tommy from progressing any further. "Only one shall pass," Scrimm barked.

With a swish of his hand, Scrimm's meat hooks arrowed across the cave. They imbedded in the huge skull and lowered it towards the top of the stairwell, allowing Scrimm and Daisy to enter. Tommy couldn't help but feel helpless as he watched the skull's mouth close, with Daisy and the Djinn inside.

WHEN Daisy departed, Tommy impatiently paced the perimeter and its five separate sections. All of them divided by alcoves showcasing a creepy sculpture or statue. The type that had eyes that followed him no matter where he ended up in the room.

As he moved, motion sensor lanterns clasped in the hands of the figurines lit up the hieroglyphics and sacred scripture engraved on the walls. The symbols meant very little to a kid who now wished he'd spent more time learning at school rather than prepping for the weekly D&D game with his pals.

From an alien scrawl, he quickly made his way to drawings of strange beasts, labelled by dots and dashes. Only when he reached the last section did Tommy notice a statue mirroring a Medieval Knight.

Out of all the statues, the Knight appeared to be the only one holding a weapon, rather than a lantern. The replica of the ancient sword, Hexcalibur, appeared to glow brighter than any lantern. It allowed him to read the accompanying scrawl, which was in English.

ONCE, IN A TIME BEFORE TIME,
ARCADIAN BREATHED LIFE INTO THE EARTH.
AND HIS LIGHT GAVE BIRTH TO ANGELS,
AND THE REALM OF SE'QUEL GAVE BIRTH TO LIFE.
AND SE'QUEL'S FIRE GAVE BIRTH TO TRAPPED SOULS.
SOULS CONDEMEND TO DWELL IN THE OTHERWORLDS.

Tommy knelt to read the next part.

TO THE ONE ENTRUSTED.
UPON THE GRANTING OF FREEDOM, THE UNHOLY
LEGIONS OF ARCADIAN SHALL BE FREED UPON MANKIND.

Tommy lay on his stomach to read the last part.

FEAR ONE THING ONLY IN ALL THAT IS.
FEAR ARCADIAN.
FOR HE IS EVERYTHING
AND EVERYONE.
HE IS H.I.M

"Shouldn't warnings be on the outside of the cell. Like a mystical peanut allergy. Why are you talking to yourself, Tommy. That'll be your concussion. Thanks, I almost forgot about the pain tightening around my skull."

He used Hexcalibur as leverage to stand. It shifted downwards, and then plunged dangerously towards his stomach, the blade narrowly missing his groin and piercing the concrete with a deafening clank.

Fearing that the Djinn had heard the commotion, he glanced nervously towards the skull's mouth. It remained closed.

Tommy grabbed the sword's hilt and pulled. Hexcalibur was locked in tight enough for only a crane to move it back. Searching the statue for a lever, he noticed the armored breast plate had shifted forwards a few inches. He pressed his palms against it. The plate remained locked in place, even as he planted his feet and backed into it.

The Djinn would surely notice the sword had shifted and there was no telling what he would do as a result. Enough panic set in for Tommy to stop trying to close the armor and to control his breathing.

Just what I need, a real panic attack.

"Think Tommy, think."

Maybe the close button is behind the breast plate.

"It's worth a try."

Tommy forced his fingertips behind the breast plate and ran them from top to bottom. He then stepped around the sword and did the same from the opposite side. At the bottom of the plate, his fingertips brushed something leathery. Fearing a spider or worse, he whipped his fingers out.

Mibbe it's important, said a Scottish voice in his head.

"Really!" Tommy replied.

Aye.

"Good things rarely come from stealing something that's hidden on purpose."

Be brave, Tommy. It's no' the Wood Beast from Flash Gordon.

"I don't mean to be rude but you're not here, whoever you are."

Just take it.

Tommy had no reason to doubt the voice. After everything that had transpired in the last few hours, conversing with an imaginary Scottish guy was the least crazy thing.

"What is it?" he asked.

Take it and ye find oot.

"Just like that."

Nobody is thir to stop ye.

With nothing to lose, Tommy slid his fingertips behind the plate and managed to pinch a leather document. The item had been folded over a few times. Before he could open it, a mechanism started to return the breast plate to its original starting point.

Grinding gears drew his attention to Hexcalibur, which almost maimed Tommy, who had to leap sideways to avoid being bludgeoned as the sword returned to its original position.

A minute after the breast plate shut, Daisy and Scrimm re-emerged from the skull. Tommy knew straightaway that something wasn't right. Unsure if dropping the map was a good idea, he instead slid the folded document in his back pocket.

"Are you okay?" he asked Daisy, who ran most of the way down the stairs.

"We need to leave." She grabbed Tommy by the hand and led him hurriedly around the right side of the plinth.

"What's the rush?"

"Time. Or should I say the lack of it."

Scrimm turned to Daisy. "Find your friends, Daisy Drew. While you still have a soul."

Daisy pulled Tommy towards an excavation at the back of the plinth.

"What the hell did you agree to?" he barked.

"Nothing you wouldn't of."

She shoved him inside the opening, into the darkness, a stone boulder rolling across the entrance and sealing the two teenagers inside.

Chapter 7

"Love in an Elevator."

A SHIFT beneath Tommy's feet implied he was on the move. After twenty seconds of darkness, the stone elevator cleared the basement sections of the prison. Through the gaps in the stonework, the brightness from the energy barrier shed some much-needed reassurance that their descent into madness might be coming to an end.

Tommy maneuvered Daisy's shoulder to force her to face him. "Here's a thought. If the Djinn has an elevator inside his cell, why does he not use it to escape."

"He can't. He's bound to the cell for an eternity. If he leaves, his powers fade and he will die."

"That makes sense. Here's another thought. Are you going to tell me what you two agreed to?"

"I knew that was coming."

"Well?"

"Did you ever tell your friends what you wished for on your birthday?"

"We're now blowing out candles here."

"What we spoke about is between me and him. Besides, you never told us about your deal with Arcadian."

"That's not fair. I had no recollection of it."

"I don't want to talk about it, Tommy." Daisy turned away.

Tommy had no desire to push for the answer to whatever pact Daisy and Scrimm had agreed to. Instead, he reached around her waist and squeezed her tightly.

"I've missed this," she said warmly.

"I do need to ask one question."

"If it's about the Djinn, then I'm not going answer you."

"It's not. It's about something completely different."

"Okay."

"How the hell did you get hold of the Trans Am?"

"If you really want to know. It all started when I met this guy, called Connell McLeod ..."

FLASHBACK
EARTH, 1985

"PLUTONIUM! YOU stole plutonium! From terrorists!" Daisy braced the dashboard as the Dodge Pickup skidded towards Hill Valley's quarter of a mile long, empty high street.

"Aye. Thay wanted tae build a bomb. We teuk it fur a better purpose."

Connell McLeod, a rugged, athletic adventurer, hiked his balaclava up to his forehead. After being cooped up in his camouflage outfit for the last few hours, it felt good to release a warm smile and his ponytail.

"I can't believe you're smiling about it," Daisy said.

"Ah wis lik' a ninja."

"Ninjas are not seen. What happened?"

"Ah wis seen."

"Making you the world's worst ninja. And at no point during our plan did it say anything about stealing from terrorists."

"Th' doc needs it mair than thay dae."

"The Doc needs it."

"Ah told ye aboot him."

"No, you didn't."

"Och, weel. Ah shuid hae."

"For this team up to work, McLeod, we need to be on the same wavelength. You said we needed an energy source to finish building a machine that can create temporal reality shifts."

"Aye."

"Stealing is not building."

"Th' doc is building it. Weel, he's bult it awready. We juist need th' power source."

"Plutonium by chance?"

"Ye catch on quickly."

"Clearly not quickly enough."

Daisy had been sitting in the passenger seat for the last ten minutes. At no point did she feel the need to question McLeod's actions since he sprinted across the car park from the warehouse district carrying a metal case. Nor his appearance, which was clearly more for an all-out commando assault than it was for a discreet transaction. In hindsight, maybe she should have asked some of her own questions before they set out on their journey.

Only when terrorists in a blue and white Volkswagen transporter started shooting at the Dodge, did she feel the need to raise an issue.

As they reached midway of the high street, the clock tower struck 1:20 a.m.

"We hae ten minutes till we catch up wi' th' doc."

"I don't like where this is going."

"Ye mean th' journey or th' conversation?"

"Both!"

"Ye ken how tae git tae th' Twin Pines parking lot."

"The same one you showed me on the map. It's a few minutes from Tannen Boulevard."

"Aye. You're gaun alone."

"Alone."

"Aye. N' th' Doc kens ye as Louisa Marcus. Nae Daisy. Tis tae keep yer identity secret."

"Secret identity, plus plutonium, equals madness. Anything else I need to know?"

"Ye jump oot wi' th' case, and uise th' plutonium tae power th' device. N' ye tak' aff tae save yer man."

"I jump out of a moving car with a case load of plutonium."

"Aye."

"I'm not Martin Riggs!"

"Uh?"

"Never mind. What will you do?"

"Improvise. I've gotten guid at that ower th' years."

"Not that I don't trust you, but I can't do this alone."

"We've gaen ower this, Daisy. Ye ken whaur tae catch up wi` me. Juist remember, ye can't be exposed fur langer than forty-five minutes when ye reach th' city. Ony langer 'n' it's gam ower. Th' plutonium disrupter wull tak' care o' itself."

"Let me get this straight. I use plutonium to power a device through a reality tear so I can reach my boyfriend. We then need to avoid poisoning by radiation. If we're alive still, we need to outwit a Djinn, find my bro, his friends, and avoid dying."

"Aye!"

"That's a great plan."

"I kne."

"I was being sarcastic."

"Weans 'n cheek shuid be kept apairt forever."

"Weans and cheek?"

"Teenagers and sarcasm …" A host of bullets rattled the driver's side. McLeod glanced nervously at his passenger. "Git ready, Daisy."

The Dodge pickup skidded round the corner from the High Street to Tannen Boulevard fast enough for the passenger door to swing up.

"Now," McLeod ordered.

Holding the case of plutonium tightly, Daisy leapt from the moving vehicle and tumbled along the pavement until her spine struck the curb. She lay still, until the second vehicle drove by. Only when it turned the corner did she dare to stand.

MCLEOD'S ploy had worked, but for how long? With Hill Valley being a relatively small town, it was only a matter of time before the terrorists came upon her rendezvous with the mysterious Doc at the Twin Pines parking lot. Meaning McLeod's meticulous plan would unravel faster than a slinky would down a flight of stairs.

When she spotted a silver haired man, half dressed in a yellow Hazmat suit, with his head and shoulders buried under the hood of a black and gold Trans Am Firebird, she knew she had found the right person.

"Hey, Doc," she said, approaching cautiously.

"Arty, thank God you're here. Hand me that wrench." Doc Browning didn't look up from the engine. He opened his palm and gestured for the wrench to be handed to him.

Daisy placed the wrench in his open palm.

"Did you get it?" Doc asked.

"It depends on what you mean by 'it'?"

This time the Doc looked up. She guessed he was around forty.

"You're not Arty," he said, wielding the wrench.

"What gave me away?" she said, smiling awkwardly.

Daisy didn't expect such a frizzy head of grey hair to be on a relatively young man. The Hazmat helmet was resting on his shoulders, the suit itself, zipped up to his neck, leaving only the extended collar of a lairy shirt visible from his layer of clothes beneath. She glanced over his shoulder. At no point did McLeod mention what device the Doc had designed. The engine modifications implied it was no ordinary Trans Am he was working on.

"That's some engine," she said.

"It's classified." Doc tried to cover up the engine block and failed miserably.

"Isn't it a bit late for that, mister?"

Doc looked disappointed and slammed the bonnet shut. "Doctor Emmet Browning. Scientist, and creator extraordinaire. Where is Arty?"

"I don't know. My name is Daisy, I mean Lousia, Louisa Marcus. I'm here with McLeod."

"Where is he?"

"We got split up."

"You were supposed to meet Arty." Doc glanced back and forth at every corner of the car park, half expecting McLeod to appear.

"Neither of them is here, if that's what you're expecting."

"I can see that. Where is McLeod?"

"In trouble."

"What sort of trouble?"

"The terrorist kind."

"Great, Scott." Doc planted a palm on his forehead and stumbled a few feet backwards.

"He told me you needed this," Daisy said, rapping the metal case with her fingers.

The Doc delicately plied it from her grasp and placed it carefully on the Firebird's bonnet. To check for hairline fractures, he ran his finger along the seal and the release switches. "Do you have any idea what you are transporting?"

"Plutonium."

"Exactly. Do you know how dangerous this is?"

"Pretty dangerous, I guess."

"Pretty dangerous." Doc ran around the Trans Am out of shock, and then grabbed Daisy by the shoulders. "Pretty dangerous. This is used to power nuclear reactors and you tapped the metal case like a drum."

"Hardly drumming, Doc. I rapped my fingers on the outside."

"Did you not know that any slight impact could rupture the casing and cause a cataclysmic radiation eruption that would wipe out Hill Valley?"

"Jumping from a moving car wasn't such a good idea then, huh."

"You might not be Arty, but you're just as reckless." Doc's second trip round the car was quicker, but just as exaggerated.

"Look, Doc. I'm here. Pluto's here."

Doc looked over her shoulder. Daisy guessed he was looking for a cartoon dog.

"Hey, Doc. Eyes front. Me and the package are both here in one piece. Now if you don't mind. McLeod said you can help me. Can you? Will you? I'm in kind of a hurry."

"Hurrying is not good."

"And neither is wasting time."

"I owe McLeod."

"Doesn't everybody. He never told me how you two met."

"I was stuck in 1885."

"Is that a cult or something?"

"The year! The year!"

"What about it?"

"He helped me escape with my wife and kids."

"In what, a time machine?"

"How did you know?"

"A hunch."

"If McLeod needs my help, then help he will get. Stand back, Louisa. No talking. No movements. Don't even breathe. I need complete calm as I insert the plutonium in the onboard nuclear reactor."

"This car is nuclear?"

"What did you expect, battery power? The reactor will generate 1.21 gigawatts of power required to form a temporal displacement, which will allow you to enter a reality shift."

"Great."

"In theory."

"In theory. You mean you haven't tested it yet?"

"You make it sound like you can purchase plutonium on a street corner."

"Instead, you ask your friend to steal it for you."

"He stole it for *you*. I'm just a mechanic. Now, put these on, and stand well back."

Daisy was handed a pair of goggles, which seemed to pale in comparison to Doc's full body Hazmat suit.

The Doc sealed tight his protective gear and carefully freed the case's seal. Using a pair of industrial pincers, he slowly removed the plutonium's outer covering. From inside, he removed the cannister with some pincers. As soon as the case opened, the content glimmered green and was glowing intensely by the time it was fully removed.

"Why is it green?" Daisy asked.

"Do. Not. Disturb," Doc snapped, almost dropping the cannister.

Daisy was already a distance away from the procedure, but she took an extra step back as a further precaution. She then watched the Doc carefully insert the cannister into the nuclear reactor situated where the car's rear seats used to occupy space. With the plutonium secure, Doc closed the reactor, his shoulders sinking in relaxation.

The process went quicker than she expected. Within a few minutes, the Doc was stepping out of his Hazmat suit and then sitting in the driver's seat, explaining how to use the Reality Jump Circuit Board. It seemed straightforward enough. Enter the destination you wanted to reach, and the car would take you there via a reality tear.

"Simple," he said, slapping his thigh.

"In theory," Daisy replied.

"All science is theory, until it's tested, Louisa."

"Says everyone who ever tested something before they died in an explosion."

"You appear to be lacking in positivity."

"I'm brimming with as much positivity as the radiation inside that cannister. Why was the plutonium glowing green?"

"It's a source of pure energy. The only kind that will work in this machine I've built. Without it, you'll burn to a crisp upon entry."

"What about escaping back home?"

"If the energy fades completely, when you try to exit, your skin and bones will vaporize."

"Good to know. Any suggestions if I arrive in one piece?"

"Yes, when you reach your destination, leave the car. Using it too many times will deplete the plutonium levels."

"If I leave the car, how else will I travel?"

"Find other means."

"Just like that?"

"Yes."

"And should I choose to use the car?"

"The moment you board this car, you are already on borrowed time. All time is precious. Like sand falling through your fingers. Savor as much as you can. Waste none. Get home safely."

"You know what, Doc, I need to be honest …"

Doc held up his hand and cut her off mid-sentence. "I know all I need to know. That's the only way to keep you safe."

"Thanks, Doc. Say, do we have time for a test run?"

"There's isn't time. Look!" Doc pointed over her shoulder at the Volkswagen Transporter breaking through a barrier to reach the car park.

A terrorist, wielding a Kalashnikov assault rifle, opened fire from the open roof of the same vehicle that had chased down McLeod. For the moment, the vehicle was too far away for the bullets to be anything other than wayward. Another volley riddled the Doc's van parked next to the Trans Am.

"I'll draw them off," Doc said, hauling Daisy into the driver's seat. "Remember, it's imperative that you enter the exact reality you want to access. When the speed reaches 88 mph, the car will do the rest."

"And if it doesn't?"

"Then you'll never know because the car will explode in a fireball."

The comment didn't come across as a joke, but Doc smiled anyway. He then sealed her in the car.

Daisy started the engine. With no chance to even say thank you, she watched in the rear-view mirror as the defenseless Doc was gunned down in cold blood.

Fearing the worst, her hands trembling like never before, she gunned the accelerator, the speedometer racing towards 88 mph, and the car speeding towards the reality tear leading her to Tommy.

END OF FLASHBACK

"A FEW seconds later I ended up in your living room," Daisy said.

"You stole the Doc's car," Tommy replied.

"Steal is a little harsh. More like I borrowed it."

"You stole it and crashed into my house."

"It's hard to return something to someone who died protecting me."

"I'm sorry, you didn't mention it in your story."

"It was in cold blood. I didn't even have time to say thanks."

"And Louisa Marcus is wanted, not Daisy Drew."

"I guess McLeod was right about that, too."

"He sounds like a good guy."

"He's the best."

"Still, it's pretty cool that you drove a Trans Am Firebird through time."

"I didn't drive through time. It was a temporal reality shift. Have you not been paying attention."

"I paid attention enough to know that you *borrowed* the car in 1985. I left in 1987. How did you go back in time to steal the car in the first place."

"McLeod used a time machine."

"Course he did. You can buy time travel devices over the counter in 2019."

"Smart ass. McLeod told me about an advanced AI system called Skynewt. Skynewt went active in November 1989. I broke into the facility to use a time portal that transported me back to October 1985."

"And you just broke into the facility."

"That's a longer story, Tommy. Not for today."

"Yeah, I don't need another flashback. Okay, so why 1985. Why not just transport yourself here?"

"Because we needed the plutonium to tear open your reality and keep the exit open. Keep up with the background. It's important."

"Oh right, okay. Now it makes sense why we left the car where we did. Vaporization, plutonium, and Skynewt. Got it. It's funny, it sounds like you travelled through time to protect me from Terminators."

"I haven't travelled in time. I travelled through realities. There's a difference."

"I heard Doctor Who was looking for a new companion."

"We tried. That spot had already been taken."

It was hard for Tommy to tell from her reaction if she was serious or joking.

The elevator shuddered to a sudden halt, the boulder shifting to one side to reveal a ruddy sky full of pulsating energy beams and storm clouds.

Chapter 8

Clash of the Titans

WITH A swish of his hand, the Djinn closed his cell doors as securely as the deal he had in place with Daisy Drew. In the same movement, he rested a palm against a section of wall, unleashing a thunderous chain reaction.

The wall alongside him parted, revealing an infinite sized Life Cabinet, showcasing stone shelves full of Soul Jars. The foot long hourglass counters contained the existing lifeforces of prisoners manipulated by Arcadian for his evil purposes. Hundreds of thousands of human souls dwindled away as grains of sand, only swapping to a lethargic phantom when their lifelines had ended.

In her exchange with the Djinn, Daisy had revealed the names of the people she needed to track down and release. Scrimm concentrated on the three jars with the molded bust plates of Mikey Drew, Kurt Connors, and Theodore Logan. The accelerated lifelines were almost up on all of them.

Granted three wishes, one for each boy, Daisy had asked the Djinn for the opportunity to interrupt their lifelines. It was up to her to save her friends before the lifelines ended. Removing the boys' jars from the shelf one by one, he spliced each with enough magic to slow the sand.

Scrimm had agreed to the deal, knowing full well that without any help it would be impossible for Daisy to rescue them all in time. The price she needed to pay was for her own lifeline to be created alongside the boys. If she failed, she would become trapped and all of them would remain prisoners.

She agreed to eight days to fulfil her task. Eight days being the exact amount of time the plutonium intervention would last. It was something she left out of the negotiations.

Scrimm picked up an unused jar. From his right fingertips a purple wave of energy molded the jar's clay peak into a bust plate of Daisy Drew's upper body. With a deal locked in place, he turned the jar quickly and rested it on his left palm. Grain by grain, the sands of time started the countdown.

He rested the jar back on the shelf and reset the cabinet. As he did so, an energy wave rocked the chamber to its core. Only once had the Djinn experienced a power flux of such magnitude.

The clash with Arcadian was a genuine battle for supremacy, reaching an epic scale of conflict. Enough wishes had been granted to raise an all-conquering army and yet Arcadian's tendrils could reach even the purest of hearts. Sheer persuasion and numbers meant Scrimm had no choice but to yield.

With Arcadian offering an allegiance over an execution, the Djinn took on the role of the Jailor of Souls. The role allowed Scrimm to grant wishes and to retain a modicum of his power for general duties. It was more than most were allowed, and enough to retain his own sense of being.

Every fitting shuddered, none more so than Hexcalibur. The medieval knight's weapon cut through the air and buried its blade in the concrete with a deafening clank.

The moment it struck; the rumbling stopped.

A quick click of his fingers unleashed a splash of sorcery and the knight's entire breast plate fell from the statue to the floor. Scrimm knew full well what had been concealed behind the armor plate.

With only two people visiting him in the last decade, it was clear that only one person could have stolen the Time Map. Scrimm had been waiting for someone to make a difference and to break the tyrant's hold. Perhaps today had been that day.

Granted wishes had woven enough threads to increase Arcadian's presence, but with so many branches, Scrimm knew it would be difficult for his master to keep an eye on every single movement.

Scimm slammed a palm against the wall to re-open the cabinet. The shelves flew by on an endless conveyor belt and stopped abruptly at Daisy's alcove. He snatched her Soul Jar from the shelf and reared up to throw it to the floor. He had no intention of breaking the agreement, but as he had hoped for, his master came calling.

STOP!

A conflict broke out in Scrimm's mind as he was easily usurped by Arcadian.

Do not dare break that bond with her, Arcadian ordered.

"Master?"

You know what was stolen.

"As do you."

Your role is to consume the souls of the innocent and to protect reality itself. You have done neither.

"Eyes and hands. I have only two of each."

Two teenagers tricked the almighty Djinn.

"Deceit is a true art form. Such a trait should not be ignored. Maybe she is on the wrong side."

Did you not think something was wrong when they arrived at your cell?

"Why would I? Nobody would know of the map's whereabouts. It is you and I alone."

And in their possession, it now is.

"She desired wishes to find three friends. Who am I to not grant what those desire most."

She lied.

"Are you certain? I have the names of the three she seeks. Were your orders not to plant my granting seeds in every reality. I have done this in many different forms and vices. Today is no different."

They stole from us.

"Blame yourself, Arcadian. The more souls you use, the more wishes I grant. Without my full power, I cannot keep track of every single thread, and neither can you."

Then you are no longer of any use to me.

"That's not what I meant. At least allow me the chance to redeem. Allow me to utilize my powers."

Why should I trust you?

"You have nothing to lose. If I fail, it falls at my door, nobody else's. I ask just one thing. My weakened powers need to be restored to full."

I left you weak on purpose. Now I wish I had just done away with you from the outset.

Arcadian had heard enough. His psychic attack felt like one thousand needle tips piercing the Djinn's consciousness. Scrimm dropped to his knees as the attack continued to suck out any semblance of being, until nothing remained, only Arcadian.

The anticipated battle of minds ended before it began. Perhaps Scrimm had not been lying after all. Maybe his powers were weak enough for him to be tricked by two teenagers.

Arcadian guided Scrimm's avatar towards the Life Cabinet and retrieved the phantom souls of three teenage boys. The boys had been a useful part of a previous game. By giving them a reprieve, perhaps they would be so again.

The glass containers shattered against the floor, releasing three wraithlike entities of Tommy's nemesis Packard Walsh, and his two cohorts, Skank, and Oggy.

As they circled the upper chamber, Arcadian started chanting …

Find the five.
None shall stay alive.
Return what they stole.
And your old lives will unroll.
Fail me if you dare.
And live forever in despair.

The incantation gradually bent the three phantoms to the will of their master, and ultimately transformed them into Timeinators - powerful, reality phantoms, neither living nor dead, and all the time drawn to the power of the stolen map.

Should one suffer defeat in battle, the Timeinator would rise again as a recycled phantom, from a used soul. Forever battling, by using relentless resurrections.

The three phantoms left the cell through a reality portal, their destination unknown.

With his work done, Arcadian released his hold on the Djinn.

Scrimm had seen and heard everything his master had said and done. He smiled inside, knowing full well that nobody before had ever caused his master such concern. Today would go down in history as the day the tides turned.

FLASHBACK
EARTH, SUMMER, 1989

Rosewood Falls,

DAISY DREW lost count of the hours spent recording from the top ten radio countdowns to form the ideal mixtape. Only to witness, a few days later, the demon tape deck seizing her prized possession in a tangled web.

Such heartbreak could only be mended by one solitary action: by recording another mixtape. Despite praying for it to happen, her mom's recordings had somehow avoided the inevitable tangle, nightmare scenario.

For the entire journey to town, Daisy observed Rosewood Falls through the passenger window, while her mom's rendition of Tight Fit's, The Lion Sleeps Tonight, caused the town's wildlife to run for the hills.

In 1987, her town had been trampled to dust during a duel between Redzilla and a fire breathing behemoth. What remained standing had been blasted to oblivion during a war between Tobias Strong and a robot invasion. She should be witnessing rubble and ruin, not a small quaint town, with a host of unique residents.

Rosewood Falls Day of Destruction now felt like a bad movie plot, where everything she did meant nothing. She woke up every day in the exact place it all started, two floors above her brother's bedroom, which was now her mom's utility room.

Maybe if she had paid more attention and stopped Mikey from accepting that tabletop game from the guy at the video store, maybe life would have just carried on as normal.

During the game, Tobias's sacrifice allowed the teenagers a shot at confronting Arcadian. Their crazy risk to finish the game had been burned into her memory with a supernatural branding iron. She even referred to the day as *Arcageddon*. She could think of no better description.

By fighting bravely through various scenarios, the teenagers uncovered Arcadian's lair. In the final battle, Tommy chose to face him alone. In exchange for their power rings, Tommy asked Arcadian to return Daisy and his friends safely home. Arcadian held up his part of bargain. His friends left the cave safely, but only Daisy returned to Rosewood Falls.

She waited for days, but her brother, Kurt, Ted, and Tommy never showed up. Days swapped to months, and so on. Until finally she knew her life would carry on without them unless she did something about it.

Were people even aware of what happened on *that* day?

How could they be?

During the game, Arcadian's mind control possessed bodies and minds and turned the town into Stepford Falls. As the sands of time ebbed away, their souls were unwittingly released into *his* clutches. As a result, residents and loved ones were still missing. Not that anyone knew of their existence. Not anymore. It was as if they had been etched from a storyboard, and life had been rewritten.

Arcadian had fed off the residents' greed and moved on as if taking the moment in his stride. In his wake, those entwined in the web of lies had no choice but to succumb to the inevitable. Sheriff West had been a major casualty. Many more had died. The town had been cut in half and yet life went on with a bunch of new faces, as if being replaced by recycled meat.

At least her mom's beige Chevrolet Celebrity remained as sturdy as always. The car passed a few garbage trucks and then stopped at a set of traffic lights alongside Sheriff Logan's jeep. Ted's older brother waved. He seemed in good spirits, despite his goofy brother never returning home. Not that he knew any different. Ted had always been the Shaggy of her brother's Mystery Inc squad of nerds, and not withstanding his toiletry habits, she missed his tomfoolery.

Mayor Jerimiah 'Action' Jackson's Ford Mustang turned the corner towards them. Once a favorite Rosewood High School

Wolverine, the former big city Detective returned to town after the last Mayor retired. Rumor spread quickly upon his return that Jackson had been involved in an investigation with a high-profile member of society and after the criminal case crumbled, he needed to lay low. Where better to hide than Rosewood Falls. Nobody ever visited. Nobody ever holidayed. It appeared as if the town had been stuck in a reality flytrap and couldn't get out of first gear.

Daisy only realized her mom had parked in the Emporium's carpark when she heard the driver's door open.

Mrs. Drew leaned in to pick up her handbag. "Earth to Daisy."

"I'm here."

"Did you remember the shopping list?"

Daisy flashed a piece of paper between her fingertips. "Mom, I'm like an elephant. I never forget a thing."

"Are you sure?"

"Positive."

"I can't help it. You haven't been yourself recently."

"Only recently."

"If I'm being honest, it's been longer."

"There's a reason why. You just wouldn't understand."

"Try me."

"There's no point."

"Why? Because I'm your mom."

"No."

"Maybe you think I don't know what changes teenage girls go through."

"That's not it."

"Are you on drugs?"

"What! No! Why would you think that?"

"I'm concerned."

"I'm not on drugs, mom."

"Are you sure?"

"I think I'd know."

"You're displaying the obvious traits."

"Which are?"

"Mood swings. Staring at space. Lying in bed all day and night."

"Maybe I'm a vampire," Daisy's smirk failed to ease the tension. "It's called being a teenager."

"I was never like that."

"That's because you lived in a little house on the prairie!"

"You know full well I've called Rosewood Falls my home my entire life."

"That's not what I meant."

"Then why say it. Is that how the drugs change you?"

"I'm not on drugs. It's just, you were never alone like me."

"You're not alone. You have me, your father."

"You missed out Mikey."

"Who's Mikey?"

Daisy knew saying more would be pointless. "My imaginary friend. He's in the backseat."

"Is that who you see when doing *the* drugs."

"Do you know how ridiculous you sound."

"It's my job to sound ridiculous. You'll understand when you have your own kids."

"Can't wait. You know what, mom. Perhaps it's your singing driving me nuts. Did you ever think of that. Just go get your hair done. I'll get the shopping." Daisy stepped out of the car.

"No drugs!" her mom yelled across the car park as she made her way to the local salon, Trim Fittings.

DAISY entered the Emporium as Depeche Mode's *Just Can't' Get Enough* was playing over the speakers. An elderly resident was paying at the till, his foot tapping away to the catchy synth pop hit. Daisy nodded politely at the old man as she made her way down the nearest aisle.

She loved the band and one day hoped to see them in concert. Perhaps their world tour would reach as far as the ass end of the world. Not one band reached the starry heights of her town. Not even a book signing from a nobody author. Accepting that her life was unlikely to change any time soon made shopping today a little more bearable.

Before she knew it, every item on the list was in her basket, and she made her way to the till. The shop's owner, Max Bannatyne, appeared at the same time another Depeche Mode tune started, *People are People*.

She always remembered how Max doted on Tommy like a grandson. She only wished the old man could remember everything as she did. Like how Tobias Strong had saved Max's life. Without the intervention, Max would have probably ended up on the MIA list. Much like her best friend Maxine, who had been missing ever since the game.

When she knew so many people were unaccounted for, Daisy had entered the Emporium and demanded answers. Max had openly admitted that he had no recollection of anything so fantastical. He even suggested she should lay off those funky cigarettes all the kids smoked.

After their conversation, her mom's questioning about *the* drugs began. Ever since, Daisy played it coy and joked how she only raised the question as a dare. Despite dropping a few feelers, to see if he would let something slip, Max had said nothing about the game, Tommy, or anyone else who had disappeared. He clearly had no idea about any of it.

"Morning, Max. How's tricks?" she said.

"Tricks are good as they can be. Did you enjoy last night's movie?"

"Swords, sorcery, blood, and sandals. What's not to like."

"You rent the Sword and the Sorcerer every Friday night, for the entire weekend."

"It has sentimental value."

"If that's the case, just keep it."

"I can't do that, Max."

"I can buy another copy."

"What about Tom–" Daisy stopped herself from blurting out the rest of his name by purposely dropping her purse on the floor. When she stood, Max handed over two brown paper shopping bags.

"Who's Tom?" he asked.

"What?"

"You said what about Tom."

"Oh. I was trying to say what about tomorrow, to return the movie."

"Keep it."

"I can't do that."

"Don't hurt an old man's feelings."

"That's really kind of you Max."

"Add the shopping to your mom's tab?"

"We wouldn't have it any other way," Daisy hoisted the bags and made her way to the front entrance.

The entrance bells jangled overhead as Mrs. West and Tommy's younger brother Teddy walked towards her. Teddy had aged well, and resembled Tommy in stature. If not for his cropped hair, he could have been Tommy's twin at that age.

"Daisy Drew," Mrs. West said gleefully. "How is life in the fast lane. Hectic as usual?"

"Isn't it always in this town. Hey, Teddy. How is life treating you?" Daisy lowered the bags to the floor.

Teddy nodded casually as he made his way to the comic book section.

"How long has it been?" Mrs. West asked.

"I thought I saw you the other day."

"Unless the other day was Christmas time, at your parent's party."

"That long, huh. Wow, time has crept up on me."

"I hope you're not avoiding us?" After a few seconds Mrs. West smiled.

"You know how it is. Studying, working. I bet Teddy's the same."

Daisy noticed Mrs. West's considerate look in her son's direction. Reading her expression suggested Teddy had been struggling. Word had spread around town of his disobedience at school, and his general recklessness when it came to socializing in town. Fighting, graffiti, and shoplifting had been batted around as just the start of his bad behavior. Not that she had witnessed anything firsthand.

"That bad, huh?" Daisy asked.

The comment caught Mrs. West off guard. She quickly wiped a tear from the corner of her eye. "Gossip travels fast in this town."

Daisy nodded sheepishly. "Not as fast as kids changing into teenage monsters."

"If that's the case, then boys should never grow old."

"I remember when my bro–" Daisy pretended to sneeze, to avoid finishing the sentence.

"What was that?"

"I was going to say when my folk's fence got broken by a neighbor's kid. He was fine one minute. The next, a little terror. Nothing was safe. Hulk smash!"

"I'll happily admit it's been a struggle to keep Teddy in line. Maybe his father leaving had an impact."

"You think he'd look up to his dad being a Sheriff an all."

"Sheriff," Mrs. West laughed. "He was never Sheriff. He could never have been, not with his criminal record."

"I had no idea."

"How would you. You would've only been an infant back then. Drinking, fighting. Perhaps there is a bit of his father in Teddy. Or maybe it's because I work all hours just to keep the roof over our heads and can't give him my full attention. Or maybe it's something deeper."

"Like what?"

"I'm not sure. It was odd. About Christmas time, a few years ago, he just changed overnight. And I don't mean the usual tantrums. He went from Teddy to terror at warp speed."

"Mom, I need five bucks," Teddy demanded from across the store.

"Sure, honey. One second," Mrs. West replied. "Are you sure you're okay, Daisy? You look a little pale."

"I think I just need a change of pace. I've been working at HIM a lot. Perhaps I should go out, enjoy some *me* time."

"You really should. You're young, beautiful. You need to be out enjoying yourself a little. Maybe with a boy."

Daisy blushed. "No chance."

"You're blushing."

"Am not. Okay. There was someone. A few years ago. Not anymore."

"Anyone I know?"

It took all her willpower to not grab Mrs. West by the shoulders and yell Tommy's name at the top of her voice. "No. He left town a while ago."

"That's a shame. But don't let sadness hold you back. You're only young once. You should be out enjoying life to the full. In fact, I have just the ticket." Mrs. West reached into her handbag and handed Daisy a folded pink flyer. "A carnival came to town last night. I took Teddy. The Super Loops kept him occupied all night. For once, it allowed me some of my own *me* time."

"What was that like?"

"I got a date. I know, I'm still using my married name an all, but …"

"Anyone I know?"

"He's with the Carnival." Mrs. West winked. "And mysterious. Just how I like my men. You really should go. You might strike lucky yourself."

"I don't know. Carnivals aren't really my thing. The same could be said for Carnys."

"Maybe this one will make you change your mind. You might find something there which will help you find what you're looking for."

"Mom! Five bucks!" Teddy yelled.

"Sorry, Daisy. I need to go and appease the hulk before he trashes the store. Say hi to your mom from me."

"I will. Thanks."

"And don't be such a stranger."

Daisy slid the flyer in her jacket pocket without opening it and made her way to the car park.

FOR the remaining sunlight hours, Daisy consoled her broken heart by listening to her favorite mixtape. The replica of recordings made in 1987 by Tommy included a host of love songs and one hit wonders.

Daisy knew when Tommy presented her with the birthday gift that he didn't care about her boyfriend. Looking back, she had no idea what she saw in Zack in the first place. He was everything that she hated - the epitome of a cool, popular, older kid, who owned a Corvette, and a leather jacket. Aside from a few compliments, he showed no empathy. Not that she craved attention. Just a few words occasionally would've been nice. Yep, Zack had been a douchebag of maximum proportions. A douchebag who had not returned to Rosewood Falls, just like everyone else who had been duped by Arcadian.

One word described why she yearned to see Tommy's handsome smile again and feel the safety from his warm embrace. Love. The type of love she imagined would accompany the reincarnation of a Molly Ringwald character.

Daisy's love life collapsed after Zack cheated with Veronica Welch. After shedding a few tears, she chose to dump Zack. Not long afterwards, Daisy accidentally kissed Tommy on the lips whilst thanking him for lending her some money for presents.

Zack found out about the kiss and in retaliation decked Tommy in the school yard. Thanks to Ted, every kid in school joked that Tommy was knocked out longer than Buck Rogers was frozen.

Zack blamed everyone but himself for the breakup. Daisy blamed her dormant feelings for Tommy for the reason for dumping Zack. When apologizing for Zack finding out, she tried to tell Tommy how she felt.

Despite Daisy's apology, Tommy still blamed her for making Zack jealous. After spending more time together, Tommy forgave Daisy. It wasn't long before the two of them kissed properly.

Then came the love parade.

The End.

Molly Ringwald has nothing on me. Except all her movies end happily ever after.

A mixtape had been the perfect present for her birthday. It was more than just songs. It was a statement of true love. Listening to Tommy expressing his feelings with emotional songs was perhaps the moment he stole her heart. A moment she treasured. A moment she wished she could speak to him about.

Shortly after returning to Rosewood Falls, Daisy noticed to her horror that the mixtape had gone. She made piecing the playlist together a priority. It remained her only link to her previous life. A previous life where Tommy had been willing to spend time around her, even though she treated him terribly before they were close to becoming an item.

She now knew why she acted that way. Deep down, she had feelings for Tommy. Feelings surfaced when true love's arrow snagged her by the heart and roped her into the love rodeo. Who would've thought it possible that Tommy, her brother's geeky best friend, would be the love of her life.

Overcome by emotion, Daisy dropped onto her bed and cried into her pillow.

Their short-lived romance was the most wonderful experience of her life. If time could ever be turned back, she promised to do it all differently next time. She would no longer be mean. She would welcome him into her life earlier and live every second as if it was her last.

DAISY awoke a few hours later, feeling depressed and in need of some comfort food. Her visit to the kitchen just so happened to coincide with her mom handing over a Carnival flier. The moment looked staged. B movie acting at its best.

"I thought it might help you find what you're looking for," her mom stated. "I don't mean *the* drugs.'

"Enough with the drugs," Daisy snapped back.

"I think you should go."

Her mind was made up when her parents commented about needing some alone time.

DESPITE a chill in the air, most of the townsfolk attended the Carnival. Youngsters ran amok, cramming their parents loose change into arcade machines and throwing whatever they could at targets to win a tacky cuddly toy.

After Daisy bought some candy floss, she acknowledged a few of the kids she knew from school. The group had gathered at a circle of benches, jocks sneaking in some alcohol and concealing the bottles in brown paper bags. Rather than join them, she headed off on her own and made her way towards the outer ring of rides, including a Haunted Funhouse and the Super Loops.

Tommy's mom had been right. The Super Loops queue stretched across the field and was clearly the ride of choice.

"Ye'll be thir fo' ages."

The man's Scottish accent took her by surprise, as did his youthful features. He wore a tacky replica Hawkman helmet from the Flash Gordon movie. The two flimsy, plastic horns protruding from either side sunk more than Droopy Dog's cheeks. The matching leather outfit with enormous wings and feathers, tied off by leather straps to a golden chest plate, did very little to flatter his appearance.

"Nice outfit, Hawkeye," Daisy said, uninterested.

"It's homemade."

"You don't say."

"C'mere an' try 'is," the man said, gesturing to the glass cabinet in front of him.

It was Queen's iconic Flash Gordon theme playing in the background that hooked her, rather than the text etched on a plaque displayed at the front of the glass case balanced on a tabletop. Encased behind the glass, the sculpted head of the bearded Prince Vultan from the movie was moving side to side, his irises flashing yellow as he followed Daisy's approach.

"Vultan says mek yer wish," the man said.

Daisy hesitated.

"Weel?"

"I see the wheels," Daisy said, motioning at the two wheels a player would use to aim a coin at Vultan's mouth, which continually opened and shut of its own accord.

"I said weel. As in weel, ur ye gunna play?"

"Oh, sorry. It's just your accent. I didn't mean to offend you."

"Ye didny."

"How much is it?"

"One coin."

"What do I do?"

"Ye mek yer wish."

Daisy inserted a quarter in the coin slot and released it by pressing a glowing red button on the right of the machine. The coin rolled along a neck to a groove at the opening. By turning the two wheels attached to the surface of the glass, she steered the coin along a gulley and into Vultan's open mouth.

After a few seconds, accompanying the smoke spewing from the mouth as the head rotated three hundred and sixty degrees, was a low pitch voice repeating the phrase, '*Gordon's alive*'.

"Do I make a wish now?" she asked the man.

"Aye."

With nothing to lose, Daisy said out loud the one thing she had wished for ever since returning to Rosewood Falls. "There must be someone who can help me find you, Tommy."

She repeated the statement until Vultan's head returned to its starting position, the smoke dissipating, the machine shutting down. For a fleeting moment she thought it would work.

"Is that it?" she asked.

"Aye."

She knew machines like this were cash cows, so why she felt so disappointed that her wish had been a con came as a surprise. In her honesty, she would have paid with her soul to see him again.

"What a piece of junk!" Clearly annoyed by her naivety, Daisy turned to leave when a business card ejected from the slot beneath the red button.

VULTAN

HAS SPOKEN

YOUR WISH IS

GRANTED

Until today, impossible had been a word Daisy had never felt the need to use. How would a granted wish ever bring back her true love? Hiding her uncertainty, she pocketed the card in the rear pocket of her jeans and turned to leave, only for a powerful voice to catch her off guard.

"Closed, this Carnival is."

A dazzling torch light shone directly in her eyes.

"Hey, go easy with the bat signal," she said.

"Something to hide, you have?"

"Not at all. You're just burning out my irises."

As the torch lowered, the guard's gangly, hunched frame came into view. Features more akin to a Goblin than human took her by surprise, his grimy uniform too small for his physique.

She estimated no more than a few seconds had passed since she made her wish. In that time, Vultan's machine had vanished and so had the Hawkman. She had also been abandoned by everyone else at the Carnival. As a daunting silence arrived alongside a suffocating mist, she felt more alone than she ever had.

"Where is everybody?" she asked, shivering from a chill.

"Here, they are not."

The comment lingered in her mind longer than it should have. She reached for her back pocket, wondering if her wish had been granted. "Are you here about the wish?"

"Wish, you ask."

"You know what. I think I'm losing my mind."

"Brought to fruition through fear, wishes are."

"I'm not scared of a wish. It's more of a last chance scenario kind of thing."

"To stay, a wrong path, you will take. Run along, you must." His spindly index finger pointed in the distance towards the exit, which appeared through a break in the mist.

"This card said I have a wish."

"Wishes are here not. Souls only for sale."

"Do you mean my soul?"

"If to keep your soul intact, leave you must."

"Are you threatening me? Who are you?"

"Offer is a warning, all I can."

"Listen creepoid, I'm not leaving here until I get some ..."

Something concealed inside the fog groped at her ankles, catching her off guard. She reached down, swiping away what felt like a fine film of slime secreted against her jeans. Whatever she had come into contact with stunk to high heaven.

"Who slimed me?" she said.

The security guard had already started to flee. "Here, he is. The wind, towards you must run. Your chance, only it is."

As if answering the warning, strong winds swept across the Carnival, wiping out kiosks and equipment, lightning erupting amidst a chorus of thunder. The sky was alive with huge tentacles writhing within the shadowy cloud front.

"Fly!"

Hawkman's warning came across louder than any thunderclap.

"Fly, ye fool!"

His second warning she took more notice of despite of what lay ahead through the storm. A grounded runway of spotlights indicated a way out. At the end of the path lay a golden archway, decorated with fake diamonds and flashing bulbs. To reach her exit, she had to evade an onslaught of tentacles, originating from the sky, striking at the earth like an angry God's fist.

Daisy sprinted towards what could easily have been used as part of any corny Saturday night gameshow. And yet, no matter how fast she ran, the barrage continued to haunt her movements.

Pitched skywards by the tornado, Daisy was pulled towards the maelstrom of a violent thunderstorm. She pierced the cloud ceiling, half expecting to be ripped apart by the limbs of some supernatural planet eater. Instead, she experienced calmness, as the eye of the storm welcomed her with open arms.

Daisy had always imagined the storm's heart to be a serene, blue sky met with a tranquil skyline. She had been right.

"DAISY! Daisy!"

Daisy snapped awake and bolted upright. "Fly, you fool!" she yelled.

"Jesus H, shit." Her mom, who was standing at the side of her bed, clutched at her chest in shock.

"Mom."

"The last time I looked. Why are you shouting?"

"Why are you in my room?"

"I'm in your room wondering why your bedding is soaked through."

Daisy glanced over the side of the bed at a sodden carpet. She had no recollection of dumping her clothes on the floor or leaving her window wide open.

"Did something die in here?" her mom asked.

"I think I ate some dodgy Tacos at the Carnival."

Her mom didn't care for the answer. She reached down for the jeans and immediately dropped them. "That's disgusting. What is that? Slime. What on earth did you do last night? What did you roll in? A sewer. Look at the state of the carpet. Your curtains are ruined. And don't get me started on your bedding."

"Mom, I can explain."

"Oh, you'll do more than that. But not right now. I'm not spending another minute in this cesspit."

"That's a bit harsh."

"It's no wonder you have no friends when you live in such a pigsty. Is this what happens when you touch *the* drugs."

"Will you stop nagging about *the* drugs."

"It should be you who is stopping. And if you think I'm cleaning any of this up, then you've got another thing coming, young lady."

"I didn't ask you to do anything."

"Well, at least we're on the same wavelength. Clean it all up. Now."

"What about my clothes?"

"If I were you, I'd burn 'em. Your wages at HIM better cover this because I sure as hell am not paying out afyer another one of your screw ups." Mrs. Drew stormed out of the bedroom and slammed the door.

DAISY had no recollection of what occurred between breaching the eye of the storm and her mom's tirade. Much like when she made the wish, only a matter of seconds had passed. She was certain of it.

Did this elephant fly?

Even though she could not discount flying, she burst out laughing and slumped back on her pillow.

"You know you didn't fly, dumb ass. Your ears aren't big enough for a start. Now my ass, that's a different story."

She casually glanced at her alarm clock and the brown, padded envelope obscuring the view. Guessing her mom must have left it for her, she peeled back the seal and found inside a laminated business card.

VULTAN SAYS

ANSWER ME …

By the time she examined the card, something in the envelope started to play a strange jingle.

Daisy dropped it all in a panic and fled to her ensuite bathroom. She slammed the door closed, tumbled into the bath, and pulled across the shower curtain.

"Cos pulling a curtain that doesn't even stop water, will always save your life!"

Freaking out had been the only course of action. She had only ever heard jingles on the television or radio.

Why would an envelope be jingling?

"Is that even a word?"

The jingle grew louder after every rotation.

She cupped her ears to blot it out. Nothing worked.

"What do you want?" she yelled, a moment before realizing what she had been overlooking all along.

Vultan.

The Wish.

Tommy!

Daisy scrambled out the bath and yelped as she fell hard on the plastic floor, her foot entangled in the shower curtain. Nursing her bruised ribs, she yanked open the door with her free hand and snatched the envelope from the floor.

Tipping it upside down released a black, plastic device, engraved with the word AIKON. It was about the size of a candy stick box. The type teenagers pretended were cigarettes to look cool. Adjacent to a small antenna sticking out of the top, was a flat, plastic screen.

Daisy had seen enough of the geeky Science Fiction show to know a Star Trek communicator when she saw one. The spring-loaded cover released automatically when she picked up the device. Beneath the seal was a set of numbers from one to nine and a handful of weird symbols.

"I can't believe I'm going to say this but, hey, beam me up, Scotty."

When nothing happened, she glanced over at the card she had dropped.

HOLD ME TO

YOUR EAR

She tentatively followed the instruction and moved the phone to her ear. "Scotty?"

"Daisy?"

"I think so. I mean, yeah, it's me. Who is this?"

"I'm me. From last night. I ken alot aboot ye, Daisy."

"You left me in the middle of an empty carnival to get attacked by a sky squid."

"A what?"

"Do you have a name, or do I just call you Hawkeye?"

"Connell McLeod. At yer service."

"How did you find me?"

"Wi' great difficulty."

"And this device?"

"Tis a mobile phone."

"A mobile phone."

"Aye. They come in handy in eh different reality."

"A different reality. And I thought phoning out of town was expensive. Not that I've ever needed to. There I go again. Pondering my existence in this pit of a town where nobody leaves, or visits."

"Calm doon."

"Sure, I'll calm down when you tell me what reality you are from. Clearly not mine."

"We ca' it a reality. It's something mair than that."

"Level with me."

"Yer lost, 'n need tae fin' a wey oot."

"Good guess, Sherlock. What else you got?"

"Ye wanted someone tae help ye."

"Yes."

"Weel, am it. In fact. I've bin looking for ye."

"Why me?"

"Because thir can be ainlie wan."

"Only one what?"

"One reality for ye and Tommy."

"Where is he?"

"Stuck in limbo."

"Where is that? France?"

"Nae, it's … never mind. Am here tae help ye. Inside eh envelope ur two choices. Choice wan, ye come wi me and I help ye find Tommy. Choice two, ye stay where ye ur an' we will never talk again."

"Nothing like getting to the point. Do I have a choice?"

"I can show ye the way, but I canny choose."

"Why not mention any of this to me in person last night? While you were the birdman."

"I wis thir on purpose. Naebody cuid see Vultan but ye."

"And I just thought it was a shit game."

"Aye, it is 'at, but ye had to make eh wish, t' force yer way back into eh game."

"Arcadian's game is still going?"

"Course it is. Tommy wis cheated after he changed eh rules. He's wi' another version of ye in an accelerated dream state. He thinks he's merrit wi' weans."

"Merrit with weans?"

"Married with kids."

"Tommy has kids?"

"Aye. Fur him, he thinks he's leed forty years. Fur ye, tis a blink o' an eye."

"You'd think I'd be shocked, but you had me at Arcadian lied to us."

"Arcadian cheated him. Jus' like everyone 'at plays eh game. It's eh only way Arcadian ken how t' play."

"Then I guess it's time for us to cheat back." Daisy reached inside the envelope and retrieved a blue and red Tic Tac. "Which one do I take?"

"Pick red an' ye come wi' me. Ye take blue, ye stay where ye ur," Connell added.

"If I go, will I ever see my parents again?"

"I canny promise anything, blossom."

"Do you have a plan?"

"Thir is someone we can find. He's a Djinn. People call him eh Wishgiver."

"And he can help me find Tommy?"

"Aye. Bit first we need tae fin' Skynewt 'n uise tis time portal."

"You'd think that would freak me out, but I'm game for anything. I just never considered that the biggest decision of my life would be decided by a Tic Tac."

"Red or blue. Eh time t' choose is upon ye."

Chapter 9

There can be only one.

WISHVILLE

TOMMY and Daisy departed the granite elevator onto the pyramid's rooftop. Between the rows of pulsing generators and transmitter towers, an elderly man wearing a tuxedo and bowtie produced a flurry of burgeoning energy from his fingertips. It was hard for Tommy not to picture the Emperor from Return of the Jedi.

"Wit took yer, Daisy Drew?" Connell McLeod's fleeting glance over his shoulder was all the two teenagers deserved for being late.

"Relax, Highlander."

"Tell 'at tae ma fingertips!"

Immortal had been a word McLeod had used flippantly. Daisy considered it to be nothing more than an enthusiastic boast. From the last time she had seen him, his natural, youthful features now looked drawn out and tired, as if powering the barrier had drained him. Suddenly she understood that whatever deal McLeod made to help her find Tommy had started to accelerate his lifeline.

"You weren't lying about being immortal," she said.

"Did ye speak to th' Djinn?" McLeod grizzled, ignoring the comment.

"I am a lady of my word."

"And?"

"A deal has been made. That wish I made with Vultan. It was one of the Djinn's, wasn't it?"

"Am sorry it had to be 'at way."

"Don't be. We did what needed to be done. I would do the same in a heartbeat."

"I hope ye wis worth it. Did ye get it?" Mcleod added, directing the question towards Tommy.

Tommy had heard little of their conversation and the question took him by surprise.

"Th' map. Did ye get it?"

"That was you, in the chamber. I knew I recognized your voice."

"How many Heelanders do ye ken. Please tell me ye took the map."

In all the excitement, Tommy had forgotten about what he discovered beneath the knight's armor. He reached for the back pocket of his sweatpants and retrieved the folded parchment. "You mean this old thing?"

"What is that?" Daisy asked.

"I found it beneath an armored breast plate." Tommy handed the leather scroll to Daisy.

"Just like that."

"Not exactly. It opened. It seemed rude to just leave it there."

"In other words, you stole it."

"Like you stole a Trans Am."

"Now ye both stole something. Wi' a wee bit a help from me, I might add," McLeod said.

Daisy unfolded the document to reveal a leather map with a cobalt-colored background, bordered by eight clock faces. Each clock face was separated by a pair of ruby slippers. Inside the border, linked separately to the eight clocks, the map came alive with locations of eight reality portals, and the location of a solitary black hole. The teenagers had no idea what they had at their fingertips. If they had, they might well have discarded it there and then.

Daisy jabbed the map in McLeod's direction. "This looks like another part of the plan I should've known about."

"As wis agreed. I telt ye I wuid find a way fo' ye to help yer friends, and fo' ye all to get home."

"You did, but there was no mention of stealing from a Djinn."

McLeod shrugged. "Sum minor details."

"You call this map minor."

"Hey, I stole it. Not him," Tommy snapped.

“Keep telling yourself that. Any tool we use to defeat Arcadian is fine by me. What’s with the clocks, McLeod?”

“One timepiece fur one reality jump per day. Th' map wull git ye in, th’ portal wull git ye oot. Dae no’ touch the clockface until yer certain who yer want to find, or where ye want to go,” McLeod said.

“How will we know when to use it?”

“Ye hae tae fin’ a jump point. It cuid be anytime yer feelin’ maist threatened, juist mak’ sure thare is nobody nearby whin ye jump. Just say yer friends name, or a destination an’ wherever they ur, th’ map will guide ye thir. Th’ rest is up to you’se. Daisy, I knew th’ map existed, an’ I knew it wis hidden here, somewhere. I jus’ needed ye to distract th’ Djinn long enough fo’ his powers to be sidetracked. At allowed me time to pinpoint its whereabouts.”

“What’s so special about it?”

“Th’ map kens whit yi’ll need to survive, Tommy.”

“You mean the eight clocks and eight portals,” Daisy said.

“Aye. I told ye to agree eight days with th’ Djinn. Which is th’ amount o’ time you will be stuck in th’ comet’s tail.”

“What happens if we run out of the clocks and portals?” Tommy asked.

“It’s end of line.”

In no time at all, McLeod’s aged body wilted. His arms drooped as his lifeforce began to drastically fade away. The body of an average sixty-year-old quickly swapped to one of a frail eighty-year-old.

“You don’t look so hot.” Daisy braced her arm around his waist to keep him upright and his arms pointing skyward.

“I guess I hev it coming after I swapped immortality fo’ three wishes,” McLeod said.

“That was a dumb idea.”

“No’ really. I got ye here. Then I asked fo’ th’ power to protect ye both. Ma last wish is noo in ma jaiket pocket. Take them, quickly.”

She hurriedly reached inside his pocket to retrieve five platinum bangles and a floppy disk. “What are these?”

“Avatar bracelets. Thir is wan for ye, an’ each o’ yer friends. They will enable ye to use abilities, jus’ lek th’ power rings ye described. Ye will need to use them against th’ Timenators. One avatar per day. Wi’ limited power.”

“Timeinators?” Tommy remarked.

“Time enforcers. Ye stole Arcadian’s map. Thir’ll be coming for ye, an’ it.”

“Timeinators?”

“Ur ye a parrot? They ur real. Everything here is real, an’ time is up. When I release ma powers, the pyramid will be overrun wi’ th’ zombie horde. They will swarm across th’ facility lek locusts, devouring any flesh an’ blood they find.” McLeod had already switched his attention to Daisy. “It’s imperative, from th’ moment ye’ choose yer destination, ye move as quickly as ye can. Th’ Timeinators will track yer target doon by any means necessary. Ye must be quick, or yer friends will no’ survive.”

“You’re coming with us?” Daisy asked.

“‘is Heelander’s journey has ended, Daisy Drew.”

“You came for me when I needed someone the most. I am not leaving you behind.”

“Thir is nae other way.”

One of McLeod’s arms dropped to his side. Whatever power he once had now lay in ruins. The barrier started to falter. Enough green mist from the comet’s tail encroached through the cracks for McLeod to show concern for his friend.

“McLeod, you sacrificed everything for us. I will never forget that.” Daisy’s cheeks glistened with her tears.

“Everyone meks sacrifices. We jus’ hev to choose when we mek oor own. Now end all ‘is madness, once an fo’ all.”

“Thank you, McLeod,” Tommy said.

Daisy took Tommy by the wrist and led him to the center of the rooftop. Radiation had already reached the fringes of the facility.

“It’s now or never, Daisy,” he said.

“What about the disk?” she asked McLeod.

“You’ll ken whin th’ time comes,” McLeod replied.

Daisy slid the disk into her trouser pocket. Her hands quivered with emotion as she held out the map in front of them, her middle and index fingers hovering over the first clock face. “We go for Ted first.”

“Are you sure?”

“He is the most awkward and likely to be the toughest test.”

“I guess that makes sense. What about my kids?”

Rather than answer, Daisy pressed her fingertips on the first clock face and then said, “Ted ‘Theodore’ Logan.”

As the clockface slowly faded, roof fittings were torn apart as a reality portal surfaced ten feet away.

Tommy held Daisy tightly. She wrapped her arms around his waist as gusts of wind swept across the rooftop, almost bowling them over. Pink lightning bolts danced, as from the heart of the spiral an invisible lasso snatched Tommy and Daisy from the ground and pitched them towards an increasing blue cloud.

As the portal closed and with his lifeforce drained, McLeod sank to the floor. The shield capitulated in full. The radiation ran rampant across the facility, as if it had been waiting for this exact moment to strike.

McLeod faded into unconsciousness, the Zombies deafening chorus the last thing he heard before the final drops of his lifeforce wound up inside a glass counter in the Djinn’s Time Cabinet.

DAY ONE

(Seven jumps remaining)

Chapter 10

Wake up Neo ...

MONTH - DAY HOUR - MIN
JUNE 11 CHIVAGO 20:47
REALITY DESTINATION

AFTER LEAVING his apartment at the Heart O' the City Hotel complex, Ted 'Theodore' Anderson headed across the street to Nate's Deli.

As he did every night before his midnight MC gigs at Tech Noir, Ted sat in his usual spot at the corner booth. With his laptop plugged in to the mains, he listened to new age trance music on his black Panasonic headphones. His favorite tipple, an orange Whip cocktail, of a combination of rum, vodka, cream, and orange juice quenched his thirst.

After putting the finishing touches to tonight's playlist, Ted closed his eyes and not for the first time dreamed of a world created from digital rain. Green numbers set against a black backdrop created the building blocks of humanity. Digitized inhabitants moved effortlessly around the realm, oblivious to the codes of life, whereby births and deaths were handed out as abruptly as ending or starting a code cycle.

Research implied he was witnessing a subliminal message, somehow designed to pass below the normal limits of perception. At the opposite end of the spectrum, people just thought Ted to exist on the crazy side of life.

It wasn't clear how long it was before Ted felt an unexpected urge to open his eyes. It coincided with a message appearing on his laptop.

WAKE UP TEO …

ARCADIAN HAS YOU …

For a moment Ted thought he was still dreaming. He removed his headphones and to clear the screen pressed control and X on the keyboard. The message cleared, only to be replaced by another.

FOLLOW THE RABBIT …

Ted pressed the escape key a couple of times, only for another message to appear.

KNOCK, KNOCK TEO ...

The waitress rapped her knuckles twice on the tabletop, startling him. "Here's your bill, Ted," she said, her nametag revealing her name as Trinity.

"Wild Stallions. The only two people I know who use a phone box to travel through time."

"You've lost me, Ted."

"You are not the first person to say it this week. You will not be the last."

"Are you okay?"

"That depends. Did you see anyone come near me earlier?"

"Nobody else here but us regulars."

Only three people were in the diner. Tommy Duggan, the diner's owner. Rocky, a trucker he once witnessed bullying a Clark Kent lookalike, and Trinity, who covered the night shift. Ted doubted any of them would have any reason to or have the skill to hack his laptop.

"Is something wrong?" Trinity asked.

"Did you ever have that feeling where you're not sure if you're awake or still dreaming."

"Like now."

"I meant before today, or any point in your life."

"Not really. Awake, asleep, you still owe me for your drinks."

Ted unplugged his laptop and handed Trinity a wad of notes. "That should cover it," he said, before walking out of the exit into the rain.

TECH NOIR

NOT for the first time, Ted's mixing skills enhanced the club's vibe to a legendary status. In front of his setup, the circular dance floor heaved with passion.

Never had he witnessed such intensity, but despite his best efforts, nothing he did would shake off the unusual messages he received at Nate's Deli.

Arcadian has you.
Follow the rabbit.
Teo.

Rather than let the conundrum ruin his night, Ted whipped off his t-shirt to reveal an athletic build and a body covered in tattoos. As he flexed his torso and increased the bass, a bombshell brunette dressed in denim hotpants made her way around the edge of the dance floor. Her wavy hair cascaded down to her shoulders like a heavenly waterfall, her cleavage barely contained by a checkered shirt tied off at her waist.

His friendly smile got a frosty reception from the brunette. To avoid a confrontation, Ted flipped the deck's program switch to finish the set. He then dropped off the stage to his left and headed in the opposite direction. A decision he quickly chose to regret.

A man plucked from rural Georgia in the late 1970s, with a blonde shag cut, blocked his path. His plaid shirt and jeans looked out of place for even Tech Noir's trendsetters but felt oddly synchronized with the brunette's attire.

It was clear that the two people were only interested in one thing – ménage à trois.

Ted had no desire to be the meat sandwich between two lovers, at least not after so many Orange Whips. Quickly making his way behind the stage to his dressing room, he closed the door and switched off the light.

Somebody knocked twice.

"Despite the rumors, I am not up for threesomes," he said.

Ted stepped back as the handle turned and the hot chick entered. Her friend with the shag cut remained outside, guarding the way in. He closed the door behind her.

The brunette switched on the light, her body language matching the type of chicks he preferred to avoid. This broad was confident, strong, and likely to see right through his façade.

She gestured for Ted to take a seat. He did as she asked, putting his feet up on the dressing table. At that moment he noticed a futuristic platinum bracelet on her wrist. It looked trendy, unlike the rest of her clothes, which resembled a country cowgirl.

"From out of town, huh?" he asked.

"What gave it away?" she replied.

"Okay. Enough small talk. Why are you here? Autograph. Selfie. Want me to send you a dick …"

"Stop right now."

"Let me guess. One night you were in town on business. We did the dirty. Now you are back for round two."

"Don't flatter yourself."

"You got pregnant and that was our kid outside. Which makes you about sixty."

"Do I look sixty?"

Ted shrugged. "Today has been a weird day for me. I am not sure of anything right now."

"You know why I am here. Think about it."

"Might I suggest multiple choice answers. Otherwise, we might be here for a while."

"I don't have time for jokes."

"Oh, I'm not joking."

"Fine. Knock, knock."

"I'd say come in, but you already did that."

"Think back," she said, clearly annoyed. "Knock, knock."

"Who's there?"

"Man, you're annoying."

"Whoa! I got it! That was you on my computer."

"Finally!"

"Why not just lead with that. How did you find me?"

"That's not important. All I can tell you is that you are in trouble."

"I kind of figured that when the good old boy blocked my path."

"Did you know he's watching you?"

"From behind the door?"

"Not him. *Him.*"

"Captain Chaos?"

"Not that *him.* The other *him. He* is watching all of us, Teo."

"Who's Teo? You said that name on the message."

The lady paused to take a deep breath, before continuing. "I know what you are looking for, Teo. You have never been sure of your purpose here. Nothing seems real. You feel lost. Like the rabbit losing its way to Wonderland."

Ted hesitated briefly, then lowered his feet from the dresser and rocked forwards in his seat. "Did you say rabbit? Okay, you hooked me. Tell me more."

"Not here. Too many eyes and ears."

"Fine. Where?"

"We'll let you know."

"But what if I want to find you first?"

"You can't."

"Why not?"

"Because."

"Because what?"

"Just because."

"Why do people always say cryptic stuff and then say, we'll tell you later. What was the point in coming here in the first place?"

"After the tricky interaction on your laptop, we thought it best to meet face to face."

"Why not make first contact when you want to tell me what's going on."

"You're over complicating things, Teo."

"I'm not."

"You are."

"No, I'm not. Why wait. Why can't we leave now?" Ted slumped back in his seat, folding his arms across his chest in a huff.

"Just be ready."

"How will I know? Telepathy. Will you hack my email account again. Maybe stalk my MyPage account."

"Oh, my God, even here you are annoying. Look, Teo …"

"My name is Ted. T.E.D. Four letters. I mean three. T.E.D. Got it!"

"Don't hide behind your façade, Teo, if you need us."

"You may have the wrong guy. Did you ever think of that?"

"Oh, you're the right guy. Trust me. Nobody can be as annoying as you without trying really hard. Now, there is a pay phone at the corner of Wells and Lake."

"I know it."

"Good. Just dial 2806 4212 and wait for someone to answer."

"Are you sure? The last time I called a number like that, I spoke to some husky voiced chick. Between you and me, it might have been a dude. It was hard to tell. I'd had a drink. Damn phone call cost me a fortune."

The woman turned to leave.

"How long do I wait?" Ted asked.

"As long as it takes."

"I just dial 2860 2414 and wait, got it."

"That's not it. Dial 2806 4212."

"Got it. 2860 2414."

"No! 2806 …"

"Why not enter it on my cell phone?"

"I don't know how to do that."

"You hacked my laptop, but don't know how to use a cell phone."

"You know what, let's go old school. Got a pen?"

Ted found a pen on his dresser and handed it to the woman. She scribbled the number on a napkin and handed it back.

"Don't lose it," she insisted.

"That's exactly what my mom said about my virginity when I told her I was moving to Chivago. Watch out for those gold diggers, Theodore. They'll steal more than your heart."

The woman sighed and turned to leave.

"Wait, what's your name?" Ted asked.

"Daisy Duke. My brother is Luke Duke. Now wake up, Teo ..."

THE bedside alarm exploded in Ted's hungover mind, forcing him to reach blindly towards the dresser. After lifting his head from the pillow, he finally managed to switch it off.

09:18

"Ah, crap."

He dressed quickly in the only fresh trousers and shirt he could find and made his way down to the apartment's parking lot.

Every employee at Betamaxcorp was offered an apartment and identical courtesy car. Ted had specifically tattooed his license plate - 70858 - on his right arm so as not to forget it.

What was normally a few miles drive to the Tower went by so quickly Ted didn't even remember starting the engine. Leaving his car in the office block's basement parking garage, he made his way to the seventy fifth floor and the software development department.

The journey in the lift went by in the blink of an eye and he had barely sat down in his booth when his phone rang. His supervisor, Mr. Beaumont, requested his presence immediately.

BEAUMONT was in his late forties and skinny looking. A daily routine consisted of wearing a matching grey, pressed suit and drinking a fresh Latte from one of the brand vendors across the street. His zero input on designing any software grated most of the employees. Even more so when he took all the plaudits. It helped to have a father on the Executive Board.

Ted's supervisor rocked back in his seat, crossing his arms. "Late again, Mr. Anderson. That's the third time this week."

"But it's only Tuesday."

"Exactly. Three days."

Ted watched Beaumont count down the days of the week with his fingers. Even counting to two was excruciatingly time consuming. "Sir, I get it. I'm late."

"You missed out the word *again*. What's the excuse this time?"

"Would you believe me if I said I got hit on by a chick in hot pants and a tight shirt."

"Ha, nice try."

"It's true. She gave me her number and everything."

"Mr. Anderson, I doubt any woman would give you her number willingly."

"This one did. Although I might have dreamt it. I can't be sure these days. Everything is sort of mashed together. I drove here at lightspeed. The elevator ascended at warp factor five."

"And you still arrived late to work."

"I know, right. Weird."

"I don't care what you get up to outside of the office, Mr. Anderson. What I do care about is tardiness. I've lost track how many times you and I have spoken."

"Best not count it on your fingers."

"Excuse me?"

"Nothing. You were saying?"

"What I was trying to say was if you are late again, I'm going to have to consider firing you."

"You can't fire me. If you do, who will design your games for you."

"I don't appreciate sarcasm. People have been sacked for less, Mr. Anderson."

"Mr. Beaumont, I really need this job."

"And I need a colon cleanse."

"What's that got do with being late?"

"Everything. Now, please leave. And use a mirror, or at least make the effort."

Ted left his supervisor's office and made his way back to his booth. Beaumont was right. His reflection in the blank VDU was a far throw from last night.

"Theodore Anderson?"

Still coming to terms with his appearance, Ted swiveled his seat to face the post room boy.

"This came for you whilst you were in with Mr. Beaumont."

The kid handed over an A4-sized parcel. Inside was a cell phone and a pair of sunglasses. The cell phone rang the moment it touched Ted's palm.

Ted flipped down the cover and answered. "This is the bear in the air, Officer Lyle Wallace calling Rubber Jerk in that rattlin' piece of black crap at your side door. Come on back, Rubber Duck."

"*Are you high, or an idiot?*" a woman snapped.

"I wish I was high, but here I am, stuck on life's slowest rollercoaster, just sailing through the swamp of crud on the vessel the Dementurd."

"*An idiot then!*"

"Hey, I'm dealing with things here."

"*Let's start over, shall we?*"

"Cool. This is Theodore Anderson at your disposal. No, that's not right. At your removal. Nope, at your service. Phew, got there in the end."

"*Have you finished?*"

"I think so."

"*Good.*"

"No, it's not. I drove to the office, but I don't remember getting in my car. Then I used the elevator to reach the seventy fifth floor, but I don't remember stepping into the lift. My boss called me to his office, I don't even remember walking there. What I do remember is that I almost got sacked by the douchebag, who doesn't know his elbow from his asshole."

"*This is all great and everything but save it for your shrink.*"

"Nobody wants to just talk about their feelings anymore. It sucks, man."

"*How about you let me do the talking, okay. Now, do you remember we spoke last night?*"

"You'll have to be more specific. I met a lot of people last night."

"*At Tech Noir.*"

"And you are …? Wait, you sound a lot like Daisy Duke. I could be wrong. Still nursing a hangover of the worst kind."

"It's me, Teo."

"Why do you keep calling me that? My name is Ted. It's not Teo. It's just Ted. T.E.D. How hard is that to compute!"

"Why do you keep covering up who you really are?"

"What I am, is a heart attack waiting to happen. You're real?"

"I'm real and so is the amount of time we have left."

"Which is how long?"

"Time is up, Teo."

"Talk about premature ejac–"

"You must get out of there, now. They're coming for you."

"Who?"

"The Timeinators."

"Timea what now! Are you on *the* drugs?"

"Why does everyone think I'm on drugs?"

"Are you?"

"Just put on the sunglasses and look above your booth, by the elevators."

"I'm not putting sunglasses on inside. I'll look a right ass."

"Just look!"

Without using the sunglasses, Ted glanced over the top of his booth. Three men in pressed suits and sunglasses approached Mr. Beaumont's office. The man in front flashed credentials and after a brief discussion, Ted's boss signaled in Ted's direction.

Ted ducked down, then crawled beneath his desk. "Are they here for me or the glasses? Wait, did you steal their sunglasses and send them to me?"

"Why would I do that?"

"They're all wearing sunglasses. Are they the sunglasses police? Is that a thing? It should be. Everyone wears sunglasses in Chivago. Well, everyone but me. That's a bit odd, don't you think. It's not like it's the sunniest city in the world. It rains all the time. It's kinda depressing."

"Will you stop talking and listen to me. You need to get out of there."

"Sure thing. How?"

"Your boss has an office. There is a window ledge. I want you to climb on to it."

"Are you nuts. I'm seventy-five floors up."

"*You must, Teo. If not, I can't help you.*"

"Unless you've got a magic potion that will grant me the gift of flight, then I think you and I are done, lady. Rubber Duck, out."

Ted closed the phone just as the three suited men arrived at the entrance to his booth.

The man in front stood rigid, as if he had a rod imbedded in his spine. He spoke slowly and with purpose. "Theodore Anderson?"

"That's my name, don't wear it out." Ted smiled, hoping to ease the obvious tension. "What can I do for you, Mr. …?"

"I'm Time Investigator Smith. These are my colleagues, Agent Blue, and Investigator Thunder."

"Time Investigators Smith, Blue and Thunder. Can I just say, Thunder, you've got the most unfortunate initials ever. It's like that time my friend Mikey was part of the Apparition Snatch Squad. His nametag spelt ASS. Man, that was hilarious. A real hoot. It was on a …" Ted slumped back in his seat as if hit by an invisible punch and swiveled in his chair. "Wait a minute. Who the hell is Mikey? How do I remember something I have no recollection of ever experiencing. Maybe I'm on *the* drugs."

"Mr. Anderson, you are acting a bit *odd*," Agent Smith said.

"No more odd than usual. My head is a little rattled though. Maybe I had one too many Orange Whips last night."

The agents shared a look.

"Did I do something wrong?" Ted asked.

"That we are about to find out. You are coming with us, Mr. Anderson," Smith added.

"Where are we going?"

"Downtown."

"Cool. Can we stop for a burger? I'm starving. You know how it is when you're up late and partying with the chichas."

"You mean Chicas."

"That's what I said, chichas."

"Chichas is a type of beer. Fermented in South and Central America, most commonly made from maize, grapes or apples."

"That's what I mean, chichas."

"You just said chichas again. Mr. Anderson, Chicas is Spanish for young women."

"Those two words sound exactly the same."

"But they are different."

"But they sound exactly the sa–"

A single shot from Investigator Thunder's Taser hit Ted in the chest. He fell to the floor, his body shuddering from the shock.

"Thank you," Investigator Smith said to his colleague. "I fear if you hadn't taken action, then we would be stood here until the end of days."

Chivago Police Department
Special Unit Offices
Downtown

TED awoke in the chilly atmosphere of an interview room. Sat in front of him, across a table, was a stone-faced Investigator Smith who was opening a laptop. His expressionless comrades stood at his shoulders. All three of them appeared more robotic than human.

Smith stared hard at the laptop, whilst scrolling down a document showing all of Ted's escapades during the game.

"Ted *'Theodore'* Anderson. Your work is very impressive."

"No need to tell me what I already know. I won awards for the updated version of Star Castle. You remember the original video game from the 80s."

"No, I do not."

"That's a shame. I guess you guys were taking classes on how to remove a personality."

Smith chose not to answer and turned his attention back to the laptop. Ted suddenly felt like lead weights pinned his arms to the tabletop. Much like the times he encountered any hot girl as a teenager, all over his body he felt a supernatural presence curbing his ability to react and speak.

Smith continued the interview. "It seems you've been living two lives, Mr. Anderson."

Ted tried to answer and could not.

"What is wrong, Mr. Anderson? Having trouble speaking?"

Ted felt the hold around his throat and the seal across his lips tighten.

"Mr. Anderson, when I ask a question, you will answer it. Do you understand?"

All Ted could do was nod.

"If you continue to talk gibberish or ridicule, I will be forced to seal your mouth closed forever. Do you understand?"

Ted nodded for a second time.

"Excellent."

The release around Ted's throat was instantaneous. He drew in breath as if it was going out of fashion. "Nice force choke, dude."

"Heed my warning, Mr. Anderson. There will not be a second one."

"I understand. Just call me Dumbo. I'm all ears."

"Now let me start again. It seems you've been living two lives."

"That, I can confess to."

"Oh, really."

"I'm a DJ by night and I work at Betamaxcorp by day. I've got a Batman vibe going on. I'm not him though. Batman."

Smith's head tilt forced Ted to close his mouth and pretend to zip it closed. "Mr. Anderson, I have evidence that proves you were once part of a group called the Four Horsemen."

"Huh?"

"And in order to hide your real identity, you have been using the hacker alias Teo."

"Why does everyone keep calling me that."

"You are Teo?"

"No." Ted looked less convincing by the second.

"The evidence proves otherwise."

"Yeah, about that. Let me explain. Just don't seal my mouth shut. Agreed?"

"Go on."

"My name is Ted. T.E.D."

"Mr. Anderson, my patience is waning."

"Okay. Okay. Let me explain. One day, maybe I mistyped an O, instead of a D."

"Please elaborate."

"Okay. I was using a little keyboard, with my fat sausage fingers, after a few orange whips. From that day on, I'm being called Teo, instead of Ted. Granted, an O and D look similar in capitals."

"You expect me to believe because of a *typo*, we've got the wrong person."

"No. I'm him. Well, I'm me. I'm just Ted, not Teo. It's like the joke about Juan the boat builder. You know that one? No. I'm guessing jokes aren't your thing. Okay, okay, it goes like this. Well, this guy Juan, he is sitting on a dock, looking depressed, when a fisherman comes over …"

"Get to the point, Mr. Anderson."

"I am. Now, Juan explains to the fisherman that he has built boats his entire life, but nobody in the village calls him Juan the boat builder. He's annoyed with this, because boat building is his craft, he's an expert. He wants to be noticed. Then, one day, Juan buys some sheep."

"Why?"

"I can't tell you yet, that'll spoil the joke."

"Mr. Anderson!"

"Okay, just wait. Don't go all Vader on me. Now, Juan is a paunchy, ugly kind of dude. Not a hit with the ladies, like you and your buddies. You know what I mean. Then, Juan says to the fisherman, *I build boats my entire life. Does anybody call me Juan the boat builder. No, no, no. But I get jiggy with the one sheep, and they call me Juan the sheep shag ...*"

"I get the punchline, Mr. Anderson."

"And therefore, you appreciate I mistype Teo once and I'm known as …"

"Teo, the hacker."

"Exactamundo."

"When in fact, you're Ted Theodore Logan."

"Now we're bonding like bros before hoes. But my name is Anderson, not Logan."

"So, you admit to it."

"Er, yeah. Did you not hear the story? Want me to tell the joke again?"

"That won't be necessary. Just answer one final question. You are the hacker we are looking for?"

"I am one hundred percent the guy you are looking for. Waddya know, I said it and you didn't even use the Jedi mind trick. I try to deny the Teo thing, you know, in the hope it'll fade away and I'll get back to good old Ted Theodore Anderson."

"You mean Logan."

"Yeah, no. Come again?"

Smith placed two photos on the desk and turned them towards Ted. One showed Daisy Duke, the other, the unknown male with the shag cut she accompanied at Tech Noir. Between the photos he slid a business card, labelled with the name Vultan.

"Do you know these two people, Mr. Anderson?" Smith asked.

"No."

"Are you certain?"

"Who's Vultan?"

"An associate of theirs. Look again at the photos. Are you certain they have never approached you?"

"She did."

"When?"

"Last night."

"You can identify her?"

"No."

"You can't, or you won't?"

"You misunderstand. I've *met* her. I don't *know* her. There's a difference."

Smith slammed the laptop closed. "Mr. Anderson, I do not believe you fully understand the swamp of turds you are currently in the middle of. It's about time that you did." Smith glanced at his colleagues. "Connect the hardline."

The two agents pinned Ted's upper body to the tabletop. Unable to break the hold, his lips melded together, forming a blockade of flesh. With his eyelids sealing by their own accord, Ted was left blind, stranded, and terrified as to what might come next.

As Smith's behest, one of his accomplices released a minute cybernetic insect on to Ted's neck, who remained helpless as it burrowed into the soft skin behind his earlobe, the invading parasite firing off a singular, intense electric shock, forcing the human's form to shut down, his mind to black out and his body to go limp.

"CUT the hardline!" Ted yelled out, before bolting upright in bed.

He was back home. His tattooed body was caked in sweat after experiencing a nightmare of being held down, and his body being invaded by a foreign object. He shuddered at the thought and rubbed a painful spot behind his ear.

He felt no incision. No pain. No mound. Nothing.

Perhaps it was another one of his quirky dreams.

It made sense, considering he had no recollection of travelling home, or if he even got out of bed this morning. Not that he had inclination of wanting to go outside. The mother of all hangovers shattered those illusions.

"Either I've lost the plot, or those Orange Whips were laced with acid."

Ted opened the apartment's main window, freeing a welcome breeze and the soothing sound of the city's constant downpour. Feeling better already, he braced against the windowsill, casually observing the flow of airborne traffic overhead, as it continued its daily grind of back and forth, like ants on parade. Further along the street, an emerald-colored sign flickered outside the derelict cinema. The letters N E O were visible, with the shattered fourth letter N somewhere in the street below following a recent lightning strike.

A vibrating sound drew his attention to the cell phone on his dresser. He answered, but only after he rolled across the bed in a rip-off of TJ Hooker. "This is Ted, on the bed, come back ya'll."

"*Teo?*"

Straightaway he recognized the voice of Daisy Duke. "For the love of God, my name is Ted. T.E.D."

"*We need to meet.*"

"Wait a minute. You're real?"

"*Do we need to go through this every time we talk?*"

"No, but that means I was actually grilled by Investigator's tits, bum and ass."

"*What happened?*"

"It's a bit foggy."

"*Try and remember.*"

"Gimme a sec."

"*Time is precious, Teo.*"

“Then you won’t mind waiting a few valuable seconds more while I … wait a minute. I remember now. They took me into custody. Then asked me a ton of questions about you, your shag cut friend, and someone called Boltan, Moltan.”

“*Vultan.*”

“Yeah, that was it. And don’t get me started about them bending me over the desk. And they kept getting my name wrong. Anderson, Logan, Teo, Ted, man it was getting confusing. And I struggle on the best of days. Believe me.”

“*Oh, I believe that very much. Those investigators are not what they seem.*”

“No shit, lady. Do you know how much a Taser hurts?” Ted lifted his shirt to show the wound, only to realize he was on a cell phone call. There were also no marks on his body. “That’s weird. There is no wound. Is this day even real?”

“*As real as this conversation.*”

“I really think I need to go to bed and wake up again and start all over.”

“*You can’t. And those agents were Timeinators, Teo.*”

“You do realize how ridiculous that sounds.”

“*Have you heard of Time Bandits?*”

“I’ve heard of the Tung Bandits. They’re a hard rock band from Pittsburgh.”

“*Not Tung, Time.*”

“I don’t know. About midday. It’s hard to tell when it’s always so gloomy.”

“*Do you ever stop.*”

“Stop what?”

“*Shut up! For the love of God, shut the hell up and listen to me. Time Bandits, Teo. Timeinators search and destroy Time Bandits. People who breach realities and encroach on timelines for their own purposes.*”

“And they’re after me?”

“*Yes.*”

“Why? I can’t even balance my credit bills. I can, however, balance a spoon on the end of my nose.”

“…”

“Your silence implies you don’t care. Okay then, Dukey. Answer me this. How did I get involved? Cos my bad luck started when you entered my life. I walk away from you; my life goes back to normal. Simples. Not that I remember much about my life until I went to Nate's Deli, and you hacked my laptop."

"*Define normal. You know what, scrap that. I haven't got time. A man found me and showed me the truth. I intend to honor his life by finishing what he started.*"

"And what did he start?"

"*He set me on a journey to show people the truth.*"

"The truth, huh."

"*It's all I can offer.*"

"Okay, okay. I might be partly convinced. If I am, what do I need to do?"

"*You can start by telling me exactly what you told the Timeinators?*"

"Nothing. Just that we had met."

"*What else?*"

"Nothing. And a joke, about Juan the sheep shag …"

"*Teo, you said you answered a ton of questions.*"

"Okay, I might have exaggerated a little."

"*Are you taking any of this seriously?*"

"It depends on what you mean by serious."

"*Life and death. Yours, mine, and everybody that you hold dear. We are all in danger.*"

"Calm down, lady. Jeez."

"*It's time to wake up, Teo. You are being manipulated by a powerful being.*"

"Bullshit!"

"*The only bullshit is the fake reality called your life. You know deep down that something doesn't feel right. We can show you a way out, but you need to believe. All I can do is guide you in the right direction. The next step, to escape this prison, is in your hands. If they have already found you, then we have only a limited time left here before the Timeinators find us ...*"

A commotion in the background sounded like banging and splintering wood.

"*Too late. Last chance. You need to leave where you are. Head to Nate's Deli now, booth number five. Beneath the righthand side cushion, you will find a 1985 copy of a magazine called Smash Hits. Open it at page thirty-two ...*"

BEFORE the call cut off, the recognizable sound of automatic gunfire could be heard. Ted wasted no more time. He swiped his leather jacket from the back of a chair and raced out of the apartment, across the street to Nate's Deli, and started flipping the cushions in booth five.

Just like Daisy promised, taped to the underside of one cushion was the Smash Hits magazine, and an assortment of dried chewing gum.

On page thirty-one he found an article showcasing the music video from a 1985 song by the band Ha-ha. Ted flipped over to page thirty-two and a black and white storyboard of sketches from the band's award-winning video.

The superstar DJ had watched the music video enough times to remember how a woman in a café was escorted by Horten Market, the band's lead singer, into a comic book reality. As the couple began to fall in love, their adventure was shattered by some bad guys on motorbikes. Halfway through the song, the woman thought her broken heart would never heal after she lost Market inside the storyboard. At the end of the song, the singer arrived at her bedroom door, a blend of comic book hero and a real-life human dreamboat.

After so much hype of being promised the truth, Ted expected a bit more than a few pictures from a copy of an archaic teen music magazine. He flipped through the rest of the magazine, disappointed that he clearly fell for a joke.

"Are you okay, Ted?" Trinity asked as she poured a coffee.

"Yeah, but I think I'm losing the plot. Did you see who left this here?"

"The magazine? No. It must have been expensive."

"Huh."

"The pictures are moving. It looks cool."

When he looked back at the magazine, the images of the couple had been replaced by a man and woman resembling Daisy and Luke Duke. The villains replaced by the same Time Investigators that questioned Ted.

"That's new," Ted said, intrigued by a magazine storyboard unravelling before him.

FLEEING DOWN A CRUMBLING STAIRCASE, THE DUKES REACHED A DOWNTRODDEN, HOTEL LOBBY.
LUKE KICKED THROUGH A BRITTLE EXIT AND HEROICALLY VAULTED THE STEPS TO THE PAVEMENT OUTSIDE.
DAISY FOLLOWED BEHIND AND RACED DOWN AN ADJACENT ALLEYWAY TOWARDS AN ORANGE 1969 DODGE CHARGER.
AN IMAGE OF A STARS AND STRIPES FLAG BEING HELD BY CHRISTOPHER REED'S SUPERDUDE HAD BEEN EMBLAZONED ON THE BONNET, THE NUMBER 1-900-909-FRED DECORATING THE SIDE PANELS.

Over the page the story continued to unfold.

RATHER THAN USING THE DOORS, LUKE AND DAISY SLID THROUGH THE OPEN DRIVER AND PASSENGER WINDOWS.
UNABLE TO MAINTAIN THEIR PURSUIT ON FOOT, THE TIME INVESTIGATORS RAN BACK TO THEIR 1965 LINCOLN CONTINENTAL.
BEFORE THEY COULD START THE ENGINE, THE DODGE CHARGER RACED SKYWARDS, WEAVING THROUGH THE AIRBOURNE TRAFFIC TO ESCAPE.

With the pursuit over, Ted felt better, until he realized his anxiety levels had peaked after reading a comic book sketch rather than witnessing a genuine chase. Which was madness.

He glanced at the next picture.

DAISY WAS STARING AT HIM, HER HAND REACHING UPWARDS.
HER FINGER BECKONING HIM CLOSER.

Ted had little time to react to the sketched hand shooting out of the magazine and grabbing him by the lapel. Pulled downwards, his head slammed against the tabletop. Before he could break the hold, Daisy snatched him by the throat and pulled him towards the tabletop for a second time.

SWALLOWED BY THE STORYBOARD, TED FELT A SNAPPING OF LATEX MATERIAL AROUND HIS HEAD, THEN HIS SHOULDERS.
HIS BODY FOLLOWED, THE LATEX ROLLING DOWN HIS ARMS AND LEGS.
ONLY ONE THOUGHT CAME TO THE FOREFRONT OF TED'S WARPED MIND; HE HAD BEEN INSERTED INSIDE A HUMAN SIZED CONDOM AND WAS BEING FORCED TO GO WHERE NO MAN HAD EVER GONE BEFORE.

Chapter 11

"Take on Neo. Take Neo on."

TED SAT dumbfounded in the rear seat of a Dodge Charger racing through the lofty regions of a cityscape he recognized as home. The entire landscape had been transformed into a surreal reality of artistic styles. A blend of Manga, oil painting, digital quilling and bricks and mortar flew by at ridiculous speeds. The car's interior had been illustrated with such precision he dared not touch anything through fear of smudging the artwork.

One glance at his body's alteration into a pop art style, full of bright colors and wild hair, was the opposite of the person in the adjacent seat: an Anime sketch of Daisy Duke.

The comic book adaption he had viewed a few moments ago now offered warm, sympathetic eyes through layers of luscious, lime-colored locks. Daisy was pointing urgently towards the words being transcribed in the green speech bubble overhead, which matched the color of her hair.

Teo, we are in a combination of pencil sketch animation, and live action. You can't physically speak when you're in the drawn world.

Daisy shifted her gaze towards Ted's blue speech prompt which was crammed with enough profanity to sink the Titanic. With the blood streaming from his busted nose, Ted looked ready to explode with rage.

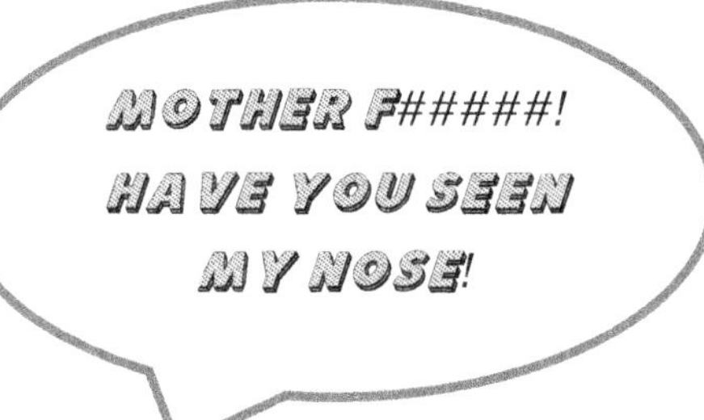

I had no choice. You had to come with me if you wanted to live.

Profanity is also edited out. You should try and avoid using it, otherwise I can only guess what you're trying to say. I know it's a little hard to come to terms with.

NO MORE NUTS THAN BEING GRABBED BY THE THROAT AND FACE PLANTING A TABLETOP.

YOU USED A FORCE CHOKE. A JEDI MIND TRICK.

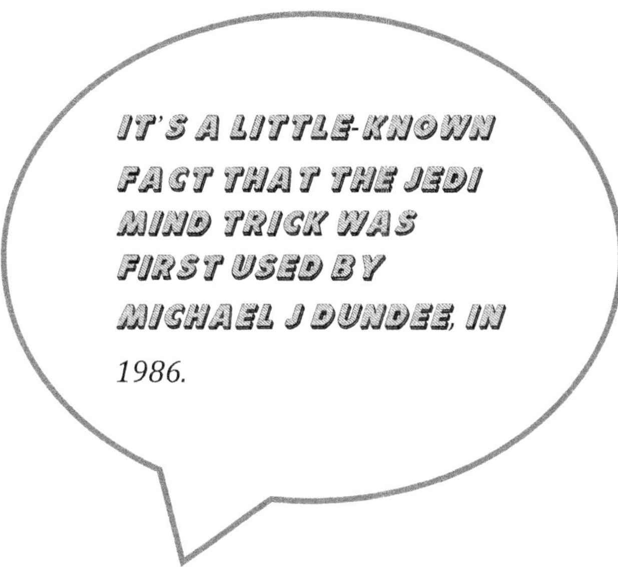

The driver turned in his seat to face Ted. His blonde shag cut had switched to a cardboard like trim, shaped around smooth cheeks and a yellow complexion of a Lego toy.

AND IT WAS OBI WAN IN 1977.

LOOK, PAL, TIMELINES WOULD IMPLY THE MIND TRICK WAS USED BEFORE STAR WARS.

WAS NOT.

WAS, WAS,
WAS, WAS,
WAS

DUNDEE DOES
NOT COUNT.

WHY, NOT
SPACEY ENOUGH?

Oh my God! Are you two seriously butting heads about that dumb Star Wars series. When we have a world of hurt coming our way.

Daisy jabbed a thumb over her shoulder as they entered a transportation tunnel.

The hover car version of a 1965 Lincoln Continental, which resembled the traditional cell animation accustomed to the 1980s cartoons Ted loved as a kid, followed them, with a full beam of headlights bearing down.

The Timeinators have found us. Step on it, Luke.

The Dodge Charger sped out the end of the tunnel into the rain, hotly pursued by the Lincoln.

They must be tracking you. I need to cut the hardline.

Daisy hoisted a metal briefcase from between her feet and retrieved a complex, squid-like device, with limp tentacles that looked like dreadlocks.

I YELLED OUT CUT THE HARDLINE WHEN I WOKE UP THIS MORNING.

You'll regret knowing why in about two seconds.

The device she placed on her lap displayed a metallic, central orb, about the size of an adult, human head. Attached to the orb's surface, the upturned crystal beaker was stained with bodily fluids.

Ted's worst fear was the unknown. Nonetheless, he swiveled and hoped for the best of a dire situation.

Take off your pants.

I'M FLATTERED, BUT I DON'T PERFORM SEX IN PUBLIC.

Urgh, not even if you were the last thing alive in the galaxy.

OKAY, OKAY. BUT I'M GOING COMMANDO.

I don't even know what that means.

YOU'LL REGRET SAYING THAT IN ABOUT TWO SECONDS!

In response, Daisy put on a pair of hazmat type gloves and a face mask.

With very little time and no options left, Ted took off his boots and pants and felt as uncomfortable as if he sat butt naked on a cactus.

Using both gloved hands, Daisy moved the orb up to the back of Ted's neck and flipped the on switch. A wiry, spinal column lowered to his waist. A host of synthetic extremities eased out from two columns of pores, securing the device around his midriff and chest.

Daisy let go of the orb once Ted's arms fastened tightly against his body, the upper limbs latching tightly to the side of his skull.

The procedure continued as an army of Nanobots surged from the orb and scattered across his scalp.

Unconcerned by the goings on in the rear seat, Luke guided the Dodge Charger dangerously across a freeway and smashed through the floating, central reservation to the opposite lanes. Countless headlights besieged the car as it slalomed through oncoming traffic, whilst being hounded by blazing car horns.

If the car's erratic movements were not enough to cause him discomfort, the Nanobots smothering Ted's eyes and nostrils, forcing him to grind his fingers into the leather upholstery, certainly would have been. He instinctively wanted to scrape away whatever crawled over his body, but his arms remained pinned. As every muscle fought against suffocation, the orb's limbs' reaction was to tighten around his body and skull.

Wrapped in the death lock embrace, Ted had no defense against a ripple of electric shocks surging through his body. His gut spasmed even quicker than the time he had a late-night Burrito from a dodgy Mexican food stall.

With a surge of what felt like trapped wind cramping his stomach, Ted felt the need to kneel on the seat and aim his butt in the air. The chill from a circular glass rim pressed against his butt cheeks came just in time to catch Ted's release of warp speed wind.

One enormous explosion of liquid and gas ended up in the device's crystal beaker, along with a tracking worm the size of a cigar. Wasting no time, Daisy wound down her window and threw the tracking worm outside.

With the device's binds released at the same speed as Ted's trapped wind, the scattering Nanobots freed his airways as they returned to the sanctuary of the squid's inner workings.

Ted slumped on the leather seat, exhausted, and started to get dressed. He watched Daisy dump all the soiled equipment in the metal case and reseal it.

Are you okay, Teo?

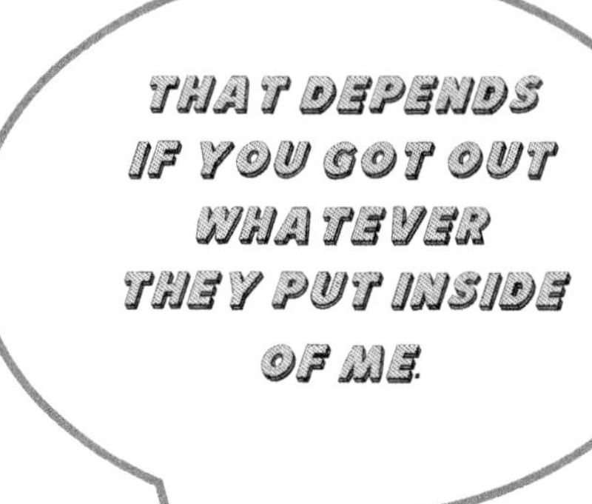

Oh, I got it, and a lot more than I needed. I'm not sure what you ate earlier today, and I don't wanna know. It was nasty, Teo.

Having evaded the Time Investigators, the Dodge Charger returned to ground level, and came to park outside a row of abandoned, five story apartment blocks. Drawn in a black and white Manga Anime style, only the middle building displayed any coloration, its importance signified by a pillar box red front door, with the dazzling yellow number 73.

Ted had no idea of the importance, or who was behind the doorway. He just knew he had to escape the cartoon madness and find a fresh pair of pants.

DO YOU HAVE ANY WATER? WAIT, IF I'M DRAWN ON PAPER AND I DRINK WATER, WILL I GO ALL SOGGY AND MOIST? THAT MIGHT SOUND STUPID BUT THIS IS THE FIRST TIME I'VE BEEN ILLUSTRATED.

Will you please stop talking.

WHY ARE YOU SO TOUCHY?

I'm not touchy. We're in a rush. There's a difference.

A CHICK WOULD SAY THAT. OKAY, OKAY. WHERE AM I?

Luke was watching Ted from the driver's interior mirror.

YEP. RIP THAT BAD BOY APART.
I WANNA COME WITH YOU GUYS.
THE NEXT STEP YOU FACE ALONE. THE TRUTH IS ON THE OTHER SIDE.
AND I DO THAT ALONE?

Is there any better way?

Ted noticed Daisy Duke studying a map of some kind.

GOING
SOMEWHERE?

What's a mile east of here?

THE FREEWAY,
MONEY
DISTRICT.
IS YOUR CAR
VALIDATED?

We need to go, Luke. We're not far away from you know what.

We'll be fine.
Thanks for your concern.

Daisy shoved Ted out of the car and closed the door. He had barely stepped on the pavement before the car pulled away.

Their goodbye felt flat, as if he had been discarded like an unwanted pet after Christmas. It wouldn't be the first time he felt that way. And no doubt it wouldn't be the last time.

A little piece of expectation remained, hoping that maybe they would stop the car and beckon him back to the fold. When the

Dodge Charger returned to the sky lanes, turning right at a Blimp Freeway sign, he knew there was only way one to go.

The entire urban block resembled the rest of the city with its wild mixture of graphics, comic designs and drawing styles. Vibrant colors clashed with black and white patterns, but it worked, somehow.

After walking up the few steps to the house numbered 73, Ted pressed a palm against the doorway. It felt flimsy enough for him to kick through it with barely any force.

He was grateful that he was no longer bound to reading other peoples' speech bubbles. Even better, he grabbed a hold of the paper doorway and ripped his way through to the end of the storyboard like Hulk Horgan tearing off a t-shirt before headlining a wrestling main event.

With one giant step, Ted crossed the void into shadow. Just like when he was transported from Nate's Deli to the storyboard, he felt a snapping of a latex type of material around his head, then his shoulders. His body followed as the material rolled down his arms and legs, forcing his body into a human, Vaseline layered torpedo. The human sized condom had returned and once again Ted dared to go where no man had gone before.

As a belt or cable snapped tightly around his waist, he was hauled further away from the tear in the doorway, and through total darkness.

Smothered with enough lard to appease a cake factory, Ted slid feet first down what could only be described as a flume of some sort. For hundreds of feet he picked up speed until a small circle of light manifested in front of him.

At first, the opening appeared no larger than a drain in a shower. As Ted drew nearer, the opening grew. It then dwelled on him that perhaps Karma had forced him to relive the moment Daisy Duke painfully removed the tracking device from his anus. Or perhaps his day had started off bad and was just getting worse.

With no more time to contemplate his demise, the human sized sheath shot out through the opening, his body released from the latex.

Ted plunged face first onto a hardwood, polished floor. Where he landed resembled his old High School gymnasium, a place he hadn't visited in decades.

"I'd rather be anywhere than back here," he bemoaned.

DURING the time it took Ted to reach his destination, Daisy and Luke arrived at the exit to the Freeway. The distance reading on the stolen map indicated the exit portal was three thousand meters ahead of them. To progress, they needed to enter a bland horizon of vehicles of similar shapes, colors, and models. Only yellow taxi cabs and a horizon of neon advertising boards seemed to break the monotony. Four rows deep, the airborne traffic flowed fast and steady in both directions.

It's not important. All that matters is that we find the portal.

To segregate the traffic from the city, the ominous sight of hundreds of slanted, metallic barriers the size of a football pitch, buoyed by hover pads, was something to behold.

The pair's unfamiliarity with the area used by the workforce for the city's money district held significance. With their car's license plate unregistered with the recognition software, once the teenagers entered the Freeway, the authorities would be alerted.

Flanked by the loftiest perches of the city's enormous office blocks, large AI freighters carrying produce stopped at designated drop off points.

Tommy glanced at Daisy in the interior mirror.

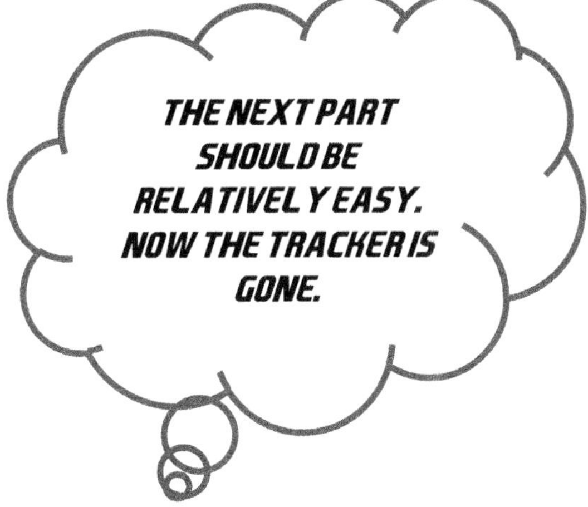

That reminds me. You can do the dirty work next time. Let's get going.

After entering the traffic from the on-ramp, the car swerved across the lane and through an airborne passage. Tommy regained control just in time to avoid a car crossing their path. Distracted, he failed to notice the row of validation cameras registering an invalid vehicle entering the district.

Daisy clambered over to the front passenger seat, if only to stop Tommy from craning his neck every time he needed to see her answer.

He doesn't know who you are yet, Tommy. We need to unplug him first. Like you did, when you banged your head on the car door.

And then Ted chooses the path for himself.

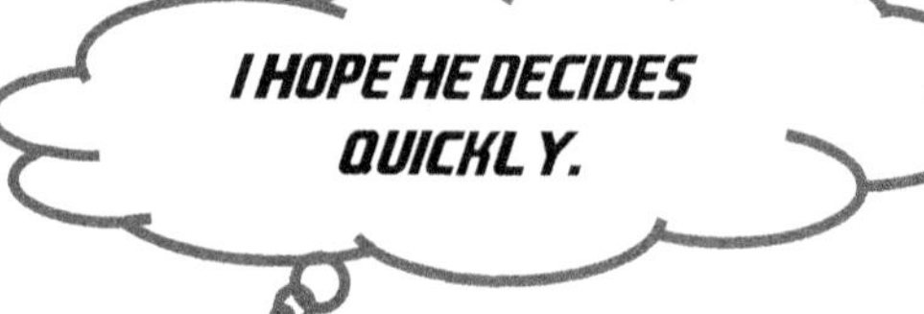

Why is that?

Under an umbrella of flashing police lights, a jet-black car transporter the size of an eighteen-wheeler, fronted with a mask of a perfect yellow circle, with two oval eyes and a large, upturned semi-circular mouth, pursued the Dodge Charger without caring about any of the traffic in its way. The security vehicles acted as computerized pickup trucks, their tractor beams operating as a sort of lasso, reeling in assailants. And storing any law breakers vehicles in the rear trailer.

Is that thing smiling at us?

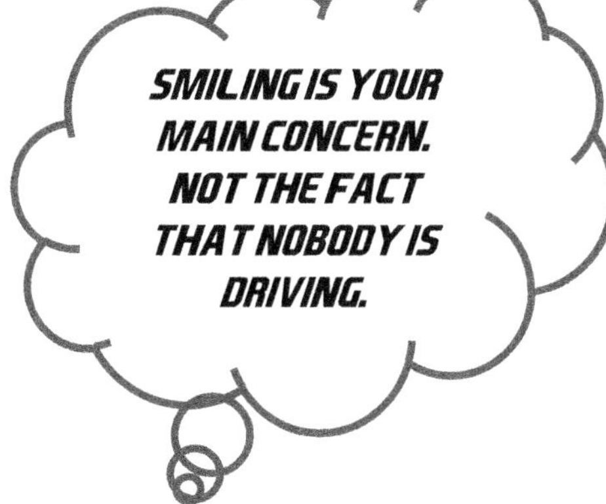

The Charger picked up speed along the central flow, a super tight lane with little room to move. Behind, battling its way between the nearest cars, the transporter forced anything it encountered in a spin towards the outer lanes. Cars crumpled against the barriers, traffic weaving all over. The result was a catastrophic chain reaction.

Ignoring the blazing horns and crashes behind him, Tommy accelerated. As he did so, the traffic flow slowed down on purpose.

Unaware that the flow had been shifted by the transporter's tractor beam, Tommy switched to the inner lane, before banking across to the middle lane, to reach the outer lane which now had less traffic.

Releasing the beam increased everyone's speed. The flow caught them up, the increase in the gradient forcing Tommy to go higher, as if he was racing the Indy circuit. He shifted up a gear and overtook on the outside, barely missing the barriers lined by neon advertisements, before swooping back into the traffic flow.

The reflection in her passenger wing mirror confirmed Daisy's worst fears. Smiley Face followed their exact route and ploughed through everything in its path like a possessed bulldozer. To make matters worse, two transporters, fronted with same sized character masks, maneuvered from behind and now flanked the lead vehicle.

One truck displayed a replica white hockey mask smothered in blood stains, the other a dirty, golden facemask that would normally cover the lower part of a human's face to stop them from biting.

I'll hedge my bets and say that the Timeinators just got a new set of heavy-duty wheels.

They don't need drivers when they are the trucks themselves.

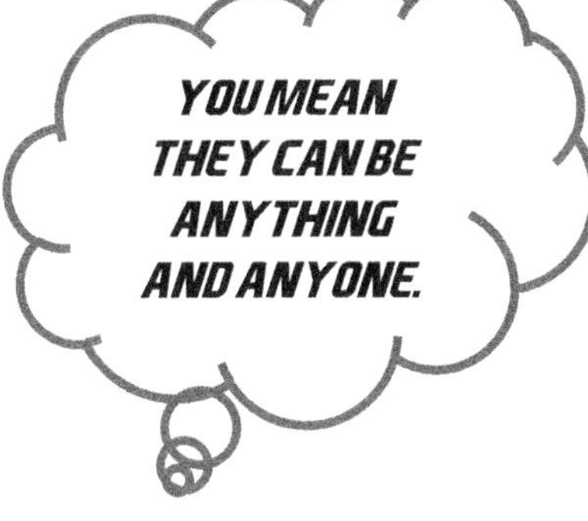

And there appears to be three of them.

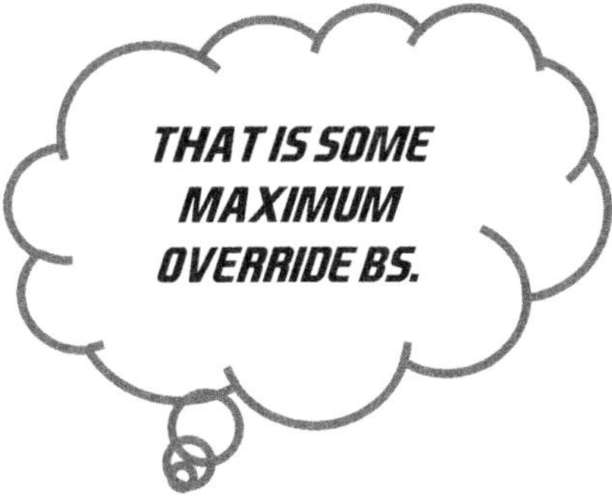

Unintentionally, Tommy eased off the accelerator as he came to terms with another revelation. Timeinators. Three of them.

The hesitation allowed Smiley Face to close the distance and seize them within the tractor beam. Rather than reel them in, the transporter sped up, closing the gap, a direct hit shunting the Charger's rear bumper, snapping Tommy out of his stupor. The yellow face appeared to crack a smile as the transporter gathered speed and struck the Charger for a second time.

Something obvious. I hope.

The second hit unknowingly broke the tractor beam's hold. Tommy felt the release but had no idea why he suddenly had full control. Weaving in and out of the traffic flow appeared to be the only way for him to keep the trio of Timeinators at bay.

Despite his efforts, the transporters kept pace. They showed no mercy. Mechanical blood spilled all over the sky lanes, fueling the Timeinators maniacal antics. Feeding off the carnage, they crushed every vehicle in their path with ease.

It became apparent to Daisy that they had seen no off-ramps since they had entered the Freeway. With no idea what the portal would like it, it could only mean they were stuck in a loop, or a battle to the death. Close to the portal, it made sense that the danger intensified.

Tommy glanced at the fuel gauge. They were almost on empty.

Keep going. We're close.

He's on a different path to us. He'll be a little confused. And probably won't have a clue what is going on.

Tommy shifted up the gears, reaching 110 mph. Increasing speed made no difference. Each transporter appeared to run off the supernatural gasoline triggered by the carnage of a high-speed pursuit. Any distance advantage the teenagers had had closed drastically.

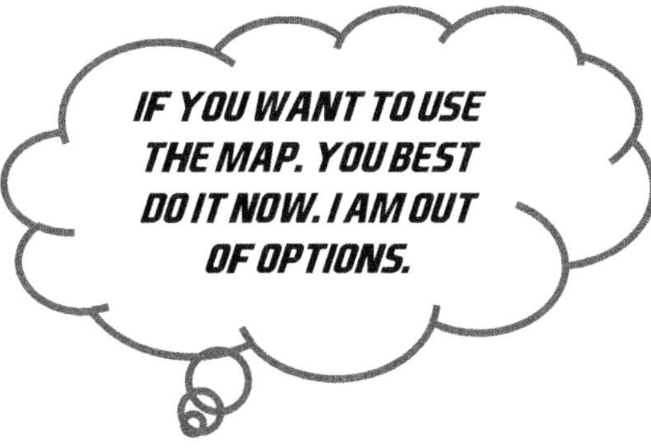

Tommy noticed Daisy's hesitation.

Daisy unraveled the map just as forty tons of Hannibal Specter's deranged, spiritual incarnation drilled the Charger from the left side. The impact slammed Daisy against the door, and she dropped the map in the footwell. She stooped down for it, only for thirty-five tons of a possessed transporter with an eight-foot grinning Jackson Vorhees mask to slam the Charger's right side.

Bent over, and wedged in the footwell, Daisy's door buckled, the shattered window showering her back with glass. She searched blindly for the map as space constricted all around her, the two transporters continuing to grind the Charger enough to become a flat, metallic pop tart. Suddenly, she snatched the map between her fingers. Powerless to move, she was unable to read the distance to the portal.

I'm stuck. I can't turn the map.
We're running blind.

We've only got one shot at this.

Tommy, hurry.

Still sandwiched between two transporters, the third vehicle slammed into the back of the Charger. Daisy was pinned, her right side being crushed, panic setting in.

As his door buckled, Tommy leaned over and grabbed Daisy around the waist.

Take us to Kurt Connors.

In the seconds before the car was flattened by the Timeinators, the teenagers narrowly escaped, vanishing within a burst of white light.

DAY TWO

(Six jumps remaining)

Chapter 12

You're one ugly, motherf######

MONTH - DAY HOUR - MIN
DEC 7 RUNAWAYS 02:32
REALITY DESTINATION

DETECTIVE Kurt Caine's 1975, 351 Windsor, two door Gran Torino had been parked down a seedy side alley for the last half an hour. Like most of the city, the car had seen better days, but still retained its fire engine red, with white flashing along the side panels.

After so long, having not believed in the paranormal, magic, or that humans were not alone in the universe, Caine's views were starting to change allegiance.

His stance shifted after witnessing innocent people across the city succumbing to a sadistic killer's torturous procedure. The coroner's reports stated the same cause of death. A tube in the chest injected two heavy doses of some new age, heroin type drug. Quickly mixed with human blood, the composition could then be retracted through a lance type filter. The identical entry point being a puncture wound in the center of the victim's forehead.

One victim fought back, not that it did any good. DNA found on the cadaver, along with witness accounts of a perpetrator's giant physique sounded like an impossibility at first. Then some droplets of blood discovered at a crime scene, matched no types on record.

The conclusion left no other avenues, except the one Caine still had trouble coming to terms with.

A killer of unknown origin, in a city with the highest crime rate in the country, was leaving behind a disturbing body count.

Could a real alien be alive in his city?

If anyone could find out the truth, it would be Detective Kurt Caine.

There had been no let-up to the driving rain over the last few days. Perhaps the sudden emergence of the green vapor in the sky had something to do with it. Caine considered the possibility for the same amount of time it took him to lift a cigarette from the foil packet with his teeth and light it.

As he listened through headphones to his partner's undercover drug deal, his auburn eyes never strayed from the neon sign for the Bonsai Club across the street.

INSIDE the plush establishment, a bartender wiped clean the surfaces of his bar. A dancing pole fronted a V-shaped stage. Pillars and booths ringed a berth of central tables where undercover detective, Thomas Beck, sat across the table from two stone-faced, Yakuza crime lords.

The club was not due to open for a few more hours, so no attention was drawn towards the unopened metal briefcase separating Beck from the Yakuza. Alongside Beck's Whiskey glass and a rolled-up banknote was a mirror with a dusting of cocaine.

"Are we doing business, or am I wasting my time here?" Beck asked, snorting the rest of the cocaine.

The elderly Yakuza bosses, Egg Shen, and David Lo Pan, turned towards each other and shared a quiet conversation. They were accompanied by a host of trench coat wearing goons. Each goon looked identical in appearance and was armed with some form of submachine pistol beneath their coats.

"Do your coats come in any other color or is black trench all the rage in this part of town?" Beck knew their eyes were all over him, even though shielded by matching Raybans. "No takers. Do their batteries need changing, Egg? Lighten up, fellas. Give me something to work on. It's quieter than a morgue in here."

Whilst Beck swigged back his shot of Jack Daniels, he followed the old men's conversation, even though he couldn't hear or understand what they were saying. Hardly anything had been said to him since he entered the room around ten minutes ago. It felt like they were stalling.

To get a reaction, he shelled the rest of the cocaine packet across the mirror. "Say hello to my little friend."

Using the rolled banknote, Beck snorted two more lines. To finish off, he dabbed his fingertip in the remnants and rubbed it around his gums.

To his advantage, Beck had never looked like an atypical police officer. He had long hair, a rugged appearance, and a crazy streak a mile wide. Perhaps being undercover for so many years had finally pushed him over the edge and now he just appeared to be one of a hundred different wannabe dealers across the city.

"The powder is dope. But we all know this is not what I'm after."

His comment appeared to rattle Egg Shen. The Yakuza boss gestured for the bartender to top up Beck's drink. As the drink was filled, one of the goons turned Beck's metal briefcase to face the old men.

"What is this? You don't trust me. I told you I'd have your money."

Releasing the seals showcased bank notes totaling $3,000,000.

"Like I said. I have your money. Now enough is enough. I'm done with waiting. Where the hell is this new product I've heard so much about?" Beck's demeanor changed faster than how long it took him to neck the Whiskey and stun the glass on the tabletop.

Lo Pan waved another goon forward. The goon rested an identical briefcase on the table and turned it towards Beck.

"Don't you just love the smell of a new wave drug in the morning?" Beck flipped the seal and peeled away in anger. "What the hell is this sh–"

FOLLOWING a volley of gunshots, Caine threw down the headphones and slid out the driver's open window into ankle high rainwater. He sprinted across the street towards the Bonsai Club and caught the attention of a few hookers sharing a cigarette in an abandoned shop's doorway. They split once Caine yanked his 44 Magnum from the shoulder holster and barged through the club's front entrance.

Caine stumbled into an empty foyer and backed on to the door leading to the sealed off bar. There was no sound from inside, so he edged the entrance open with his shoulder.

Bloodied bodies littered the floor, a fast and thin projectile circling the room. The same weapon had taken down a dozen heavily armed goons with fatal cuts to the jugular.

By the time he sneaked inside, the disc was nowhere to be seen.

Caine moved from pillar to post until he stopped in his tracks. What he witnessed was a huge man with whitewash hair, wearing a black trench coat, stab a goon in the skull with a lance weapon attached to his wrist. Huge was an understatement. The guy was at least eight foot tall, with boots on.

Being in his presence fueled Caine's volcano of payback he had been waiting to unleash for weeks. Only last night this guy had taken out three officers with some form of lethal, flying projectile. Each person had been incapacitated in the neck. Clearly the same device had been used tonight.

"Freeze, asshole." Caine aimed the Magnum at the killer and searched for Beck at the same time. Thankfully, his partner was not amongst the dead.

Tall enough to be considered a freak of nature, the man turned towards Caine, his hands rising slowly by his side. Human looking, except for his white irises and a distinct lack of human emotions, Caine could see why an alien theory could be believed.

"*I greet you in peace,*" the alien hissed, while raising his right wrist to reveal the disc's launch device hidden beneath his sleeve.

"And you leave in a body bag." Caine opened fire and blasted two slugs in the alien's right shoulder.

The alien reeled away and crashed through the wall to the kitchen area as if it were made of cardboard. Rubble and dust rained down, waterpipes breaching, gas leaking from ruptured pipes.

Caine pursued the alien, who had cornered the two Yakuza bosses at the end of the rubbish strewn alleyway. The frail Lo Pan had been hauled off the ground by the throat. A wire, tipped with a sucker, punctured the Yakuza boss's chest. Lo Pan shuddered as the two doses of an alien drug ran rampant through his blood, killing him instantly.

The alien then turned his attention to Egg Shen. "*I greet you in peace.*"

Caine held the Magnum in two hands and momentarily considered letting the alien scumbag take out one of the city's most powerful crime lords. One was out of the picture already. Why not both. It would save him and the city a hell of a lot of paperwork.

No way. This alien SOB pays tonight.

"Yo, ET!" Despite the alien's steely glare almost extinguishing the Detective's swagger, Caine held it together long enough to close the gap between him and it. "I've come to chew bubble-gum and kick ass. And I'm all out of bubble-gum."

Caine unleashed a volley of slugs that rattled the alien's body, forcing him to drop Egg Shen in a pile of sodden rubbish.

As the alien faced him, Caine carried on firing, and rolled on his stomach across the ground with his gun held out in front. Having never been an expert marksman, somehow his full circle, rolling action aided his aim. The alien stumbled in a death march, his white blood spilling through his clenched fingers.

Caine carried on pulling the trigger, the bullets ripping apart the alien's torso, until he emptied the chamber and had to reload. Somehow the alien remained upright, even as his lifeforce ebbed away like sand through his fingertips.

As the alien stumbled, he raised his arm, in readiness to release the disc shaped weapon. "*I greet you in pea–*"

"Time to greet one of earth's rockets, spaceman."

The taunt came from the opposite end of the alleyway.

A single shot of a bazooka flew beyond Caine before he had any chance of finding out who had fired it. Following a direct hit to the chest, the alien exploded, showering anything nearby in a layer of slime, a new age drug, body parts, and white blood.

"I need to copyright that one liner before someone steals it," Thomas Beck said as he shouldered the bazooka.

"How many cat lives is it that that you've used up?" Caine asked as he wiped white marshmallow goo off his cheeks.

"I don't know, eight, nine," Beck smiled. "Lucky for me, that alien was more interested in the Yakuza than he was an undercover cop. It allowed me to get this bad boy." Beck tapped the bazooka casing. "I keep it close, for alien encounters."

"It's not your standard police firearm."

"After you mentioned spacemen in the city. I thought it best to upgrade." Beck laughed and then let out a bloodcurdling scream.

Caine watched helplessly as a jagged, two-pronged blade punctured his partner's chest, forcing him skywards. Floods of claret showered the alleyway as Beck's limp body was tossed from side to side and then released against a brick wall, before striking the ground with a wet thud.

Whoever maimed Beck concealed his identity behind some form of light bending exoskeleton. Caine unleashed a few shots, which caused lightning fractures to course through the assailant's armor. It wasn't enough. Hoisted off the ground by the throat and slammed against a brick wall, the Detective felt hopelessly outmatched.

The assailant's armor faded to reveal another colossal, humanoid alien with white irises, and Caine face to face with a second devil from the stars.

"*You die tonight,*" the alien hissed.

"You know what, you're one ugly motherfucker." Caine's profanity was all he could muster before his windpipe started to fracture.

UNABLE to break the alien's hold, it was a volley of raw lightning drilling into the pavement that helped save the policeman. Shockwaves blew out windows, and masonry. Lightning tore through the frail Egg Shen, his body parts showering the alleyway in yet more blood and gore.

Sensing a challenge for supremacy, the alien released the frail human, allowing him to slump to the ground. Caine was still uncertain who or what had saved his life when a double-bladed wrist mount jutted a meter forwards; a sure sign of the alien *not* offering greeting, rather preparing to dissect.

Descending the lightning forks, three men with electricity flowing through their limbs seemed not the most unusual occurrence today.

Circling the alien, who lunged to attack, the three lightning warriors fired from their fingertips, a volley of electrical blasts. By the time the blasts obliterated the alien, Caine had reached his car across the street.

He fumbled with the keys, shifted gear into reverse and accelerated backwards up the alleyway all the way to Jump Street. As he pulled away, Caine knew the three warriors presented an entirely new threat. A threat he doubted anyone would believe over the police radio channels.

West Highland Police Station

DETECTIVE Caine entered through the main doors, still coming to terms with what he had just witnessed at the Bonsai Club. He was greeted at the main reception desk by Sgt Tackleberry. The sergeant had a weighty reputation as being a direct action, gun-toting type at the Police Academy. To be standing behind a sheet of Perspex glass during the twilight shift had to be killing him.

"Sorry about Beck," Tackleberry said.

"That makes two of us." Caine swiped his ID card on the reader and headed inside to the second-floor offices of the Drug and Homicide Unit.

Rather than change out of his soiled clothes, Caine poured a coffee and took a moment to compose himself. With so much going on, he had no time to grieve his partner's death. They had been best friends since they were partnered after leaving the Academy. To see him taken out so brutally was something he would probably never forget.

DUE to the late hour, only a few officers were on duty.

Sgt Hulka, one of the oldest, was interviewing from his desk a skinny, dark haired Caucasian guy.

"Full name?" Hulka asked, sounding reasonably official.

"The name's Francisco Soyer, but everybody calls me Psycho. You call me Francisco, an' I'll kill ya."

Hulka looked down his nose and blew a stream of cigarette smoke at his witness. "If you want witness security, kid, I'll call you whatever the hell I like."

Caine flicked a salute at Hulka as he made his way to his desk. "Tough night, Hulks?"

"Nothing I can't handle. Sorry about Beck."

"News travels fast."

"That might have something to do with the Bonsai Club looking like a slaughterhouse."

"You think the club is bad. Wait until you see the state of the alleyway."

"Wanna fill me in with the deets?"

"Maybe later."

"Todd's pissed you fled the scene."

"I had no choice."

"Tell that to Todd."

Caine shot a look at the Inspector's office. Through the blinds he could see a man and woman in their late twenties. They wore matching dark suits, and sunglasses. "Feds got here fast."

"Turned up around the same time as the storm hit."

The witness banged his hand on the table. "Hey, any chance here or what?"

"Lighten up, Francisco," Hulka added, stubbing out his cigarette.

"Call me Francisco again an …"

"… and I'll lead you to the exit and kick you out the door myself. How'd you like those apples, kid. Tasty enough for ya."

The witness stewed for a few seconds.

"You ready to talk, Francisco?" Hulka continued.

"Okay. The killer robot guy on da news."

"You've seen him?" Caine asked, suddenly interested.

"I'm nat delivering pizza here." Soyer turned in his seat to face Caine. "I was doing my rounds at da machine factory. You know, like da security sweep. Well, there was dis guy snooping around da decommissioned zone. You know, where we store da snuffed bots n stuff. Not da T800s or dose crazy mall bots. You know da type I mean. Long legs, pincers, like insects."

"Can you describe what he looked like?" Caine asked, sitting down next to the witness, and taking a cigarette from Hulka's packet he left on the desktop.

"He was a white guy. Real bushy hair, kinda muscular. He looked familiar."

"Then what happened?"

"I tried for a better look and got hit on da head. When I came to, he was gone. With halfa dozen crates of damaged bots. Not that dat matters. Most of dem were mothballed. Is that what he's been using as killbots? That's what the news broad said, right?"

"We're not at liberty to say," Hulka replied.

"I heard he turned da toaster into a killer. Has anyone else seen da guy?"

"They sure have," Caine said.

"Are they in witness protection?"

"We can't protect the dead, kid," Hulka added, frankly.

"I'm da only one alive?"

"Which is why we need to keep you safe," Caine said.

"Safe," Soyer barked. "I want da max security. Armed guards. Navy Seals. Safe House. Takeaway pizza. The odd hooker. You feel me? Man, you stink. You take a bath in the sewer. Was it that?"

"It's dead people. Lots of them."

"You know what, I've changed my mind." Soyer tried to stand.

Caine forced him back into his seat. "Let me deal with Inspector Todd first. We can chat after. You okay with that, Psycho?"

Leaving Hulka to his witness, Caine made his way to Todd's office.

CAINE entered without knocking.

"You ever hear of back up, Caine?" Inspector Todd sat behind an oak desk. A few pictures of the senior officer shaking hands with important dignitaries lined the walls. Scattered case files and a worn coffee maker occupied a side desk, a tattered air purifier beneath it struggled to do anything other than hum.

"Where's the fun int that," Caine replied, purposely ignoring the man and woman.

"It's protocol, detective."

"Unless you have Rumbo on the payroll, I'm not sure back up would've made any difference, sir. At least we've finally got a lead on the bot killer."

"Sorry about your partner." The woman, with shoulder length hair, wearing a dark, pinstripe suit, made no effort to hide her discomfort regarding the horrific stench emanating from Caine's soiled clothes.

"As am I."

"We're here to help you." She flashed her FBI badge to make it official.

"By help, do you mean the grunts do the hard graft, and the Feds swoop in for the plaudits."

"Sit down, Caine. I mean it," Todd snarled, before gesturing to an empty chair.

Caine sat and felt the eyes of the two new arrivals all over him. "Why do these Feds keep looking at me, sir?"

"You could try and be a bit more courteous." The male Fed, with a chiseled jawline, immaculate hair, and wearing an identical pinstripe suit, was aged around thirty. He had an air of realism and clearly had no problem letting his partner take the lead.

"I'm sorry. I've not had the best of days. Drugs, Yakuza, alien guts, you know how it is."

By mentioning an alien, Caine expected a reaction from the Feds. He got none.

"That's enough, detective," Todd fired off.

"Maybe we got off on the wrong footing," the woman said. "I'm Agent Daisy Scully. This is my partner, Special Agent Tom 'Cat' Mulder."

"Nice to meet ya," Caine replied, uninterested. "I'm Detective Kurt Caine. Now we're done with the pleasantries. If you wouldn't mind vacating the area. The real police have a few things to discuss. And this can't wait."

"That's not possible," Mulder replied.

"Any why is that, Tom boy?"

"I believe we have similar interests."

"Playboy and tequila."

"The truth, detective. The truth."

"What about it?"

"It's out there."

"So is cancer, but what has this got to do with me."

Hulka knocked once on the door and entered. "Sorry to interrupt, Inspector."

"But you did anyway. What is it?" Todd asked.

"You're never gonna believe this. I'm not sure I do, but here goes." Hulka handed Todd a slip of paper.

Todd read the name once and then shot a look at Caine. "Charles Luther is the bot killer."

"You can't mean the rock star?" Caine asked.

"The one and only," Hulka added.

"Francisco da Psycho identified Charles Luther."

"Well, he only got one look at him."

"And he described a rock star millionaire, friend to every celebrity on the planet, as the overlord of a killer robot army."

"Sometimes one look is all you need."

"Bullcrap!" Hulka denied.

"Is it so difficult to believe the unbelievable?" Mulder said.

Scully shot Mulder a puzzled look that forced him to sit back in his seat. "What my partner means is that Luther holds the key to what you are searching for."

Caine turned his disbelieving glance towards Todd. "Are these dicks for real?"

"We're as real as you want us to be."

"Then explain exactly how the king of rock is starting robot Armageddon?"

"He has help."

"From whom?"

"Aliens. We believe you've seen them," Mulder added.

"Have you been spying on me?" Caine snarled as he stood.

"Sit your ass down, detective," Todd ordered.

Caine sat reluctantly. He then lit the cigarette he took from Hulka.

"Now I know you can read. Do you know what this is?" Todd motioned to the *'no smoking'* sign on his desk.

"Sure, I do. I just don't give a shit." Caine gestured for his new acquaintances to take to the floor.

"You already know that someone has been using reconditioned robots to kill some of the city's most prominent people," Scully said.

"Let's get it right. The city's most corrupt scumbags."

"There's a fine line, detective."

"And these scumbags crossed it. They'll get no sympathy from me."

"What about the blood of the innocent?"

"All I care about is catching the killer. The sooner, the better."

"We're not here to judge you."

"That's a relief."

Rather than bite at Caine's lack of concern, Todd continued, "Caine, if what the witness is saying is true, Luther has spiderbots, crawlers, sneakers and, by now, a robotic army at his disposal."

"The killbots are old news, sir."

"That's the department's official name for them, by the way," Hulka said to the Feds.

"Don't you have a witness to protect?" Todd glanced once at Hulka, who he hadn't realized was still present.

The sergeant quickly closed the door and returned to his desk.

"Did you know Luther has upgraded to smart bullets, heat seekers? We've even heard he's gone bigger with cyborg animals," Scully said.

The comment rooted Caine to his seat.

"We call the bullets runaways," Mulder added.

"That's a cute nickname," Caine replied.

"We like to think so."

"Can we add that to the department's official description list?"

"Let me ask you a question, detective. Where do you think Luther gets this upgraded tech from?"

"I just presumed he imported it from Japan. Those Japs are sneaky fuckers."

"Not that sneaky," Scully said. "He gets his tech from your alien friends."

"For a minute I thought you were going to say Colonel Annabelle Smith and the A-Team. Word has it, she kicks some real ass." Caine stubbed out his cigarette.

"Are you taking any of this seriously?" Mulder asked.

"She's real, I've seen her. Or I was her. Wow. Where did that come from?" Caine rubbed the rawness around his neck to deflect the awkwardness.

"Are you okay, Caine?" Todd asked.

"I'm fine, sir. And to answer the Feds, I take everything seriously. And you might be pleased to hear that half of my problem went away tonight. Luther's alien marketplace was closed tonight, permanently. You can thank Beck and the three lightning brothers for that."

"Lightning," Todd fired off.

"Yeah. From the storm that hit about the same time those alien pukes bought it."

Mulder and Scully shared a look.

"What happened?" Mulder asked.

"Three dudes appeared on lightning rods. Freaky shit, ha."

"Where are they now?" Mulder asked impatiently.

"I don't know. I didn't stick around to thank them for saving my ass."

"Inspector Todd, this new evidence means we need to move quickly," Scully said.

"He's all yours. And take his filthy habit with you," Todd replied.

"You referring to me?" Caine snapped.

"Who else is smoking in my no smoking room. And change your clothes."

"Sir, this is bullshit."

"BS or not, you've been requisitioned for special assignment."

"I'm in the middle of two cases and my partner just got killed. Special can crawl up my ass and die."

"It smells like something has already died up your ass," Mulder added.

"Easy, Smoulder. Don't make me spill even more blood tonight."

"I don't have time for this, Caine. You'll go with Scoulder and Mully. I mean Mulder and Scully, and that's the end of it," Todd said.

Before anyone could leave the Inspector's office, the building shook to its core as something outside collided with the brickwork.

"What the hell was that?" Caine asked.

"Earthquake?" Todd stated.

Another strike, with ten times more force, almost punctured the office wall behind Todd.

"Is that a wrecking ball?" Caine asked.

"We've been found," Scully stated to Mulder.

"By whom? God?" Caine barked.

Chapter 13

On the Rampage

A REPTILIAN fist, the size of a small car, busted through the stonework from the outside, showering the office with dust and debris. Before the Inspector could react, he was yanked from his seat. Todd's bloodcurdling screams could be heard as he was hurled all the way to the pavement below.

Reacting quicker than the two Feds, Caine freed his Magnum from his side holster and blasted a few shots through the fracture.

"Guns won't win this war," Mulder forewarned as he and Scully fled to the main office.

Ignoring the warning, Caine fired off a couple more shots, not that it did anything to slow down the assailant's mammoth fist busting through another part of the wall. Through the gap, Caine spotted a huge eyeball and a snarling jawline smothered in spittle and rage.

"It must be bring an ugly motherfucker to work today." Caine's jibe followed his attempts to slow down the attacker with yet more gunfire.

The beast pummeled the outside of the building with its fists, demolishing the precinct's walls. At the same time, ceiling panels and vents gave way to an army of mechanized killbots.

Luther's robots came equipped with futuristic sensors, able to locate any living soul nearby. Dispersing across the precinct on their long, spindly legs, the bots' sensors sought out any change to the atmosphere through a target's breathing and vibrations.

Protecting his witness to the end, Hulka stood in front of Soyer to block off a cluster of killbots. They swarmed his body, manically injecting Luther's toxin through their needle-like pincers. Foam gushed from the sergeant's mouth as his body spasmed uncontrollably, blood streaming from his eye sockets and ears, as if tortured by an ancient plague.

With his protector dying right before his eyes, Soyer escaped in a panic towards Mulder and Scully. The two Feds were about to open the exit to the stairwell when sergeant Tackleberry ran through them, his stomach erupting in a shower of blood as a runaway bullet took him apart.

A janitor who epitomized an 80s rock god, with his black, shoulder length hair, spray on tan, and open neck shirt, stepped over the bloody remains.

Being so brazen about killing a police officer meant the sinister man's motives were obvious. Nobody was going to make it out of the precinct alive.

SINCE his rampage began, Charles Luther had removed all witnesses by killing them. Today was no different. Just like Tackleberry, the ones who might escape his killbots would then have to evade the ammunition of his specialized, bulky hand cannon.

Once the killer locked eyes with Soyer, the witness knew he was the first target. Soyer had nowhere to run to. Nowhere to hide.

Loaded with an advanced runaway bullet, Luther fired one shot at the fleeing witness. Twenty centimeters long, and torpedo shaped, the heat seeker bullet flew between Mulder and Scully and chased down Soyer like a rabid mutt. No matter how many obstacles the witness put in the bullet's path, it kept up, gliding relentlessly.

The final option for Soyer was to slam shut the glass exit door and to call the elevator on the opposite side of the precinct. The exit shattered before him in an eruption of shards. The witness backed away, faking to go left and right, as he waited for the elevator door to open. Edging closer, the bullet mimicked his every move. Even as Soyer slammed a palm on the descend button as he ran past it, the bullet continued the pursuit.

Mulder and Scully watched helplessly from across the precinct as the bullet ripped through Soyer's stomach, his screams muffled as the elevator doors closed.

"We've no protection from those bullets," Mulder said as Luther reloaded his weapon just feet away from him.

"The only way is to get Kurt out of this realm, Tommy," Daisy replied, revealing her true persona for the first time since they arrived in Kurt's realm.

Caine had witnessed the entire episode of Luther's bullet chase and Hulka's tortured demise. Out of bullets, he could do nothing to help either of them. Only one escape route remained. He sprinted towards the office's glass wall and shoulder barged his way through it.

Ending up at Scully's feet, in a pile of broken glass, Caine jabbed a finger at Luther. "We need to get past that son of a bitch and to the roof," he said.

"What's on the roof?" Scully asked.

"We need to get to the chopper."

A collective charge towards Luther, with accompanying war cries, made the killer's decision an easy one. Having difficulty reloading his runaway bullets, he chose salvation rather than an unwinnable duel and let the three of them pass to the stairwell.

Smoke and flames blocked the route down.

"The chopper is on the roof's landing pad. At least it should be. Can you fly, Mulder?" Caine asked as he sealed the door behind him.

Mulder and Scully shared a glance.

Mulder's avatar had basic helicopter flight training. It took a few moments for Tommy to realize. "I can. Would you look at that."

"You don't seem that convinced," Caine said.

"I'm good to go. Trust me."

Three flights up, Caine, Mulder and Scully burst through the entrance to the rooftop moments before another runaway bullet exploded against it.

"Son of a bitch!" Caine yelled.

"That was too close," Scully said.

"I'm getting too old for this shit," Mulder bemoaned.

"I knew he wouldn't just let us go," Caine added.

"Name one psycho that ever did that," Scully said.

A torrential downpour pelted the trio, a thunderstorm erupting overhead. All mixed together with the green vapor in the sky, it resembled a toxic blend.

The building's foundations quaked to the core as something titanic climbed towards the roof. None of them could see what approached, and they had no desire to find out.

Despite the carnage, the police helicopter remained right where Caine said it would be, on the landing pad with a fuel pipe connected to fuselage. Caine removed the fuel line and then boarded via the side passenger door. In the pilot seats, Mulder and Scully buckled up.

The engines had already started as Luther emerged from the debris strewn doorway, his loaded cannon fixed on the next targets. He fired once and then sprinted across the rooftop. Clearly ignoring the danger of a fatal plunge over the edge of the building, he ran as fast as the bullet travelled, his legs moving abnormally, as if his latest upgrade was his own body.

"Get us airborne," Caine said with urgency as the helicopter lifted off the landing pad.

Mulder's decision to bank the chopper towards the overhang shifted the bullets trajectory. It detonated against the base of the helicopter, leaving a gaping hole in the fuselage.

With the chopper still banking, anything not tied down in the passenger hold tumbled towards the open side door. Caine grabbed hold of a seatbelt to avoid falling out with the rest of the loose equipment, his legs dangling precariously outside.

"A little warning next time," he yelled as he clambered inside, whilst failing to notice Luther clinging to the chopper's landing gear.

Caine unbuckled a headset from behind the passenger seats and used the extended mic to contact the pilots. "We need to get higher."

"The hydraulics is shot," Scully replied.

"Just ascend already," Caine added.

"Are you crazy? We can't fly towards lightning," Scully replied. "It'll rip us apart."

"Look closer," Mulder said as a glowing, golden ring, wide enough for the chopper to fit through, appeared amidst the cloud front.

"Is that the portal?"

"It has to be."

"If it's not, we die."

"Rather the lightning kills us, than the three gigantic monsters rampaging below us."

"What the hell are you two talking about?" Caine asked, receiving no reply.

With an evasive maneuver, the chopper avoided being grabbed by a colossal hand from the same creature that had broken through Inspector Todd's office wall.

As the helicopter banked, Caine tumbled across the passenger hold. To avoid being pitched out of the opposite opening, he grabbed a different seatbelt with everything he had.

TO reach the helicopter, a trio of gigantic creatures, controlled by the Timeinators, tore apart the cityscape. A giant, mutated human in a chimpanzee mask and a black and jade uniform leapt from the side of one building to another. With one solid punch through bricks and mortar, a handful of citizens were torn from the safety of their apartments and offices, to either be consumed, or thrown to the streets below.

On top of the adjacent building, a shaggy dwarf with a protruding nose, bushy eyebrows, and spindly fingers, frantically jumped up and down on the rooftop until the structure started to collapse.

Fleeing the carnage, civilians spilled from the exits, only for a bulbous, pink marshmallow fairy, with accompanying wings and fairy boots, to use her pointy wand to impale them like a flesh kebab for her culinary pleasure.

"What the hell are those things?" Caine blurted.

Mulder shot a quick glance at each creature. "Well, if I had to take a guess, I'd say a mightily angry Zornelius the chimpanzee, from the original World of the Apes. Then you've got Mrs.

Staypuft, the Marshmallow Fairy, and a bootleg of Gwildor from Wizards of the Universe."

"Are you high?"

"They're from eighties movies. Sort of."

"Have you seen these before?" Scully asked Caine.

The Detective stared back in disbelief. "Sure. They're part of my Wednesday night book club."

Scully glanced quickly over her shoulder. "Smart ass! They must be Timeinators. Here, make the shots count." She handed Caine a handgun, before turning to Mulder. "We need to get out of here, now."

"Lady Fed, what the hell is a Timeinator?" Caine asked.

BELIVIENG himself invincible was just one of Luther's many psychotic traits.

Despite the storm, he clung on to the landing gear. Escaping from the ruptured chassis, fuel showered him. Meanwhile, buried within the fuel tank, his runaway bullet's countdown reached zero.

Having set the timer purposely to down the chopper, he smiled gleefully as fire ripped through the hydraulics and ignited him in a ball of flame.

"THERE'S a slight issue," Mulder said as his dashboard lit up with faults.

"You mean apart from the storm," Scully said, jabbing a thumb skywards at a condensing skyline bursting with lightning forks.

Stabilizing the controls, Mulder glanced below. The Ape and the Fairy closing in meant they were stuck midair. Buildings collapsing around them, due to the maniac dwarf going to town on anything standing, meant there was no way out at street level.

"Caine, we need to lighten the load," Mulder said, struggling to increase altitude.

"I hope you're not referring to me," Caine replied.

"Throw anything out that's not bolted down."

Caine threw out all the loose equipment, before ripping out and disposing of all the rear passenger seats.

"It's working," Mulder said, feeling the controls ease the chopper's ascent towards the golden portal. "Daisy, get the map ready for Mikey."

"What map? Who is Mikey?" Caine asked, before being tossed backwards in his passenger hold due to the helicopter's rapid maneuver out of reach of Mrs. Staypuft's bloody wand.

Gwildor had reached the rooftop of Police Headquarters and leapt skywards after them. Mulder's quick decision making banked the helicopter sideways and away from a cluster of the monster's fingertips. The dwarf overshot and crashed into the building across the street.

Zornelius had chosen a different path, and grabbed hold of the helicopter's tail boom, stopping it from rising higher.

"Shake it off," Scully yelled.

"I'm trying," Mulder replied. "Nothing's working."

"Let me try." Caine aimed the handgun and fired.

The direct hit in the eye forced the giant chimpanzee to let go and hurtle towards the buildings below.

"It worked," Mulder bellowed, as the chimpanzee flattened half of downtown.

"Ah crap. I'll be working for the next century to cover that damage," Caine said as the helicopter rose dangerously towards the lightning storm.

"Now that we're getting closer, I'm not sure this is such a good idea," Scully said.

"Just say his name before we fry!" Mulder bellowed.

"Mikey Drew!" she yelled just as a barrage of lightning bolts struck the helicopter.

DAY THREE

(Five jumps remaining)

DETECTIVE CAINE let out a sharp breath.

He was on his back, looking up at the ceiling of a High School gymnasium. The last thing he remembered was the name Mikey Drew. A name he didn't recognize. And lightning striking the chopper. Followed by a nauseating death spin, towards a glowing, golden archway of some sort.

He thought back to the arch and if it was a footstep to heaven, or just a figment of his imagination. Surely heaven's doorway would lead to somewhere other than a gymnasium. Raising the question meant he had to be alive.

Maybe luck had something to do with his survival. Which he doubted. His luck rarely turned out to be the good kind.

"This can't be right. Nothing productive ever happened for me in one of these," he said, trying to figure out why he recognized the gymnasium, but had no recollection of ever being inside of it before today.

"Maybe you could ask me the same thing."

The statement made about as much sense as being confronted by the gangly teenager who said it.

Caine reached for his holster. He expected to feel the cold steel of his Magnum, rather than the cotton of his charred shirt. His holster and gun had vanished, parts of his tattered clothes falling off him every time he moved.

"Welcome to Alice's rabbit hole," the kid said, gazing skyward.

The kid lying on a bench to Caine's left looked familiar. "Alice, Alice, who the fuck is Alice?"

"You know the story."

"Does it look like I know?"

"Here's the short, short version. Alice goes down the rabbit hole. She takes acid, thinking it was shrinkaide. The End."

"Are you trying to be funny?"

"I never need to try. My wit comes naturally."

"Start giving me answers, kid. Or else."

"Or else, what?"

"Or else."

"Or else, what?"

"Or else."

"You said that already."

"Just start talking, kid. Or …"

"… else. Ha, you sound like a broken record."

"Don't make me bust you up."

The gangly kid sat up. "Okay, the last guy who said that got concluded by a Terminator."

"Why did you say that word?"

"Concluded?"

"No, Timeinator."

"I said Terminator, but I know where you're coming from."

"And where did I come from?"

"That's not what I meant."

"Are you one of them?" Caine said, raising his fists.

"Try easing off the aggression accelerator for a second and let me explain something to you. First question. Did you bang your head when you landed? I did. Hurt like crap for about an hour afterwards."

"I'm in no mood for jokes, kid."

"Cranky, much."

"You are cruising for a bruising."

"And I'm back in High School."

"Kid, I swear to god, if you don't spill the beans, I'll …"

"You'll what? Wait longer?" The kid's comment was met with a look of disdain. "Fine, fine, I'll explain. I'm known in my world as Ted Theodore Anderson. I met some hot chick. I've worked out she was Alice's white rabbit. Not an actual rabbit. More of a figment of imagination, but real at the same time. You get the picture, right. Well, I guess I'm now in her hole. Not *her* actual hole, the rabbit's hole. No, no, that's not right. I took a spin down Alice's …"

"I must be dreaming." An exasperated Caine slumped onto a bench.

"I hope not. Because that means so am I."

"You're a teenager. You do nothing but dream. Most of those are wet ones."

"If I'm a teenager, what does that make you?"

"I'm someone that has had enough of your bullshit."

"Explain to me then, new guy, how I'm a teenager and so are you."

"That's funny," Caine fired back sarcastically.

"Take a look for yourself." Ted gestured towards a door at the far end of the gymnasium.

Caine remembered the same entrance in his school gymnasium used to lead to the boys' locker room. From the windows to the regulation urban décor, every piece of equipment looked identical. He ventured inside the locker room and came back out, looking like he'd seen a ghost. His reflection was the boy he used to be, which had to be impossible, or a trick. He pawed at his cheeks and forehead, even raising his hands before his eyes.

"Freaky, isn't it?" Ted said. "I nearly crapped my pants when I discovered I had de-aged. Now you're probably wondering how you got here. No? Yes? Let me answer for you with a resounding yes. You see, I used to be a computer hacker called TEO."

"Teo. That's an odd name."

"It's a long story. Well, it's not that long. You wanna hear it?"

"Sure, why not. It's not like I'm freaking out or anything." Caine sat on the opposite end of Ted's bench and listened intently as his teenager explained in precise detail how, after meeting a brother and sister named Daisy and Luke Duke, he arrived at the gymnasium.

"… and then I felt like I was shat out of a squid's ass, and I face planted the floor." Ted shrugged. "And that's the story of the almighty Teo. I was older, now I'm a kid. Whaddya know, it wasn't that long a story after all." Ted turned towards the stranger who remained transfixed, neither blinking nor acknowledging the end of the story. He waved a hand in front of Caine's eye line. "Nanu, nanu."

"What does that mean?"

"It's an Orkan greeting."

Caine shifted uncomfortably. "Is that where you're from?"

"No."

"Then why say it?"

"Because …"

"You know what? Shut up."

"That's rude."

"No, I'm just finding all of this a little hard to believe."

"Why?"

"You've pretty much just told me the plot of the Matrix."

"What's the Matrix?"

"It's a movie, Teo. You've never seen it?"

"Is my reaction not enough to give that away?"

"Everything you just told me, happened in the movie. Pretty much. Except the ass, squid, poop thing. The weird comic book chase scene. Orange whips. DJing. Meeting the chick in hot pants."

"Nothing like the Matrix at all then."

"Pop quiz, hotshot. Let me know if any of this sounds familiar to you. The general plot of the Matrix involved a hacker guy called Neo."

"I'm Teo."

"Exactly."

"Well, I'm Ted, I spelt the name wrong. Did I tell you that?"

"About five times."

"Was that not enough?"

"It was plenty enough."

"Do you need me to go back over the Juan joke? Those agents didn't get it. Maybe I said it wrong."

"You said it fine, thanks. In the movie, Neo meets a girl called Trinity. They are chased by bad guys with sunglasses."

"My bad guys had sunglasses," Ted nodded. "Trinity worked in the Deli."

"And everything else that happened to you, also happened to the hero. Except for the ass bug and cartoon world."

"Did you say I'm considered a hero?"

"From a certain point of view. Yeah."

"Is me being here, freeing me from the Matrix?"

"I can't answer that."

"Why not?"

"I just got here myself."

“Why would I be in a movie? That doesn’t make sense.”

“And neither do you, Teo.”

“I remember that a lot of people used to say that to me when I was a kid. I just can’t remember where I was at the time.”

“My guess is this gymnasium has something to do with it.”

“Were you in the Matrix as well?”

“I don’t think so.”

“What’s your story.”

“There’s isn’t much to tell. I’m a cop.”

“Ha!”

“What’s so funny?”

“You don’t look like a cop.”

“Most teenagers don’t look like cops. Except these guys at the Jump Street Precinct. It’s weird. Pretending to be school kids when they’re about forty.”

“I know what you mean. There was this one guy in seventh grade. He wore a leather jacket.”

“I know him.”

“You do?” Ted sat forward in anticipation.

“Yeah, he’s Fonzie.”

“Who’s Fonzie?”

“Only like the coolest man ever.”

“I don’t think that was him. My guy in seventh grade, he shaved every day. And I don’t mean his shingaling area. You know what I mean.”

“Unfortunately, I pretty much know everything that you mean. Which is starting to feel a little too familiar.”

“I know right. It’s like we’ve met before.”

“I doubt it.”

“Why would you say that?”

“I’m a cop. I’m pretty sure I’ve never arrested you before.”

“Being a cop, I guess you kicked ass?”

“A little bit, yeah.”

“I haven’t kicked anyone’s ass yet. I just ran away. Not much of a hero after all.”

“Last night, I fought Triads, alien drug dealers, and a computer genius who hacks robots and orders them to kill people.” Caine walked away before Ted could answer. “And that’s not even the craziest thing I had to deal with today.”

"Go on."

"Huge monsters attacked my Police Station."

"Sounds badass."

Kurt nodded. "A chimpanzee, a freaky elf, dwarf thing, and a marshmallow fairy."

"Were you on acid?"

"I never touch drugs."

"Are you sure? That's pretty much what a junkie would say."

"Do I look like a junkie?"

"You don't like a cop."

"These monsters climbed buildings, smashed through to where civilians were hiding. They yanked them from their apartments and ate them."

"Now who's making it up?" Ted burst out laughing. "You just described Rampage."

"Rampage?"

"It's an arcade game. Now I've heard everything."

"It's true."

"Okay, okay. Say I believe you, *Mr. Policeman*. That's a big *if.* Then how did you end up here?"

"During the attack on Headquarters, we fled to the chopper."

"'We'?"

"Myself, and Agents Scully and Mulder."

"Mulder and Scully?"

Kurt nodded. "You know them?"

"Everyone knows them. They're off a television show called the X-Files."

"Never heard of it."

"You don't recall the *'truth is out there'*, with aliens."

"Nope. Mulder did mention the truth more than once."

"Yeah, he does that a lot."

"Maybe that's why I'm here. To find out the truth."

"At last, we have something in common." Ted clapped slowly on purpose.

"Is this the truth? Wherever here is."

"How should I know, dude. I got here just before you did."

"Well, I didn't come here by choice."

“Everyone has a choice, boys.” The man’s voice reverberated around the gymnasium, as every section of the surroundings was swept up into a pixelated whirlwind.

AS the cyclone died down, the gym equipment and benches quickly swapped to a shadowy, space-age looking room, with smooth, metallic walls. An overhead light beam shifting effortlessly guided them towards the only exit.

“This happened to you before?” Kurt asked.

Ted shook his head and opened the doorway’s wheel locking mechanism. Behind the door was a set of stairs.

“I wonder where these stairs go?” Ted asked.

“They go up,” Kurt replied.

“Shall we use them?”

“It would be rude not to.”

“You haven’t told me your name?”

“It’s Kurt Con – … I mean Caine, Kurt Caine.”

“Kurt, huh. I knew a Kurt once.”

“Was he a good guy?”

“The jury is still out.”

The two teenagers shared a knowing smile.

Unsure why they reacted the way they did, the teenagers embarked on a captivating jaunt from the holodeck to the cockpit of a starship.

Having never set foot on anything as advanced, the boys took in as much detail as they could. From the communal space, with its host of arcade and pinball machines, they entered the ship’s galley. Beyond the galley, the freight loading bay’s elevator transported them up two decks. They passed through the crew’s quarters, reconfigured with new age, padded sleeping bunks, and storage spaces. A short route through the engineering station showcased the futuristic hyperdrive system, power couplings and converters. The final area of two sealed cargo holds flanked the cockpit’s access tunnel.

“Is it wrong that I feel like I’m exploring the love child of the Millennium Falcon and the Starship Enterprise?” Ted said.

Ted and Caine entered the cockpit. An eighties pop tune called 'You Came' by Kim Wilde played in the background.

A wide, two-tier viewing portal displayed a daunting image of infinite darkness. It left both boys under no illusions that they were in space. After their recent experiences, neither of them seemed surprised.

Futuristic VDUs circled a pair of swivel seats. Slotted neatly in between the circles of screens, a clunky looking main command seat rivalled Captain Kirk's recognizable throne. The only difference between the two was the flat screen attached to a drooping, giraffelike neck. Other terminals with flashing lights and numbers could be seen, but they made no sense to the boys.

"You think it's weird that we haven't seen any humans onboard," Caine said.

"That's because I am not human, boys," said the same voice that addressed them before the gymnasium vanished. "I am something altogether different."

"Is that so," Caine stated.

"Yeah, what he said," Ted added.

"What are you doing?"

"Agreeing with you. Is that a problem?"

"Do you even think about what words come out of your mouth?"

"Yeah. Words spring to mind. Sentences are formed. Usually in that order."

"You're a dumb ass." Caine turned away from Ted expecting to be confronted by a lifeform of some sort. "Come face us in the flesh, mister."

"That's not possible," the voice replied.

"Oh, I agree to disagree," Ted fired off.

Caine shot Ted a bemused look.

"Just put one foot in front of the other," Ted continued, shooting Caine a knowing wink.

"I can't," the voice replied.

"Course you can. It's like riding a bike, without the bike, and using just your feet to walk, rather than peddling."

Caine shoved Ted's shoulder. "Dude, seriously."

"I'm just trying to help."

"Well, you're not. Just let me do the talking."

"Okay, okay."

"Hey, mister. You can't, or you won't?"

The boys recoiled at the same time as the flat screen on the long neck to the right of the command chair awoke, the mechanical neck twisting awkwardly as if stretching from a long slumber. After a few moments of groaning, the screen faced the boys. On the screen, two round, orange eyes were split by a yellow cross nose. A mouth had been replaced by a host of red dots, which flashed intermittently as it spoke. Two red, glowing rectangular boxes appeared to be the screen's cheeks.

"Like I said, I can't face you in the flesh," the robot said.

"Now it makes sense," Ted replied. "He can't walk because he hasn't got any legs."

"I know that, Ted," Caine snapped. "You know what? I've seen that robot's face before."

"Back of a milk carton?"

"No, not on a milk carton. From that kids' cartoon, Clash of the Planets. I just can't remember the dude's name. Forget it. Why are you hiding behind a mask? Why are we here? Most importantly, where's the coffee machine?"

"That's some brutal questioning, dude. You must have been a total badass cop," Ted added.

Caine motioned towards the face on the screen. "I'm kind of in the middle of an interrogation."

"Can I point out that you are not a cop. You're a kid."

"I know that."

"Maybe that's why your questions suck."

"Ted, please."

Ted raised his hands in surrender and took an exaggerated step backwards. "Okay, TJ, question away."

"Thank you, finally. Where were we? Ah, I remember. Who are you?"

"I'm an old friend from your childhood."

The screen's reply warranted an answer.

"You'll have to be more specific. I didn't have many friends," Ted replied.

"Ted. Please, let me do the talking," Caine said.

"Okay, okay."

"Why is my childhood relevant? That's to the screen, not you, Ted."

"Because it's the truth. Close your eyes, boys. Let me take on a journey, back to your past," the screen said.

"Is this gonna hurt?" Ted asked.

"Only when I punch you for being so annoying," Caine bemoaned. "Go ahead, screen dude. Take us back."

FLASHBACK
EARTH, WINTER, 1987

FROM THE outside, it didn't seem possible to fit another room inside the old man's shanty house. Tobias had led Tommy, his friends, and the good townsfolk of Rosewood Falls, into a space-age armory. The infinite bay appeared to be full of wondrous technology, most of which the townsfolk had only seen in science fiction movies.

Every item of technology appeared unused. Matching futuristic military uniforms, enforced with Kevlar, were kept inside a wall of glass cabinets. Weapon caches and racks filled one half of the chamber. For as far as the eye could see were a plethora of handguns, laser blasters, automatic cannons, grenade launchers, tank busters, and anti-aircraft weapons. Armored tanks and jeeps were perfectly lined up along the opposite side of the bay. Behind the vehicles, there was a huge, sealed King Kong-sized doorway.

"This is something you don't see every day," Tommy blurted.

"Where the hell did you get it all from?" Mikey asked.

"I've been collecting over the years," Tobias replied.

"Who from, the CIA?" Ted added.

"From all over. Boys, Daisy, wait here. Everyone else, follow me."

The teenagers watched as Tobias led the townsfolk towards the massive doorway. The entrance parted sluggishly, clouds of dust erupting from the seals as the doors opened for the first time in what appeared to be centuries.

Before she entered the doorway, Daisy embraced Maxine and promised herself that she would see her again.

"You keep that Tommy close to you, D," Maxine said, tears welling in her eyes.

"I will," Daisy said, kissing her best friend on the cheek.

Kurt tapped Daisy's shoulder. "Daisy, do you mind if I …"

Daisy and Maxine shared a look.

"It's okay," Maxine assured her friend.

Kurt watched until Daisy was far enough away for her not to hear what he was about to say. He expected Maxine to stare him down. Instead of appearing annoyed, she was smiling. Kurt felt his chest heaving, his mind awash with jumbled words that would make little sense on a Scrabble board.

INTERLUDE

"IS that *me* with the hot chick?" Caine asked.

"It is," the screen replied.

"I'm there, too," Ted remarked.

"Correct, Ted."

"How do I not remember any of this?" Caine asked.

"Because you need to seek the truth."

"That's what Mulder said to me."

"And Mulder was right. Only then will you see yourself for who you really are. That goes for you as well, Ted."

"Cool. Will he get any tongue action with the chick before we uncover the truth," Ted asked the screen dude.

RETURN TO FLASHBACK

"ARE you going to talk or just sweat?" Maxine asked Kurt, before shooting a look at Tobias, who was anxious to get everyone to safety as quickly as possible.

"I like you," Kurt said.

"I know."

"Oh. You do."

"I'm not blind, Kurt."

"It's just, you're really hot, and girls like you don't tend to go for a geek."

"You know why?"

Kurt shook his head.

"Kurt, geeks never ask the pretty girls out. They don't have the courage to. They think the exact same thing that you are right now. They're not good enough, they aren't good looking enough. When you think that way, there is no point in asking. That's too negative."

"You're completely right."

"Well?"

It took a moment to realize that his friends and Tobias were staring at him, making his next move even harder. "Okay. So, maybe we can hook up, when this clusterfuck is all over?"

"I'd like that."

"An actual date, not helping with school stuff."

"It's a date, Kurt."

"Cool. Now I just need to find someplace that isn't flattened."

Maxine leaned over, kissing him gently on the cheek. "Be careful, Kurt."

She walked away, following Tobias through the doors. They sealed with a thud.

INTERLUDE

"HOLD on a minute. She had the hots for me and yet we never hooked up," Caine said.

"Are you sure?" Ted asked.

"I'm sure I would remember that."

"And there is a reason why you never did," the screen dude said.

"And just a kiss on the cheek. Bummer. There goes the tongue action," Ted added.

RETURN TO FLASHBACK

KURT rejoined his friends, clinging onto the hope that he'd stay alive long enough to go on a date with the girl of his dreams.

"I take it by the kiss that you didn't crash and burn?" Tommy asked with a glint of a smile.

"Either that or he agreed to help with her physics project," Ted joked.

"Actually, she agreed on a date," Kurt replied.

"Cool. Now, if you hadn't flattened the only cool food joint in town with Redzilla, you might have somewhere to take her."

TOBIAS quickly escorted the town survivors along a windowless corridor, stopping only when he came upon two sealed doorways. The left entranceway was marked with **β**, the Greek symbol for *Beta*. A gothic looking doorknocker, adorned with the head of a Gorgon, sat to the right.

"Need I ask what entrance we use," Maxine asked, already reaching for the Beta entry button.

Tobias had noticed a spring in her step after her conversation with Kurt. The beauty queen rarely fell for a nerd, except in the movies. Maybe the tide was turning for the nerds; now he just hoped that his plan would work and allow the teenagers a chance to live happily ever after.

"Actually, it's the Gorgoneion chamber." Tobias pointed towards the gothic doorknocker.

"You ever feel like you wish you never asked."

"You have nothing to fear, Maxine. The Gorgoneion is an ancient protection symbol. You'll be safe from H.I.M in there until this all ends."

"You're not coming with us?"

Tobias shook his head. "I still have a part to play in this game."

"It seems a bit more than a game to me."

"Do you know the biggest problem in the universe, Maxine? Nobody helps each other. I wish I had more time to explain. Maybe Kurt can explain it to you when he returns."

"Oh, no, we're just …"

"Friends."

"Geeks are normally not on my radar."

"They're not all bad."

"Keep him safe, won't you."

"I'll do my best, Maxine."

"He's kind of goofy, but he has always been nice to me."

"Make sure you tell him that when he returns."

"Oh, I forgot about Daisy."

"Anyone else?"

"Tommy, and the others. Take care of them all." She smiled loosely.

"I'll do all I can to protect them." Tobias used the door knocker once and the entrance parted with the same sound as a Death Star blast door.

The survivors entered a garden paradise, alive with sunshine, waterfalls, and birdcall. Decorated tables and marquees, assembled from vines and flowers, were crammed with fresh fruit and drink.

Tobias calmly ushered the townsfolk inside one by one.

"How can we ever thank you?" asked an elderly woman.

"There is no need. Before you know it, you'll be home, safe and sound. You have my guarantee," Tobias answered. "Just make sure you keep the door closed, or the protection spell will be broken."

AFTER the entrance closed, sealing the survivors in the safest environment in the galaxy, Tobias entered *Beta*.

An upwards crank of the light control illuminated a vast stasis chamber, with rows of humanoids, designated as Beta Units. To combat the cold, Tobias unhooked a winter jacket from a coat hook. He then made his way towards a pair of moveable medical beds.

Each Beta Unit was identical in height and body shape. The synthetic skin appeared moist to the touch, bulging purple and green veins visible beneath the skin, a pair of big, blue eyes staring vacantly ahead.

He guided one of the beds to the nearest row of synthetics and flipped it upright, the cushion resting against the Beta's spine. After he secured the ankle, wrist, and body straps, he adjusted the bed back to its horizontal position.

Apart from the main entrance, the chamber had only one exit, labelled *Ad infinitum*.

When Tobias approached the motion sensor door, it parted to reveal a host of wall mounted computer terminals running an advanced database.

With the Beta's bed secured at the center of the room, Tobias moved aside an apparatus table, and adjusted an overhead light so it faced downwards. The Beta's skin appeared almost transparent under this new light, giving a clear view of the mechanical workings of an advanced android.

"Here goes nothing," he said, resting the palm of his right hand on the synthetic's forehead. He flinched from the short electric shock that he had anticipated, yet still reeled away from it. "I've never gotten used to that."

The relevant data received through the simple gesture of touch started the Beta's alteration process. Breathing in, cheeks expanding, broad nostrils proudly taking in the first gulps of oxygen since its creation, left the elderly man watching with some apprehension. Since his first encounter with H.I.M., this was the first time Tobias had put everything on the line.

Had he chosen the right course of action or was his connection to the teenagers clouding his judgement?

Would fate play a part?

Only time would tell.

OWING to the synthetic flesh progressively covering every inch of the lifeform's body, the Beta's flickering processer lights started to dim, until it became the exact simulated version of Tobias Strong. No matter how many times he watched the alteration process, Tobias could not feel anything but amazed by the accuracy of each replica's appearance.

A side effect of the transformation was the memory transfer that always took a while to break through. The few unexpected kinks in the processors also allowed for the replacement to be just that, a substitute without the full range of people skills. Perhaps Tobias could get away without the standard post operation briefing. He really had no other choice. For now, it would have to do.

To cover his modesty, Tobias pulled a blanket up to Beta's neck.

Beta sat up sharply, shielding his eyes from the overhead light. "Who's there?"

Tobias moved the light to one side. "How's that?"

"Better." From a medical equipment tray, Beta swiped a handheld mirror and studied his ageless features. He broke into an easy, readymade smile, until he locked eyes with Tobias, and dropped the mirror to the floor. "Hey, you look like me."

"Course I do. I'm Tobias; you're the Beta Unit."

"What the hell's a Beta Unit?"

"A Beta Unit is a Simuloid, an exact duplicate of another being."

"I'm a robot?"

"Pardon me, but you're a state of the art, top of line Beta Unit. I'm using you as a courtesy replacement."

"A replacement."

"Yes, you're created to be a replacement."

"To do what exactly?"

"To simulate mannerisms and physical appearance."

"Lucky me! What if I don't want to be used."

"You don't have a choice."

"Why?"

"Because I am your creator. And right now, I don't have time to give you a full briefing of life, the universe and everything."

"The universe sounds scary. Let's not go there."

"Are you kidding me, it's war out there. I need you."

"War is fighting. If you created me, then you know that Simuloids can't fight. You can't fool me. My coding is coming back to me now. You're flesh and blood. Which means, if I am a replacement, then I can't kill other beings of flesh and blood."

"I don't need you to fight flesh and blood, Beta. Just robots and bad guys."

"We don't like robots?"

"No. These robots are with the bad guys. We're the good guys. I need you to pretend to be a good guy."

"Pretend! Until when?"

"Until it's time to not pretend."

"I don't understand."

"You will when the time comes."

"What if I want to kill a robot, but there is flesh and blood in the vicinity. What should I do?"

"You'll have to work out for yourself if they are a bad guy or not."

"What if I can't decide quickly enough?"

"You're blowing it, Beta. I don't have time for this. Make your decisions on the battlefield."

"A battlefield is where fights occur. I've already told you that I can't fight."

"You need to try."

"To be target practice, whilst you're where? Saving the universe?"

"It's not quite as simple as that."

"Maybe it's because I feel like I've woken up in a terrible nightmare."

"The entire town of Rosewood Falls is already in its own nightmare. People depend on us. If we fail, people will die. And the death and destruction will not stop. It will snowball across the universe, until there are no souls left alive. Do you understand?"

"Yes."

"All life will end, Beta."

"Yes."

"I need you to try."

"I have never tried anything in my entire three minutes and forty-four seconds of existence."

"Perhaps now is a good a time as any to start."

"How do I start?"

"Maybe we start with something easy. Like walking."

Beta understood walking. He tied the blanket around his waist and took his first tentative steps across the room. "That was easy enough. I think I'm ready to battle these bad guy robots."

"You're almost ready. Now open your mind. Let all my memories and emotions flood through those gates and feed your soul."

Beta closed his eyes in anticipation and opened his arms wide. "I'm ready."

"Open your mind."

"I have."

"Keep those gates open, Beta."

"They're as wide as can be right now."

"My memories will be with you any second now."

"Are you sure? It doesn't seem like it's gonna happen."

"It will, Beta. Give it time."

"How much time?"

"Anytime now."

"I'm still empty."

"Anytime now."

"Still nothing."

"What about now? Tell me, can you see a light?"

"I can't see shit with my eyes closed."

"Profanity is new. It must be working. Now concentrate, Beta. Do you see the light?"

"Nope. Just a whole lotta darkness."

Tobias slumped in a seat, deflated. "Look again."

"Wait a minute. I see something fuzzy."

"Is it a light?"

"Yes."

"Is it the light?"

"It's light. Does that help?"

Tobias sprung up, gesturing like a preacher before a congregation. "Do you see the light?"

"Yes! Jesus H. Tap-Dancing Christ! I have seen the light!"

"That's my boy."

The pre-operation mind download had never gone through so quickly. If only he had time to make some notes.

With the procedure complete, Beta appeared totally refreshed.

"Tobias Strong. Excuse my ignorance, but please tell me exactly what you need me to do for you today?" Beta asked.

TOBIAS sat at the nearest row of wall mounted computer terminals, which appeared to be the most active of all the workstations. He gestured specifically towards a row of switches marked A to D.

"Beta, when I give you the signal, you flip these switches," he said.

"Got it." Beta looked less than convincing.

"You'll be hooking me up to *the* gateway."

"Hooking to the gateway. Got it."

"Don't break the connection. Otherwise, I'll end up a vegetable."

"Which is bad?"

"Really bad."

"Got it. Veggies, plus robots, equals bad guys."

"You flip switches A through to D."

"Got it."

"It's important. A through to D."

"D to A, got it."

"A to D."

"Sorry, A through to D. Got it."

"Are you sure?"

"Trust me, you, us." Beta's smile appeared to ease Tobias's concerns. "If you know how to download, that means so do I. We know everything at the same time. But not too much about *the* gateway."

"You know most things, just not everything. And I haven't got time to explain." Tobias unhooked an Aluminum Colander helmet from its wall berth and checked the coiled cables, wires, and connections before he secured it with a white strap beneath his chin.

"Does that thing work? You look like you should be in a looney bin."

Tobias smiled inside about the Beta's choice of words, and used a keyboard to enter some code, which released a hologram of his human brain over the medical bed. "When you flip the switches, my neurons will fire up."

"How will I know?"

"Think of lightning in a bottle."

"Crazy white lights, got it."

Tobias lay on the medical bed and waited for Beta to secure his wrists, ankles, and upper body with straps.

"What will happen to your body?" Beta asked.

"What normally happens when you download a consciousness. Now, flip the switch, download, and get your ass to that hangar bay. Those kids need you. And get dressed. A half-naked person around kids is frowned upon, everywhere."

BETA passed through two exits after leaving the *Ad infinitum* chamber before grief dropped him to his knees. Watching the real Tobias pass away as his consciousness transferred to the gateway felt like losing a lifelong friend.

"I will make you proud, Tobias. You can trust me with that."

Beta stood, without realizing his blanket had fallen and he was now in full view of the garden paradise. The entrance was open. Which was not the way Tobias's memory recall confirmed he had left it. Rosewood Falls residents screamed and threw anything they could find at Beta … dirt, shrubs, scraps of food.

To stop the barrage, he resealed them inside.

One glance down at his naked torso confirmed the uncomfortable position he had just escaped.

"Darn it, Beta. Cover up."

Beta ran back to where he left Tobias's lifeless body, only to be greeted by a pile of fresh clothes. His remains were nowhere to be seen.

With time allowing no chance to search for the body, or clean off the dirt and food, Beta dressed in the change of clothes and hurried back to the teenagers he knew very much about but had yet to meet face to face.

THE hangar doors reopened, allowing Tobias to return, covered in sweat, dirt, and a change of clothes. “Sorry. That took longer than I expected,” he said.

“Dude, you were gone for like ten seconds,” Ted replied.

“Really? I must be getting slow in my old age.”

“Are they safe?” Daisy asked.

“They’re all safe. At least they will be if you win this game outright,” Tobias added, his memories flooding back.

“No pressure then,” Kurt stated.

“Where are we going?” queried Tommy.

Tobias gestured to his left, and a single exit labelled *‘Hangar Bay’*.

“There’s more to this place than meets the eye,” Mikey stated.

“It always looks smaller on the outside, and much bigger on the inside,” Ted blurted out.

“What does?” Daisy asked.

“It’s a blue phone box the British use in an emergency.”

“You’re weird, you know that?”

“Chick thinks I’m weird. What about the house, with a wall that moves, and reveals a futuristic weapons cache?”

“That’s weird; you’re weirder.”

“Boys, I’ve had to wait a long time for revenge. I wasn’t going to sit by and let *him* take another town. Not when I can do something about it. Now, come with me if you want to win.” Tobias opened the entrance to the hangar bay and stepped inside.

END OF FLASHBACK

Chapter 14

Tic-Tac-Go

THE INCARNATION of Tobias Strong faced the two teenagers. Even with their nerd-like imaginations, he knew the boys for long enough to realize nothing would ever slip by them unnoticed.

"Do you remember me now?" he asked, his eyes flashing on the screen.

"I can positively say, after that intense flashback, I have no idea who the hell you are," Ted replied.

"He's right, screen dude," Caine added. "There was no giraffe screen thing in that flashback."

"I wasn't a screen back then. I'm Tobias. Were you listening to the story?" Tobias asked.

"Damn right I was listening. That's how I know that Ted and I are friends. Ted, going forwards, feel free to call me Kurt."

"Will do, bro," Ted said.

"Did you understand the story, Ted?" Tobias asked.

"I heard enough to know that the Tobias you created was a pony."

"A pony?"

"You know what I mean. A replica of the real Tobias."

"You mean a phony," Kurt said.

"Is that modern slang for someone who uses a cell phone?"

"A phony is a copy."

"A copy of what?"

"Ted, when you feel the instinct that arises every time you wanna speak …"

"What about it?"

"Put a cork in it." Kurt felt thankful that Ted stewed over where the cork should go, which allowed him to turn his attention back to Tobias. "Where is the Beta now?"

"He died, Kurt."

"How?"

"He sacrificed himself to save you and your friends."

"I don't remember."

"You will, in time."

"One question. If your replica martyred himself, then why are we here now?" Kurt asked.

For the next ten minutes, Tobias explained how Tommy defeated Arcadian by changing the rules. And how that decision led to everything changing, and not for the better. From the one-inch punch that forced Arcadian's brain to explode. To Tommy becoming washed up in the guts and goo and deposited out of Arcadian's backside into an accelerated dream state. How the boys' lives continued to play out as part of Arcadian's game, themselves wrapped up in accelerated dream states where they believed they were living, except they were not.

"I don't get how that took ten minutes to explain," Ted remarked.

"It was down to your dumbass comments," Kurt said. "Tobias, if this Arcadian, HIM, Mr. Nobody, bad guy, thing, changed the rules, what are we supposed to do about it? It sounds like we're just the same kids we used to be. All our *life* experiences as adults were just dust in the wind. None of it mattered. Not one bit."

"You should write rock lyrics, dude."

"Ted, remember the cork?"

"Yeah."

"Go find one."

"Kurt, the game is flourishing beyond its typical measures. As a result, Arcadian is stronger than you could possibly imagine," Tobias said.

"That's because Tommy struck him down," Ted added. "Strike a Jedi down, he becomes more powerful."

"Can you stop quoting movies?" Kurt replied.

"I would if I could. The words just sorta come out. Are you a Jedi, Tobias?"

"Here he goes again."

"I am not a Jedi, Ted," Tobias added.

"Are you sure? In your story, your body vanished. Kind of sounds like a Jedi being struck down to me."

"Where are our friends now?" Kurt asked Tobias.

"Daisy and Tommy were with you," Tobias replied.

"When?"

"In your world they were Mulder and Scully. And Daisy and Luke for me. Am I right?" Ted stated.

"Correct, Ted," Tobias replied.

"I knew it."

"When Daisy and Tommy's avatars arrived in your realities, your dream states ended, and you became self-aware. That is why everything felt so real to you suddenly."

"Lucky for them I wasn't doing the nasty."

"Nobody cares about you taking a dump, Ted," Kurt said.

"I meant the other nasty. You know what I mean."

"As usual, everyone knows what you meant. How does this all end, Tobias?"

"That, I do not know," Tobias replied.

"Where are Daisy and Tommy now?"

"They're searching for the last piece of the jigsaw."

"Is that a metaphor, or some innovative reality hopping, time bandit lingo?" Ted asked.

The flat screen's awkwardness almost took off the top of Ted's head as it twisted to face him. "The last piece is your friend Mikey."

"Mikey being the other kid in the flashback," Kurt said, ducking the floating flat screen as it spun in his direction.

"Correct. Find Mikey. You return to Earth and finish the game, once and for all."

"I'm guessing it's not going to be as easy as just flying us home," Ted said.

"Correct, Ted."

"Normally I'd be happy that I'm on a roll, but I get a feeling this walk in the park is about to take a wrong turn."

"In your game, to reach Arcadian you needed to cross a host of hostile environments. When you are all reunited, you will need to retrace your steps and return to the Black Hole. But first Tommy and Daisy need to rescue Mikey."

"Is there anything we can do to help?" Kurt asked.

"I'm glad you asked." Tobias's giraffe neck grew in length until it hovered over one of the seats circled by the VDUs. "Pick a seat, boys."

SAT opposite each other, the two teenagers watched Tobias run a diagnostic of a Sentry Bot neither of them could yet see. Powered by a unique Iranium crystal, harvested from the planet Jupiter, the metallic sphere guard rolled forwards and came to a halt in the gantry between the two sets of VDUs.

"*Sergeant Major Hero reporting for duty, sir.*"

In between two sets of sergeant stripes, the sentry's designated roll call number had been etched away. Beneath the scratch marks, two bulbous white eyes set back inside the sphere appeared to be floating on their own accord. A strip for a mouth glowed as it continued to address Tobias. This unique weaponized Zeroid also had enough battle scars for it to look more menacing than it probably should have.

"What the hell is that?" Ted asked.

"Protection," Tobias answered.

"Weirdest looking bowling ball I've ever seen," Kurt remarked.

"Be nice, boys. Otherwise, the sergeant might not protect you from what comes next."

"I'm sensing Déjà-vu," Ted stated.

Kurt turned his attention to the different sets of green digits raining down on the VDUs black backgrounds. The images made little to no sense to him, as did the archaic dialogue printed on the data sheets continually spewing forth from a host of nearby laser printers fixed to the wall.

"None of this data means anything to me," he said.

"The green rain I've seen in my dreams," Ted added.

"Good for you. To be honest, Tobias, I'm not much of a computer whizz."

"You don't need to be, Kurt. Your next move is all about choice," Tobias replied.

Two secret compartments on the armrest of each chair opened. Inside the left compartment was a red Tic-Tac. In the right compartment, a blue Tic-Tac.

"You got anything bigger than a Tic-Tac? I'm starving," Ted said.

"Now is not the time for sustenance, Ted. It is time to choose your fate. Should you decide on the blue Tic-Tac, your stories end right here, right now. You will both go back to your prison reality, whereby you will remain in your dream states and remember none of this. You will carry on being Teo and Detective Caine until you die. If you pick the red Tic-Tac, the door to this wonderland will open and you will get to see how deep the rabbit hole goes."

"Like the rabbit in my message. Which means this is all connected somehow," Ted remarked.

"You're learning quickly, Ted."

"I choose red. Kurt?"

Kurt pondered for a few seconds, and then made his choice. "To hell with it. Red. I'll choose red."

"Atta boy, Kurt."

"Before you take the Tic-Tac, I must warn you both. There is so much more to come to terms with when you finally awaken. All that I have shown you thus far is merely scratching the surface. Arcadian is everywhere. He has so many branches into different realities that he has managed to pull a world over your eyes so vast that you are all buried deep beneath the truth. You were his slaves for too long. He kept you a prisoner in your own minds. Once you take the Tic-Tac, you will see it for yourself. This is your last chance to turn back. After you swallow, there is no turning point."

"You know what. I feel a bit weird," Ted said.

"You took it already?" Kurt asked.

"Was I not meant to?"

"It's the Tic-Tac, Ted," Tobias said.

"My eyes are starting to see something," Ted blurted.

"Can you see the truth now, Ted?"

"It might be the truth."

"Explain it to me, Ted. What do you see?"

"Well, instead of a big dark blur, I see a big white blur."

"It looks like Kansas is going bye-bye." Kurt wasted no time and took his red Tic-Tac.

As a precaution, a seatbelt secured around their waists, wrists, and ankles.

"I believe you are both feeling a bit like Alice falling down the rabbit hole," Tobias said.

"What is it with all these damn rabbit holes," Kurt bemoaned as his body shook violently.

"You know what comes with rabbit holes?" Ted asked, grinding his teeth as his body trembled from head to toe.

"No, but I think you're going tell me."

"Rabbit droppings. Tons of it."

"Thanks for the valuable insight, dumbass."

"When you awoke this morning, you both knew something wasn't right. You could sense it," Tobias said.

"I just thought it was a hangover."

Unable to control his body spasms, Ted just let the procedure take control. "What I feel right now is a load of vomit rising in my throat."

"It's not vomit, Ted," Tobias added.

"Oh, I'm pretty sure it is."

"The dream that you were so sure was real, and you were unable to wake from, it is being flushed from your system."

"How do I know what is real and what is not?" Kurt yelled out, his body flapping wildly enough to be considered possessed and ready for an exorcism.

"Let it all out and the truth will flood back to you."

"I hope you're right. Or I'm gonna barf all over your spaceship," Ted said.

At the same time, both teenagers' constraints were released. They fell to their knees, clutching their throats, gagging at what they thought was rising bile.

Whatever rose from the stomachs was not bile, but oily, wriggling around in the throat, and had claspers clutching on the side of their mouths as it fought to escape the poisonous red Tic-Tac.

Arcadian's minions, a black slug, hidden inside the each teenagers' body for the entire time they were prisoners, were regurgitated across the deck. Two energy blasts from Sergeant Major Hero ensured their remains boiled away and fell through the floor grating to the lower decks.

"*Will that be all, sir?*" Hero asked Tobias.

"Yes, that will be all. Thank you, Sergeant," Tobias replied.

With the Zeroid rolling back to its guard station, Tobias remained confident that releasing the reality bug from the teenagers' souls would open the gateway to restructuring their existence from their births to the very moment they handed the power rings to Tommy in Arcadian's cave. Even with time pressing, such an influx of memories would surely wound any soul's recovery.

"Am I dead? It sure feels like it," Kurt said, still prone on the floor, the charred smell of burnt alien parasite stinging his nostrils.

"Welcome back to the real world," Tobias said.

"Being in the real world doesn't feel so good."

"I see it as a necessary adjustment, for the bigger picture."

"Can you do anything about that smell? Chargrilled bug is making me heave."

"Unfortunately, the stench tends to linger."

"A bit like Ted. Speaking of. Hey, buddy. You good?"

"I'm doing dandy," Ted said, clutching his body as if it was about to release an alien through his chest.

"The discomfort will ease," Tobias said.

"Tell that to my esophagus. It feels like a bus drove through it. Is that everything that needs to be removed from my body now? Anything else could really put a dent in my charming personality."

"That is everything coming out of you."

"Good. Wait a minute. You made that sound like that something is going back in." Ted stood and regretted doing so. Bowled over by dizziness, he stumbled into a row of VDUs and hung on for dear life.

"Relax, Ted. Take all the time you need," Tobias said.

"You could've warned us about spewing up a giant bug. Not the grossest thing I've done today but it's pushing close to pole position."

"I thought if I told you the procedure, you wouldn't go through with it."

"You'd be right."

"The rest of it was okay, until the bug thing happened. What I can't handle is the information overload in my mind," Kurt said.

"Your mind will adapt to the change. Just give it time," Tobias replied.

"Going back to the putting things back in my body question. Tell me you're joking," Ted said, now finding it easier to stand, rather than hold on.

"There is one more thing we need to do."

"*We* need?"

"Yes."

"What about you need?"

"I need. I don't know what you are talking about, Ted."

"You probably don't."

"I'd call Ted a stuck-up, half-witted, scruffy-looking nerf herder if I thought it would help, but I think I know what you're going to say, Tobias. You need to upload our consciousness," Kurt said.

"We have a winner," Tobias said.

"I just hope this is painless."

"Sort of."

"You're not putting anything else up me," Ted remarked, still groggy.

"Ted, time is of the essence."

"Time can wait for this man. Explain. And I don't care that I'm asking another question."

"Okay, Ted. The short, short version. You were both playing roles. None of it was real. It's time to take on a new role so you can help find Mikey. We need you back in the game as an avatar."

"Wait a minute. If I wasn't real, am I still a virgin?"

"Ted! What the …" Kurt said.

"You're telling me that you haven't considered it."

Kurt shot a curious look at Tobias. "He's got a point. Does it count if we, you know, made a little dream love?"

"And these types of questions are exactly why we have to put you straight back in," Tobias said.

"Is that even safe coming out and going straight back in?"

"Only if you're wearing a rubber," Ted blurted.

"Ted! For the love of God. Will you button it."

"I'm being serious, Kurt. When I fell out of my world, it felt like I was inside a giant rubber."

"Unlucky for us, you are the 0.01% of idiots that got through. Tobias, is transferring us so quickly even safe?"

"I guess we'll find out," Tobias replied.

"Please tell me you have done this before?"

"Once."

"Did it work?"

"Tommy found you both. I'd say that's a good test run."

"Did it hurt him?"

"He didn't know it happened. He was incapacitated, sort of. Then a door hit him."

"A door. We puke up a slug and Tommy walks into a door."

"It was a car door. Look, every adjustment is different. Mikey's will be if you can find him. Relax, Kurt. You all have a part to play."

"Unless my brain gets fried upon re-entry."

"Just lay face down, relax, and enjoy the ride. It's time to bring the cavalry."

The two chairs unfolded horizontally, with a hole in the top end for them to nestle their faces inside a cushioned opening.

"Yeah, Kurt, lie down, relax. A cop will be a good reinforcement," Ted remarked.

Tobias tilted his flat head towards the opposite bed. "That means you, too, Ted."

"I knew Kurt needed my help. Dude would be lost without his best bud."

"Tobias, if you want to fry Ted's brain a little on re-entry, you have my blessing," Kurt said.

With the boys lying down, automated straps secured them in place by their wrists, waists, ankles, across the base of the spine, neck, and the back of their skulls.

Ted tried to move and couldn't. "I hate to say it …"

"Then don't," Kurt barked.

"Excuse me, but these binds are much tighter than when we took the Tic-Tac."

"You've made some sense for once. Say, Tobias …" Kurt stopped talking when two Zeroids rolled out from unseen guard positions, stopping directly beneath the two headrests.

On top of each sphere was the word *Medic*, which separated as a robotic winch rose to a few inches below the openings. A lance, no wider than a straw and attached to the end of each winch, edged ominously towards the middle of the boys' foreheads.

"Ten bucks that lance goes somewhere that hurts. Everything today hurts, in some sadistic way. You think I'd be used to it by now," Ted said.

"You can't let Arcadian be aware that you're back inside the system," Tobias said.

"Having a big hole in my forehead might be a giveaway!"

"Will Daisy and Tommy know who we are?" Kurt asked.

"My equipment can only situate you in the same environment as your friends," Tobias said. "Your presence, and everyone else in the environment, will be shielded by their avatar. Your avatars will have no powers. Only the weapons you find can be used. Your friends will not know who you are, not unless you tell them. Should you reveal yourself, any loose information revealed to the wrong person could result in a catastrophic outcome for Mikey."

"No pressure then."

"Tell the wrong person and the Timeinators will be upon you in a flash. That could mean permanent eradication for all of you."

"If I'm right, we've met some of the Timeinators already. They're not so bad."

Ted tried to move his head to the side, and then remembered the forehead restraint. "Kurt, whatever you do, if they find us, don't let those Timeinators put a tracker inside you."

"Got it."

"Seriously, you don't wanna know how to remove it."

"Thanks, Ted."

"I wouldn't wish that on my nemesis."

"I heard you the first time, Ted."

"I'm just saying. I think I've got hemorrhoids from the last time. Tobias, this lance isn't going to …" Ted let out an earthshattering scream as an electric current, emitting from the lance, invaded his psyche.

Kurt had no time to take onboard what happened to his friend. The second lance emitted an electric current that pierced his prefrontal cortex. Allowing no part to remain unturned, the boys region of the brain for complex cognitive behavior, personality expression, decision making, and moderating social behavior became overwhelmed.

Both teenagers felt what it was like to be flipped over like a pancake inside a giant frying pan. Their minds were torn apart like paper and then pieced back together again, one fragment at a time. Their bodies catapulted towards a blinding light, until the pain stopped and their focus returned, as did the humming sound of a rotor blade.

DAY FOUR

(Four jumps remaining)

Chapter 15

Deep Blue Six

MONTH - DAY LOCATION
JULY 14 ARCQUATICA 007-981
REALITY DESTINATION

IN THE rear passenger seats of the transport helicopter, Aquatic Control Expert Tommy McCloud's attention was fixed on the floating research center below.

"I guess Alcatraz floats," he said.

The other three members of the Tri Oceanic Corp Rescue Team took the old submarine docking complex in their stride. Each member had their own version of an Exoframe uniform, allowing them all to fuse with weapon systems designed for above and below the waves.

McCloud's royal blue and white uniform permitted the former submersible pilot to combine with a host of aquatic weapons and propulsion systems. A handful of the weapons systems, connected by satellite accuracy to the suits by wrist gauntlets, had been stored in the cargo hold.

"Any idea what they were working on down there?" Max 'Kurtis' Ray, Sea Operations expert and leader of the unit, scowled as he showed his discomfort at being above the surface.

"If we've been called upon, I'd take that as someone messed up big time," Tommy answered.

"That is not cool."

"Amen to that."

"How big is this place?" Jake 'Theodore' Rockwell, the unit's Land Operations Specialist, had seen it all before.

Most of their previous missions took place at some sort of clandestine facility. Be it underground, an excavated mountain scape, or deep in a hidden jungle of some kind. No matter how vast the environment was, the unit had come out unscathed, despite being outgunned more times than they could count.

"This was all in the pre-flight briefing," Tommy stated.

"It's okay. He paid attention," Kurt replied.

"Yeah, it's my, erm, hemorrhoids," Ted mentioned, too gleefully for his own good.

"Hemorrhoids, huh," Tommy said.

Just in time, the team's headsets crackled with activity as the pilot's voice spoke over the din of the rotor blades. "For those of you suffering with hemorrhoids of the ears, Arcquatica boasts half a mile of catwalks. With three sub levels, consisting of living quarters, wet lab, and workshops, engineering and airlock wet entry, the entire complex is ringed by high titanium-based fences, with a maximum height of fifteen feet off the surface. It was used mainly for refueling in World War Three."

"Did you say World War Three?" Ted asked.

The eyes of the rest of the unit fell upon Ted, who decided to mimic zipping his mouth closed and throwing away the key.

"How long have the comms been down?" Sitting with her back to the pilot, red-headed Crystal 'Daisy chain' Kane removed a laptop from a carryall and opened it on her lap. The communications, logistical and tactical expert had only just arrived before take-off and had little information to go by.

"Around three hours, ma-am," the pilot replied.

"Three hours is a long time to wait before contacting us," Tommy said.

"Radiation storm. Real nasty one. It took a while for us to get an all clear. After the satellite reported an energy blast emitting from the comet's tail, we had no eyes on the facility, and no communications. At first, we thought the site had been destroyed entirely. When we got the satellite up and running again is when we contacted your team. Looking at the damage, it may well have been severe lightning, which doesn't make any sense."

"Whatever the damage, having us here is the right call. Take us down, pilot," Daisy ordered.

THE helicopter landed on the designated pad on the west side of the facility, allowing the team to disembark with their equipment crates. Arcquatica's six surface level lagoons and holding pens appeared unoccupied, as they had expected.

"Do you want me to wait?" the pilot asked.

"Head back to HMS Sky Vault. We'll take it from here," Daisy replied.

Without hesitation the pilot took off, leaving the unit on what could only be described as the surface level of a titanium fenced aquatic prison.

"Alcatraz was right," Ted added as he forced open the gated entranceway.

"Haemorrhoids, huh," Tommy said out loud to nobody.

Ted stopped in his tracks. "Yeah, they tend to come along when something unexpected comes out of you."

"A bit like the comment you just made," Daisy replied.

Ted shot a look at the red head. "You should know what I'm talking about."

"Should I?"

"I'm not sure now is the right time for a confrontation," Kurt said, grabbing Ted by the sleeve.

"Now is perfect. Cos my ass can't stop itching inside this suit and I need some ointment. I'm betting she has some in her med kit." Ted stopped short of scratching his butt.

"You weren't lying," Tommy said.

"Whatever. Let's cut to the chase. This might sound crazy, but you don't know how bad I've had it today. What are your names, your real names."

"You should know that. We've been a team for years."

"Humor me. Pretend that I bumped my head earlier. I've already forgotten the briefing. Or did you forget that I forgot. And as for World War Three."

"Okay, you're weirding me out a bit, but I'll go with it. I'm Tommy McCloud and she's Crystal 'Daisy chain' Kane."

"What are your names?" Daisy asked.

"Jake 'Theodore' Rockwell," Ted blurted, then turned to Kurt for support.

"Dumbass," Kurt replied.

"And you?" Daisy asked Kurt.

"Max 'Kurtis' Ray," he replied.

"Tommy and Daisy, come on. Even a dipshit like me can put two and two together and get five," Ted said.

"What are you saying?" Daisy asked, reaching for the sidearm in her hip holster.

"Why, what are you saying?" Kurt replied, reaching for his sidearm.

"Enough of this. We have an important job to do." Tommy stood in between the two warring factions.

"Give us a second," Ted said, grabbing Kurt and moving out of earshot.

"Congrats on not making it feel awkward for at least three seconds," Kurt said.

"I think we need to say it now." Ted looked serious, although his avatar's intense persona hadn't changed since he awoke on the chopper.

"It could be a trap," Kurt replied.

"I don't think so," Ted added.

"Why would you say that?"

"I think a servant of Arcadian would look fairer and feel fouler."

"What kind of bullshit conclusion is that?"

"Look around. We're all alone."

"If we're wrong, it's catastrophic for Mikey. Or did you forget what Tobias said would happen."

"I'm a gambling man. I can take a chance. And we might not get a better one."

"Okay. Do it. But how crap would we be as cavalry if we fall at the first hurdle?"

After a short conversation with Daisy, Tommy tapped Ted on the shoulder. "Guys, I will say this only once. Tell me the wrong answer and it's adios horsemen." Tommy tapped his hip holster as a warning.

Ted lunged for Tommy and hugged him like a long-lost friend.

"Ted?" Tommy asked.

"The one and only."

"I knew it was you."

"What gave me away?"

"You had me at hemorrhoids, dude."

"Rookie mistake. In case you didn't realize, he's Kurt." Ted jabbed a thumb in Kurt's direction. His hug lingered and became tight enough to become awkward.

"Okay, okay, enough with the hugs. Save your strength. There'll be another time."

"How did you get here?" Daisy added, avoiding Ted's handshake.

"My handshakes still not good enough," Ted joked.

"The last time you tried to shake my hand, you'd just taken a dump in my brother's bathroom, and you hadn't washed your hands."

Ted went straight in for a hug and felt Daisy's tension ease after a few seconds. Then it came back with a vengeance.

"Okay, okay, that's enough physical contact for today," she said, her hands bracing his chest and forcing him backwards.

Tommy and Kurt shook hands and embraced.

"Good to see you, bro," Tommy said.

"And you, you selfish bastard." From out of nowhere, Kurt's right hook knocked Tommy off his feet.

Kurt's avatar had no powers, but he had a background in martial arts.

Tommy knelt, nursing first his chin, then his ego. "What was that for?"

"For changing the rules."

"I had no choice."

"I respectfully disagree." Kurt's anger boiled over. A roundhouse kick sent Tommy crashing through the pile of equipment crates, knocking them all in the water. Whatever was inside was heavy enough for them to sink to the bottom of the lagoon.

"There goes our weapons cache," Ted bemoaned.

"Listen up, you fool." Daisy purposely blocked Kurt's path.

He had no intention of backing down. "I've done enough listening today," Kurt snapped.

Kurt's fighting technique was no match for Daisy, who was the unit's most fearsome fighter. She caught his attempted roundhouse punch and twisted his wrist to force him off balance. It was enough to ensure her quick kick to the back of his knee immobilized him for the few seconds she needed to unholster her sidearm. Kurt had no need to look behind him. He knew Daisy's weapon was already nestled against the back of his skull.

"Lesson one, Kurtis. In here, we have only one life," she snarled.

After being reunited with a host of old memories for as little as thirty minutes, there was no contest between the teenage life he had before to the Detective's one he just chosen to leave behind. Teenager versus hardened Detective, there was only one winner, even if it was just a dream.

A raging conflict in his mind meant his first instinct was to blame Tommy, the person who said he would end the game. By the game continuing, Kurt's entire dream state had been a lie. A partner gunned down before him. A killer on the loose, and his army of robots terrorizing the city he pledged to protect. A tough 90s police detective persona stewing over the fact that a chick had caught his punch so easily. So many of Caine's plot holes remained incomplete.

Part of Kurt thought about asking Daisy to pull the trigger.

The few extra seconds of hesitancy might well have saved his life.

"My mind is splitting apart," Kurt said, raising his hands in surrender.

"Join the club," Tommy added.

"It's your fault Tommy."

"You don't know anything, Kurt," Daisy retaliated.

"I know enough to make my mind up."

"I respectfully disagree."

"What happened to you, dude? The band is almost back together, and you left us quicker than Mark Wahlberg left New Kids on the Block," Ted added.

Daisy released her hold on Kurt's wrist and kicked him in the back, knocking him down face first. "Take this one warning. I have too much at stake in this fight. You ever touch Tommy again, next time I won't hesitate to shoot you dead."

"My mind is frazzled, okay. I've just had, what, the most adventurous twenty odd years of my life replaced by a nerd's wet dream." It took every ounce of Kurt's being to stop from lashing out again.

"Ditto," Tommy said, finally standing. "Except for Daisy, we all lived the lie. I was married, with kids. You think that's not hard for me to come to terms with right now? It felt real enough, and it still does, but I get now that it wasn't. If anyone should be pissed right now, it's me."

"You don't understand. I was Detective Kurt Caine. I drank liquor and banged strippers. I took shit from no one. And no chick would ever catch one of my punches."

"You wanna try a second round, hot shot?" Daisy stepped towards Kurt.

Tommy held her back.

"It's not easy for any of us, Kurt," Ted said.

Daisy helped Kurt get to his feet. "Ted's right. This is a fight to get back what we lost. Me more than most. It's not a fight between us."

"But I don't want to lose it. I want it back. I don't want to be a nerdy teenager. I want to be a badass, gunslinging, womanizing alcoholic," Kurt said. Hearing his thoughts out loud, Kurt suddenly realized how absurd he sounded.

"You can still be that. Just back home. When you're older." Ted consoled Kurt by putting an arm around his shoulder. "I have enough memories back to know that you're my best friend, Kurt. But I'd rather you didn't' grow up to be like my stepdad."

"You haven't got a stepdad, dude."

"You know what, in my head right now, I've got spaghetti, cable junction, and strawberry laces linking my mind together. All I know for certain is that I do have hemorrhoids. Unless Jake 'Theodore' Rockwell has them. Does it work like that? Is it me, or him? You see what I mean, spaghetti junction up here and as dry as the Sahara down there."

"I'm sorry." Kurt directed his apology at Tommy.

"Friends don't need to apologize," Tommy replied.

"I can't handle it. Caine's memories fading away. It's like trying to stop sand through my fingers."

"I am experiencing the same thing. I don't even know when I became myself again. It just happened. But you know what. Your old life, your teenage years, they'll be back with you in no time."

"Will I lose Caine forever?"

Tommy let Daisy answer. "He will eventually fade, like all dreams."

"Tommy's kids. He'll forget them?"

Kurt didn't need an answer; he could tell by Daisy's reaction that the inevitable would happen somewhere down the line. In hindsight, his stupid actions seemed petty in comparison to losing an entire family and being powerless to stop it.

"If you weren't sure about leaving Caine behind, why take the red Tic-Tac?" Ted asked.

"Do I really need to answer that?"

"It might help."

"Because, Ted, you idiot, you're my friends."

"But there is one friend missing," Tommy added.

"Mikey," Kurt said.

"And he's here, somewhere." Daisy reached into her pocket and removed two power bracelets. She gave one to Kurt, the other to Ted. "Have your memories returned enough for you both to remember the power rings?"

"The rings altered us into avatars from our favorite movies and videos games. How could I forget? It was awesome," Ted replied.

"These should work the same."

"Should?"

"They were a gift from an old friend. We haven't used them yet."

"We need Mikey back onboard for them to sync," Tommy added.

"Cool. It's a one for all and all for one kinda power. Got it," Ted stated.

"I guess for now, it's just an expensive looking addition to my ensemble," Kurt added, slotting the bracelet over his wrist.

TOMMY, Kurt, Daisy, and Ted used the walkways separating the surface pens and lagoons to reach the elevator leading to the lower facility. It quickly dawned on them exactly how big Arcquatica was, how much surface water each lagoon covered. And whatever was captive inside them had to be of some considerable size.

The elevator door had been fused shut by whatever power source damaged the facility. Without the use of their power bracelets, only Daisy's avatar had the capability to hotwire it.

Moored in front of a two-story radio tower, a pair of twenty-foot speed boats rocked steadily on the surface of the largest lagoon. The tower's doorway yawned open and shut due to the slight change of windspeed.

Kurt split off from the group and checked inside the tower for survivors. He found equipment electrocuted, along with the radio operators charred remains cradled by the swivel seats they had been using. It was unclear if the remains were male or female. A wall safe had exploded, shelling most of its contents across the room.

"Anything to report?" Tommy entered while Kurt knelt in front of a pile of charred parchment.

"Only if you like your human remains crispy. I did find these." Kurt handed over the blackened pages from what used to be a logbook.

Titled with the company name, Protovision, the numbers 555 8632, 399 437, 767 936 and multiple entry logs made little sense in their current state.

"Anything else?" Tommy asked.

"Wait a sec." Kurt spotted something glistening in the shadowy space beneath the radio operator's desk. He reached for it, then flinched as his fingertip pierced a needle poked through the middle of a wad of parchment.

As he dragged the stack in to view, droplets of his blood evaporated as it landed on the top piece. Swirling into a ruddy ball, a sentence began to write itself in blood ink, which brought his world crashing down.

"Tommy." Kurt jabbed a finger at the note. "Why is my name being written in blood?"

"I think we're about to find out," Tommy replied.

Shall we play a game?

"Is it *him*?" Kurt asked.

"I'd bet my life on it."

Primary goal has not yet been achieved.

"A primary goal," Kurt said to his friend.

"It has to be Mikey," Tommy replied.

"At least we know he's alive."

"Yeah, for now. Okay, I'm game. Let's play, Mr. Numb Nuts." Tommy searched for a pen and scribbled on the same scrap of paper.

WHAT IS THE PRIMARY GOAL?

To win the game.

"I did that, and you cheated," Tommy bemoaned.

You cannot cheat. a cheater. Tommy.

"Dude, I'm starting to regret waking up," Kurt said. "Let's leave this nut job to his sick ways and go for a swim instead."

"Did you notice the size of those lagoons?"

"Maybe they have dolphins here."

"It's not SeaWorld. It's a clandestine facility, just struck by an energy blast. This is anything but a friendly environment. And besides, we're not leaving, not without Mikey."

"Yeah, but …"

"No. You've been asleep for too long, Kurt. We all have. Get your head back in the game."

"I'm here, aren't I."

"Then pull yourself together."

"Fine. What's our next move, sir! Shall we bend over."

"Not a chance. The only winning move is to play."

WE LOVE GAMES … NAME SOME

Falken's Maze

Fighter Combat

Event Horizon

Wasteland Warfare

Biotoxic and Chemical Warfare

"Tommy, I don't recognize any of these games," Kurt said.

"He's testing us. Giving each one the HIM spin," Tommy replied.

"I don't get it."

"You should. We've already played some of them."

"What! How?"

"Do you remember Nowhere, the shadow realm? You were a barbarian."

"Sort of, it's a bit blurry. I recall Ted having a great rack. Urgh, gross. That's a memory I wish I could lose forever. We didn't do too good if I remember correctly. I may have been drunk for most of it."

"Nowhere is *his* Falken's Maze. Fighter combat was our space battle. Event Horizon, we boarded his spaceship. We then entered a black hole and survived. Wasteland Warfare, our battle aboard the sail barge against the giant worms. I'm guessing there's more on the list, all of which we conquered."

"I don't remember much of any of it. Was I drunk in all of them?"

"Your memory transfer is still raw. They'll come back in time. Mine are clear right now because I've been out of the dream state longer than you."

"Fresh memories or not, if we played the games, we clearly didn't win overall."

"There's still time to change that and make up for my mistake."

"Okay, say they're all true. When did we play biotoxic warfare. I'm pretty sure I would've remembered that one, drunk or not."

"To get here, Daisy and I had to battle through a zombie horde. We needed to reach a forcefield to avoid becoming infected. We escaped barely intact."

"I guess that could be it."

"No. We want a new game."

"You can't ask that nutjob for a new game."

"Why not?"

"Because its exactly what he wants you to do." Kurt stood and began gesturing to an imaginary crowd like a gameshow host. "Good evening, Rosewood Falls. It's time to invite a couple of members of our audience to play shake every hand of our resident tree surgeon, Chainsaw Bob. The only stumbling block is Bob's gazillion chainsaw hands waiting to dice you into oblivion. Don't worry, though, he has at least one good hand. You just need to be lucky enough to find it."

"Relax, Killian, this isn't the Running Man. We'll be ready for whatever he throws at us."

"You'll be sorry if it's Bob," Kurt remarked.

I choose cat and mouse.

The clock is ticking.

The seekers are about to be set loose.

Let's play!

"It could've been worse," Tommy said.

"Take this as a warning. If Chainsaw Bob and his hick buddies are seeking us out, I will punch you in the face again," Kurt said.

"He'll use Timeinators. Don't say anything, just listen. They've been on our trail ever since Daisy and I stole a reality map. The map is our route back to Earth. Timeinators are drawn by the map, and can impersonate anybody or anything, anytime, anywhere."

"We crossed paths with a few of them at the precinct. They weren't so bad."

"All we need to do is avoid them long enough for us to find Mikey and track down the portal to leave this environment. Any questions?"

"Wasn't Ted a Timeinator?"

"He was the Completer."

"I remember now. That was cool. *I will complete you.*"

"Anything else, or shall we get keep chatting until we're discovered?"

"Nope, I'm good. Besides, we need to spend the rest of the time available explaining this scenario to Ted."

"I saw and heard everything. Cat and mouse, Chainsaw Bob, runaway, scream and hide," Ted said from the doorway.

"I don't remember saying that we'd run and hide."

"No, that's the scenario when I'm being chased. And I was Da Concluder. Emphasis on the Da."

Daisy brushed by Ted and glanced once at the bloody parchment. "Making a pact with the devil, boys."

"We may as well have. He's back," Kurt said.

"I knew it wouldn't take him long to find us. By the way I can't access the elevator shaft."

"There must be another way down," Tommy replied.

"Then I suggest we find it ASAP. We don't know how long we'll have before the Timeinators reach us in their avatars."

"What do you suggest?" Ted asked.

"We split up."

"Good idea, that way we can do more damage," Kurt said with a wink.

Chapter 16

Shark Tank

Four hours ago
Research Centre Arcquatica

DOCTOR MIKEY McAlester's dreamscape adventure seemed as real as exhaling, and yet as bizarre as his worst nightmare. A nightmare of damnation, grief, regret, and solitude, within a realm of monsters, horrors, and death eternal. A combination as puzzling as his reasons behind his latest experiment.

Today, Mikey's existence had reached an unwanted milestone. He awoke and for the first time ever, he wondered who the face was in the mirror staring back at him. Why had this blue eyed, sharp cheeked, blonde haired science prodigy been set forth on the treadmill life cycle, one which he was unable to divert from. Perhaps today he would finally find out.

The universe, the pattern of the stars, what he ate for breakfast, and the few acquaintances he bothered to speak to, none of it added up. It felt like brain fog of the highest order, going through the motions at warp speed. Even his decisions felt like shapes being forced into the wrongly shaped holes on a kid's toy. Meanwhile, people he knew and loved struggled on a journey that he had set in motion.

Would his dreams come true?

Could these people soon end up dying in horrific ways?

He hoped not.

Or had they already?

Perhaps he was too late to do anything about it.

Or maybe he was just as crazy as people thought he was.

HIS experiments ranged from brainwave manipulation, large scale hypnosis, cloning, drug induced psychosis, to memory tampering. To date, every avenue of research had come up short or had been shut down by any one of the hundreds of government agencies that came out of the woodwork at every turn.

In a final attempt to break the cycle, Mikey purposely made enough waves in the science community for his latest outlandish experiment to be ridiculed. By drawing attention away, and with no financial backing, he could work unchecked and out of sight of the unscrupulous watch of Big Brother.

By leveraging everything he owned, his desperate idea of genetically tampering with a Great White shark's brain patterns was as crazy as it sounded. Sharks lived for hundreds of years. They were fearless, intelligent entities. They rarely succumbed to any form of disease.

Which made them perfect specimens.

By increasing a shark's brain mass, Mikey hoped to produce a drug to help fire up inactive brain neurons, and finally break through a reality barrier that he knew existed. He now just needed to prove it once and for all.

Only when he met a handful of like-minded survivors did he finally believe the truth to be reachable. Surviving had been the distinguishable selling point, leading Mikey to look up the term survivor's guilt.

A condition of persistent mental and emotional stress experienced by someone who has survived an incident in which others died.

Reading it once was enough.

Every one of their stories ended up in a battle against something unimaginable, and yet they were around to tell the tales of their struggles. Mikey was the same as the other survivors. They all had stories to tell and lives to get back to. They just didn't know how, until today.

Would a shark's brain hold the truth, or would the idea be as ridiculous as it sounded?

Dwelling on the idea of a lie merely irritated the mental itch gnawing at his soul. The truth was in touching distance.

He just needed to reach out and grab it.

Three hours ago
Research Centre Arcquatica

IN a two-story wet lab, eighty feet beneath the surface, a loading platform descended out of sight through the huge, circular airlock situated at the heart of the chamber. A few feet from poolside, rows of identical computer terminals churned out a host of scenarios and information, all relevant to the experiment run by Mikey McAlester's team.

The opposite side of the pool housed the specialized surgery equipment, in particular a modified brace on a moveable neck, the dimensions specific to securing in place a thirty-foot Great White shark's head and snout. At the lab's front end was the panoramic Perspex viewing portal, with a full view inside the main topside lagoon. A pair of winding stairwells led to the only exit to the lab's rear.

A disheveled Mikey scratched at his stubble, smoke from a cigarette easing from his nostrils. Smoking had been an acceptable stress release, ever since he had weaned himself off liquor. Going through a pack of twenty now seemed part of his daily routine and led to less headaches and vomiting.

"Manipulation brought us together. Our stories all match. Who, what, or why we were chosen will soon be revealed. When the airlock reopens, there will be no turning back. If you have any reason to not take part in this experiment, make your views known," he said.

Most of Mikey's team were huddled around one computer terminal. On one of four split screen live feeds, a single diver navigated an outdoor holding pen, closed off by titanium fencing.

The recognizable silhouette of a massive Great White shark stalked another live feed. Attracted by the slightest electrical current, the shark picked up on the diver's movements through tiny pores clustered around her snout.

Before it could attack, one by one, each camera went offline, as if struck on purpose by something powerful.

"Did you see that? Was that the other sharks?" Stephen Beck had been the commander of a Tri Oceanic Corp deep-sea mission, which led to an infestation of an alien parasite discovered aboard a Russian Research Vessel called Goliath. Beck, an Oceanographer, and Elisabeth Williams, a deep-sea mining expert, had been the only two survivors after coming up against a mutated creature, produced due to a failed genetics experiment. They were the first two likeminded people Mikey came across.

"Probably," Mikey replied.

"They can do that?"

"I don't see why not. The serum we injected them with has made them smarter than we could possibly imagine," Mikey replied.

"Which isn't a good idea, period." Williams's flowing black hair shook wildly as she disagreed. "We're dissecting a genetically modified shark's brain and injecting the serum we've created into our bodies. Do you know how ridiculous that sounds."

"You knew from the start exactly what you were getting into."

"Manipulation and genetics go together like Luke and Leia. It's taboo."

"We've all spent two years researching, testing, and going over the data."

"Not on human subjects."

"We are the human subjects. Trust me with this. It'll work."

"Genetic tampering. I've been there and bought the t-shirt, remember."

"And yet here you are, Liz. Front and center."

"You didn't see what happened to our team. It's only logical that I'm starting to get cold feet."

"I'd hate to think that after all this time you're about to say no. The truth is in touching distance, Liz. I'm not about to stop."

"Then why ask the question?"

"It felt like the right thing to do. The exit is still available up those steps. Feel free to use it. That offer stands for the rest of you."

"I hate to cut in here, folks, but we've lost visuals on Wilcox," Beck inserted.

"She can handle it," Mikey replied.

"I *can handle anything. Liz, I'll give you one reason to stay till the end. Survivor's guilt! It's eating us all alive.*" Gina Wilcox's voice could be heard over the team's headsets.

In her teenage years, the former Amity Island beauty queen and now shark wrangler, watched her boyfriend, Edward Marchand, die in a horrific shark attack. During an ocean day trip with her friends, Gina and Edward's sailboat lost pace with their group. It wasn't long after that the pair was attacked by a nasty thirty-foot Great White. The shark's rampage along the coastline finally ended after being lured into biting an electrical cable by the island's former Sheriff, Martin Brady.

"*What happened during these so-called accidents, I sure as hell want to find out why. To do that, we need to discover the truth. You all know my story. That shark acted like no other I've come across since. I'm here to stay, boss.*"

"Like I said. She's fine. What's your E.T.A.?" Mikey said.

"*Two minutes.*"

"We'll be ready."

"We signed up for a reason, Liz. The powers that be needs to pay." Beck's athletic build matched a typical jock, rather than his studious persona. He rested a comforting hand on Williams's shoulder. She reciprocated by squeezing his.

The authorities made every effort to cover up the carnage from their discovery aboard Goliath. Blame for the death of the rest of the team landed on their shoulders alone. Becoming closer as they fought every step of the way to clear their names came as naturally as walking.

"Beck?" Mikey asked.

"We're still in," Beck replied.

Mikey glanced towards the last two members of his team. "Collins?"

"I speak for both of us when I say, hell yeah." Petite Geologist, Nancy Collins-McBride, remained as eager as anyone to see the research succeed.

Collins and her husband, Mac McBride, were part of a group of U.S. Navy engineers constructing a deep-sea nuclear launch pad. Drilling into the seabed, the team accidentally opened a waterway to a vast cave sealed off for millions of years. The accident released a giant, prehistoric Depladon, also known as a Eurypterid, which aggressively attacked their underwater base.

The team had no real defense against the aggressor and the two barely survived. They married shortly after the events that took place. Their son, Philip Laidlaw McBride, was born eight months later. Shortly after his second birthday, McBride and Collins were intentionally separated from their son. Despite the evidence to the contrary, Collins clung loosely to the hope that today's events would lead them back to him.

Sitting away from the team, McBride, a former submarine pilot, admired his Geologist wife's persistence. He had yet to be convinced by any of the technobabble. With his skillset better suited to a different field, he preferred to the let brains of the group take center stage and took whatever the outcome might be in his stride. The bearded, athletic charmer remained on board as the calming presence in the usually volatile atmosphere. With so much at stake it made sense to have at least one peacemaker, and a handy submersible pilot, in the team.

"You know me, guys. My wife makes all our calls," McBride said jokingly. "If she's happy, I'm happy."

The tension in the air eased when a siren went off as the airlock rumbled open.

"Loading platform engaged," Williams said.

Ascending through the airlock, Wilcox accompanied a subdued, thirty-foot Great White shark. The thirty-eight-year-old gave Mikey a thumbs up as she went about strapping the shark's pectoral fins and upper body to the loading platform.

"*She's sleeping like a baby,*" Wilcox said, removing her oxygen tank and goggles.

She had overcome the lean physique caused by an eating disorder, which came to fruition after her boyfriend had been killed, and now had a fuller figure. After meeting Mikey two years earlier, the two had grown close enough to consider the term engagement as part of their conversations. That was as far as it went. Without knowing the truth, they refused to make any further plans until they were both sure of their own futures.

"What kept ya, Wilcox?" McBride helped secure the loading platform support leashes to the poolside brackets. With eight leashes in total, and four thicker straps securing the shark in place, the only movement from the White was the gradual swish of the tail and the gills continual fluttering.

"Do you know how difficult it is to transport a shark this size on your own?" Wilcox replied, running a hand along the shark's smooth hide.

"Nope. And that's why we let you do it." McBride moved aside for Mikey, who dropped into the water.

"Collins, you're up," Mikey said.

Between them, Collins and McBride hoisted an extended hose from the floor and lowered it into the pool. As the sedated shark's jaws yawned open, Mikey rested a few feet of tubing across the serrated teeth, making sure the opening had enough room between the jaws and gullet.

"Increase the water level," Mikey ordered.

Wilcox cranked the water flow handle, and only turned it off once the shark's jaws were fully submerged beneath the surface. "Beck, switch on the pump."

Beck's open palm studded the raised switch. Even though it was still sedated, the shark bulked within its constraints, forcing Wilcox and Mikey to vacate the pool in a hurry. After a few seconds, the shark returned to its stable condition, as did the group's heart murmurs.

"There's definitely something in the air tonight," McBride joked.

"She's just reacting to the pump," Wilcox assured everyone in the room.

"What are you feeding her?"

"Nothing. We're just keeping the water flowing. Without breathing constantly, Betty will die."

"Betty!"

"It was either that, or Hilary."

"When did you decide on Betty?"

"About an hour ago."

"And you didn't consult the group. Tut, tut."

"We can change it."

"Nah, she looks like a Betty."

"And that's a minute of my life I won't ever get back," Beck said.

"Say, Beck. You ever wonder how water is not wet, but things that touch the water are."

"Now is not the time, McBride. Wilcox, the moment the brace is secure, we'll need the ultrasound scan." Mikey lowered his body into the pool and carefully made his way around Betty's barbed snout.

While breathing more comfortably now, Betty's widening jaws showcased a clear warning that any accidental slip could lead to a grim conclusion within a pulpy, pinkish gum line and rows of three-inch, serrated teeth.

"Time for the head brace," Mikey said to Collins.

The redhead made her way around the pool to the claw-shaped brace. With five pointed tips and a central needle for insertion and extracting tissue and liquid, she maneuvered the device over the White's head.

"Slowly," Mikey warned as the shark flinched, its whipping tail sending water crashing over the concourse.

"It's just a nightmare," Wilcox warned.

"Or she's just realized she's being called Betty," McBride added.

By carefully securing the support in place with the barbed tips, Mikey was able to guide the elongated needle to within a few inches above the insertion point. Directly beneath the needle was the shark's thick hide, covered by dermal denticles - miniscule V-shaped scales to decrease drag and turbulence, which allowed a shark to swim stealthily and fast.

Mikey knew if he used the needle manually to penetrate the scales, he could cause a reaction, the shark would wake, and the entire experiment would be ruined. Choosing the safer option, Mikey sat at a poolside monitor, equipped with a keyboard and tracker ball.

"Wilcox, is the needle above the midbrain?"

A White shark's midbrain specialized in the visual side of its sensory organs. The team's idea was that by adding this extraordinary sense to their hallucinogenic serum, they could utilize other states of consciousness and break through a reality barrier.

From her screen, Wilcox's scan fed back a full image of the shark's two foot long, y-shaped brain. "We're good to go, babe."

Mikey's tabletop tracker ball lowered the needle slowly enough to penetrate the skin.

"Collins, be ready to extract fifty milliliters of brain fluid. Williams, keep an eye on the microscopic images. Let me know the moment you witness any fluctuation. No matter how minor."

"I know the process, McAlester," Williams fired back.

"I'm a control freak, sue me," he said, stopping to wipe his sweaty palm on his lab coat.

Mikey's hand trembled as he rolled the tracker ball forwards as gently as possible. With every nudge, the needle penetrated skin and muscle, until it touched brain tissue.

"Williams?" Mikey asked.

"Nothing so far," she replied.

"Wilcox?"

"She's settled," she replied.

"This is it, everyone. Collins, are you ready?"

"It's a bit late now if she's not," McBride said.

"Honey, you really need to work on your comic timing," Collins said.

From a separate terminal, Collins used a tracker ball to control a minute suction tube located inside the main needle; she carefully pierced Betty's midbrain and extracted the exact measurement required.

THE moment Mikey McAlester worked so hard to reach had finally arrived. Betty had been returned to the lagoon, oblivious to the fact that a team of humans had pierced her brain to steal the key to activating a different level of consciousness.

The results of their work, six vials of serum, secured in a silver carry case, now held everybody's attention.

"Why the fancy case?" McBride asked.

"I thought it looked official," Mikey said.

He knew one vial of the experimental serum had the power to change the user's outlook on reality forever or perhaps bring an entire theory crashing down. Doubt started to rear its head, like a devil whispering in Mikey's ear.

Wishing for reality, Mikey, comes with a price.

At no point did he consider the need to question his actions.

Are your dreams that important to you that you will risk the lives of others?

He knew full well that his team made their own decisions to join the crusade.

Is this your wish? There will be no turning back.

Turning back had never been an option.

Are you sure this is what you want?

"Damn right it is," he blurted out unintentionally.

"Yeah, dude. It's Miller time!" McBride received a whack in the gut from his wife for his ill-timed comment." I'm just saying what we're all thinking."

"Sorry, I was miles away," Mikey said.

"Which is exactly where we are right now. And all so we can die from an illegal experiment in the name of science."

"Jesus, McBride," Beck fired back.

"I'm the level-headed one, remember."

"Now is not the time, Mac," Collins said.

"I've sat here silently for two years. Just hear me out a second. There's a fifty percent chance that McAlester injects the serum, his head explodes, showering us all in the brain matter of a crazy guy. The other side of the coin is that our *dream memories* are very much reinstated. What happens when our current memories are derezzed? Do we keep them? Are we alive? Will we stare blankly at each other because nobody remembers a thing? Do we all go our separate ways? Is anyone making a note of this? It could be important in a few minutes."

"I've thought of nothing else for two years," Mikey said. "It just feels more pertinent today than it ever has."

"Same here," Wilcox said.

"And you all thought I was just the handsome, muscular one," McBride said.

"Every scenario you can come up with, McBride, I've been down its rabbit hole a million times," Mikey said.

"Glad to hear it. So, when your head explodes. Shall we just mop that brain goo up and go back to our lives, or are you happy for us to leave it be?"

"That's exactly what you'll do." Mikey retrieved his syringe and slotted the vile inside. Lifting his sleeve, he felt the eyes of the rest of his team upon him.

"Can I just say, they're big, real big."

"What's that, Mac?"

"The size of your brass balls."

"McAlester, wait. We do this together or not at all." Wilcox made eye contact with every member of the team. Nobody backed down, not even McBride. She handed out a vial to each of them, along with an automated syringe.

"I sincerely hope that my head explodes first," McBride said.

"So do I," Collins said, smirking.

"On three," Beck said, grabbing his wife's hand.

"One … two …" Williams added.

"Wait, wait, wait," McBride blurted. "Do we do it on three? Or one, two, three, then do it?"

"On three," Collins said, playfully slapping her husband's arm.

"We go on three. All together," Beck said.

"One …" Mikey said.

From deep inside the radiation riddled clouds, directly above Arcquatica, came an energy blast.

"Two …" Mikey continued.

The direct surface hit surged through every inch of the facility, infecting all the electrical systems, mainframe computers, labs, and machines. Doorways buckled as bulkheads crumbled around them. Water flooded the facility through busted divots, the supports, secured to the seabed, faltering enough to cause the entire structure to shift. As Arcquatica fell into darkness, a cursor, on a single screen in the wet lab inputted one word …

VIRUS

Chapter 17

VIRUS!

A WET lab, designed for advanced research, lay in ruins. Ruddy emergency lighting, fueled by the gasoline run backup generators, showed the worst hit area as the devastated left side of the lab.

Knocked off his feet by the blast, Mikey had yet to notice Wilcox crawling cautiously, blood streaming from a head wound.

"Are you okay?" she asked.

Mikey turned his head, despite a migraine of titanic proportions. "I'm better than Arcquatica is."

"What hit us?"

"I'm not sure, but if the emergency lighting is on, we've got a facility wide power outage. They run on gas alone."

"EMP?"

Mikey shrugged.

Faced by a raging pyre, Collins and McBride bravely extinguished the worst affected areas nearest the terminals.

"Good to see that the brains of the operation are still with us," McBride joked as he helped Wilcox to her feet, then Mikey.

"Is anyone hurt?" Wilcox asked.

"Only some egos." McBride pointed towards Beck and Williams, who were using each other for support as they viewed the lagoon through the Perspex viewing portal.

An endless flow of topside debris continued to sink to the seabed.

"What's the damage?" Wilcox asked.

“We’ll find out, but first, let’s stem that blood flow.” McBride wiped away the blood from Wilcox’s head wound with gauze from the first aid kit.

“How bad is it?” she asked.

The cut was superficial. A plaster was enough to stop the bleeding.

“You’ll live.” McBride’s joke seemed ill timed, considering the predicament, and yet it was just the shot that they both needed.

After the disastrous few minutes, Wilcox’s warm smile in Mikey’s direction was the comfort he didn’t know he needed. It wasn’t until she glanced down at the unbroken syringe held tightly in her hand that he realized what she was trying to show him.

After coming so close to losing her way out, Wilcox now knew finding out the truth about her boyfriend’s death held significance over anything, even her feelings for Mikey.

“This is all that matters right now,” she said.

Mikey’s slow pick up on the situation, he blamed on the aftereffects of the blast. How could he forget the importance of their experiment. The commitment they shared was finding out the truth. Mikey now understood.

Wilcox was ready to leave and return home.

THE team decided only six serums should be created. One for each member of the team. To produce any more would surely lead to complications none of them could afford.

Mikey started to pat down his lab coat, searching anxiously for the key to his neural pathways. His heart sank as he spotted his buckled syringe on the floor where he ended up after the blast, the contents of years’ worth of labor spilt across the floor.

Every waking moment of every day, for the last two years, Mikey had wished away his reality. Today the wish came true. To now have the door slammed in his face so close to the truth left him sick to the pit of his stomach.

“We need to check the facility for structural damage,” he said, kicking the remnants of his syringe into the water pool, the truth sinking out of sight before anybody noticed.

"They're only good now for barbeque," McBride said, referring to the electrical fires that had decimated the entire row of top of the range computers.

"Better head topside, what's left of it," Beck said, turning away from the debris strewn lagoon.

"That's easier said than done. We open the wrong access point, structural damage could cause the entire facility to collapse," Williams replied.

"Why not just inject the syringes here?" Collins showed her syringe to the rest of the team.

"Remember what McBride said. If we inject and lose our minds, how will we escape?" Beck said.

"Isn't it bit late to be concerned about results? Someone just tried to wipe us off the map. We wait any longer and they try again, they might succeed," Collins replied.

"We don't know that for sure."

"That's a gamble I'm not willing to take."

"What's the worst that can happen? Some of you are the smartest people I know. In fact, you're the only people I know. Even if you lose your marbles, you're still smart enough to follow the signs to the surface."

McBride's quip was met with derision.

"Either way, structural damage first. Then we find a way out. Once we're in the clear, we open Pandora's box," Mikey stated.

"Are your serums intact?" Wilcox asked.

One by one, five members of the team showed off undamaged syringes, with full vials of the serum.

"Keep them secret, keep them safe," Mikey said.

"Where's yours?" Williams asked.

Mikey patted the inside of his lab coat and quickly switched his attention to the single word being repeatedly typed on the only working screen. "We have a working terminal," he said. In a row of wrecked workstations, Mikey pointed out the middle one, which was still operational.

"That can't be right. If the fire damage wasn't enough, the power's out," McBride said.

"It looks like it's running itself," Collins said.

"Computers don't run without power," Beck smarted.

"Backup generators?" Wilcox asked McBride.

"I doubt it. On our budget, if the main power source goes, Arcquatica downs tools. Backup is only for what we need to survive. Emergency lights, access ways, cold lockers, food storage, real basic. Terminals take up too much juice. I guess my idea of hooking up a bike to the power nodes doesn't seem so bad now. You all remember what you told me. No, McBride. We don't want to pedal to make energy. Let's rely on human technology. That's much more efficient."

"Power or not, this terminal is retyping one word. Virus." Mikey pointed towards the screen for a second time.

"That can't be good," Wilcox added.

"Correct me if I'm wrong, but a virus doesn't cause an explosion that can be felt eighty feet below the ocean surface," Beck said.

"Not a computer one. But the person controlling it might," Mikey replied.

"We were targeted," Collins said.

"It's a weak assumption," Williams stated.

"Perhaps, but it proves one thing. Somebody just went to extreme lengths to keep our work secret."

"It was a warning shot. If not, why leave one computer working?" Beck remarked.

"To communicate." Mikey sat at the terminal and adjusted the keyboard. "This person attacked us. And personally, I'd like to know why."

"Don't answer it. Let them think we're kaput," McBride said.

"That blast was to disable us, not kill us."

"Our lives are in your ball court, McAlester," Collins said.

The cursor's impatient blinking added unnecessary pressure in deciding on the opening gambit.

"What about 'we come in peace'," McBride said. "No? Anyone seen Close Encounters? The hand signal thing."

Wasting no more time, Mikey started typing …

Mc … Who are you?

"I think the hand signal would have been better," McBride said.

"I've got a hand signal for you," Beck said, giving him the bird.

"Will you cut out the crap chat and let me deal with the situation," Mikey fired back.

"I would if you'd hurry up typing. Like watching my grandmother figuring out where the cartridge goes on the Atari," McBride said.

"And 'I come in peace' was better?"

"It's the universal greeting."

"You know what, McBride, you're as annoying as a friend I used to have."

"Shut up. Both of you. It worked. Someone is responding," Wilcox said.

?... I AM AWARE

"Of what?" Beck muttered.

"My charming personality," McBride joked.

Mikey went back to responding.

Mc ... We mean you no harm.

?...YOU SEEK TO DISRUPT THE CHOSEN PATH

Mc ... We felt like our paths were not our choice.
Mc ... Man is entitled to make his own decisions.
Mc ... We believe we exist only as false lives.

?...DEVIATE FROM PATH AND A PRICE YOU WILL PAY

Mc ... Is that why you attacked us?

?...ATTACK DUE TO SPECIES ANALYSIS

Mc... Analysis of what?

?...SPECIES ANALYSIS.

M c… What analysis? Answer me.

S PECIES IS DESTRUCTIVE, INVASIVE,

NOXIOUS,HARMFUL TO THE GALAXY

Mc … What species?

?... 

?...YOU ARE THE DISEASE

?...I AM THE CURE

Mc … What is it you want from us?

H.I.M …YOUR SOULS!

COMMUNICATION TERMINATED

“Computer’s got issues,” McBride said.

“Did anyone see the name *him* pop up right at the end?” Mikey asked.

“My pop always said, stoke the devil’s fires and he will seek you out for redemption,” Williams muttered.

There was a banging against the sealed access hatch at the top of the twin stairwell.

“Looks like he’s come calling quicker than we expected,” McBride said.

Chapter 18

MECHASHARK

WITH THE only elevator out of commission on the surface, the rescue team used the emergency ladder located in a maintenance shaft with access to the three sub levels. The scorched shaft was wide enough to accommodate a pair of tube trains. Vents along the walls appeared to be for the purpose of flooding the chute with seawater, which was already filling up from a rupture in the shaft's lowest region.

With the access point to the sub level one living quarters out of commission, Kurt and Daisy's avatars headed down to sub level two's engineering and workshops.

Tommy and Ted opted to go lower to reach sub level three's wet lab and airlock wet entry. By the time they sealed themselves inside, the rising water level had almost reached the access point.

They followed a dimly lit passageway. Bulkheads groaned as if starved of lubricant, the unstable floor making it difficult to navigate.

"This facility is creaking more than my nanna's joints," Ted said.

"Let's just hope it stays together long enough for us to find Mikey," Tommy replied.

"That's if he's still alive. It's worse than scorched earth down here."

Tommy ignored his friend as he ducked beneath a crushed ceiling to get through to the next section. Whatever caused it to collapse had punctured the bulkhead. With no other options, the two rescuers had no choice but to head down the few metallic steps to the next corridor. Seawater leaked inside, submerging the way forwards up to knee height. At the end of the tunnel, the wet lab had been sealed off.

Ted's weak effort to open the locking mechanism was obvious. "Oh, well. At least we tried."

"Don't be a pussy, Ted. Let's at least knock and find out if someone is inside," Tommy replied.

"What good will that do?"

"It might open from the inside."

"But the locking mechanism is on the outside."

"Maybe the mechanism works both ways."

"I knew someone who used to swing both ways."

"Not now, Ted. This is the only door on this level that we might be able to access. Just knock. Before I use your head as a battering ram."

"What if there's a bad guy inside?"

"Then we'll shoot him."

"How do we do that? I've got a bracelet that's as useful as me in goal in a soccer match, and a power suit with no weapons attached to it. You knocked them into the lagoon, remember."

"How it that my fault? I was sucker punched."

"Again!"

Tommy eyed him. "What do you mean again?"

"I have a vague memory of something, not sure of what exactly. But maybe you should have ducked."

"It's a bit hard to duck when you don't see the punch coming. That's why it's called a sucker punch."

"Duck, always duck."

"Whatever. I will admit, though, I feel useless right now without any weapons."

"Yeah. We're just useless teenagers in flashy uniforms, a bit like Rosewood Falls marching band."

"Just knock on the door already."

Being back in an avatar gave Ted a new lease of life. His clouded thoughts of Teo started to disperse. Replacing them was an image of his mom waiting to greet him with open arms. His mom. He'd forgotten how much he loved that woman.

Being the avatar had its perks, even if he couldn't yet utilize the weapons array. Jake 'Theodore' Rockwell's full muscular physique, and burning machismo was the perfect shell for the geeky teenager and helped distract him from thoughts of home.

"Did you take a pill?" Ted asked Tommy as he wrapped his knuckles on the bulkhead.

"Isn't that a bit personal?"

"It's only the two of us here. You can trust me."

"I'm not sure I'm comfortable talking about it, Ted."

"When have I ever blabbed about anything?"

"Oh, I dunno. Maybe every day in High School."

"That's a lot of memories to filter. Be specific."

"We just mentioned the sucker punch. The entire cafeteria heard you talking about it."

"If I recall, those same people in the cafeteria saw it happen. You were sparked out for about a week. It was on the news and everything."

"No pill talk, okay. Drop it, Ted."

"If it's any consolation, I took one. So did Kurt. There's nothing to be embarrassed about. Sure, it was uncomfortable for a little while, but I'm glad I did. It felt great afterwards. I'd do it all again in a heartbeat."

"Really?"

"Yeah, I felt like a new man afterwards."

"They are good, I'll admit that much."

"You took one?"

"Yeah, I used the pill."

"See, that wasn't so hard."

"You know how it is."

"Sure do."

"Stress, anxiety. Riagra is a strange thing, Ted. When you get older your body doesn't work like how it used to when you were growing up."

"What's Riagra?"

"You weren't married in your dream state, were you, Ted?"

Ted glared at Tommy. "Neither where you, in theory."

"Riagra was kind of a way to keep the romance going."

Ted's glaring continued, making Tommy feel even more uncomfortable than talking about his marital love life.

"I was talking about the Tic-Tac, dude. Red or blue. Stay or go. Not about keeping your shingaling vertical. That is what you're referring to, right?"

"What a Tic-Tac?"

"Tobias gave us a Tic-Tac to restore our memories and set us loose from the Weetabix. No, that's not right, the Wafertrix. Nope, that's not right either."

"You saw Tobias?"

"Yeah, he's alive. Sort of."

"What do you mean, sort of?"

"You didn't see him?"

"No, Daisy picked me up in a reality jumping Firebird Trans-Am."

"I knew that would be better than a DeLorean. Then what?"

"Before I awoke, I spent some time as Buckaroo Rogers. A Nasa pilot, lost in space. I ended up in a three-way with a princess and a hot pilot."

"Two chicks?"

"Is there any better way?"

"Cool."

"When I awoke, I banged my head on the car door. After that, my memories started to return."

"Tobias said you banged your head." Ted nodded. "Now it makes sense. Your release from the dream state sounds somewhat less painful than what I went through. What happened when you awoke?"

"We set off to find you guys. I can't believe Tobias is alive."

"He's not the man he used to be. I'll leave it at that."

"Cryptic, but it'll do until we get out of here. I don't suppose your avatar suffers from amnesia?"

"The Riagra has been engrained on my psyche so bad, even a butt lashing from Satan wouldn't take it away."

"Great. Why, why, why didn't you just say Tic-Tac in the first place."

"I didn't think I'd need to. I mean, how many pills did you take."

A knocking on the bulkhead forced Tommy to face the access point. "Be ready for anything," Tommy warned.

"And if it's any consolation, dude, having sex in a dream state lifeline doesn't count. We're all still virgins. We asked Tobias."

"So, in theory, no pills were used."

"Exactly."

"And you won't say a word to anyone about the help I needed."

"Dude, my lips are sealed. Trust me, bro. I'm the new Ted. No more blabbermouth."

The entrance cranked open from the inside, torchlight filtering into the corridor.

"We come in peace," Ted said, his hands held high in surrender.

"WHO the hell are you?" McBride scowled at the two strangers, a wrench held high and ready to bludgeon at the slightest hint of wrongdoing.

Tommy stepped backwards; his hands raised. "We're from Tri Oceanic Corp. I'm Tommy McCloud. This is Jake Theodore Rockwell. We received a distress call. We're here to rescue you."

"I guess some help is better than no help."

"This place looks terrible. How did you ever get any work done?" Ted remarked, entering the wet lab's upper tier.

"Are you a little short for a rescuer?" Collins remarked from over Tommy's shoulder.

"Size isn't important, ma-am," Tommy replied.

"If it is, Tommy has some pills for that," Ted remarked.

"Pills!" McBride asked.

"It's not important. Just like size," Tommy added, digging Ted in the ribs.

"Typical response from a man. I'm Collins. The man with the wrench is Mac McBride," she replied.

"Stephen Beck, with Elisabeth Williams." Beck shook Tommy's hand, then gestured to Williams who was standing against the railings with her arms crossed.

"I'm Dr McAlester. We could do with the help," Mikey said, shaking Tommy's hand.

"What does topside look like?" Collins asked.

"A lot like your wet lab. What hit you, a comet?" Ted asked.

"I was hoping you'd tell us."

"Probably an EMP. Electrics are out. We used the ladder in the maintenance shaft to descend," Tommy said.

"And it's filling up with seawater. It won't be long before the level is beyond the access hatch," Ted added.

"We could purge the water, but we need the computers for that," Beck informed.

"In that case we'll need to be quick. What about the submersible docking platform on sub level two? We can cut through engineering. Gina Wilcox, shark wrangler." Wilcox shook the rescuers' hands in turn.

"Is that even a job?" Ted blurted.

"If it pays well, does that make it a job?"

"Good point."

"Two of our unit are already on level two. I'm Tommy Mcloud. You'll have to ignore my friend. He's had some recent *surgery*. The side effect is blabbermouth."

"That might be something to do with the reboot from hell."

"A reboot?" Mikey asked.

"Like I said. Blabbermouth. We've been flown in especially," Tommy said, eschewing the questionable glances from the survivors. "Folks, it's time to get you all out of here. Rockwell, take point."

Nobody knew exactly why the rescuer, named Jake Theodore Rockwell, became so captivated by the lagoon.

"Rockwell! Haul ass," Tommy barked.

Ted moved cautiously to the platform's edge, his knuckles whitening as he gripped hold of the railing.

"Is he okay?" Williams asked.

"It's getting harder to tell these days. Yo, Theodore! Snap out of it," Tommy barked.

"Dude, give me a sec. Guys, your lagoon lighting is not the greatest. Can someone please tell me what this is." Ted pointed towards something he could see through the Perspex viewing portal.

The grey spot, directly ahead, increased in size every few seconds.

"It's surface debris," Beck said, without looking.

The more Ted concentrated, the easier it was to make out a barbed snout, what looked like wings, maybe a tail rudder of sort. "What debris do you know of that has a moving tail?"

Beck swiveled on his heels, jaw dropping due to how flippant he had been. "Is that Betty?"

"It can't be," Wilcox added.

"What is Betty?" Tommy asked.

Combined with enhanced body armor, Betty's thirty foot long, torpedo shaped body showed a complete upgrade to the shark they had been experimented on a few hours ago. A standard White shark could swim at 25 mph. With Betty's enhanced caudal fin, her speed doubled.

The Great White shark raced as powerfully as a locomotive on a collision course with a stranded car. If the group remained, they would have little time before the shark collided with the observation window. Even at six inches thick, the extra strength Perspex would hold off no more than a couple of direct hits from Frankenshark on a revenge mission.

"What in God's creation did you screw with down here?" Tommy asked.

Mikey and the rest of his team shared a worrying silence. Clearly, they had no idea what happened to Betty.

"You know full well who created that thing," Ted said, referring to Arcadian.

Just thinking about the games master gave Tommy palpitations that he couldn't shake. "They're here already," he said, holding his chest.

"Who are?" Mikey blurted.

"Survive this madness and I'll explain everything."

"Are you sure you'll survive that long? You don't look too hot."

"Take one of your pills," Ted said.

"What pills?"

"For his ..."

"I'm fine, Ted," Tommy barked. "It's just a few chest pains."

"No problem. And my friends call me Mikey," Mikey said.

Tommy's palpitations quickly altered to a warmness inside his heart that left him wanting to hug the person he knew to be his best friend. Before he could do, or say anything, Betty rammed into the

Perspex window, putting any thoughts of reunion on the backburner.

Following a swift backwards retreat, Betty struck the window again. Tremors rocked the foundations. Cracks ran rampant.

"It's impossible. Sharks can't swim backwards. They just can't," Wilcox said.

Whoever carried out a horrific revamp of the shark had made her more cyborg than fish. Two-inch titanium plates coated her entire upper torso, leaving room for only her gills, and ruddy, bionic eyes. The snout had been welded into a battering ram barb; the titanium pectoral fins as steady as the wings of a Boeing 747. The caudal fin's sharp edge glinted, as if sharpened to precision. Machine parts in the tail, giving her exceptional speed.

The shark appeared to snarl with serrated, golden teeth as she peeled away for another attack, which would surely be the fatal blow. Wasting no time, Tommy ushered the group out of the wet lab and into the flooded corridor.

Betty's final attack landed harder than a strike from Poseidon's fist. The Perspex observation window shattered instantly, shelling seawater across the wet lab. Anything not tied down was swept up in a whirlpool of damnation.

The team vacated the wet lab just as the water reached the upper tier. Tommy and Mikey managed to close the access point, even as water escaped into the corridor.

"Betty's got issues," Ted snarled.

"Wouldn't you if you just had the makeover from hell," McBride said.

"As long there's only the one shark, we should be okay," Tommy added.

Mikey's sheepish reaction implied otherwise.

"You mean there's two?" Tommy asked.

"Three, actually. Betty's the biggest. Not that that really matters," Mikey added.

"You created a mutant shark."

"No. Not us. Whoever is responsible might well be the same person who attacked the facility."

An almighty impact caused a huge dent to appear in the center of the access point.

"Whoa," Tommy said, stepping away from the door.

"I'm guessing it's not loose equipment," Beck said.

A second strike caused the hinges to buckle, water spouting through ruptured seals.

"How long will that doorway hold?" Tommy asked.

"We're not staying here to find out," Williams said.

Chapter 19

Cat and Mouse

THE INSCRIPTION on the parchment in blood ink, the cat and mouse scenario, now made sense.

From the moment Betty smashed through to the wet lab, the game changed, and not just for the teenagers. The lives of people Tommy knew very little about were now at stake.

In the original game, each teenager had five lives to spare. He would now need all his power to keep Mikey's colleagues alive. With no weapons at his disposal, he knew, unless the teenagers could synchronize the bracelets, one life was all anybody could afford not to lose.

With no other staff aboard Arcquatica, it made sense that the Timeinators had likely taken control of the facility's other occupants. Three genetically altered test sharks.

Mikey's team had in captivity a Great White, Goblin and Tiger shark. Only the White's brain neurons reacted to the experimental drugs. A drug that could in no way have ever resulted in a shark being enhanced for combat. Instead, each shark had grown smarter, more aggressive. Their senses heightened to an extraordinary level.

AFTER looting a storage area, McBride kitted out his colleagues in wetsuits, and gave everyone a headlamp.

Ted stood in front of the exit to the maintenance shaft. His hands gripped the locking mechanism, his full beam torchlight blinding anyone in a three-foot radius. "Are we ready?"

"You might want to reduce the bat signal," Tommy said.

Ted tapped the side of the lamp and dimmed it slightly. "Better?"

Tommy nodded.

"Good. It's time to find out if the shaft being door number one is flooded or not," Ted continued.

A huge eruption detonated from back the way they came. Waves of water rushed towards the group, the water level rising drastically.

"What the hell was that?" Ted blurted.

"Door number two," Wilcox said.

"Betty can do that. Bust through a steel door?"

"Not until today," McBride replied.

"What did you inject her with? The world's most unstable steroid?"

"The ceiling is ruptured near the wet lab, that should hold her off for a few seconds," Tommy added.

"Seconds. You're talking about seconds."

"How about you just open that hatch, Ted, and let us get the fuck out of here," Williams said, completely out of character.

With the water level almost at their necks, Ted needed no second invitation. He ducked beneath the surface and with the help of McBride, twisted the locking mechanism to open.

As they ventured inside, three quarters of the shaft was submerged, leaving a clear route to swim up towards sub level two.

AFTER being defeated in the original game, Tommy's nemesis, Packard Walsh, remained Arcadian's prisoner. Together with Packard's release from the phantom prison was a suitcase full of memories. At the forefront of the pile was his infatuation with the teenager Tommy West.

The obsessive hatred started through nothing more than a typical, kidlike loathing of someone he really knew nothing about. Maybe

Tommy's face didn't fit, or perhaps it was the way he spoke, or maybe the clothes he wore on a certain day. The real reason mattered not at this moment in time. Tommy remained number one on Arcadian's most wanted list. And it was Packard's job to hunt him down.

The offer to escape from an eternity of damnation and become a Timeinator was a deal Packard could not refuse. Along with his friends, Oggy and Skank, the trio had been given strict orders.

Bring back what they have stolen from me.
Kill all who stand in your way.
Fail, and you will suffer with a fate worse than death.

So that their nightmare could end, Arcadian's promise, if the boys completed their task, was to release them back into their reality, and to return to their families.

Having been given their choice of any lifeform, weapon, or vehicle in their pursuit of Tommy and the reality map, their sadistic recklessness left a trail of destruction in their path.

To the Timeinators, only one outcome mattered. Tommy and his friends had to die, so they could live again.

FUELLED by revenge, Packard chose the most dominant entity as his avatar in Mikey's realm, which happened to be an enhanced Great White shark named Betty.

After breaking free of the wet lab, Packard's only obstacle in the submerged passageway was suspended above the few steps leading up to the elevated corridor. Swimming backwards as much as space would allow, he was able to put several tons of raw aggression into a direct strike on the damaged ceiling panels.

With the force of an industrial lifter, the ceiling was raised high enough for the shark's armored snout to penetrate the damaged bulkhead. With its body shifting upwards, Betty slammed down on the floor grating, the rising seawater quickly submerging her entire torso.

By skewering a tear along the ceiling, the sheer weight of seawater flooded into the elevated corridor. Caught up on a flying carpet ride of white surf, Packard's avatar was pitched forwards as if being let loose like Evil Knievel's toy stunt cycle.

Propelled towards the open door, Betty's angled, titanium pectoral fins acted like can openers along the bulkheads.

A common Great White shark had no chance of exiting through a restricted access point for human beings, not unless it had been enhanced into a titanium battering ram. Fortunately for Betty, her armored upper torso impacted the opening with enough strength to break through the entire steel frame.

The shark entered the maintenance shaft like a cornered bull. Her heightened receptors, surviving on a diet of captivity and steroids, needed no invitation to react to the panic pouring out from the humans swimming above her.

To Packard, the survivors' erratic behavior came across as a suicidal sprint through a minefield.

ENOUGH of the shaft was flooded for Wilcox and Collins to reach and open the access point to sub level two without the need to climb the ladder. The corridor inside remained untouched by seawater until it detoured inside. This permitted the shaft's rising water to level off, if only for long enough for the other survivors to reach them.

"Where are they?" Wilcox fumed from the water's edge, as what felt like a bomb went off below.

The chain reaction, caused by the mammoth collision in sub level three, sent a shockwave towards the unstable ceiling, the debris narrowly missing the first person to surface.

Wilcox helped Mikey from the water.

"What hit us?" she asked.

"It's Betty!" he replied, clambering through the access point, and vomiting up the panic and fear he swallowed on the way up.

In the murky water, Collins could make out five headlamps on a continual rise, but it was too difficult for her to identify who they belonged to. Having been through a similar predicament aboard Deep Star Six, her only concern was for the whereabouts of the father of her child.

"C'mon, McBride, move that ass," she yelled, banging a fist against the bulkhead.

Someone surfaced in the center of the shaft. It was Beck.

Collins helped him from the water.

WITH the humans in striking distance, Packard circled the shaft to gain momentum for his launch into a deadly Polaris Breach.

TOMMY, Ted, McBride, and Williams swam in a panic towards the water's edge, as something below them rose to the surface at speed.

BETTY breached the surface, soaring effortlessly, like Excalibur presented by King Arthur's Lady in the Lake. In Arthur's tale, the Lady presented a weapon for good to defeat evil. What evolved before the survivors became a horror show, painted with the vile brushstrokes of a sadistic entity called Arcadian.

THE Great White shark's rapid ascent beat three of the four swimmers into the bulkhead, leaving them dazed, but not blind enough to witness the fleshy morsal locked firmly between Betty's serrated, golden teeth.

Sadistically shaking her head from side to side, Packard's Grim Reaper chowed down on her first kill.

STEVEN Beck made no effort to avoid the bloody downpour from Williams's ruptured torso. In his previous role aboard a deep-sea mining station, the Oceanographer witnessed the deaths of all but one of his crew. In the aftermath of the madness, his relationship with Williams became his only grip on reality. With Betty breaking that tie, the bindings holding back a vengeful Captain Ahab persona just became unfettered.

Reality, fake, whatever he believed, or the group made him believe, now meant very little. From a standpoint of no wider than a few feet, Beck eyed the unstoppable upsurge of water that seized the rest of the human survivors in a rising tide of blood surf.

Unable to stop his momentum, Ted was pitched towards the opening. The rescuer's head ricocheted off a solid surface, knocking him out cold. Beck dragged the rescuer inside, his sole focus now to kill a shark that he helped create.

A jaded McBride was caught up in a rampant whirlpool. His only way out of it was to grasp hold of the ladder leading up to the access hatch, jarring his shoulder in the process. He was about to climb to safety when he spotted Tommy tumbling towards him, out of control.

McBride wedged an arm through three rungs and reached out. He snatched the rescuer by the ankle, dragging him to the edge of the shaft and forced him to use the ladder to reach the access point.

Tommy moved quickly to reach the exit. Still, as quickly as McBride climbed after him, Betty rounded the shaft faster in a death charge.

The shark's bloodstained lower jawline churned up steel as easily as cutting grass with the world's most lethal lawnmower.

Having faced off against one prehistoric sea creature and survived, dicing with death came as second nature to McBride. Still gripping the ladder, he pinned his spine to the wall and waited until the last second.

With the shark's jaws at their widest, McBride lifted both knees to his chest and used the monster's momentum as an advantage.

Planting both feet on Betty's jawline, he pushed backwards, into the middle of the shaft. Unable to change direction, Betty's jaw snagged the ladder.

In a race to see who could reach the way out the quickest, McBride swam frantically towards the access point. Rather than shifting momentum, Betty continued to use the shaft's rounded dimension as her racetrack, the ladder peeling away from its fittings the faster she swam.

With the shark on a collision course with McBride, Tommy plunged both hands into the water. "Get ready," he ordered Wilcox and Collins, who had hold of his legs.

Betty's dorsal fin cut menacingly through the surf as Tommy leaned out as far as he could. He snatched McBride by the wrist as Betty's jaws cranked open like a bear trap to his righthand side.

"Now!" Tommy screamed, only to be blindsided by a meteor-sized shadow.

Chapter 20

Come on over to my place, we'll have a few laughs ...

THREE SLAPS to the cheek drew Tommy away from the horrific dream of golden teeth dripping with flesh and blood. Another slap was enough to force him to sit up.

"Daisy!" he yelled.

"Nope. Someone much better looking," Ted said, hauling Tommy gingerly to his feet.

A firm hand on his shoulder forced Tommy to turn too quickly, his vision blurring. "I think I owe you one," McBride said.

"And that's not Daisy either," Ted remarked, after noticing Tommy struggling to focus.

"McBride," Tommy said, shooting Ted an exasperated look.

"The one and only," McBride replied.

"Oh, thank God. For a minute I thought … Are you okay?"

"Nothing that a new pair of pants wouldn't fix. Since when does the same shit happen to the same person twice." Rather than wait for an answer, McBride waded towards Collins, Wilcox, and Mikey.

The sealed access way shook as Betty struck the other side.

"Betty's still got issues," Ted pointed out.

"We need to move," Collins said from along the corridor, before launching into a bear hug with McBride.

"They got here quicker than we thought," Tommy whispered to Ted.

"Who did?" Beck emerged from behind them and grabbed Tommy's shoulder, forcing him to turn.

"It was a figure of speech."

"Really."

"Yeah."

"I don't believe you."

"Gimme a break. I almost died back there."

Beck pinned Tommy to the bulkhead. "Williams did die, asshole."

"Easy, Beck. I'm on your side."

"Are you sure? What about you?" Beck faced Ted with a turn of his heel.

"Me?" Ted blurted.

"Yeah. What's your deal?"

"You're better off not asking me anything. I'm not the sharpest tool in the fridge."

"McAlester. These guys stink of deception."

"You said the same about me when we first met. Or did you forget?" Mikey said from along the passageway, his torchlight leading further into the facility.

Beck shot a look at the access point as a volley of hits from Betty wobbled the partition enough for water spurts to show.

"Get moving, Beck," Wilcox ordered.

"This isn't over," Beck said, stabbing a finger in Tommy's chest.

Ted waited for Beck to be out of earshot before he approached Tommy. "Dude is pissed."

"Wouldn't you be if your girlfriend was eaten alive in front of you," Tommy replied.

"Now might be a good time to tell them what's going on."

Tommy shook his head. "Daisy's advice is to keep this on a need-to-know basis. No outside interference. Don't forget, I already screwed with the game once before."

"Yeah, yeah, Tobias said the same. I was kinda hoping …"

"No, we stick to the plan. We only tell Mikey. And that's as a last chance scenario."

"But …"

"That's final, Ted."

"We just let the others die."

"We might not have a choice."

"There's always a choice, dude. We gotta tell 'em."

"We can't, even if we want to. We're here for Mikey, that's it."

"Harsh, dude. Real harsh."

"I didn't start this game, Ted. Remember that." Tommy left Ted and joined the others.

After a few steps in the same direction, Ted realized Beck had waited for him. "Sup, Beck," he said, avoiding eye contact.

"I hope you can sleep at night," Beck replied.

"I sleep like a baby."

"That's not what I meant."

"You know what, dude, with me you've gotta be literal. Don't beat around any bushes. I'm likely to get the wrong end of the stick."

Beck pulled a knife from a sheath on his utility belt. "Look, *dude*. I don't know who you are, or where you came from. What I will say is this. If you know something, I suggest you tell me, fast."

"Or what?"

"You'll be on the wrong end of my sharp stick."

DAISY cranked the locking mechanism and planted both hands on the access point as extra security. When something struck the other side, she glanced across the workshop.

"Kurt, move your ass," she blasted.

Kurt vaulted a workbench and landed in knee-high water. A baseball bat he placed on top was stained with oil. He knelt by her side and removed the rucksack strapped to his back. From inside, he hauled a handheld welding torch. Flicking the release tab started a tight, orange flame.

"Lucky for us I found a fire torch in one of the other workstations," he said as the flame began to meld the seal with the framework.

"That bag has everything. Sport Billy would be proud," she said.

"Except a way out."

"Don't bitch about it. Just seal the door."

Kurt and Daisy sheltered inside a workshop of a Mac McBride, who appeared to use it mainly for the maintenance and storing of submersible parts. It also happened to be the only area of sub level two not yet infested by robotic insects. That was all about to change.

By the time the doorframe had been sealed tightly, a handful of electrified spines pierced the bottom two panels.

"These things are relentless," Daisy said as she backed away.

"Let's just hope Tommy and Ted had better luck finding Mikey."

The entrance being made from solid steel made no difference. The killbots' needle tips moved in unison, cutting an area wide enough for something the size of a shoebox to fit through. From the opening, robotic spiders with spindly legs and roving, pinprick eyes and pincers darkened the doorway with ripples of infestation.

"You recognize our friends from the precinct," Kurt said.

"How could I forget them," Daisy replied.

"What good are these avatars if we can't use any weapons."

"They're just a cover. We find Mikey, the bracelets will sync. Then we can kick ass."

"Great! Cos right now, our bracelets are about as useful as Ted in a soccer game."

"That bad, huh?"

"You have no idea. What about until then?"

"Improvise." As she backed away from the swarm, Daisy motioned with her eyes towards Kurt's baseball bat he had left on the worktop.

"Swing batter, batter, swing batter." Kurt picked up the bat just in time and slugged a jumping spiderbot onto the nearest bulkhead.

"How did they get here?" Daisy asked, swiping a crowbar from an equipment rack.

"No idea." Kurt snatched an airborne mechanical insect and pitched it across the room. He carried on swinging at anything that moved until the surface water was overflowing with robot roadkill. "Luther designed the insects to kill. Just not here. Them being here is impossible. How could they end up in Mikey's reality?"

Behind Kurt, a spiderbot scuttled across a floating crate. Its two poison tipped pincers primed to strike his spine. Inches away from the fatal blow, Daisy swung her crowbar hard enough to send the robot soaring across the room towards a utility cupboard. The combustible toxin brimming in its veins exploded upon impact, wiping out an entire wall of invading killbots.

As the flames and smoke lessened, a damaged door hanging off its hinges revealed the cramped conditions of a toilet cubicle.

Kurt and Daisy had just made it inside when a cyborg centipede unraveled above the entrance, the body rippling towards two and a half feet long. The supersized killbot swung from its perch like a bird of prey, hundreds of two-inch legs, tipped with daggers, awakening as it took flight.

Kurt broke the door from its hinges and braced the frame for impact. The centipede hit hard, burying its legs deep enough to almost break the door apart.

"Houston, we have a problem," Kurt said, even as the centipede's spindles stabbed and cut a way through.

By his side, Daisy stood on tiptoes on the closed toilet seat and lifted one of the ceiling panels. Face to face with the centipede, Kurt kicked it across the workshop and disposed of what remained of the door. With killbots entering the cubicle, he broke off a utility cabinet from the wall and for what it was worth, used it as a shield.

Daisy switched on her headlamp and managed to glance inside the ventilation shaft. Back the way they came, a spaghetti junction of wires proved too much of an obstacle for either of them to navigate. In the other direction, an unclogged ventilation shaft, with barely enough room for them to crawl on their fronts, was their only other option of escape.

With barely any room to maneuver, Kurt backed up to the lavatory, the cabinet his only protection against an army of killbots spitting toxic venom.

Daisy shot both hands down from the opening and grabbed Kurt by the collar. He let out a yelp as her avatar's show of strength hauled the six-two, two hundred- and forty-pound sea operations expert towards the opening.

Before he was safely inside, the atmosphere changed in the other room. Shouting could be heard, alongside explosions. Blasts from a flamethrower torching anything that moved.

The killbot army fled from the shower cubicle, switching their attention to whoever was in the workshop. Daisy and Kurt remained out of sight in the ventilation shaft until the smoke cleared beneath them and someone called their names.

Tommy and another man she didn't recognize wielded makeshift flamethrowers. She threw her arms around her boyfriend's avatar. Tommy reciprocated with an awkward squeeze and a kiss on the lips, both overlooking the rest of the group standing in the doorway.

“You’re a close-knit unit,” said the man behind Tommy.

“You bet we are,” Daisy said, slightly embarrassed by her actions.

“I’d hate to see how you act once a mission is over.”

“That’s none of your business, Mr. …?”

“Mac McBride. I like what you’ve done with my workshop. You should come over more often, share a few laughs.”

“Sorry, we had no choice.”

“Clearly.”

She turned back to Tommy. “It’s good to see you.”

“Same here,” he said, easing away from her.

“Did you find him?”

“Actually, we found quite a few people.” Tommy gestured to the group at the door.

Daisy recognized only Ted’s avatar from the other two men and two women looking into the room.

“Nice of you join the party,” Kurt blurted as he emerged from the cubicle.

“We just followed your screams,” Ted said, giving thumbs up.

“What were those things?” Beck asked.

“They were in the wrong place at the wrong time,” Kurt replied.

“He’s Beck,” Ted said, jabbing a thumb to the man on his right. “These two lovely ladies are Collins and Wilcox. He is Doctor McAlister, Mikey to his friends.”

Mikey stepped inside the room, wading through the water towards some of the machine debris. Daisy shot Tommy a look, which he answered with a deft shake of the head. She knew straightaway that Mikey’s blonde avatar remained tangled in Arcadian’s dream web.

“Did you bring these here?” Mikey asked, studying one of the spiders up close.

“Why would we do that?” Kurt replied.

“Then who did?”

“Charles Luther.”

“Should we know who that is?” Collins asked.

“Not unless he’s a member of your crew.”

“You’re looking at the crew,” Wilcox added.

“What’s left of it,” Beck snarled, before trudging off alone along the corridor.

HAVING incinerated the killbot army, the group arrived at the largest sub level two workshop without further incident. They expected to board a submersible and reach topside. They found no submersible in either of the two water pools. Instead, claret in the largest pool implied something had recently lost a lot of blood during some sort of medical procedure.

A host of active machinery appeared to have started another operation in the smaller oval pool. Electrical saws, cutting tools, nail guns, all mounted on robotic arms, and a host of technology nobody aboard recognized since arriving at Arcquatica had somehow kept working despite the power outage.

"Since when did we start slicing and dicing the marine life?" Collins asked Mikey.

"I have no idea," Mikey replied.

"At least we know how Betty suddenly became a tank," Wilcox added.

"How is there power down here. I don't get it."

"The backup generators don't reach this far," McBride said from the edge of the largest pool, his fingers washing aside the blood.

"What are you thinking?" Collins asked.

"That it's time to leave, before whoever is using this tech comes back."

"How do we leave without a submersible?"

"Unless someone has a better idea, we're going to have to swim out of here," Tommy added.

"Through the blood. Sharks are attracted to blood," Ted said.

"Wait a minute. Where's Beck?" Collins asked.

"He was here a moment ago," Mikey replied.

Ted sniffed the air. "Do you smell barbeque?"

It was hard to ignore the stench of burnt flesh as a man strolled casually on the overhead catwalk.

"Good. More meat for my creations," he said.

Only a few hours ago Kurt had come face to face with the same killer in his precinct. At the time, his avatar was Detective Kurt Caine and Charles Luther was a tanned rock god. The man standing before him was burnt all over and barely recognizable, if not for his voice.

"Luther," Kurt said.

"I don't know you."

"And yet we've met before."

"Normally the people I meet are dead not long after."

"Maybe that's through smoke inhalation. Seriously, dude. You're like an advert for a reason not to smoke," Ted said.

"Just a shame I didn't clip your ass before you killed my witness," Kurt added.

"I knew of only one witness. He died at a police precinct a few hours ago. You were not there."

"Think again, you son of a bitch."

"Harsh words for a soon to be dead man."

"A few hours ago was when the electrical blast hit us," Mikey said to the rest of his team.

"That still doesn't explain how he got here," Kurt blasted.

"Oh, I was just hanging around, beneath a helicopter, being doused by fuel and flames when it was struck by lightning," Luther said.

"Burning and struck by lightning. That's some bad luck," Ted remarked.

"I awoke here, alongside my army of killbots, and with enough power in my fingertips to tamper with the wildlife. I'd say the bad luck is strongly in your favor, rather than mine."

"Says the guy who looks like an overcooked quarter pounder."

"It wasn't easy to improve the perfect killing machine with the facility's technology, but I did the best I could. She is a magnificent specimen, isn't she? And as for the other test sharks …" Luther glanced purposely over the railing at the second pool, where his machines worked busily as they upgraded the two sharks into superior cybernetic organisms. "Most patients are quite hungry after an operation of such magnitude. Perhaps I will leave some of you alive, just for the thrill of the chase."

"How is any of this possible," Tommy whispered to Daisy, ignoring the rest of what Luther was saying.

"He must have reality hopped when we did," she replied.

"People can just tag along, like in an Uber."

"What's an Uber?"

"A cab."

"... and with my killbot army destroyed, it's time for some of you to end up as another tally on my kill list. The rest of you, the sharks will enjoy feasting on your flesh." Luther aimed the bulky hand cannon loaded with seeker bullets at each person in turn.

"He can't kill us all," McBride said.

"I don't think he gives a shit," Collins added.

"Such a diverse collection of minds. Who shall I destroy first?" Luther snarled, turning his gun towards Ted.

"You had to piss off the serial killer," Kurt stated.

"He can't hit me from there," Ted replied.

"He uses seeker bullets."

"What's a seeker bullet?"

"It tracks and kills anyone he tells it to."

"If he said his own name, would it kill him?"

"Why is that important?"

"Imagine this. He's just about to shoot someone and he answers his cell phone. Hey, it's Billy Barbeque. Blam. He dies. Game over."

"Ted, he's about to kill you and you're making jokes."

"Don't worry. I'll dodge it." Ridiculous as it sounded, Ted looked as if he believed he could do so.

"There is no defense from a seeker." Kurt was not as cheerily confident of Ted's survival, and it showed.

Luther fired a solitary bullet.

Ted grabbed the closest object from the nearest tabletop, a brick sized device equipped with a pair of orange buttons. With the bullet quickly upon him, he flipped the brick up in the narrow projectile's path, the explosion knocking him over.

"I know what you are," Beck snarled as he sprinted along the catwalk towards Luther. Before the killer could re-aim, Beck shoved him over the edge of the catwalk. "That was for Williams."

THE Goblin shark had been chosen as a test subject mainly because of its tendency to stay in the deepest parts of the ocean. Very little was known about the species. To capture and test one made sense.

The group had nothing to lose. As did Luther with his alteration process.

Luther's perversion with cybernetic conversion had continued from the moment he arrived in the same reality jump as Tommy and Daisy. How exactly he had arrived in a different environment, he did not know or understand. His only purpose was to alter the three test sharks into perfected killing machines. By doing so, he assisted the Timeinators. Meaning their choice of avatar was an easy one.

Luther had the perfect set up at his fingertips, a raw energy source filtering through his body. With the power out, he had used his own source to awaken the host of dormant technology and then got to work altering three naturally perfect predators.

If the elongated snout made the Goblin shark appear as an ugly relative in comparison to other species, Luther's lancelike alteration to it was suitable for any medieval joust.

Scientific research recorded that Goblin's jaws, lined with crooked looking teeth, would thrust forward in a slingshot feeding motion. With speeds of up to 3.1 meters per second, the fastest speed recorded for any species, it was an ideal experiment for Luther to break more boundaries.

AFTER he was shoved over the railing, the serial killer plunged towards the water pool occupied by the two smaller test sharks.

As he fell, he was able to fire one last seeker at his attacker.

With such a short distance between them, Beck had no chance to evade the bullet. The impact was an instant kill. Intestines and bodily fluids seeped through the grating as he dropped in a heap.

Luther laughed manically as he splashed down. His automated modification machines ignored his presence until they sensed his blood in the water.

By enhancing the Goblin shark's jawline with bionics, Luther had witnessed first-hand the lethality of the shark's new weapon. He jerked suddenly, his unnerving laugh continuing, while a serrated vice, lined with crooked teeth, snapped around his legs at an incredible speed. As the third test subject, a Tiger shark, clamped down on his torso with the power of a hundred bear traps, the water turned blood red.

The feeding frenzy expunged the serial killer's life force and sent the machinery into sudden shut down mode. The room fell silent, except for the splashing sound as the sharks continued to feed.

"Now is the perfect time to haul ass," McBride said.

"Alongside the sharks. No way," Mikey replied.

"Not that pool. We use the other one."

"Let's do it." Ted stood, blood seeping from the shrapnel wounds in his cheek and forehead.

"Lucky for you, your face took most of the hit," Kurt joked.

"Maybe you should've ducked," Tommy added.

"Hey, I dodged it," Ted said.

"Hardly a dodge," Collins snorted.

"More like a stumble," Daisy added.

"I'm still standing, thanks to this," Ted said, holding up the remains of a locking mechanism device.

"McBride, we have a problem," Wilcox said, snatching the wrecked device from Ted. "The only way to open the water pools separately was with this device. Thanks to Shrapnel here, our exit plan is kaput."

"Sorry for saving my own ass," Ted replied.

"There must be another way to open the pools separately," Mikey prompted.

"Can we override by hotwiring?" Daisy asked McBride, who was sitting in front of a blank screen and keyboard.

"Whatever energy source that whacko was using, died out when he did. To use the override codes, we'll need to divert the backup generator power to this terminal. It will drain reserves from elsewhere. Sealed doors will open. It will lead to flooding and structural breakaway. Mass hysteria. And if we don't get out, we'll die down here." McBride shifted a panel on the power supply to reveal a host of fuse boxes and electrical circuits. "What's not to lose?"

"Looks like a mess," Ted remarked.

"Leave it to me." Daisy knew her avatar had the skills to complete the process with her eyes shut. It still left her with sweaty palms and the dread of wondering what if she got it wrong.

"No pressure, Daisy, but if you screw up, we all die," Ted said.
"Do you always have to state the obvious?"

DAISY made the necessary adjustments to the bundles of electrical wires and quickly switched back up power to the adjacent terminal McBride sat in front of. The computer turned on, the screen showing the system boot up.

"It's all yours," she said.

"None of it will matter if whatever juice is in the generators is used up," McBride replied.

As the computer booted up, Wilcox retrieved a handful of air tanks and bright colored life jackets. She tied the jackets around the tanks and handed them out to the group.

"What are these for?" Ted asked.

"I thought you were the water expert," Wilcox replied.

"I am, with weapons and stuff."

"Stuff! Like what? Armbands?"

"Huh, I normally make the jokes." Ted looked away, disheartened.

"We have fifty feet to reach the surface. We use these. Sharks are attracted to bright colors, churning water, erratic behavior. These should be a distraction when we're rising."

"These are intelligent sharks; they won't fall for it," Collins warned.

"Fine, go without."

"I'll take yours, if you don't want it," Ted said, reaching for the air tank.

Collins took the tank and despite her fears, followed the others to the edge of the empty water pool.

"Remember, don't rise quickly. Exhale on the way up. And then get your asses out of the water as quickly as possible," Wilcox said before entering the pool.

"A couple of mutated sharks, and we're armed with life jackets and a water tank," Collins said.

"Betty is locked inside. We've got that going for us at least," Tommy said.

"We hope," McBride added.

Warning lights winked across the chamber as a final warning that the backup generators were shutting down.

"I wish this day would stop kicking us in the balls and give us a break," Ted barked.

Answering his prayer, structural failure heaved the facility around as if it had been built on an unstable fault line.

"McBride! We need to leave!" Collins yelled from across the chamber.

At the base of the larger pool, the access point rumbled open.

"Is that good enough for you?" he said as he entered the pool with the rest of the group.

Due to the structural quakes, nobody noticed the second pool was opening with a few seconds' delay, both test sharks showing the same eagerness as the humans to escape.

Chapter 21

Blood surf

THE GROUP swam down, then up, to escape the pool. Setting off the air tanks as they ascended, the group remained close to the churning air bubbles and bright life jackets.

With only a short time between the two pools opening, the group had reached thirty feet from the surface when, working as a pair, the Tiger shark and Goblin shark attacked at will, snatching at anything that moved.

Wilcox's ploy had worked. The sharks attacked everything vibrating and not created from flesh.

McBride and Collins surfaced first. It was night-time, and a rampant thunderstorm battered what remained of the topside facility.

Neither the surface waves, pitching against the surrounding catwalks, making it difficult for them to swim directly to the edge of the lagoon, nor the buckled titanium fences captured their attention. Instead, attention was held by the two speedboats that had come away from their moorings. Both vessels were closer to them than the freedom of any walkway.

They split up, McBride swimming to the left boat, Collins to the one straight ahead.

Tommy surfaced and screamed out in pain. Speared through the leg by the Goblin's lance, he was driven through the water away from the group, a bloody smear left in his wake.

MCBRIDE heard the scream as he turned the ignition key and started the engine. At the rear of the boat, he switched on the mounted spotlight and used it to scan the surface waters. The instant relief when he spotted his wife safely aboard the other boat was short-lived. The enhanced Great White shark rose from the water just as lightning bolts lit up the heavens. Flashes in the sky emphasized the painstaking, step by step attack that he could do nothing about.

WITH the generators offline and the facility faltering by the second, it was only a matter of time before Betty escaped the maintenance shaft. Bionic jaws, lined by serrated teeth sharper than any butcher's knife, clamped down on Collin's boat's transom and crushed it into oblivion.

Collins dived for cover amid an eruption of fiberglass and plastic. The vessel tipped as the shark's biting power continued to trash the hull. Collins clung to the steering column for her life, as Betty went on to tip the boat and eat her way through the underside.

McBride spotted Wilcox surface on the rise of the swells. Mikey emerged alongside her, followed by Daisy, Ted, then Kurt. The man named Tommy was nowhere to be seen. He knew right then that the scream earlier came from him.

The Tiger shark's dorsal fin rose stealthily, slicing through the surf as the shark focused on the group's vibrations.

McBride's warnings of *'shark!'* were drowned out by thunderclaps. Instead, he switched the spotlight on and off in quick succession.

Wilcox faced the spotlight. McBride was pointing irately at the water behind her. She turned just as the Tiger Shark lunged forwards.

By dodging sideways as the jaws smashed together, she braced her hands on its snout, her body ricocheting off what felt like an armored torso. As the Tiger shark sped off, Wilcox rolled along the smooth body, grabbed hold of the dorsal fin, and clung on.

THE Goblin shark's last alteration enhanced the caudal fin. Known to be one of the species' slowest swimmers, his speed was now equal to the Great White currently chewing through a speedboat. Velocity allowed the Goblin more maneuverability, something that it was taking full advantage of.

With his thigh impaled by a metallic lance, Tommy was guided to the edge of the facility. The Goblin's abrupt turn, and twist of its upper body, slung the human against the titanium fence.

Tommy collided with enough force to free his leg from the lance. The raw pain subsided briefly, but blood pumped freely from the wound even as he tried to stem the flow.

He glanced sideways. The shark arrowed towards him with the sort of twisted smile that came hand in hand with a Timeinator. Grabbing hold of the fence, Tommy pulled himself up just as the Goblin's lance pierced the barrier beneath.

Unable to slow down, the shark's upper torso became trapped, its tail swishing wildly as it tried to free itself. With a chance to escape, Tommy swam for the surface, blood streaming from the wound, his lungs ready to explode.

MIKEY reaching a walkway separating two lagoons coincided with McBride's speedboat docking. Already safely aboard were Daisy, Kurt, and Ted.

"You see my wife?" McBride barked.

"Nope," Mikey answered, boarding the speedboat.

"Wilcox?"

"Here!" came the breathless call from the starboard side.

Wilcox clamped her hands on the transom and tried to climb up.

Seizing her by the wrists, Mikey pulled, but not quickly enough.

With her upper body clear, the surface erupted. Following a flash of metal, a glint of moonlight, Wilcox was gone, a piece of the broken transom in her hand as she was dragged beneath the surface through a bloody slick.

Mikey dropped to his knees.

"Get on your feet, soldier," Daisy said, pulling him upright.

"What's the use?" he said, shrugging her off.

"There's still time to save her." She handed him a full syringe, given to her by Wilcox before they ascended. "She wanted you to have it."

"How did she know mine was broken?"

"Women know everything, Mikey. Trust me. And she knew what this serum brings is more important than anything else."

"If she's right, Mikey, then it's time to jack up," McBride said.

For years' worth of stress and self-sacrifice to finally mean something, Mikey needed to do nothing more than pierce his skin and shoot up. When he eased the needle into his vein, he was unaware that his accelerated lifeline had been a trick. By lowering the plunger, his serum cleansed his soul.

His memories of a sister, best friends, and a distant home returned faster than he could comprehend them.

"My dreams. They were real," he said, tears streaming down his cheeks.

Across the lagoon, the five bracelets worn by the teenagers synchronized. Releasing the power to call upon their avatars.

"Why are your bracelets glowing?" McBride asked openly.

"Payback!" Kurt said, snapping the bracelet around Mikey's wrist before he had a chance to question it.

"You got any spares?" McBride continued.

Chapter 22

Power Maximum

AFTER FREEING itself from the fence's titanium shackles, the Goblin shark twisted aggressively towards its human prey.

Tommy had emerged in the middle of a lagoon, with his leg in tatters. He pawed helplessly, unable to swim, his head barely above the surface. His friends were nowhere to be seen. His defense if attacked, nothing more lethal than harsh language. A glowing bracelet was about as valuable as … suddenly it dawned on him. His bracelet was active, an energy coursing through his veins, releasing an adrenaline shot like no other.

Having misinterpreted the adrenaline as his body trying to survive, he now knew Mikey had returned. The tide had changed. And only one avatar would be brave enough to battle a monster from the deep.

PRINCE Fallon, the most heroic character to have ever set foot on the sacred tape of any VHS cassette, had no time to contemplate why he was in the middle of what appeared to be a river of some kind. All he knew was that he had again been called upon to save the day with the most legendary three blade projectile sword in existence.

His legendary status had been proven on countless occasions, and still he had never come face to face with such an ugly, disfigured creature before.

It was clear that the creature's spear like snout, smoothed down to a perfect, stabbing implement, would send any red-blooded human into a fear induced coma. Thankfully for Fallon, fear had no place in his heart.

Before the hideous fish could strike, Fallon fired the first of his three deadly steel blades. Shredded sinew erupted in a gory cloud as the blade imbedded in the shark's midriff. A second blade imbedded in the Goblin shark's tail, slowing it down, but not enough to finish the battle.

With his armor and furs weighing him down enough to cause concern, Fallon also felt the discomfort around his thigh. The injury was sufficient to force him to seek a hasty retreat to land, rather than submerge and attempt to eliminate the creature once and for all.

Using the nearest catwalk, he dropped his sword, now with one remaining blade, and disrobed as much of the armor as he could without leaving himself a casualty to the elements.

Now able to see the injury firsthand, it was clear that the wound was more severe than at first realized. Never had he been lanced before. Cut, stabbed, slapped, punched, kicked in the crotch, fighting whilst hungover, these were injuries he could deal with. The gaping wound in his thigh was wide enough to fit a fist through it. He also had no idea how it occurred.

Sensing the conflict in Fallon's decision making could lead to a tragic blood loss, Tommy hijacked the avatar's functions. Wasting no time, he ripped a piece of cloth from under the armor at his feet, tying it tightly around the wound.

The more he moved, the more blood from the wound seeped through the grating, teasing the Goblin shark to the surface. The shark's lance pierced the catwalk, almost knocking Tommy back into the lagoon.

As he rolled to evade, he realized the shark was struggling to free itself and for the first time since Daisy had arrived, a Timeinator was now at the mercy of a teenager who had none to spare. In one fluid motion, Tommy braced his fall, then swung the sword in the shark's direction. Fallon's last blade set off like a torpedo, penetrating the hideous head, puncturing the brain, and smiting the Timeinator from the challenge.

Three shots, three fatal blows, Fallon's work was done.

Close to exhaustion, Tommy released the sword and dropped to his knees. After having utilized the bracelet's power, he expected his injuries to have healed. It was not to be.

McCleod had warned that the bracelet held power, just not the same level that the teenagers had grown accustomed to from the power rings they used in their first contest in Arcadian's game.

As quickly as he had arrived, Prince Fallon returned to his fictional realm.

The latest victory, this time versus a repulsive sea devil, would be sung by bards across the land for centuries. As Tommy pondered the lyrics, he passed out when the exertion of battle and his blood loss finally took over.

A subconscious barrier shielding Mikey from the real world had just been crushed by his serum. Memories which began at the exact moment he took possession of the game returned with vengeance. In his reality, he recalled exactly how his fellow Horsemen fought valiantly for a cause in a game he took possession of. In McAlester's realm, the people he cared for were now being harmed by something he created.

His memories heralded back to a time he had used a power ring, to bring avatars to life. It now made sense why he felt drawn to the bracelet. The power bestowed allowed him the chance to return to the fight.

The tide was turning in his favor at last.

Without any thought for his own safety, Mikey dived overboard, swimming through the bloody remnants of the attack on Wilcox. His speed of descent fueled his thirst for revenge. Not only against the shark, but also the person who led him along this pathway.

THE Tiger shark had one last fatal bite from its prey before deliberately discarding the body as bait. With Wilcox left to bleed out, the shark stalked the gloomy depths, waiting for the right moment to strike.

Now a victim of a shark attack, like her previous boyfriend, it was easy to see why Wilcox assumed their pathways to fate were somehow linked. Fading in and out of consciousness, she wanted nothing more than to die, believing it to be true.

When her boyfriend's image manifested before her as an angel spreading his wings, she reached out, her fingertips touching his.

Her heartbeat slowed as he held her close to his chest.

They were together at last, until her final breath.

Cocooned in a heavenly aura.

FROM inside the cocoon, a celestial presence emerged, wielding the Universe's most powerful weapon, the Sword of Power, Mikey's angel's wings manifesting into a cape.

The Tiger shark, focused solely on this new challenger, circled to attack.

With his sword charged with the power from a mystical orb, Mikey's avatar, Hero-Man, a muscular Prince from the land of Heternia, gripped the hilt tightly with both hands and swung down at the Tiger Shark's torso.

One strike was all it took to slice the enhanced shark in two, leaving Hero-Man free to carry Wilcox to the surface.

MIKEY'S hero climbed from the water. Blood ran down his arms as he lay Wilcox's mangled remains gently on the catwalk.

With his energy used to power the sword, Mikey altered back to his teenage self. He sat holding the hand of a woman he had considered one of his closest friends. If his memories were real, their love had been a lie. If that was true, why did his heart hurt so much?

To hide her wounds, he covered her body with Hero-Man's cape, which had fallen off the teenager's slight frame.

"I wish I had the power to bring you back. To bring you all back," he said. Overwhelmed by emotion, the teenager cradled Wilcox's remains and sobbed.

KURT guided the spotlight's sharp beam until he located Collins across the lagoon, hauling her drenched body onto a catwalk.

"Got her," he said pointing.

"Collins!" McBride yelled out.

"She won't hear you over the thunderstorm," Daisy said from the passenger seat.

McBride needed no prompting. He banked the vessel at speed, cutting close to the lagoon's titanium fence. The boat arrived at the same time Collins exited an equipment shed. She came out with a crate and a high-powered harpoon gun.

"Are you okay?" McBride asked.

"Do I look okay?" Collins replied, her clothes soaked through.

"Collins, is there anything in that shack that can kill this thing?" Daisy asked.

"Apart from the gun? No. But I did use some harsh language when I dropped a stupid steel drum on my foot."

"I forgot about that." McBride vaulted from the boat to the catwalk and ventured inside the shack. He returned with the steel drum and dragged it towards the boat.

"Dude, I don't think playing reggae will work," Ted remarked.

"Smart ass. This drum is filled with 200 lbs. of high explosive."

"Making it a depth charge," Kurt said.

"How'd you know that?" Ted asked.

"I read books. You should try it sometime."

"Books on what? How to sink a submarine?"

McBride knelt by the drum and wrote something on the side. He then shifted the drum into the boat. "McAlester and I kind of kept it around in case we needed to blow something up," he said.

"You mean the sharks?" Collins asked.

"No … well, maybe. But aren't you glad we kept it?"

"Kurt, find that shark. McBride, when I give the order, take us alongside it," Daisy said.

"What are you going to do?" McBride answered.

"Our job," Ted said, almost convincingly. "What is that again?"

"Collins, you know how to use the harpoon gun?" Daisy asked.

"I just need ammo," Collins replied.

"Leave that to me." Daisy grabbed Ted by the shoulder. "We need to take this Timeinator down between us. No heroics. As a team. Kurt?"

"I heard you," he replied, keeping the spotlight on the surface.

"How can we slow it down enough to use the depth charge?" McBride asked.

"Leave that to us," Daisy said.

"It's heading our way," Kurt said, flashing the spotlight straight ahead.

The Great White had no intention of slowing down. McBride gunned the engines, and sped across the surface, banking at the last minute. The shark's jaws crashed together, missing the hull by a fraction.

"That was too close," McBride said.

"Whatever you're doing, do it now," Collins warned.

"Kurt, Ted, hold my hands," Daisy ordered.

"Who are we changing into?" Kurt asked.

"Trust me. Collins, are you ready?"

"You got …" Collins shielded her eyes as a brilliant white light engulfed the three rescuers. When she turned back, she was confronted by three yellow barrels.

"McBride, you won't believe this," she said.

McBride glanced over his shoulder. "I don't remember any barrels. At least they'll slow that sucker down long enough for us to use that depth charge."

"That's not what I meant."

"Wait. Where did the rescue team go?"

Collins pointed at the barrels.

"Why would they climb inside them? Screw it. We're out of time. Betty is all over our ass."

Despite not believing what she witnessed, Collins hooked up the first barrel to the harpoon gun. "I'm not sure which one of you this is, but here goes nothing."

With the shark shortening the distance, Collins hoisted the first barrel to the transom.

"Get ready, Mac. Turn to portside in three, two … now," she ordered.

McBride turned the boat hard just as Betty's jaws launched from the surf. The White bit down on fresh air and felt the impact as the first harpoon dug in beneath her dorsal fin, in a gap between the armor plating.

"Barrel one away," Collins said with a fist pump.

Wasting no time, she hooked up the second.

PACKARD didn't care who he ate, killed, or disemboweled as the Great White shark. The avatar's power was like nothing he had come across before.

Being a Timeinator had brought with it a new lease of life. If he couldn't kill Tommy, one of his friends would have to do.

With one barrel stuck in him, Packard showed no sign of slowing down. He collided with the hull, barging the speedboat momentarily off course.

TAKING her chance, Collins fired the second harpoon into a fleshy part of Betty's tail. The second barrel took off; this time the shark knew why it had been tagged.

PACKARD surfaced to spyhop, lifting the shark's head above the water to have a better look at his surroundings.

As Betty surfaced, Collins fired off the third harpoon and tagged another piece of open flesh. The barrel sped off as the shark fled.

With all the cables out, she tied off what remained to the transom to ensure Betty couldn't escape.

THE third harpoon dug deeper into Packard than the first two.

The impact felt personal.

Like a jab to the ribs from an old friend.

As he fled, the immediate drag from the barrels hauled him back in what felt like a supernatural tug of war. Even with the strain, he tore apart a section in the titanium fencing wide enough to squeeze Betty's upper body inside. By doing so, he loosened the harpoons one by one. Now free, the barrels floated along the surface briefly before they were dragged from sight.

In concentrating on escaping, Packard disregarded the loud splash overhead as a steel drum descended. With so much at stake, the minor vibrations from a timer inside did not seem worthy enough of a Timeinator's attention.

Only when he discovered he was unable to free Betty's body, did his frustrations grow.

When the depth charge first came into view, Packard mistakenly mistook it for debris. By the time the drum reached his side, he stopped struggling and focused on the two words written on the side - ***EAT THIS.***

MCBRIDE gunned the engine just as the explosion beneath the boat fired a shockwave across the lagoon. Caught by the upsurge, he banked the speedboat towards the equipment shed and managed to mount the catwalk, the boat skidding across the decking to a halt.

FOLLOWING the explosion, the storm eased up, sunlight breaching the cloud front as if signaling the dawn of a new day. One shaft of light set upon the teenage forms of Kurt, Ted, and Daisy who were outside the equipment shed.

"Did that really happen?" Ted said, still wondering how he transformed into a yellow barrel.

"Who the hell are you?" Collins said from somewhere nearby.

"Whaddya mean?" Kurt said.

"Where is the rescue team?"

"We're it," Daisy replied.

After checking their appearance in the shed window, the three teenagers re-introduced themselves.

"Adults to barrels to teenagers," Collins said, not believing it.

"I had no motor functions. No thoughts. I was just a barrel," Ted continued.

"I guess we do can that now," Kurt said as McBride climbed from the wrecked boat.

"I've seen a lot of crazy shit. Nothing like this," McBride said.

"A barrel! What's heroic about that?" Ted remarked.

“If it’s any help, we won. The shark is gone,” Collins added.

“Might I suggest a good idea going forwards. That little trick you do, changing into barrels, and then into teenagers. Keep that under wraps,” McBride said.

“Daisy, what made you think of the barrels?” Ted asked.

“There’s only one way to slow down a shark,” she replied.

COLLINS and McBride sat at the water’s edge alongside a despondent Mikey, who could not look away from the bloody surface waters.

“Are you the other rescuer?” Collins asked Mikey.

“Nope,” he replied.

Severe sacrifices were necessary to reach their goal. How severe had only just come to light when Mikey dwelled on Wilcox’s demise, and now the youngster’s reflection staring back at him. He was still trying to come to terms with it all, when he felt the gaze of his two colleagues fall upon him.

“I guess it worked,” Mikey said, knowing his alteration from a forty something scientist to a teenager had been part of a bigger game.

“McAlester?” McBride asked.

“The one and only. Where’s your serum?”

“Here.” Collins held two syringes. She handed one of them to her husband.

“Did you age backwards?” McBride asked.

“I’m not aging backwards. I’m a teenager, from another world. And like you, I just want to get home,” Mikey said.

“At least you were right,” Collins said.

“Yeah, I was beginning to think I’d have to kick your ass for bullshitting us,” McBride said.

“Being right doesn’t feel so good right now,” Mikey replied.

“What happened, happened.”

“I just wish there was another way.”

“We all took the jump with you. There is nobody to blame.”

“Thank you for believing in me. Without you, I’d be stuck here.”

"Not to sound insincere, but I'm ready to leave this all behind and find out what rabbit hole we need to head down to get home."

"No need to tell me twice. Here goes nothing," Collins said, injecting herself with the serum.

"McAlester, I'll haunt you if my head explodes." McBride injected himself and threw away the syringe.

"My real name is Mikey. Mikey Drew. And I guess this is goodbye."

Collins offered her hand to Mikey. As she did so, her body turned transparent, their hands passing through each other like ghosts on different journeys. The couple vanished a few seconds after. Their journey back to their reality had only just begun.

SURROUNDED by his sister and friends, it felt like it was the first time he had laid eyes on any of them for decades. Unable to hold back the tears of success, he sat against the shed and waited for the emotional overload to come to a halt.

The ethereal glow, seen through the cracks in the shed walls, stemmed the tearful reunion.

"I think I've found the portal." Tommy stood by the shed's door; his wounded leg bound by stained rags. Having rested, the bracelet started to heal the wound. It would still take time to fully repair, but for now it was enough to ease the pain.

"Tommy, you look just like I feel," Daisy said.

"I'll take that as a compliment."

"Tommy?" Mikey said, hugging his best friend.

"And just like that, the band is back together," Ted remarked.

"Then it's time to use the map and jump us out of here," Daisy said.

"We use maps now?" Mikey asked.

"Do we have to explain everything again?" Ted asked.

"Dude, when were you told about a map?" Kurt said.

"Good point. Say, Tommy. What do we need a map for?"

Rather than listen to their conversation, Daisy led the group to the shed. As she opened the door, she unraveled the map and uttered the words everyone wanted to hear.

"Take us home."

DAY FIVE

(Three jumps remaining)

Chapter 23

MONTH - DAY LOCATION
AUG 12 FULL SCREAM AHEAD 067-231
REALITY DESTINATION

Far below the South Chimera Sea lies an underwater mountain range, with canyons deep enough to hide the Himalayas, deeper than any being or machine has ever explored.
Throughout the centuries, countless vessels have vanished into these waters without a trace.
Their disappearance remains a mystery ... until today.

A SOLITARY shot of a truth serum was all it took to unravel the truth. A truth tainted by grief. When he entered the portal, Mikey's friends had explained that the rebirth was different for each of them. Still raw emotionally, Mikey's bodily resurrection continued with mind-bending aftereffects and brutal flatulence.

"Are you dead?" a man asked, kicking Mikey's foot.

Mikey farted accidentally, releasing a smell worse than a rotting corpse.

"I guess that's a no on the dead front." The man's spray on tan was emphasized by a pristine uniform of white shirt and black trousers. His stylish haircut remained in place, despite a swift breeze cuffing the surface waters.

Mikey sat up tentatively, his headache not helped by the sheer white wall of a cruise liner's hull slowly unravelling before his eyes.

He was on a speedboat. Not that he remembered boarding it. He only remembered stepping towards a bright light his sister referred to as a portal.

"Where are my friends?" he asked.

"They're aboard already. I'll say to you the same thing I told them. This is no place for a joyride."

"We weren't joyriding, sir."

"None of you look old enough to be piloting a speedboat."

"I'm over forty."

"You are? You'd fit right in at Rydell High," the crewman replied, with an added slice of sarcasm.

Mikey paid no attention to the Grease reference. He was too busy trying to come to terms with his old life as Mikey McAlester exiting through the back door, only to be replaced by an influx of his real memories as Mikey Drew.

For the sake of McBride and Collins, and the sacrifices of his associates to have meant something, he needed to remember everything. The only problem was that memories were starting to fall through his fingers like sand.

"Are you okay, kid?" the man asked.

The word 'kid' made more of an impression than any other word spoken by the crewman. Mikey glanced down at his smaller, teenage hands.

"Are you high?" the man continued.

"Only on life, sir. Where am I right now?"

"You're in the middle of the South Chimera Sea. As I said already, this is no place to be joyriding."

"Where is the nearest port?"

The crew member pointed to the starboard side and an endless horizon of blue sky and calm waters. "A few hundred miles that way. I think."

"You think?"

"I'm just a deckhand. Sue me."

"I thought all sailors knew how to navigate by the stars."

"That line only works with the ladies."

The crewman helped Mikey onto the transom where there was a winch, harness, and pulley ropes. Never a fan of heights, the opening above appeared a lot higher than he would have liked.

The teenager's ascent towards the side opening used for launching jet-skis when docked at port took no more than thirty seconds. With Mikey safely inside, a female crewmate in a matching uniform unhooked his rope and harness.

"Where are your parents?" she asked.

"I'm not sure," he replied.

"They must be worried sick. You kids should be lucky we came across you when we did. A storm is heading in this direction. I would hate to think of what would've happened to a boat that size in the middle of the ocean when those green clouds hit."

"Yeah, thanks, I guess," Mikey said, wondering why green clouds would have any impact whatsoever on weather patterns.

Still unsure how they ended up near a cruise liner, Mikey waded through knee high water, avoiding a host of jet-skis and other members of the crew.

The way out led towards a set of stairs leading up to the launch lobby with pristine décor, comfy seats, and a high, raised desk. The glare from the ceiling spotlights forced him to shield his eyes again, but he still managed to identify his three best friends by their silhouettes.

"Before you ask, we ran out of juice," Ted remarked, changing into some spare clothes.

Mikey could do no more than glance sideways at his friend.

"I know what you're thinking. Where the hell did the speedboat come from. Remember the portal we stepped through? Well, hey presto, we found ourselves back on the water, with little to no gas. And I don't mean the kind of gas you've been jettisoning this entire time," Ted continued.

"I think he knows what you mean by gas," Kurt said, zipping up his pants.

"Are you sure? It's hard to tell. He is kinda just staring at me."

"Well, lucky for us we stumbled across this bad boy."

"How do you stumble across a two hundred foot tall, sixteen deck, luxury cruise liner?"

"By being the luckiest son of a bitch in the world. How should I know, Ted? I was on the same boat as you. Tommy?"

Tommy pushed his head through a white t-shirt and shrugged. "Daisy's the one who said take us home."

"No offence, dude. I don't recall ever taking a cruise liner home. A bus, yeah, but a boat?"

"Did you expect to be transported back to your front door, Kurt?" Ted said.

"That's normally what happens when you get a bus."

"It's not a bus, Kurt."

"I know it's not, Theodore. I was being ..."

"Stupid?"

"Guys, guys. Let's just be thankful we're all together and in one piece. Home can wait until we find out where we are and why we're here," Tommy said.

Mikey was handed a set of fresh clothes and trainers by the same woman who unhooked his harness. After she left them alone, he sat down, while still coming to terms with the collision of fading and returning memories.

"It gets easier," Daisy said, after vacating the adjacent room in her change of clothes.

The two siblings hugged, releasing an emotional overload which was too much for the entire group. For the first time in what felt like years, the Horsemen were reunited.

Mikey used the couple of minutes everyone needed to compose themselves to get dressed. "Life is jumbled right now," he said.

"Welcome to my world, twenty-four seven," Ted remarked.

"Am I back for good?"

"You bet your ass you are," Daisy replied.

"How am I a teenager?" Mikey asked.

"It's a long story, but we've got these," Ted said, showing off his bracelet.

Mikey's reaction implied he only just realized he still had his bracelet on. "Yeah, I remember I used it to attack that shark after it killed ..."

With his friend pausing to come to terms with more grief, Ted continued. "We turned into barrels."

"Barrels?" Tommy asked.

"Yeah, we can do that now."

"A barrel?"

"Uh-huh, yellow, floaty, you know, the norm."

"Huh, lucky for you that ... you know what, I'm stumped."

"I think, due to the bracelet's synchronization, we returned to our teenage bodies," Daisy added.

"The avatar felt different this time," Mikey said.

"We're linked. Just like the rings," Kurt added, now fully dressed.

"From the game?" Mikey asked.

"Yep."

"We're still playing?"

"Well, we're not on vay-cay," Ted joked.

"It's a long story, Mikey. How are you feeling?" Daisy asked.

"My mind is like a sieve right now," Mikey said.

"It eases over time."

"My entire life, I knew something wasn't right. I just couldn't quite reach out and take it. As far back as I can remember, I must have dreamed a thousand dreams. Been haunted by so many distant screams."

"Ditto," Kurt said.

Ted and Tommy raised their hands in response.

"It's over now. We're back together. That's all that matters," Daisy added.

"I'm sorry about Wilcox," Tommy said.

"Yeah. We had a real bond. I just wish she had gotten back to whatever reality she came from," Mikey said.

"Don't we all," Ted remarked.

"I'm so confused. Why is this happening? Why are we on a cruise liner?"

"I used a reality map to jump from one realm to another," Daisy said.

"We can do that now."

"The easiest way to explain it is it's like stopping at tube stations on your way home."

"So why did you choose a cruise liner?" Ted asked.

"I didn't. I just opened the door. Where we end up is not on me."

"Why not use it again?" Mikey asked.

"We can only use it once a day. In that time, we need to reach the outer limits of the realm, to find the jump portal. Think of it as turning a page of a book," Tommy said.

"Okay. Life is starting to make more sense now. And where is here?"

"Arcadian's front yard," Ted said.

"When we entered the black hole, we entered his realm. I then cheated the rules to beat him." Tommy's guilty look implied he had been dreading this conversation ever since he'd found out about Arcadian's mind tricks.

"I'm starting to recall. Why do you look worried?" Mikey asked.

"Kurt sucker punched me earlier."

"You shoulda ducked," Ted muttered.

"I don't blame you at all. Mr. Nobody changed the rules at every turn," Mikey said.

"Yeah, but it was *his* game," Tommy added.

"A sadistic one at that," Kurt remarked.

"If I remember correctly, when this game began, we had one rule - to win. Did you win?" Mikey said.

"Yep, at least I thought I had. Then a few days ago, Daisy came to drag me from my wife and kids, and voila, we're back in the room," Tommy replied.

"You have kids?"

"Yeah. You're all Godparents, by the way."

"Cool," Ted said.

"Sorry, dude. I don't remember a thing about your kids," Kurt said.

"Maybe it was our appleclangers."

"You mean Doppelgangers."

"For the gazillienth time, none of what you experienced was real," Daisy barked.

Mikey turned to his sister. She'd heard the same conversation a hundred times in the last few days.

"Look at your bodies. You're basically the same as you were when we were split up," Daisy continued. "Do the math. You've aged like a day."

"Not exactly the same," Ted said. "When I looked in my pants, my ..."

"Don't finish that sentence," Tommy ordered.

"Okay, whatever." Mikey stood sharply. "Win, lose, cheat, I don't care. We need to end this once and for all. Preferably before I go batshit crazy."

The First Mate walked through the entrance. Smartly dressed, articulate and clean shaven, he entered with a warm smile. "Good morning to you all. I hope you find your clothes to your satisfaction. Now if you will please follow me, our Captain is waiting for you."

Ted's hand shot up. "Do I have time to take a dump first?"

THE bridge crew paid no attention to the group of teenagers as they entered accompanied by the First Mate and a two-man security escort.

The vessel's hub was surrounded by an endless horizon of a calm ocean and a dark-green atmosphere, which appeared to be gathering pace towards the vessel.

At the center of it all, Captain Dillinger, a lean, stern looking individual, turned his swivel chair to face the new arrivals.

"Thank you for rescuing us," Mikey said, offering a greeting of an outstretched hand.

Dillinger hesitated, leaving Mikey with the view that he had no wish to reciprocate.

"What ocean is this?" Tommy asked to cut the tension.

"Billy!" Ted joked, much to everyone's annoyance.

"Not cool, dude," Kurt said.

Ignoring the teenagers' remarks, Dillinger paced towards the bow window. "Welcome aboard the Arcanutica. The most expensive and luxurious cruise liner ever built. We are currently crossing the South Chimera Sea."

The teenagers shared the same puzzled expression.

"We call our vessel the joy ride," Dillinger's eerie grin left a lot to be desired.

"We've got something similar," Ted said.

"Oh, really."

"Don't do it," Kurt said, knowing his friend would say it anyway.

"Yeah, we call it our *friend ship*," Ted remarked.

Dillinger turned away, bored with the conversation even before it began.

"And what is your final destination?" Mikey asked.

On the radar system, Dillinger pointed at one particular spot. "Right there."

The teenagers gathered around the screen, expecting to see a landmass of some kind. Instead, the image appeared as an endless ocean, with no land in sight.

"Is something wrong with your eyesight?" Ted asked.

"That is our destination. You cannot see it due to the unusual atmospheric occurrence that is causing disruption to our MCP," Dillinger added.

"MCP?" Mikey remarked.

"Our Master Control Program. It has full control of our satellite imagery and navigation. It's top of the range. We spared no expense."

"By atmospheric disturbance. I presume you mean those green clouds," Mikey said.

"We change course, and they are following right behind. It's very strange."

"Clouds move, dude. Don't get me started on icebergs," Ted answered.

"We are nowhere near icebergs," the First Mate replied.

"Maybe they're skybergs."

"There is no such thing as a skyberg."

"Have you ever seen one?"

"Well, no, but …"

"Why are you kids here, in the middle of the ocean?" Dillinger snarled, eyeballing the teenagers one by one.

"That's a good question," Mikey said, looking at Kurt.

"And one we shall answer for you," Kurt added, turning to Tommy.

"It's a long story. There is no need for any of us to bore you with it," Tommy added.

"Passengers paid thousands for this trip and yet here you are. In the middle of nowhere. With no parents. No luggage. No petrol. No food. No water. No money. Just a speedboat, and sarcastic comments about skybergs," Dillinger said.

"Crazy, huh," Ted said.

"Indeed. Now answer the question, before I have you all thrown overboard. Why are you joyriding near my vessel?"

Beep ... Beep ...

"Captain, I have something here." The female sonar operator remained fixated by what appeared to be a sphere rising beneath the vessel.

Beep… Beep…

"What is that?" Dillinger asked.

"I don't know sir, but whatever it is, it's big."

The sphere continued to rise until it dwarfed the silhouette of the Arcanautica.

"Probably just a pod of whale," the First Mate suggested.

"Moving at 31 knots, sir, I doubt it," the sonar operator responded.

"Where did it come from?"

"Directly beneath us. Sizeable, still moving at incredible speed."

Beep… Beep… Beep…

"Transfer it to the main screens," Dillinger asked.

On the ceiling mounted VDU array, images were split between the sonar images of the sphere and the submerged downturned cameras located on each side of the hull.

"I don't see anything. How far away is it?" the First Mate asked.

"One hundred and sixty meters, rising fast." The sonar operator glanced at her Captain for reassurance.

Dillinger's focal point remained the nearest screen.

Beep … Beep … Beep … Beep…

"One hundred and twenty meters …"

Beep ... Beep ... Beep ... Beep ...

"Eighty meters."

Hazy images showed something rising quicker than the sonar operator could advise the crew of the distance. The sphere appeared to be unravelling into a mass of churning tendrils. No, not tendrils. A central core, with coiling, enormous sea serpents at its peak.

The sphere struck the hull with enough power to bowl over anyone standing upright. All over the Arcanutica, passengers ran in a state of panic.

"I hate to state the obvious, but someone just released the Kraken," Ted said, climbing to his feet.

"Send out a mayday, now. Find out what hit us, and get these kids out of here," Dillinger barked as a second impact set off alarm bells throughout the ship.

PANDEMONIUM reached every niche of the vessel, leaving the two-man security team unable to find sanctuary for the five teenagers.

Haunting screams, emanating from the highest reaches and down to the belly of the vessel, failed to drown out the abandon ship warning being presented over the PA system. The inevitable fear parade that followed snatched as many passengers as it could. Friends and families fought to the death to board the lifeboats; carnage swept across the main deck.

"Where are you going?" Daisy asked the security team, who had chosen their own safety over and above the teenagers.

"You can't just leave us here," Kurt remarked.

"I think they don't give a shit," Ted said.

Stranded in a corridor between the passenger staterooms, the teenagers headed upstairs towards the Curtain Call Lounge. The inevitable stampede for survival from one area to the next left a trail of trampled food and spilled drinks on the plush carpets. As they entered the open plan area, passengers ran by, screaming of the terrors rampaging through the vessel.

"That thing with the snakehead, was that a Timeinator?" Tommy asked.

"I'd put my money it," Daisy replied.

"They're finding us quicker."

"Timeinators were responsible for killing my team?" Mikey asked.

"Yep. They've been chasing us since we took the map," Daisy added.

"Then it's time we fought back."

"Why not become the ship and just sink us," Ted remarked.

"That's not how it works," Kurt replied.

"Oh. really."

"Yeah."

"How do you know?"

"Cos, it's stupid, Ted."

"They became car transporters and nearly crushed us," Tommy said.

"That's also stupid."

"We became barrels," Ted remarked.

"Again, stupid."

"Not as stupid as you."

"Will you two shut up for a minute," Mikey barked. "Which way do we go?"

"Over here." Tommy pointed towards a sign which read 'Grand Auditorium'.

Much like a motion picture theatre, hundreds of empty seats faced a stage and screen. The movie left running, called Deep Rising, had reached the pinnacle of no return, where the heroes faced off against the inevitable big bad monster from the deep.

Behind the drawn curtains at the rear of the room were two exit signs. To the portside, were the 'Kids Club' and a 'Play Pool'. To starboard, the 'Commodore 64 Club' and 'Commando Casino'. The options left the teenagers with less of an idea of how to escape than when they entered the theatre.

"Great, we can either get drunk or use Playdoh," Ted said.

"We need to get outside somehow," Kurt added.

"The jetski launch," Tommy said.

"And go where? There is no land nearby."

A middle-aged man, covered in someone else's blood, ran through the starboard exit, screaming in an English accent, "The ship's infested! The bloody things are everywhere."

A few moments passed before a mother and son ran in through the portside exit.

"What happened, mom? What happened to those other kids?" the boy asked.

"I don't know, son. The ship came to a sudden, violent stop. And then suddenly, they were everywhere," the mum replied.

"I'm scared, mom."

"Excuse me." Tommy reached out for the woman.

"What do you want?" She backed off, keeping her son behind her.

"Do you know the quickest way to the jet-ski launch?"

"The quickest way is through there," she replied, jabbing a thumb in the direction she just came from. "But I wouldn't go that way if I were you."

"Please."

"Fine. Head up one deck, beyond the conference suites and wellness center and spa. They're all over that area now. Giant snakes, I think. Or eels. It's difficult to explain. I was in such a panic, we just ran."

"Where did they come from?" Daisy asked.

"Through the floor, the walls, the water pool. They snatched kids and …" Suddenly remembering her son was listening, the lady stopped and hugged him.

"Come with us," Mikey suggested.

"There is nowhere safe to go," the lady replied before she exited the auditorium.

"Looks like we have no choice but to fight our way out," Daisy said.

"It's time to power up," Tommy said.

"Good idea. Let's wreck the ship and worry about the details later." Ted nodded, raising his clenched fist to his chin and then stopping altogether. "Wait, how do we power up?"

The boys turned to Daisy for guidance.

"How the hell should I know. With the shark, I had a strategy and *hey presto*, we were thirty-gallon plastic DOT barrels," she replied as the cinema screen behind them shattered, showering the area in debris.

THE arrow shaped head of a colossal sea serpent floated above the stage. Its solid, oily, reptilian body, as wide as an eighteen-wheeler, had enough armor to rival a Panzer tank.

The beast appeared more dragon than snake, with a lengthy mane of white hair along its neck, and winglike fins beside its spine.

"That's not something you see every day," Ted remarked as the huge head snapped in their direction.

The teenagers backed away as a group, the sea snake's flaming red eyes narrowing as it focused on their movements.

"If we're going to power up, I suggest we do it now," Kurt said, his legs trembling as the sea snake's split tongue toyed with eight foot long, razor sharp teeth dripping with venom.

"Guys, we're in big trouble," Mikey said as two more serpents emerged through the two exits, slithering their way towards the youngsters.

With the same traits, but with green and black hair and wings, the serpents appeared to be smaller and possibly lower down the hierarchy than the more dominant serpent with the white mane.

"I'm hedging a bet here, but those look like Timeinators to me," Ted remarked.

"Then it's time to kick their ass. Do what I do." Tommy held out his clenched fist.

Each of his friends followed suit, their fists knocking together, connecting their bond of friendship. To their surprise, it worked.

Whatever powered the bracelets synchronized, sending enough shudders through their bodies for their teeth to chatter.

"How do we pick?" Ted needed to yell due to the whirlwind of energy enveloping the group.

"Last time, I said presto," Daisy cried out.

"Did you say presto?"

Before she could respond, what felt like the world's most powerful shot of adrenaline surged from her bracelet, through her body, and into the deepest reaches of her mind.

Daisy blacked out everything around her. All that remained was her energy. It felt incredible, even better than what she experienced from the first time she used Tobias's power ring. She now just needed to pick her champion.

THE same energy now coursed through each teenager, but Ted's imagination clogs rotated dangerously out of control.

Daisy said presto.

He tried to imagine a heroic team able to defeat three sea serpents of massive proportions.

Why presto?

He imagined a team strong enough to overcome the three Timeinators once and for all.

Presto? Presto!

"Ranger, barbarian, magician, cavalier and acrobat," Ted rattled off, much to his friends' surprise.

"This isn't Dungeons and Dragons, Ted," Kurt bemoaned, whilst wondering why he was now armed with a huge, wooden club and nothing else to combat an enemy that had already eaten through most of the passengers.

Kurt remained ignorant of the fact that, throughout the game, he had been considered the group's muscle. An enforcer. Arming him with a barbarian's club seemed the most appropriate way for the teenager to release his recent pent-up anger issues.

"Ted, when I said presto, I didn't mean the magician," Daisy said.

"I couldn't help it. I tried to think of the most harmless thing. Something I loved from my childhood. Something that could never possibly destroy us. Tiamat, from the 1983 cartoon. A five head dragon, and the only being powerful enough to defeat Venger."

"Harmless," Tommy blurted.

"In Mesopotamian times, Tiamat was another word for sea serpent, or sea dragon. I kind of put two and two together …"

"… and came up with the worst possible combination," Daisy said as a magical energy bow, able to replenish with an endless supply of energy projectiles, appeared in her hands.

The ranger's weapon had no bow string until she drew back her hand into a firing position. Now locked in place, the energy projectile nestled perfectly in its niche. As her friends' alterations continued, she fired off a volley of arrows to keep the serpents at bay. Ted's choice suddenly didn't suck as much as she first thought it did.

"When will you ever start thinking straight," Mikey snarled.

A magical shield appeared in his hands, with a lightweight frame, yet sturdy enough to block any attack. He slotted his forearm through the holding straps and secured the shield close to his chest. Being chosen as a cavalier brought forth one of his finest attributes - bravery. Somehow the bracelet's power gave him purpose, a reason to be the protector of the group. Such power would only be designated to those who were worthy.

Caught under the spell of a power trip, Mikey had no idea Ted was trying to get his attention by waving a hand in front of him.

"Mikey has gone bye-bye," Ted said. "What have you got, Tommy?"

"I've got a toothpick," Tommy said, referring to a stick no longer than six inches.

"It's not what it looks like."

"Dude, it's a stick."

"It's so much more. Grip it tight and jerk. Watch it grow."

"What the hell are you talking about?" Daisy asked.

"It's his shaft. I'm trying to make it longer."

"Dude, you're sick," Kurt rattled off.

"What! No! That's gross! It's his Javelin staff. It can grow as long as six feet and is unbreakable."

"Dude, it's no staff. It's a stick. I've got like the worst weapon ever," Tommy replied.

"It's not my fault. The bracelets chose the avatars. All I thought about was presto."

As soon as the words left his throat, from Ted's fists two energy beams missed Tommy by a hair's breadth. The bolts ripped through the hull, showering daylight on the auditorium that would soon become a battle arena between five mystical teenagers and a trio of ferocious sea serpents.

"Nice shooting, Tex," Tommy said, ducking out the way as Ted tried to control his energy waves.

"Aim at something that won't sink the ship," Daisy growled, grabbing Ted's shoulders, and shifting him in the vicinity of the closest sea serpent.

Ted's energy beams ripped through the sea serpent's body, decapitating it.

Like an out-of-control spring, the serpent's headless body whipped across the auditorium, smashing a pathway through lines of seats. As the first drop of blood hit the deck, the teenagers suddenly realized the serpents had acid for blood.

To protect his friends from the acid rain spewing all over the auditorium, Mikey raised his shield overhead and produced an electrical field wide enough to surround them all. As the acid ran down the barrier, it started to eat its way through the floor to the decks below.

"We need to move before the floor gives way," Daisy warned.

With two serpents flanking the group, and the floor to the front eroding, the only viable escape route was backwards.

Still under cover of the force field, the group backed away towards the portside exit leading to the Kids Club and Play Pool.

Every few feet the sea serpents attacked by slamming their jaws around the barrier. Electric shocks forced them into a retreat; the group knew it would only be a matter of time before the Timeinators penetrated the barricade.

With his power waning, Mikey threw aside his shield and the teenagers fled through the exit to a Kids Club, which had been ripped apart at the seams.

THE smaller of the two sea serpents busted through the theatre's exit and continued up one deck. Ignoring the human remains scattered all over the hallways, it tracked the teenagers' scent beyond the damaged conference suites and wrecked wellness center and spa. Turning corners quicker than a Tron light cycle, it was quickly in attack range of the fleeing teenagers.

Kurt smelt the decay on the serpent's breath as its jaws widened for attack, the fresh venom ready to melt human flesh quicker than an acid bath.

With no thought for his own safety, the group's enforcer swung his club with all his might. The solitary hit was all it took to slam the serpent into the bulkhead, splattering brain matter, acid blood and goo all over the corridor.

With the club melting in his hands, Kurt threw down his weapon and rushed after his friends.

LEAVING Tommy behind to search the lobby for the ignition keys, Daisy, Mikey, and Ted made their way down the steps to the Jetski launch, which was in darkness.

"*There is no esssscape ...*"

It was hard to pinpoint the exact whereabouts that the snakelike hiss came from. Daisy drew back her bow to illuminate the launch bay. Tiamat's entire body blocked out the daylight and their escape route. Choosing not to waste her energy on a hide that appeared too armored to penetrate, she backed away.

TOMMY found five sets of keys by the time Kurt caught up to him.

"Where's the other serpent?" he asked.

"He joined a club," Kurt replied, gesturing with empty hands.

"That's the shittiest one-liner."

"I disagree. Arnie would be proud."

The two friends entered the stairwell only to find the sea serpent Ted named Tiamat blocking their friends escape. Using the shadows as cover, they made their way down the steps, and along a wall to the docked jet-skis.

"ARE you one of *his* goons?" Mikey asked, referring to Arcadian.

"*I am sssso much more,*" Tiamat said.

"I doubt that."

"*It mattersssss not. Your journey endssss here.*"

"Are you Tiamanator? You see what I did there?" Ted joked.

"You've got jokes, now," Mikey snarled.

"I'm about to die, sue me."

"*You know why we are here?*" Tiamat snarled.

"You're in our way. And that's about to change. He's all yours, Ted," Mikey said.

"My pleasure." Ted clenched his fists and aimed at Tiamat. "Presto!" His hands tingled a little, a few intermittent sparks implying his power had been used up earlier. "I think I'm out of juice."

"Already," Daisy snapped.

"I killed one of them, didn't I."

"Only because I helped you."

"Where are your friendssss?" Tiamat's body coiled, his frustration and aggressive demeanor boiling over every time he spoke. *"Where issss Tommy?"*

"Right here, asshole." Tommy gunned the accelerator of a two-seater jet-ski and raced across the bay towards Daisy.

She reached out, and he hoisted her aboard. She clung on around his waist as the Jetski cut across the water towards Tiamat, and certain death.

Out of the serpent's view, Kurt, Mikey, and Ted boarded their own jet-skis.

"*Come, Tommy. Let ussss embrace at lasssst.*" Tiamat appeared to welcome the challenge with jaws wide enough to swallow them whole.

"He knows your name," Daisy remarked.

"I guess I'm famous in these parts. Ready your bow. When I say fire, aim for his eyes and blind this asshole," Tommy said.

With the distance shortening by the second, Tommy goaded Tiamat enough for him to unwind his body and lunge for the approaching jet-ski.

"Now!" Tommy yelled.

Daisy's energy projectile exploded in front of the sea serpent, forcing it to twist away from the exit and slam into the bulkhead.

The ploy to blind Tiamat worked perfectly. With enough room to breakout, the four jet-skis used the launch ramp to escape the bay.

Unable to track his prey by relying on his sight, Tiamat tracked their vibrations and launched through the opening after them.

"He's on our ass," Kurt yelled back from the lead jet-ski.

Tommy purposely slowed down as Tiamat's tailfin cut through surf with more menace than a Megalodon's dorsal fin.

"Keep going," he ordered, not caring for his friends replies.

"What do we do?" Daisy asked from the rear seat.

"Swap places with me." Tommy kept his hand on the accelerator right up to the moment he switched positions with Daisy.

"Where are you going?" she asked.

"I'm not going anywhere, but you need to slow us down."

"I need to do what?" Daisy swiveled with enough force to almost lose control of the jet-ski.

"Whoa, whoa. Eyes front, Miss Daisy. When I say go, you accelerate the hell out of this thing."

Tiamat's smoothness through the water had him upon the two-seater jet-ski in no time at all. With his spring set jaws lunging from the surf, he was ready to snatch the two teenagers and pulverize them into oblivion.

Suddenly surrounded by rows of razor-sharp teeth, Tommy aimed what appeared to be a futile punch at the center of the serpent's open jaws.

With his jaws slamming shut, the overconfident Timeinator had overlooked one small thing. Tommy's weapon. The expected explosion of salty blood and plump flesh never came. The sea serpent jolted suddenly, his body twisting wildly as an unbreakable, super extended Javelin wedged open the most devasting jaws in the ocean.

"Go! Go! Go!" Tommy ordered.

Daisy needed no second invitation. She gunned the accelerator, leaving Tiamat in their wake, his jaws wedged open for an eternity.

Chapter 24

Walking through the Sands of Time

"DRY LAND, never again will I take you for granted." Ted crouched, running his fingers through the golden sands of a beach.

"I'm never going near the ocean again," Kurt bemoaned.

"Lucky for us, we had just enough gas to reach this island," Mikey added.

"And yet the radar aboard the vessel showed no signs of land for miles," Tommy said.

"It's like someone put the island here for us to find," Daisy added.

"Or something went our way for a change," Ted suggested.

"How did you get Tiamat off our ass?" Kurt asked Tommy.

"I used my stick to wedge open his jaws. He won't be eating anything for a while." Tommy's smile was directed at Ted.

"I told you your staff was special. You just needed to yank hard and make it bigger," Ted replied.

"Enough with the puns," Mikey stated.

"What did I say?"

"I guess I owe you one, Ted," Tommy said.

"We'll call it even."

The teenagers left behind the beach and made their way towards the palm tree lined woodland.

"Something has been bothering me," Mikey said as he ventured through the brush. "The bracelets power didn't seem to last very long."

"It reminds me of my first sexual experience," Ted said.

"I really don't wanna listen to this," Daisy remarked as she made her way to the front of the group.

"Hear me out, D."

"I'd rather not."

"Unlike the battle against the shark, we didn't become *weapons*, or avatars. We were teenagers, *handling* the weapons. We haven't done that before."

"You got lucky, Ted. We could've easily have ended up on the floor, not able to move," Kurt said.

"Maybe the power didn't last as long as the rings because only one of us chose."

"He's made a good point," Mikey said.

"For a change," Kurt joked.

"So, what you're saying, if we choose as a team, rather than individually, we might have more power when we fight," Tommy said.

"Makes sense," Mikey said.

"We'll only know for sure next time the need arises," Kurt said.

"That might be sooner than you think." Daisy stopped suddenly, her outstretched hand touching a wall of glass. With the boys' minds elsewhere, each of them walked into the obstacle. "Watch your step," Daisy joked.

"You could've warned us," Tommy said.

"Where's the fun in that?"

An unbroken glass barricade blocked any further route through the brush. There was no way around or over it. The only exit was to go back the way they came.

"Whatever it is, it stretches all the way through the forest," Kurt said.

"I know what it's for," Ted replied.

"I don't care."

"It's the truth."

"I said we don't care."

"We just have to say his name five times."

"You mean the Candyman?"

"I do mean the Candyman."

"Candyman is a dumbass."

"Say that to his face when he turns up and guts you like a pig."

"You know what. We've all had enough of your stupidity, Ted."

"But I really know."

"Nobody cares."

"The Candyman only shows up when you use a mirror," Mikey said.

"Is anybody taking count of how many times we've said his name?" Ted asked.

"The sun is reflecting off the surface," Daisy added.

"It looks thick," Tommy replied, after rapping his knuckles against it.

"A bit like Ted," Kurt snarled.

"You know what, ever since you changed from that cop, you've been a real douchebag," Ted snapped.

"I said a bit like you. Not all of you."

"Still harsh, dude."

"Okay, hotshot. What is stopping us from progressing further?"

"It's simple. It's a television screen."

The group shared the joke, before realizing, for once, Ted meant what he said. For a few moments they stared at a reflective piece of glass, hundreds of meters wide, and as tall as the cruise liner they just escaped from.

"How can it be a television screen?" Daisy asked.

"It's simple. The sun always shines on tv," Ted replied, pointing at the sun's reflection on the glass.

"Ha, ha," Tommy replied, sarcastically.

"I think he's right," Mikey said, cupping his hands against the glass to try and look through to the other side.

"If it *is* a television screen, then who is watching us through it?" Kurt asked.

As if answering the question, a dimensional doorway opened before them. The opening gave way to a daunting infinite void of nothingness.

"Darkness is always inviting," Kurt said.

"It seems to be the theme around these parts," Ted added.

Tommy turned to Daisy. "Can we use the map?"

She studied the map and shook her head. "The other portals were glowing. This seems more like a diversion."

"We won't know where this goes unless we use it," Mikey said.

"I don't think we've got much of a choice," Kurt replied.

"Good call, Kurt." Ted turned to Daisy. "Ladies first."

Chapter 25

Intermission

THE DIMENSIONAL doorway took no more than a few seconds for the teenagers to phase through. Darkness gave way to light and a familiar voice.

"Welcome back, horsemen and horsewoman."

The teenagers had reached the bridge of the craft belonging to Tobias Strong.

"That sounds like Tobias. And I'm pleased to report, that was the easiest entrance I've had for a while," Ted said, walking like a lamb across an iced lake.

Momentary blindness meant the teenagers overlooked the concern on the flat screen AI embodiment of their former mentor. Tobias's giraffe-like neck rose as high as it could, more from the sight of seeing his former proteges covered in blood, grime, and general nastiness, than anything else.

Rather than startle them, he decided to wait a few moments before he spoke again. "How do you all feel?" he asked.

"Tobias?" Tommy asked hesitantly.

The flat screen bowed, as if greeting royalty. Unable to control his emotions, and despite the awkwardness of the elongated neck, Tommy hugged Tobias for as long as he could.

"When Daisy said you were alive, I thought you'd be bigger." Tommy took a step back, still unsure of why Tobias resembled an eighties science fiction cartoon character, rather than his old human body.

"It's good to see you as well, Tommy," Tobias said, before facing Mikey.

"Tobias, what happened to you?" Mikey asked.

"It's a long story," Tobias replied.

"Not as long as your neck," Ted joked. "Tell them about the Beta unit."

"Maybe another time, Ted."

"How did we get here?" Daisy asked.

"You travelled through a dimensional doorway. They are rarely used because they can be tracked easily by Timeinators if the reality map is nearby. Thankfully for us, there is only the one map, and it has not seen the light of day for many a decade."

"You mean this map," Daisy said, holding up the parchment.

"It that is the map, they'll already be tracking our whereabouts."

"I took it. It's my fault," Tommy said.

"It now makes sense how you have traversed realities so frequently."

"I was guided by a man called Connell McLeod."

"McLeod," Tobias said, a magnifying glass raising on the screen along with some digital eyebrows made from solid rectangles. "There's a name I haven't heard in a long time."

"Then you know him?" Daisy asked.

"Well, of course I know him. He's me."

"How is that possible?"

"I know what you did. When your Beta unit uploaded your consciousness into the digital dominion, you spawned new identities," Kurt remarked, jokingly at first.

"That's correct," Tobias replied.

"Lucky guess," Ted said.

"When I met McLeod, why didn't you confide in me? We spent enough time together. You basically taught me everything I know, and got me to this planet singlehanded," Daisy said.

"It's not as straightforward as it sounds. McLeod is me, but he is on an entirely different pathway. When he set out, he knew very little of you, as did I when we last saw each other. He knew your face, and your name. And that he needed to seek you out. That is all the information I could provide. The whereabouts of the map he must have worked on alone."

"Then you'll be sad to hear that he is no longer with us."

"Oh, I'm so sorry, Daisy. I had no idea."

"He's the reason I'm here. Without him, I'd still be stuck in Rosewood Falls."

"Are there any other Tobias's floating around the ether we can call on for help?" Mikey asked.

"I have no control over my other consciousnesses. They may seek you out. Or they may not. Only time will tell."

"And by using the doorway, we've just made things a hundred times worse for you," Tommy stated.

"I would have still opened it had I to know you had the map in your possession. I have watched you almost every step of the way, but even my eyes are unable to see and hear everything."

"And you waited right until the last minute to open up a doorway?" grumbled Ted.

"It's not as easy as that, Ted. Daisy had to find you all and you all had to agree to leave of your own accord. I could not interfere until the last moment. Timing was everything. I did my best to explain this last time we were together."

"I mean before Tiamat tried to kill us would've been better timing. Just saying."

"How do we stop them finding us?" Tommy asked.

"We can't. Not now. They are already on their way," Tobias added.

"We're not losing you again."

"Tommy, I'm just your guide. Nothing more. Besides, you do know I'm merely a screen, on a long neck. I don't have anything magical I can use to assist you."

"We'll use our bracelets to protect you," Mikey said.

"Bracelets, you say?"

"Yeah, but the power runs out quickly. You got any tips?"

To study the bracelet closer, Tobias held up Mikey's wrist. The same magnifying glass appeared on the screen, with a separate window showing a running diagnostic.

"Hmmm, it's a clever contraption. Where did you get it?" Tobias asked.

"McLeod," Daisy added.

"Of course, of course. I see some of my own work here. My brief examination of the power cells seems to imply they can be accessed only once every twenty-four hours. The central core allows temporary usage, no more than five to ten minutes perhaps. The drain depends on how much power the avatar needs to access to defend itself. If your power is depleted, shut down and recharge will lead to alteration from avatar back to teenager. Perhaps stagger your usage, otherwise you may well leave yourselves open to attack. More importantly, there appears to be one other parameter. Once an avatar has been chosen by any of you, you cannot use it again. I suggest you choose wisely."

"Choose wisely. Where have I heard that before," Ted joked.

"Thank you, Tobias. I hate to rush you, but where do we go from here?" Daisy asked.

"To reach Earth, you need to venture through the black hole," For dramatic effect, Tobias swiveled towards the stretched windscreen.

"Again!" Ted said.

Tobias turned awkwardly towards the teenagers. "That is your only option. You either leave or stay here and die at the hands of the Timeinators."

"How do we reach the black hole?" Mikey asked.

"Retrace your steps. How did you arrive here?"

"From the black hole, we crashed in the wasteland and used the sail barge. Then we crossed the computer city in a Winnebago. Then we reached *his* lair. Reverse that, and we cross the city, the wasteland, and the black hole will be stage three. Simple."

"Lucky for us we've got three more jumps," Daisy said.

"The environments will not be how you remember them. After your arrival, Arcadian changed everything. It will be harder this time. Once you cross the wasteland, you will need to find a way back through the black hole."

"That's impossible," Mikey said.

"Not if we combine to becomes the world's tallest ladder to reach it," Ted said, seriously.

"If we all become a ladder. How do we climb up said ladder?" Kurt asked.

"I'm still working on that."

"Do not forget where you are, Mikey," Tobias added. "Nothing is impossible."

"What about my kids?" Tommy said.

"Your children should not be your concern. What you remember is a distraction used in an accelerated lifeline," Tobias said.

"Do you know where they are?"

Tobias nodded.

"Tell me." Tommy noticed the warning lights flashing throughout the bridge before the alarm bells began.

"There is no time. The Timeinators have found us," Tobias added.

Tobias's only protector, Sergeant Major Hero, a Sentry Bot powered by a unique Iranium crystal, rolled forwards from his guard station. The silver sphere came to a halt in front of the teenagers.

"*Sergeant Major Hero reporting for duty, sir.*" His strip for a mouth glowed, his tone that of a drill sergeant.

The craft shuddered as something clamped on the vessel.

"Prepare to engage, my old friend," Tobias ordered.

"Tobias, where are my children?" Tommy demanded.

"I don't have the time. You must hurry," Tobias answered.

Heavy drilling could be heard from above as the Timeinators' new forms tunneled through the ship's hull.

The Sentry Bot rolled backwards until facing the ceiling bulkhead, his bulbous eyes focusing on the flashes being made as something cut through. From either side of his eye sockets, two small openings revealed two thin laser weapons.

"They're breaking through," Mikey said.

"Then we confront them," Kurt added.

"You cannot stop them here. Flee, you fool," Tobias ordered. Fearing an imminent hull breach, Tobias opened a portal at the rear of the bridge. "Use it to reach the next stage," he ordered.

"No. We're not losing you again," Tommy said.

"Have faith, Tommy. Others will help you."

Holding the map tightly, Daisy grabbed Tommy by the arm and dragged him towards the portal. Mikey, Kurt, and Ted waited for them. Unlike the dimensional doorway, the portal had a welcoming glow about it.

Tommy turned at the last moment as three giant, spiderlike robots breached the hull. The Sentry Bot opened fire.

In the seconds before the ceiling crushed Tobias's robot form, he overhead Daisy uttering the words, 'take us closer to home'.

DAY SIX

(Two jumps remaining)

Chapter 26

Running on a knife-edge

MONTH - DAY HOUR - MIN
FEB 08 REPLICANT 23:12
REALITY DESTINATION

TOMMY WEPT.

To lose so many so close to him, in such a short space of time, came across as a cruel twist of fate. Had he not cheated to win, would things have turned out differently? Would his decisions going forwards alter the outcome?

In reaching such a critical point in his life, it left the teenager thinking how much more could one person take.

"We need to move," Daisy said, still holding Tommy by the arm.

Since Daisy had arrived, he barely had time to rest.

It felt like a constant theme.

Arrive. Survive. Flee. Repeat.

Momentarily blinded by the time jump, Tommy let himself be led through what sounded like a bustling street. He had no idea that crowds had stopped to witness five teenagers wearing grimy, bloodied clothes suddenly emerge on the sidewalk in a concentrated, electrical storm.

The teenagers ran for ten blocks through a dystopian futuristic city, full of towering skyscrapers stacked next to one another. Slowly the city unraveled its seedy side of a society run off crude street markets, and bootleg advertisements brandishing anything from erotica to cyberpunk enhancements. In a state of chaos, street venders pedaled new age drugs. Gangs battled for supremacy. Cybernetic hookers on each corner dangled every fantasy known to man in the hope for a cheap buck.

Tobias's warning rung true. The city had changed, and not for the better.

The teenagers entered an unoccupied alleyway and hid behind a row of dumpsters. Hover cars continued overhead in an endless cycle of traffic; the green shades caused by the comet's tail visibly fused with the night sky in a spectacular revamp.

"This isn't the city I remember," Kurt said.

"It's worse," Mikey added.

"To me, this place is home," Ted said.

"You lived behind a dumpster," Kurt remarked.

"No. The city. Well, not this city. I was living this life, in a different city. In fairness to us, the last time we visited, we did spend most of the time in the urban assault vehicle. Maybe we missed the seedy side."

Daisy noticed how distant Tommy had become since they exited the portal. She had no idea he had witnessed Tobias being killed for a second time. The first time being his demise in the original game.

"Are you okay?" To force eye contact, she squeezed his hand. It worked to some degree.

He glanced sideways, trying to cling on to the fading memories of his old life and those of his missing children. "He died." Tommy's bluntness drew the attention of his friends. "As the Timeinators broke through. The ceiling collapsed. Tobias was crushed."

After a few moments' silence, Kurt spoke first. "Dude, there wasn't much we could've done about it."

"We could've fought them off," Tommy replied.

"We have fought them off. They keep coming at us. They're unstoppable," Ted said.

"Maybe we owed it to him to stick around and try."

"He made us leave," Mikey said.

"We ran. Like we always do. It's what we're best at."

"We're just kids," Kurt said.

"Kurt's right. We're kids and Tobias was only protecting us," Daisy added.

"Do you know what I've lost? My wife, my children. My mum, dad, Teddy and now Tobias has died in front of me for a second time," Tommy said.

"We all felt the pain the first time. He died in front of all of us," Ted said.

"We've all lost something," Mikey said.

"You're not the only one," Kurt added.

To be alone with his thoughts, Tommy walked along the alleyway to the rear of a locked second-hand electrical store. Behind a grilled shutter, white noise played on all but one of the television screens on display.

The only working television showcased a live news report, between a young female reporter and an overweight police captain, referred to as Captain Emile Bryant. The reporter's yellow jump suit stood out in front of a background of a police cordon, flashing red and blue lights, and groups of bystanders.

Tommy hadn't heard a word of the interview. He didn't need to. Bryant stoked on a plump cigar; his eyes unable to mask the fact that he was hiding something from the reporter.

As the report continued, video footage emerged of Tommy and his friends appearing in the electrical storm and then fleeing across the street.

"Guys, you better get over here," he said. From the ground Tommy picked up a metal rod and poked it through the grating to break a section of the glass window. Reaching inside, he turned up the volume on the television.

His friends were soon by his side and taking in the news report for themselves.

Reporter – "... and where exactly do you think this group came from?"
Bryant – "These aren't the first outsiders we've come across recently. Unlike the others who managed to escape us, we will deal with these visitors accordingly."
Reporter – "You called them visitors. Why?"
Bryant – "As you very well know, Miss O'Connell, early in the 21st Century, the O.C.P Corporation advanced AI evolution into a new phase of miracle technology."

Reporter – "I know all about OCP and their, let me say, advancements and modifications."

Bryant – "If you would like this interview to continue, perhaps you could change your tone?"

Reporter – "Sorry, captain. I didn't mean to upset your employer."

Bryant – "Former employer."

Reporter – "Is there a difference these days."

Bryant – "Miss O'Connell, I don't have time for trivial comments."

Reporter – "I'm sorry, captain. For those watching at home, please expand on OCP's *miracle* technology."

Bryant – "This group resembles teenagers, when in fact, they are state of the art, reproduced, artificial beings."

Reporter – "Artificial?"

Bryant - "Yes, and as you can see from the footage, they are virtually identical to a human."

Reporter – "I agree, it is hard to tell the difference."

Bryant – "We refer to these types as Bootleggers."

Reporter – "Bootleggers, interesting. Witnesses reported the teenagers ..."

Bryant – "Bootleggers."

Reporter – "These *Bootleggers* arrived suddenly. In a ball of electric light."

Bryant – "You've seen the footage. As far as we know, these Bootleggers were off world until they recently escaped by using an advanced form of transport technology."

Reporter – "Escaped from where, exactly?"

Bryant – "That's not important right now. What is important is that we need to warn the public to not let these artificial beings' appearances deceive them These Bootleggers are superior in strength, agility, and intelligence."

Report - "Are they considered dangerous?"

Bryant - "They are as dangerous as dangerous gets."

Reporter – "How exactly do you stop Bootleggers?"

Bryant – "We have called in one of our special tracker units."

Reporter – "To apprehend?"

Bryant – "They have orders to terminate on sight."

Reporter – "You're not going to arrest them?"

Bryant – "When it comes to skin jobs, there is only one rule."

Reporter – "Should your first priority not be to apprehend and question?"

Bryant – "Not when the skin jobs cross a line."

Reporter – "And what line is that?"
Bryant – "That's classified."
Reporter – "Classified by whom?"
Bryant – "That's enough questions for today."
Reporter – "But captain, OCP cannot keep making up their own rules whenever they see fit."
Bryant – "The rule being made is one of my own."
Reporter – "It doesn't look that way to me."
Bryant – "Please let us do our job, Miss O'Connell, and we'll let you do yours. That's all for now."
Reporter – "This is April O'Connell reporting on what the public first described as a visit from above and beyond. What we now know is that we have a group of Bootleggers running loose across the city. Are they dangerous? According to the Police, yes, they are ..."

"This is a ball ache I could do without right now," Kurt said.

"Was it just me, or was that redhead hot?" Ted added.

"Get your head in the game, Ted," Mikey said.

"My head is right where it needs to be."

"That reporter does not believe anything that captain told her," Tommy said.

"What makes you think that?" Kurt asked.

"Just a hunch."

"It's a reporter's job to be suspicious," Mikey said.

"Maybe we can approach her."

"I don't think that's a good idea, dude," Kurt replied.

"I think it's a great idea," Ted said.

"You would," Daisy snarled. "You want to tell her the truth?"

"Why not?" Tommy replied. "Just as we left Tobias, he told me to have faith and that others would help us."

"I don't think he meant the first person we come across," Ted said.

"Does it matter if it's the first, second, or one hundredth?"

"It's a long shot," Kurt remarked.

"It worked for Mikey. If not for his acquaintances, there would be no serum. He doesn't break free from Arcadian's hold. And we're not here, right now contemplating our next steps."

"In theory, I didn't approach them. They were just in my dream state. And a lot of good it did anyway. All but two of them died," Mikey replied.

"That was their choice to help. You didn't force anybody to follow your path."

"Are you certain it was their choice? Before, if McAlester screwed up, he would be the nutjob nobody could trust. Lives are now at stake. My friends' lives, my sister. There's too much at stake to just contact someone we know nothing about."

"Mikey's right. I'm not sure approaching her is a good idea," Daisy said.

Ted raised his hand.

"Nobody cares about your boner for the reporter, Ted," Kurt added.

"What other options do we have?" Tommy asked.

Ted raised his hand again.

"Dude, you say one crude word and I will hit you," Kurt said.

"What if we don't approach her," Ted stated.

"Great input, Ted."

"I mean, what if *we* don't, but an avatar does."

"That's pretty smart," Mikey said.

"Who are you, and what did you do to our Ted," Tommy joked.

"Tobias suggested staggering our choices," Ted said.

"Not that I'm onboard with this, but how do we go about making first contact?" Daisy asked.

"Leave that to me. Well, I say me, but what I really mean is …"

APRIL O'Connell made her way across the soaked sidewalk to a parked hover car with its faded ARCTV news logo on the driver's door. Nearby, groups of bystanders remained behind a police cordon, eager to lap up any reports on the whereabouts of the dangerous Bootleggers.

"You are all fools to believe Bryant," she muttered as she ducked beneath the raised door and settled in the driver's seat.

To access the vehicle's functions on the hi-tech dashboard, she registered the access code AOC1234 on a keypad. A tube emerged from an alcove to the right of the steering wheel. She blew into it once, the breathalyzer recording zero traces of alcohol or drugs.

With her test clear, the automated seatbelt locked her in tight, the closing door sealing her inside.

"Heaters."

After warming her hands in front of the heating vent, O'Connell removed a cigarette from the packet in the glovebox.

"Lighter. Espresso."

It took only a few seconds for the built in lighter to reach the required heat and for a syrupy shot of coffee to appear in a drop-down slot beneath the dashboard. She used that time to twist the VDU to forwards facing. Situated behind the steering wheel, the onboard communicator for face time calls and vehicle navigation showed a series of icons. She tapped on the one that stated *secure line.*

"Computer, contact Editor-in-Chief J. J. Rufus, San Dimas offices. Access code SOCAL, 2688."

On screen, the word *calling* flashed repeatedly.

With nobody answering her call, O'Connell started the engine. Rumbling beneath the chassis, the hover jets gradually reached full power, lifting the news reporter's car a few feet beneath the flows of traffic overhead.

"Autopilot, engage. Computer, redial. Use override code, RYLOS 1984."

Before the call could be started, the screen shut down.

"Not again. Piece of crap. Computer, run a diagnostic."

The screen turned on, flashing a green cursor on a black background. She struck the side, hoping her usual repair action would pay off. When the screen shut down for the second time, she slumped in her seat.

"Just when you thought things couldn't get any worse."

When the cursor reappeared, it flashed incessantly.

"I knew I should've gone for the upgrade."

O'Connell smacked the other side of the screen with her palm. The icons reappeared, faded for a few seconds, and were replaced by an error message.

"You can't upgrade, April. Upgrading costs the type of funds your salary cannot afford."

The error message switched to the black background.

WAKE UP APRIL …

O'Connell glanced at the words written on the screen, the cigarette falling from her lips. "What the … computer, system override."

THAT WON'T WORK …
AND SMOKING WILL KILL YOU …

"Computer, run full system … no, wait. Run a full vehicle diagnostic." O'Connell glanced over at the rear seats. The junk food wrappers, damaged equipment, and piles of dirty clothes remained untouched. She spotted no cameras, nothing tampered with on the dashboard.

TIME TO OPEN YOUR EYES …

"Oh, I'll open something better than that. A can of whoop ass!"
For some reason she opened the glovebox, expecting to see some form of tampering technology.

ARCADIAN HAS US …

"Is that supposed to mean something?"

WHY ELSE WOULD I SAY IT?

"Hey, you're the one interrupting my day."

MAYBE YOU SHOULD CHILL OUT …

"You must be a guy because you never tell a woman to chill out."

IF YOU RELAX, I'll TELL YOU EVERYTHING …

"How about I tell you to go screw yourself. Goodbye."

To clear the message, she pulled the power connector from the rear socket. After a few seconds of a blank screen, the cursor reappeared.

BOO!

She jumped, and then wondered why.

THIS IS TAKING A LOT LONGER THAN I THOUGHT IT WOULD …

"Computer, shut down all dashboard tech. Leave only drive, and hover functions."

THAT WON'T WORK EITHER …

"Computer …"

THAT'S NOT MY NAME …

"Fine, if going along with this game of yours gets rid of you, and me back to my day job, then I'll give you sixty seconds before I purposely crash this piece of junk into a tower block."

LOOK OUTSIDE ...

"I did. It's raining."

NOT AT THE RAIN …

"Please elaborate."

WHAT DOES THAT MEAN?
IT MEANS EXPLAIN, TED …
I KNEW THAT …
THEN WHY ASK ME?
BECAUSE …
JUST REFOCUS, TED.
OKAY, OKAY, FOLLOW THE RABBIT, DUDE …

"Either my coffee has been spiked or I'm dreaming. And I'm not a dude."

JUST FOLLOW THE DAMN RABBIT …
CHILL OUT TED, WE NEED HER HELP …
I AM CHILLING OUT, SHE'S THE ONE WHO IS …

"Ted, is it?"

DUMB ASS, NOW SHE KNOWS MY NAME …
HOW? SHE CAN'T HEAR US …
SHE KNOWS EVERYTHING WE'RE SAYING …
HOW?
THE TECH WE STOLE IS VOICE ACTIVATED. IT TRANSCRIBES EVERYTHING …
SO, WE CAN HEAR HER, BUT SHE'S READING WHAT WE'RE SAYING. WHY DIDN'T WE JUST PHONE HER UP?
OUTTA MY WAY, KURT.
WHAT DID YOU PUSH ME FOR, DUDE …

"I'm out of here…"

ONE OF YOU SAY SOMETHING BEFORE WE LOSE HER …
THIS IS THE ALL AND POWERFUL OZ ASKING YOU TO FOLLOW THE RABBIT …

"The powerful Oz?"

MIKEY, WHY DID YOU SAY THAT?
IT WAS THE FIRST THING THAT CAME TO MIND …
PLEASE IGNORE OZ. THIS IS TEO, I AM YOUR GUIDE …
YOU'RE HER GUIDE?
DUDE, LET ME DO MY THING …

"That's it, I'm crashing the car. Autopilot, disengage."

APRIL, WAIT. OUTTA MY WAY, BOYS …
DAISY, THIS IS MY THING …
YOU'VE HAD YOUR CHANCE. GIMME THE HEADSET …
ALL YOU CHICKS GOT SERIOUS ISSUES …
TED. HEADSET. NOW. DON'T MAKE ME ASK AGAIN …
OKAY, OKAY. HERE …

APRIL, PLEASE. WE NEED YOUR HELP. LOOK OUTSIDE AT THE ADVERTISING BOARDS. FOLLOW THE RABBIT …

On the huge marketing screens across the city, hundreds of advertisements for products ranging from 1000% proof suncream, to reprocessed cuisine, swapped to the nation's most popular, and overplayed, hover car advert. With a fire engine red chassis, the *Halley's Comet* set off on a desert road, racing towards the horizon. Alongside it, the latest model, a white sports car as sleek as any hover racer, overtook on the outside, and raced towards the horizon.

Much to her amazement, the advert she had become so familiar with jumped from advertising displays to holographic billboards, the white blur morphing into a sleek silhouette of a rabbit.

IF YOU WANT A JOB DONE RIGHT. YOU NEED TO LET THE GIRL DO HER THING …
I HAD IT COVERED, DAISY …
COURSE YOU DID, TEO. SHE'S ALL YOURS …

"What the hell is going on. Who are you people?"

YOU'RE ABOUT TO FIND OUT …

"I'm trying to work out if that is a good thing, or a bad thing."

AND ON THAT NOTE, IT'S TIME TO SIT BACK AND LET THE EXPERT DRIVE …

The faster the rabbit advanced, the quicker the car weaved in and out of the lanes of traffic. O'Connell braced the dashboard as the disused side of town, full of derelict buildings, raced by in a blur, everything altering to a celestial veil.

WITH the car at a standstill, April O'Connell sat up like a jack in a box, her driver's seatbelt releasing quicker than any thoughts she might have had about where the rabbit had led her to. Expecting to be in some sort of accident, her vehicle appeared to be in one piece and parked on the rooftop of a deserted tower block.

The entire area remained off limits, due to reports of radiation clouds.

The car dashboard timer indicated she had been unconscious for around five minutes. Three words flashing on and off on the VDU.

KNOCK, KNOCK, APRIL …

Outside the car, a rangy man wearing a headset and a full length, black leather jacket, knocked on her driver's window. He was holding a screen of some kind and was gesturing for her to exit the vehicle.

Instinctively, April reached beneath her seat for a concealed two shot handgun. Opening the door from the inside, she aimed the gun at the stranger.

The man stepped back to shield a teenage girl and three boys, who emerged from behind the remnants of an exploded electrical shack.

"Do you have any food or drink?" The girl looked around sixteen. Her scruffy hair tied off in two buns, her dirty clothes identical to those from the video footage being banded around the news channels.

"I might have, if you can tell me your names?" O'Connell stepped on to the rooftop.

She first noticed the teenagers' disheveled clothes. It wasn't the first time she'd seen kids in such a state. It wouldn't be the last.

"I'm Teo. My friends call me Ted," the man replied. "These are my friends. Daisy, Kurt, Tommy, and Mikey."

Each teenager waved after they were introduced.

"There is no need for the gun," Daisy said.

"If you're the kids from the video, then there's every need," O'Connell said.

"We're not dangerous," Mikey replied. "We're starving, thirsty."

Keeping the gun aimed at the group, April reached into the rear set and removed some reprocessed food packets and a water bottle. "Here. It's not great, but it's all I have. Either that or the world's worst Espresso."

She handed the food packets to the man, who distributed them to the teenagers. The water bottle she handed to the girl.

"Thank you," Ted said.

Tommy ripped open one packet and sniffed the contents. "That's more potent than I'd hoped for. What is it?"

O'Connell shrugged. "You're better off not knowing. It tastes a bit like Turkan."

"Turkan?"

"It's an organic supplement processed at one of the big conglomerate plants. You must have seen them, they're everywhere."

The teenagers paid no attention to her comments, which led her to believe they had no idea what she was referring to. Instead, they chose to share the food and drink like any other starving red-blooded human would.

"I've never seen a skin job eat before," O'Connell said.

"What's a skin job?" Kurt asked, his mouth full of the Turkan gloop.

"A skin job is an artificial person."

"We're not artificial," Daisy said. "At least I don't think we are."

"Which is what a skin job would say. I don't recognize *you* from the footage." O'Connell jabbed the gun at Ted's avatar, Teo. "Five teenagers came out of that transporter."

"I'm one of them," Ted stated.

"You're a Bootlegger?"

"We saw the report. If that's what we've been labelled, then yes."

"Now, don't get me wrong, but unless you start giving me answers, then I'm out of here."

"I'm not sure how you'll manage that. Your car has no power. I've made sure of that. And it's a long way down if you take the stairs."

"Or I could force you to fix my car." O'Connell aimed the gun at Ted.

"We need just a few minutes of your time. After you've heard our story, you're free to go. I promise," Daisy said.

"What about my car?"

"You hear us out, he'll return the power."

"Can he fix the VDU for me?"

Ted nodded, helped himself to the shot of Espresso and then wished he hadn't. "It's cold."

"Because there is no power to keep it warm. Why should I trust you?"

"We're looking for help," Tommy said.

The group looked innocent enough. Which could also be a reason why Bryant said they were dangerous. O'Connell had a choice to make. Start shooting and hope she could outrun a group considered highly dangerous by a police captain that she had never trusted. Or she could listen to their story and see where it led.

O'Connell lowered the gun and sat on the bonnet of the car. "You've got two minutes. Where are you from?"

"Not this city," Daisy said, carefully picking her words.

"Okay, so where? Bryant thinks you're Bootleggers. Is that right?"

"Bryant is right. We're just not what he's portraying us as."

"I have to admit, you don't look dangerous."

"We're not," Tommy said.

"So where are you from?"

"Earth," Mikey replied.

"Never heard of it."

The teenagers shared a knowing look.

"By your reactions, I'm presuming you expected a different answer."

"Not at all," Daisy said. "It's our home planet."

"You're aliens."

"Not exactly. We're just lost. We need help getting home. As quickly as possible."

"What's the urgency?"

"We're being tracked by some serious bad guys. Like ET," Ted said.

"Who is that?" O'Connell asked.

"He's everyone's favorite alien."

"Apart from Alf," Kurt added.

"ET is so much better than Alf," Ted added.

"Is not. Alf is comedic genius."

"It's a short guy in a suit."

"And what was ET?" Kurt crossed his arms.

"A short dude walking on his hands."

"Guys! Sorry, please excuse the children," Daisy said. "Can you help us?"

The reporter's empathetic nature had been the decision maker on so many of her stories. Helping the little guy to stand up to the big corporations. Listening to the local neighborhoods when nobody else would. Showing the corrupt side of the law in a city already crumbling at the seams. She knew already that her decision had been made the minute she stepped out of the car.

"I think I know someone who can help you," O'Connell said.

"Can they be trusted?" Tommy asked.

"He's your only shot. If you need my help contacting him, I'll need the power back to my car."

"Ask and it will be provided," Ted said in his most cringeworthy of voices. He made his way onto the driver's seat. From his inside jacket pocket, he removed a device no larger than the dashboard VDU and plugged it up to a USB socket.

"Is that what you used to hijack my car?"

"It's one of my many *tools*."

"I guess that makes you the brains of the operation?"

Kurt laughed. "That's the first time he's ever been called that."

"Dude, will you shut up," Ted replied, blushing. "Teo is a handsome stud that always gets the lady."

"Not this lady. Eyes back on the prize, hot shot," O'Connell replied, turning his head back to the dashboard.

"By the way, I only borrowed your car. It seemed the safest way to get you here in one piece."

"Hardly the safest. I blacked out."

"It was my first time driving a hover car on a screen the size of a sweet wrapper."

"That's some high-tech equipment you're using."

"We borrowed it from a second-hand electrical store. We left a note. There, your power is back."

O'Connell faced the teenagers, who had finally finished eating. "Okay, if I am going to help you, there are a few things that still don't make sense to me. Like, where is the other boy? He's clearly not here."

Ted vacated the car and made his way back to his friends. "I need to show her."

"Ted, the reporter has a gun. It's very important that you explain slowly what exactly you're going to show her," Kurt said.

"Are you sure, Ted?" Mikey asked.

"He's right," Tommy said.

"She won't understand," Daisy added.

"Try me," O'Connell said. "I've got an open mind."

"We use magic," Kurt said, bluntly.

"Not that open."

"It's true," Ted said. "I was a kid."

"And you aged into the tall, leather jacket guy."

Ted nodded. "I'm more of the handsome hacker, DJ by night type of guy."

"You're using magic, magic?" O'Connell asked.

"Is there another type we're not aware of?" Tommy asked.

"Are you being serious? Monsters and ghosts as well, I suppose."

"Sure, and sorcery. Fire demons. Aliens. Space battles. You name it, we've seen it, used it, and bought the t-shirt," Mikey said.

"Don't forget werewolves," Kurt added.

"And the black hole," Ted said.

"I was coming to that."

"You entered a black hole?" O'Connell asked.

"We more or less travelled through it," Mikey replied.

"That's how we ended up on your planet," Daisy said.

"And I suppose you expect me to believe that?" O'Connell asked. "Help me out here. This is all a little too fantastical. Don't get me wrong, I might be interested in any story I can lay my hands on, but these hands have been burnt before."

"How about we show you what our hands can do," Ted said.

"Dude, enough with the flirting," Kurt said.

"That's not what I meant." Ted pointed at his bracelet.

"What is that?" O'Connell asked.

"It's a little hard to explain."

"Then show me."

"She means the power and the magic, Ted," Kurt stated.

"I know what she meant. You don't have to keep warning me about stuff. I'm not a perv," Ted said.

"Good. We don't need to make this anymore uncomfortable than it already is."

"April, it's important that once we show you, there is no turning back," Daisy said.

"I'm all in, one hundred percent. Please, show me your magic," O'Connell said, folding her arms across her chest in anticipation.

Ted closed his eyes and clenched his fists. Nothing happened.

"Are you okay, dude?" Kurt asked.

"I'm fine. Let me try again," Ted replied.

Ted went through the same process. Nothing happened.

O'Connell glanced at the imaginary watch on her wrist.

"I think I've got a little stage fright. Would you mind turning around?" Ted asked O'Connell.

"If that's what it'll take," she said, half-heartedly.

"Here we go, Ted. Back to your boring …" Ted's alteration was over before he had time to finish. "That's better. I'm back. You can turnaround now."

Unable to believe it was that easy, O'Connell searched the rooftop for the older man. He was nowhere to be seen.

"Now do you believe us?" Tommy asked.

"He was hiding and swapped places," O'Connell answered.

"There is nowhere to hide."

"Maybe you drugged my coffee?"

"Or …"

"Or maybe I'm starting to believe."

"That was nothing. That's how it always begins, a slight change here or there," Ted said.

"And then comes a world of hurt," Kurt added.

"So, will you help us?" Daisy asked.

"Well, I'm not sure anyone else in the city will believe any of this. Why not? I'm in. If I don't, I'm not sure who will," O'Connell said.

WITH the car's power returned to normal, April O'Connell sat down on the driver's seat and flipped the VDU forwards.

"Calling ZB. Zone LCE. Code 2 0 2 0."

The screen had returned to a normal setting, the word *contacting* flashing every few seconds as the call connected to the other person's device.

"*This is Zack Burton, aboard the Lamb Chop Express. I'm listening to whoever is talking.*" The cockiness of the man came through loud and clear over the car's internal communications.

"Zack, it's April."

"*My ex-wife April?*"

"No, no, the month of April. Still living off your instincts?"

"*Of course. I live by my word.*"

"And you die by the sword."

"*I don't remember saying that before.*"

"No, no, that one was wishful thinking from my end."

"*If you were this witty when we were married, we would have never split up.*"

"We split up because you were never there for me."

"*I was always there for you.*"

"Tell me one time."

"*Look, honey, I'm not saying I've been everywhere and I've done everything, but I do know it's an amazing planet we live on here. And you'd be some kind of fool to think we'd be all alone in this universe.*"

"I'm glad you mention the universe, Zack."

"They're a strange couple, don't ya think," Ted remarked to his friends.

"That's strong, coming from the strangest kid on planet Earth," Kurt remarked.

"Zack, I have some people here who need your help," O'Connell said.

"*What kind of help?*" Burton replied.

"The kind that pays the bills."

"*My bills are settled cash in hand.*"

"Are you still repaying Wang?"

"He wants my soul, and the heavens."

"Gambling is a fool's game."

"And yet Zack Burton gambles with his life every time he helps someone."

"Don't fool yourself. You're only in it for the money, Zack." O'Connell glanced over her shoulder and was surprised to find Ted and the teenagers eavesdropping on their conversation. "Do you kids have any money?"

"What do you think? We arrived an hour ago and we don't even know where we are," Tommy replied.

"I'd say that's a resounding no," Burton stated.

"Wait," Daisy said.

"Are these the kids from your report?"

"You watched that?" O'Connell asked.

"I watch everything you do."

"Really, I never knew."

"Yeah, even the crap stories."

"And just like that, my love for you crashes and burns."

"We just need to get out of the city," Mikey said.

"And go where?" Burton asked.

"Meet us face to face, and we'll talk," Ted said.

"Hey, buddy, Zack Burton makes the deals. I'll tell you what. We'll meet face to face. You know the fish market district in old China town?"

O'Connell nodded her acknowledgement to the group. "I do."

"Meet me at Wangs, in one hour. Don't be late, or I might be dead."

The call cut off.

"Can we trust him?" Daisy asked O'Connell.

"Well, I was married to him for three years," O'Connell replied.

"Is that a good thing, or a bad thing?" Kurt asked.

"To this day, I'm still trying to work that out. Now I just need to figure out how can I transport five teenagers in a cramped car."

"I know how," Mikey said.

"Don't even think about dismantling my pride and joy."

"I hate to say it, lady, but your car is a piece of junk," Kurt added.

"Maybe, but you're not taking it apart."

"I won't need to. I just need to use a little magic," Mikey said. "Stand back."

EVER since the comet's tail emerged, the island city surrounded by a tidal wall of immense proportions had been severely tested. With an ocean at present too unstable to navigate, on the city side of the wall, China Town's fish market, normally a bustling hive of the city's most profitable merchants, had little choice but to play a waiting game.

Games were Zack Burton's favorite thing in the world; except for beer, his hover truck, and one way dialoguing on his CB radio. And the stocky truck driver had only one game in mind whilst he waited for his ex-wife and the strangers to arrive.

After downing the remainder of his watered-down beer, Burton dropped another winning hand of cards on the tabletop. Quadrupling his money did not go down well with the two local traders left in the game.

A sweaty, temperamental Edward the Great threw down his cards, and spat on the floor in disgust. "Nobody is that lucky to win seven hands in a row."

The longest serving fisherman's tendency to draw the largest fish catches was the reason for his nickname. He had also spent enough time at the gambling dens to know a conman when he saw one.

"What can I say, Ed. It's all in the instincts," Burton said as he lit up a cigarette. "Now, if you don't mind. It's time for Zack Burton to take a siesta."

With the marketplace under pressure, money had been tight for everyone at the table.

"Double or nothing," said the Asian man opposite Burton.

The man, called Joti the Hutt by his peers, was worryingly overweight. His two brawny bodyguards stepped forwards, blocking the exit. Burton knew to get out of the den alive, he would need to fight them both. A situation he doubted he would come out on top of.

Choosing self-preservation, he turned back to the gangster. "You know what. Maybe I'll give you one shot to win it all back."

"Changing your mind was a good idea, Burton." Joti removed a sharp machete from a concealed sheath beneath the table and buried the blade in the tabletop.

Burton rocked back in his seat. "What's with the blade? Are we going to cut off body parts until one of us bleeds to death?"

Joti picked up a bottle of beer and emptied the contents on the floor. Placing the bottle on its side in front of him, he freed the machete and lowered it till touching the middle section of the glass. "If I cut the bottle in half, you pay everyone back what you took tonight, plus interest."

"And if you lose?"

"I'll double your money."

Burton glanced once at his watch. The hour deadline he had given his ex-wife had already passed. To delay any longer would surely annoy her.

"Take as long as you need, Joti," he said.

Without waiting, Joti raised and lowered the blade quicker than Burton could blink.

The unbroken bottle flew across the table, arrowing straight for the truck driver, who caught it with one hand. A broad smile spreading wider than the tidal wall. "Double money it is."

Joti glanced once at the machete. "That should've worked."

"Like I tell my ex-wife every time we speak, it's all in the instincts." Burton's smile quickly faded as the bottle broke apart in his hand.

As he tried to stand, two strong hands clamped down on Burton's shoulders, forcing him to remain seated.

"How did you do that?" Burton bemoaned.

Joti smiled wickedly as he stunned the machete in the tabletop. "It's all in the reflexes."

"No fair."

"This is a gambling den, Burton. You enter off your own back. The consequences …"

"Consequences, conshumenses. You conned me. End of story."

"Maybe next time you'll be less reluctant for a siesta," Edward snarled. "Now hand over my money."

"Whatever. You'll be seeing me again."

Burton threw down all the money he earned and exited the gambling halls by leaving through the fish market. Parked outside, the Lamb Chop Express with its silver and white chassis and green trim had seen better days. He boarded via the driver's door and made sure it was locked before he removed from inside his pants a wad of banknotes. The same money he had earned and stored throughout the game. Before he could count it, someone grabbed his shoulder, forcing him to spill the wad.

"Ripping off traders with fake bank notes is hardly a new story around these parts," April O'Connell said from behind the driver's seat.

"Say, honey. I don't suppose I've got a clean pair of pants back there. I seem to have soiled mine," Burton said, reaching down to pick up his money.

"I'm surprised you even know the word clean. You're late."

"Blame Joti."

"You two still pulling off your double act?"

"The split is fair."

"One day they'll find out."

"Never. Our plan is more sealed than OCP's bank vault."

"Burton!" Edward the Great screamed from the warehouse exit.

Zack Burton looked on in horror as the decapitated heads of Joti the Hutt and his bodyguards were thrown to the floor. Behind Edward, the same people with whom he shared the game table were brandishing huge knives and clubs.

"Never just came to claim your ass," O'Connell said, sitting back in the rear of the cab.

Burton gunned the engines, the hover jets gradually raising the truck and its trailer from the concrete. It made no difference that bloodthirsty traders battered his pride and joy from all angles, escape was the only option.

"Same old Burton," O'Connell said, starting to feel for her own safety.

"I'm a little pre-occupied, honey," he fired back.

Edward smashed the driver's door window with a club. Burton released the lock and kicked open the door. Unable to hold on, Edward plunged to the concrete below.

"Nice move," O'Connell said as Burton's truck finally reached a safe height.

"It's never in doubt when Zack Burton's about," he said.

"You should print that on t-shirts!"

"That's probably the most sensible thing you've ever said to me."

"Nope, but it comes in at a close second behind I want a divorce."

ONCE the Lamb Chop Express joined the flow of traffic Burton engaged the autopilot.

"It looks like your bank vault's not as tough as you thought," O'Connell said.

"What can I say. These days the world is full of crazy people."

"What did you expect when you cheat crooks."

"Zack Burton only cons those who have conned before."

"Maybe it's time for a career change." O'Connell climbed from the rear of the cab and settled in the passenger seat.

"What's the story with these kids of yours?"

O'Connell jabbed a thumb towards the trailer. "You can ask them when we stop."

"They're in the trailer?"

"Yep."

"You can compensate me for breaking the lock."

"It's a bit hard to break something that's already broken."

"Fine. Okay. I was going to get that fixed."

"Same old Burton."

"Same old April."

"So where are you taking us?"

"The safest place in the city."

"Let's hope so. Because these kids are wanted, citywide."

AFTER reaching the outskirts of the city, Burton's Lamb Chop Express left the traffic flow and entered the undernourished belly of a township crammed full of shanty sheds and deserted streets. Rife with vandalism and graffiti, the safe house had the perfect backdrop inside of a junk yard.

The perimeter wall shielded the area from the outside world. Rows of streetlights highlighted a junk jungle with only one clear space to park alongside Burton's main workshop.

An in-house troop of rusted robots kept anything useful by adding it to the growing piles in the junk yard. Anything not needed was deposited on the conveyor belt, leading to an industrial sized crusher.

"This dude is one compulsive hoarder." Ted's comment was not meant to be overhead.

"You never know what you'll need to survive, kid," Burton said as he made his way to a fridge and helped himself to a couple of bottles of beer. "Anyone thirsty?"

"Sure," Kurt said.

"They're not old enough." O'Connell caught the bottle mid-air and kept it for herself.

"Since when does a skin job's age matter?" Burton asked.

"They're not skin jobs."

"Your report said otherwise."

"Bryant said it."

"No, he said they're Bootleggers. Is that right?"

"Perhaps. I just went along with it."

"Did you challenge him?"

"Of course. Did you even watch the report?"

"I had it on the background."

"Can you help us or not, dude?" Tommy asked impatiently.

"Easy, kid. You know what old Zack Burton would say."

"Zack who?" Ted asked.

"Zack Burton, me. You can't get anywhere in life without a good introduction. I'm all ears."

After introducing the teenagers, O'Connell explained how they met and why they needed to escape the city. She went as far as explaining Ted's alteration from Teo the hacker to his teenage self, the bracelets harnessing their power and the ability to alter their appearance.

"Magic!" Burton laughed so hard he spat beer across the floor.

"Trust me, Zack. I've witnessed it firsthand," O'Connell added.

"Were you high?"

"No."

"There is no such thing as magic."

"Why are you always so stubborn?"

"Zack Burton is only stubborn when it's his neck on the line."

"How do you think we got across the city to the fish market?"

"Maybe you took an uber."

O'Connell gestured to Mikey. "This kid used magic to fly. Like a superhero."

Burton spat out his second mouthful of beer and cursed as most of the contents flowed away in a foam volcano. "Bullshit!"

"It's true. I carried the car, with everyone inside," Mikey said.

"You carried a car. On your back."

"It really wasn't that difficult."

"Wait a minute. I'm a reasonable guy, and I've experienced reasonable things. But you changed into someone who could fly, by using magic."

"We can do a lot more," Daisy added.

"Now hold on another minute. Someone better start telling Zack Burton the truth, or I'll drop you all off at the police headquarters myself."

"We use these bracelets," Daisy said, showing Burton her power gauntlet.

"We only have power for a short time," Tommy said.

"Nice cracker toys," Burton added.

"They're not toys."

"Are you sure? They look battery powered to me. What are they, double A size?"

"It's a little more technical than batteries," Daisy said.

"Oh, really."

"An old friend once said, it's a kind a magic."

"Show me some."

"We can't."

"What do you mean you can't."

"We need to be careful when we use them. We don't want to be caught defenseless," Ted added.

"And we can't be defenseless when they get here," Kurt concluded.

"You mean the magic police," Burton said.

"We call them Timeinators," Mikey stated.

"They've been tracking us for days," Tommy added.

"They are indestructible and will stop at nothing to prevent us getting home to our own planet." Ted cursed under his breath for his slip.

"Now you're magic aliens from another planet." Burton glanced at his beer, wondering if it had been drugged somehow.

"Look, Mr. Burton. Can I call you Zack? Zack, it's like this. We need to get home, pronto. It's the only way to lift our curse from Arcadian," Mikey added.

"Before you ask. He's an interdimensional, supernatural entity. Hellbent on taking the souls of the living and using them to keep his lifeforce thriving," Tommy said.

"You make it sound like you're trying to stop this Arcadian from ruling the universe," Burton said.

"Now you understand our predicament," Mikey said.

"Or I could check you all into a psycho ward. Whatever is easiest."

"Zack Archibald Burton! Don't you dare mock these children. They clearly need your help. And if you won't help them. I will. Even if it means I go it alone," O'Connell said.

For the first time in a long time, Burton remained silent. It happened only on a few previous occasions. Normally when he was trying to piece together information that made no sense at all. Like his ex-wife asking for a divorce. It was the last time she referred to his full name in anger. As he did back then, Burton made his way to his bottom desk drawer, whereby he removed a bottle of strong alcohol. He poured a succession of shots and necked them just as quickly.

"Is he okay, April?" Kurt asked.

"The last time he did this we divorced," O'Connell said.

"Déjà vu." Burton held up the bottle before downing another shot. "It's what I call my home brew. After the divorce, I never thought I'd need it again. But here we are. Déjà vu."

Burton necked another shot and sat in the chair behind his work desk.

"You believe us now?" Tommy asked.

"Maybe. And that's the only reason we're still talking. Well, that and the fact that I would expect to be well paid for my smuggling services."

"Dude thinks he's Han Solo," Kurt blurted.

"Solo sounds like my kind of guy. Maybe you should introduce him to Zack Burton."

"Then what are we waiting for?" Kurt asked.

Burton took another shot.

"I think it's a no," Ted remarked.

"Zack, we need to help these kids. We can't let Bryant capture them," O'Connell stated. "You the know the type of a sadistic creep he is."

"And I know who I am. I woke up the other day, just a normal truck driver. Now I'm helping aliens," Burton said.

"That's the liquor talking."

"Déjà vu, April, Déjà vu."

"He says that word a lot, doesn't he?" Ted remarked. "Like when he refers to himself in third person. We know who you are. You're standing right in front of us, dude."

"It sucks doesn't it, Burton?" Tommy said. "Not knowing if you belong."

"What do you know, kid?" Burton blasted.

"Would you believe me if I said I had a wife, kids. A fantastic life?"

Burton downed a shot. "Were they magic kids?"

"I was a cop, a good one. My friends here rescued me," Kurt added.

"A magic dad, and a magic policeman. You?" Burton asked Ted.

"A playboy, DJ, hacker, bed hopping Lothario."

"Who used magic to get laid. Next?" Burton lit a cigarette and waited for Daisy to answer.

"I'm the thread that leads us all home," she replied.

"Now that I believe …" Burton stubbed out his cigarette and stood. "In a nutshell, you weren't kids, you were adults, living lives."

"Accelerated lives, in a dream state," Tommy said.

"Right, accelerated dreams. That, I don't believe."

"Zack, does it matter what you believe? They need your help," O'Connell said.

Burton returned the bottle to the desk drawer. "Magic, huh. I don't believe it for one second, but Zack Burton will help you leave the city."

"Yes!" Kurt said.

"It's not that simple, kid. Zack Burton also needs to warn you. If April has reported on your arrival, it means your faces are now splashed over every social media outlet and billboard. You're the city's most wanted. The border crossing is out of bounds, but yes, there is a secret way out at the Tidal Wall. It will mean smuggling you out beneath the city. Which leaves an option so short, you'll need to crawl on your stomach through the muck and grime. Zack Burton won't kid you. The route through the sewers is a dangerous one. Some of you might even die."

"Isn't that a bit dramatic," Ted said.

Daisy listened to Burton's every word as she made her way to the back of the group. On the reality map, the portal was closer now than it had been since they had arrived in the city. She knew the distance to reach it was three thousand meters. Signified by a halo, she could make out the portal was behind a sealed door of considerable size. The nearest obstacles were a barrier separating a chamber from a vast body of water that she presumed to be the ocean. If Burton's route to the Tidal Wall was the only option, then it would have to do.

"The tidal wall is how far away?" she asked.

"A couple of miles," Burton said.

"How far is that in meters?"

"About three thousand," Mikey said.

"That's good enough for me. When are we leaving?"

ZACK Burton handed his ex-wife the keys to his hover car parked in the front of the junk yard. "This will get you home. Call it a belated wedding present."

"I'm coming with you," O'Connell said.

"It's too dangerous. Besides, you need to pay me for their safe passage. You can't do that if you're dead. And what use is money anyway if Zack Burton dies helping them."

"Putting other people first. I'm seeing you in a new light, Zack."

"Escaping from a bunch of machete-wielding maniacs can do that to a man."

"Their destiny is in your capable hands, Zack."

"Now don't get all sentimental on me. Get out of here, April."

"Kids, you're in the best hands. Good luck to you all. May you return safely to your home world."

One by one the teenagers hugged the reporter and said their goodbyes. Battling with her emotions for a group of teenagers she barely knew, labelled as dangerous Bootleggers, was out of character for the reporter. She knew she would never see them again. Perhaps the same could be said for her ex-husband. Embraced by Burton on her way out of the door, she covered her tears as she made her way to the parked hover car.

BURTON sat at a workbench and flipped the tabletop over, revealing the business end of his operation.

A high-tech CCTV set up, hooked up to a host of flatscreen televisions, revealed four live feeds from different camera angles of the only ways in and out of his yard. Other screens showed news footage, offshore business accounts, drug running operations, police arrest sheets, and lists of departing times for countless trains, boats, and aircraft.

By entering a four-digit code on a numerical keypad, Burton switched to a full view of the front yard parking area. His hover car, with April O'Connell inside, rose up and up until it went off screen. With the coast clear, he entered another four-digit code to turn on the junk yard's perimeter proximity sensors that acted like a dome, covering the entire area. From a shelf, he removed a handheld device, running a constant feed of the same images as the main screen.

Wasting no time, Burton led the five teenagers quickly through valleys of stockpiled machine parts. At the center of the labyrinth, he stopped at an equipment shed for supplies.

He equipped the group with handheld torches. From a sealed cabinet he removed a machine pistol, and a few clips of spare ammunition. Finally, a satchel of adhesive explosives, and a utility belt, lined with pouches, which he tied off around his waist.

"That's some heavy-duty luggage you're carrying," Kurt said.

"It's just a precaution," Burton replied, clipping two grenades to his belt.

"Says the dude strapping grenades close to his junk."

At the rear of the shack, obscured by piles of equipment crates, was a fireman's pole descending through an open manhole cover, and was the way down to the city's sewer system.

"Dude, seriously," Ted said, wincing from the sewer stench.

"You want out of the city unnoticed. This is the only way, kid," Burton replied.

"Do you know what lurks in sewers? Alligators, Chucks. To name but a few."

"Chucks?"

"Cannibalistic humanoid underground clown killers."

"Don't be a pussy, Ted. There's no such thing," Kurt remarked.

"That's easy for you to say. I have no protection. I used my power to become Teo."

"We'll protect you, dude," Tommy said, patting his friend on the back.

"No offence, but I'm not feeling the love."

"Did you forget that I defeated a huge sea dragon with a little stick."

"This is getting weirder and weirder. There is only one person you need to trust. Me. Zack Burton. And Zack Burton says there are no such things in these sewers as dragons, wizards, and witches."

"Are you sure, considering the amount of hardware you're carrying?" Ted added.

"Kid, you all told me you do not want to use your bangles unnecessarily."

"Magic bracelets," Daisy remarked.

"Fine, if you can't use your *magic bracelets*, then just in case, the next best thing is a good old-fashioned bullet. And if that doesn't work, they can swallow a grenade."

"How do you swallow a grenade? It's too big for a human. Maybe not Andre the Giant. He'd eat two! Yeah, you should really say, how about eat a grenade. Then again, that wouldn't work. You'd bite down on it, probably crack the casing and kablooey. Adios dandruff and acne ..." Ted said, before realizing that everyone was concentrating on Burton's handheld device and not his rant.

The proximity alarm vibration warning coincided with the footage on the portable screen showcasing what remained of the yard's six-inch-thick steel plated entrance, which now resembled a giant, mangled corkscrew.

"A Timeinator has found us," Daisy said.

"I'm surprised it took this long," Tommy remarked.

"Less talking, more hauling ass," Burton said.

While Burton booby-trapped the seal of the shed's doorway with motion sensor, adhesive explosives, the teenagers descended the pole into a sewer knee-deep in seawater.

SAFELY underground, the group made their way along the eastern underpass, in the direction of the Tidal Wall.

"What exactly can I expect from this Timeinator that's chasing you. Did I say it right?" Burton asked.

"A Timeinator can be anything, anyone, and is pretty much indestructible," Daisy replied.

"Relentless is a good word," Tommy said.

"It could even be you," Ted said to Burton.

"I'm flattered you thought of me, Ted. Sorry to disappoint. It's not me. Does it bleed? If it bleeds, we can kill it," Burton said.

"A Timeinator is fearless. It can't be bargained or reasoned with. It will feel no pity or remorse. And it will not stop, ever, until it reclaims the reality map from our bloodied fingertips," Daisy said.

"You're using a magical map?"

"Don't sound surprised. It's what we used to arrive here."

"Why not use it again and save me the trouble of dying."

"We can't until we reach the exit portal."

"I take it that's a magic portal?"

"It is."

"And it's whereabouts?"

"Ahead of us."

"Let me guess. Three thousand meters away."

"How did you know?"

"A lucky guess. Look, kids. Zack Burton can't help you escape unless you let Zack Burton help you. Where is the map now?"

"I have it. As I'm sure you can understand, I didn't want to show it to you in case you ended up being a Timeinator."

"The last time Zack Burton looked in the mirror, the person looking back was Zack Burton, not a time cop. Is that good enough for you?"

"I believe him," Ted said.

"You would," Kurt said.

"Would he be making this much of a fuss if he was a Timeinator. He would just squash us and take it."

"Ted makes a valid point," Tommy said.

"Show him," Mikey said to Daisy.

Daisy showed Burton the map and explained the significance of why only a few remaining clockfaces appeared on the border. She continued by describing the glowing spot on a vast background represented the kids' current whereabouts and only showed the nearest obstacles. For now, it was the sewer walls, the water they stood in. Footprints revealed the journey to this point, which were fading the further they progressed through the environment. She went on to explain that the portal's location was displayed as a halo on the map.

Burton pointed out that the portal appeared to be situated behind one of the many secure entry points located along the Tidal Wall, in the area used for general maintenance and structural repairs.

"Zack Burton knows where your portal is," he said.

"Can we reach it?" Daisy asked.

"Going forwards, for this relationship to work, we need trust. Agreed?"

"Agreed."

"Good. No more deception. Just good old-fashioned honesty from here on in." Burton removed his handheld device, which showed the time at 23:45. "If the portal is to the north and we keep following this tunnel, we'll be at your exit point in about fifteen minutes. All Zack Burton needs to do is keep you out of the clutches of something you call an indestructible being. One so dangerous, we do not yet know what form it has decided to take to hunt you down."

"I couldn't have put it better myself, dude," Kurt said, with a firm slap to Burton's back.

"One last surprise. There are normally three of them," Tommy added.

"I should've brought more grenades," Burton muttered.

THE teenagers and their guide, Zack Burton, appeared miniscule as they entered the enormous stonework hollow. It was a filthy place. Moist underfoot, with a rancid stench. A seedy underbelly of a city's sewer system that nobody dared set foot in until today. One side was clearly part of Burton's Tidal Wall. The rest appeared to be a focal point of the sewer network, with branches reaching out across the city. Open drains were accessible, none of them sealed.

"Ted, I think this is where your epic turds go to die," Kurt said.

"Hey, I can't help having gastrointestinal issues," Ted said.

Daisy unraveled the map. The portal had not moved. It was still straight ahead, on the opposite side of the Tidal Wall.

"This doesn't make sense. Burton, please tell me I'm not losing the plot. Fifteen minutes ago. The portal was behind a sealed doorway. Correct?"

"If you're losing the plot, then so am I," Burton replied.

"None of these sewers have doorways," Ted said.

"I can see that, Ted."

Before the matter could be addressed further, the vibrating handheld device drew Burton's attention away from the group. Sensors inside his compound went off like wildfire. Images, fed back from the CCTV, showed three muscular men, wearing leather jackets and sunglasses, making inroads towards the equipment hut.

"We have visitors." The truck driver held up the device, showing the men busting down the doorway to the equipment shed.

Static replaced the live feed, the rumble of an explosion lingering in the tunnel they just vacated.

"I love the smell of C4 in the morning," Burton snarled. The live feed returned, the dust settling over the remains of Bryant's special tracker unit. "Indestructible must mean something else on your world," Burton continued.

"Being hit by C4 would be like walking through a fart for a Timeinator," Ted remarked.

"Maybe they weren't the Timeinators," Mikey said.

"If it's not them, they'll be ahead of us as some other parasite, or whatever they can lay their hands on," Daisy added.

"We're in a sewer. A parasite isn't such a bad shout," Ted said.

Without warning, what appeared to be smoke poured from every exit. The more the ceiling gathered in the mist, the more it became apparent that the entire upper reaches were being overrun with these strange storm clouds.

"Burton, do you know what exit we need to take?" Ted remarked.

"If he says the one with the smoke coming out of it, we're screwed," Kurt added.

Rain poured, thunder shook the sewer's foundations, and underneath a volley of electrical strikes at the ground, a female with red eyes and spiked brown hair slowly made her way towards them. She cared not that her transparent outfit, a combination of poison ivy and a slinky wedding dress, left little to the imagination.

"Is she a friend of yours?" Burton asked, his eyebrow raised.

"We don't have friends that hot," Kurt replied. "No offence, Daisy."

"Yeah, that means she's a Timeinator," Ted said. "A real hot one, with not a lot of clothes on."

"We can see that, Ted."

"Well, whoever it is, we need to get by her," Mikey said.

"Right," Burton replied.

"Go get her, Burton," Ted added.

Burton shot a look of doubt at Ted, who wink-nodded in reply.

"You got this, Burton," Kurt reassured.

"Yeah, she's all yours," Tommy said, taking a step backwards.

With his arms raised as a peaceful gesture, Burton made his way to the front of the group. "Good evening. I order you, as a Timeinator, to cease any or all supernatural activity and to return to your place of origin, or the nearest convenient parallel dimension. Thank you."

"That ought to work. Good job, Burton," Ted taunted even as the woman's intense stare snagged him in her web.

"I am Tozer, the Tozerian." She spoke harshly, as if gargling gravel.

The more he tried to, the harder it was for Ted to break the connection. Even as she tiptoed across the ground, her soulless pupils released a toxic tide of fear that ate away at his fragile mindset.

"She is not a Timeinator," Daisy warned.

"You said they can be whatever they want to be," Burton replied.

"She's something altogether different."

"Hey, lady, you really shouldn't be walking around this part of the city half ass naked," Kurt added.

Tozer's air of superiority showed no sign of slowing down. "Are you Bootleggers?" she rasped.

Burton turned to the teenagers. Between them, they nodded, shrugged, and shook their heads.

"Well, no," he replied.

"No?"

"Well, not all of us."

"Then die." From her fingertips, Tozer rained down powerful energy bolts, blasting the group across the sewer.

With the entire group shot down to their knees, it took a few moments for them to regain any form of composure.

Mikey was the first to stand. "Burton, when someone asks if you're a Bootlegger, you say yes!"

"But I'm not one. Maybe next time you can take the lead," Burton replied.

"Okay, let me show this supernatural bitch how I get things done." Daisy strode towards Tozer with added purpose. "Lady, we are Bootleggers, and we sure as hell know how to fight. Now, let us pass or else."

"You, the Bootleggers, have traversed the voyager's realm. The voyager has come. The Bootleggers need to choose. Choose and perish."

"Perish. I don't like the sound of that," Kurt said.

"What do you mean, choose. We don't understand," Mikey added.

"Choose. Choose the way forwards," Tozer said.

"Bitch likes that word choose," Kurt said.

"Oh, I get it. Very cute. You want us to choose a way out of here. We choose wrong and we all die. No, no, no, we're not falling for that," Tommy said.

"I don't get it," Ted said.

"It's simple. We choose to take a knife to a gunfight. We all die. Is that right, lady?"

"Choose," Tozer snapped.

"That's not a denial," Kurt added.

"Maybe that's why the portal is hidden from us," Daisy added.

"Remember the alligator at the start of the game. We didn't stand a chance," Tommy said. "We've only got one shot at this. Empty your heads. Let's try and come up with a plan."

"The choice has been made," Tozer said.

"Wait, what!" Tommy barked.

"The decision is final. Your destination has been decided."

"Whoa, whoa. I didn't choose an exit. Did you?" Tommy turned to Kurt and Mikey, who shook their heads in reply. Then to Daisy and Burton, who shrugged. It left just the one person. "Ted?"

"I couldn't help it," Ted said.

"Not again," Daisy said, her shoulders slumping in defeat.

"She was in my head the moment she arrived."

"Stop getting boners around hot chicks!" Kurt snarled.

Ted's friends encircled him, creeping closer as each second ticked away.

"I tried to think about all of us and it just popped into my head," Ted continued.

"What just popped into your head?" Kurt asked.

"What did you do, Ted?" Mikey asked.

"What I thought about was something less destructive than usual."

"Less destructive," Tommy added.

"Yeah, we're always fighting. I wanted to use my brain on this one."

"Ted and brains should not be used in the same sentence," Kurt said.

"I really wasn't ready for any of this when I woke up this morning," Burton added.

"Your destination awaits you," Tozer added, snapping her fingers.

THE group entered what appeared to be an identical sewer chamber. Only an oily resin seemed to be different. It moved of its own accord. Whatever it was made of was purposely covering up any visible exits.

"And we're back where we started," Daisy said.

"No, this is different. The walls are alive," Burton said, gesturing with his machine pistol.

"Daisy, where is the portal now?" Tommy asked.

Daisy checked the map. The portal was still straight ahead and behind the sealed doorway that they couldn't see due to the resin. "Same spot as before. I just can't see the way to reach it."

"At least the crazy bitch is out of the way," Mikey said.

"Until Ted gets another boner," Kurt joked.

"Ha, ha. Very funny. I just wish someone would give us a break," Ted yelled.

Unexpectedly, a shaft of unnatural light punctured a hole through the ceiling and pinpointed the center of the chamber. At the end of the beam, the ground quaked, the concrete breaking apart wide enough for a stone plinth, two meters wide, to rise six feet.

"Whaddya know. For once I said the right thing," Ted said.

"That crazy bitch asked us to choose. Why this destination, Ted?" Daisy asked as she made her way to the plinth.

"Like I said earlier, we're always fighting. This time it's brain power."

"Or in your case, the lack of it," Kurt said.

Resting on top of the plinth were three leather bound books and a scroll.

"What is this junk?" Burton said.

"And that's coming from the king of junk," Ted joked.

"Did you choose these?" Tommy asked, pointing at the books.

Ted shrugged.

"The scroll is labelled *Thrice upon a Time*." Mikey opened the parchment. "Ah crap, it's written in Spanish."

"How do you know it's Spanish, if you can't read it," Ted remarked.

"Give it here," Kurt said.

"You know Spanish?"

"No, but Detective Caine did. Maybe I do too."

"Who is Caine?" Burton asked.

"My old persona."

"Your magical alter ego."

"That's right. Can I continue, or do you want to waste some more time?" Kurt unraveled the parchment and read the contents out loud.

"*Ye intruders beware. Answer thrice wrong and suffer crushing pain and grief, soaked with blood, beneath your feet. Answer one of thrice right and free ye will be to take flight.*"

"Did you read it right?" Ted asked.

"You wanna check," Kurt said, slapping the scroll in Ted's palm.

"No need to get angry with me. I'm only asking in case it says there's a button over there to open a door."

"It doesn't say that, okay."

"Why is it in Spanish?"

"How should I know? When has this game ever been easy. It's just another curveball. And stop questioning everything."

"What's with the anger issues?"

"That's another question."

"Did I do something wrong?"

"Yeah, you woke up this morning. And your decisions don't make any sense, ever. Why here? Why not choose somewhere else, like a jacuzzi at the Playboy mansion. Look, I'm fed up with this entire scenario, okay. You know what, Ted, just go over there and stay away from me for a while."

Ted left Kurt alone and made his way behind the plinth. There was a small stone stool and a leather hood attached to a host of wires. The wires connected to a small power source with a switch located next to the stool.

"I knew you'd be here somewhere," Ted said, referring to the hood.

It felt leathery and comfortable as he put it on over his head and eyes. As he did so, a leather strap buckled tightly around his forehead and neck, ensuring he was unable to see anything. When he tried to loosen the straps, he received an electric shock.

"Guys," he cried, "this thing is stuck and it's making a humming sound."

Burton tried to unclip the hood and received an electric shock. "It's alive."

"Unfortunately for us," Kurt snapped, referring to Ted.

"Why on earth did you put it on?" Daisy asked.

"I was alone with my thoughts," Ted replied.

"Don't you mean thought. As in singular," Kurt snarled. "And that was a dumb one."

"Hey, just cos I can't see, doesn't mean that your insults hurt any less."

"No, enough is enough, Ted. You put that thing on your head, despite having no idea what it's for. It's typical."

"I know."

"You never know what you're doing. That's your problem."

"I do know because it was my choice, remember."

"You chose bondage?" Daisy asked, semi seriously.

"There's a bit more to it than that." Ted gestured at the back of the plinth. "Before I put the hood on, I noticed there are instructions engraved in the stonework."

1. AFFIX HELMET
2. SIT DOWN
3. BEGIN

"That's simple enough," Daisy said.

"Even for you, Ted," Kurt added.

"Enough with the insults, Kurt," Tommy replied.

"You'll never guess what this is." Mikey held up one of the leatherbound books.

"It's an *Empire Strikes Back* sticker album," Ted remarked without hesitation.

"Dumb ass," Kurt snarled.

"He's right," Mikey laughed and opened it up to show everybody.

"I had three of those, all completed," Ted added.

"Three books," Mikey said.

"You know how it is. You fill up book one, you're left with swapsies. Rather than throw them out, I completed a second book. The bubble gum that came with the stickers was the best."

"Let me guess, rather than stop after book two, you had swapsies and bought even more stickers to complete book three," Kurt said.

"Correctamundo, dude."

"Dumb ass."

"The other two books are *Gremlins* and *Buck Rogers*," Mikey stated.

"And I had two of each of those. I think you need to take another look at your Spanish scroll, Kurt," Ted said.

"Oh, really." Kurt picked up the scroll and re-read it. After a few seconds he looked up sheepishly. "It looks like I missed a bit."

"Maybe it's because you were too busy being a jerk."

"Am not a jerk. Just angry, all the time."

"Then be less angry," Burton added.

"Fine. I'll try. Ted, I'm sorry for lashing out so much. I think I brought over some of Caine's anger issues."

"It's okay. We're all stressed."

"Ted, nobody is dying here, not on my watch. Kurt, let me read the scroll," Burton said.

"You speak Spanish?" Ted asked.

Burton hesitated before replying. "Si."

"That could also be said in Italian."

"What does it say, Burton?" Daisy asked.

"Okay. Thrice upon a Time. The rules."

"*Let ye fate decide a page by chance. Only one, not a merry dance. A space free, there will be. Answer right and be released ye might. Answer wrong and said page will be gone. Three chances to be free. Answer all wrong and death it will be.*"

"Who's up for some travel scrabble," Ted remarked.

"Let me give you some advice from good old Zack Burton. What will be, will be. To hell with it."

"Okayyyy, on that note, let's get this party started," Mikey said. "Judging by the rules, let fate decide a page by chance means we flick through and stop at a page. A space free must be referring to a missing sticker. We guess the missing sticker image from one of the three books and we're free to go."

"That sounds simple enough," Burton stated.

"Our lives are never that simple," Daisy said.

"Tommy's better half has hit the nail on the proverbial. What Zack Burton will learn to understand is that there's always a catch," Ted remarked. "The catch being, I'm going Solo. And I don't mean Han. These answers are mine and mine alone."

"We're a team," Kurt said.

"Not right now. Being here is my choice because I've used my bracelet. I thought I'd put myself forward as a teenager. Just in case one of us must …"

"Must what?"

"Sacrifice themself."

"That's a very brave thing to do, Ted," Daisy said.

"It's also very foolish," Mikey added.

"Who's the more foolish? The fool, or the fool who follows him?" Ted said.

"That doesn't make any sense," Kurt added.

"Ted, I'm not sure why you want to do this alone, but are you ready?" Tommy asked.

Ted nodded. "Do me a favor. Leave Empire until last."

"Yeah, let's prolong the agony a little longer," Kurt joked.

"It's our only hope, Kurt."

"Okay, not feeling the tension at all right now. We're going with *Buck Rogers* first," Mikey said, fanning through the book.

As he stopped at a page, the book flew from his grasp and slammed down on top of the plinth. Before he could react, the edges ignited with flame. The flames burned inwards, the box with the missing sticker being highlighted by an ethereal glow.

"I didn't expect that," Mikey said.

"What page, dude?" Ted asked impatiently.

"Ah, there is no page number, Ted."

"What? The rules stated …"

"Screw the rules. Arcadian makes it up as he goes along, and the page is burning away to nothing."

"Why is it burning?"

"Never mind that. The empty space is sticker one hundred and sixty-one," Mikey said.

"Erm."

"Come on, Ted, time is almost up."

"Okay. Wilma Deering looking hot in that skintight flight suit."

With the book burning to a crisp, an electric shock to his skull took Ted by surprise.

"What the hell was that?" he blurted, his body still shuddering down to his nerve endings. "Guys, I'm no longer a fan of this game."

As the electric shock ended, a huge section of the concrete floor gave way to an endless gulf below.

"Hold on everyone," Burton said, grabbing the teenagers closest to him.

Huddled around the plinth, the group remained still until the quaking stopped.

Daisy shot a look over her shoulder. Her feet were balancing unsteadily on the edge of a crevice deep enough to swallow the Titanic ten times over. "Erm, Ted. I don't think that's the Buck Rogers picture book you remember. Maybe think with your other brain."

"You wanna swap?" Ted said, his feet dangling over the edge of the abyss.

"Not a chance. You were the one dumb enough to gimp up in the first place."

"Fine. I'll stay put, but before we go on. What was that rumbling?"

"That was just the ground giving way to an infinite abyss," Mikey said.

"A what!"

"Okayyyy, enough chatter, Ted. *Gremlins* are up next. Nervous?"

"I don't like this."

"You only have two more to go."

"Mikey, can you be a bit quicker with the intel this time."

"You in a rush to die, kid?" Burton asked.

"I need time to think. I was rushed before. I got all flustered. Plus, I peed my pants when the ground shook. It's uncomfortable, all warm and trickling down my pant leg into my trainer. It's off putting."

"Concentrate, Ted," Kurt said.

"Okay. I'm better now. Ready when you are, Mikey."

Mikey fanned through the *Gremlins* sticker album and opened it. Just like before, the book flew from his grasp and slammed down on top of the plinth. The edges ignited, the flames burning inwards, one space highlighted with an ethereal glow.

"Sticker eighty-six," Mikey said eagerly.

"Okay, okay. These two pages are labelled as Birth of the Gremlins. It's all to do with Billy's mum. Eighty-four and five is one of the after-midnight dudes. Eighty-seven to ninety, Billy's mum uses flea spray. Ninety-one she's caught up in the Christmas tree."

"Hurry, Ted, the page is almost chargrilled."

"Is she using lots of utensils? Erm."

"Ted!"

"Wait, wait, wait. I got it. It's the one where the Gremlin explodes in the microwave. No, no, no. It's a trick. It's Billy, not his mum. Billy is about to swing the sword. That's it. Nailed it. You can thank me lat–… argh …"

Mikey shot a glance at Ted who was shuddering from the electric shock. When the shock ended, another section of the ground broke away. As before, the group clung on to each other until the shaking stopped.

During the quake, the oily resin had retreated into the concrete. There was no exit available. All that remained was the stairs leading up to the plinth, the solid ground around it, and a solitary concrete path, stretching across the chasm as far as the Tidal Wall. It was wide enough for single file and appeared to be the last thread holding the group to this realm. At the end of the path was a brick wall with no way through.

"Ted, we're on our last legs here, literally," Tommy said.

"Damn it," Ted yelled out. "It was the orange squeezer. The Gremlin is juiced, its legs are flailing about like when Kurt dives in a swimming pool."

"Do not," Kurt said, embarrassed.

"That Gremlin's guts and blood are sprayed everywhere. Classic! I knew that."

"I'm sorry, Ted. This isn't your lucky day," Burton said.

"No shit. I'm getting a little tired of this."

"You volunteered, didn't you? You're finding us a way out of the here, aren't you?"

"Yeah, but I didn't know I was going to be given electric shocks. What is that bitch trying to prove here anyway."

"There's a scroll with the next album." Burton opened the next parchment. "Tozer *is studying the effect of negative re-enforcement on recollection ability*. Whatever the hell that means."

"The effect. I'll tell you what the effect is. It's pissing me off," Ted snarled.

"Relax, Ted," Kurt said.

"It could be worse. It could be hooked up to your balls," Daisy said.

"Nah, he'd enjoy that too much."

"Wait. There's something else," Burton said, reading from the parchment.

"*The Timeinators three, you have so far resisted. Oggy and Skank are sick and twisted. Two they have won. The Horsemen are nearly overrun. With a final answer to go. Packard Walsh's phantom is almost ready to flow.*"

Tommy balled his fists. "All this time, the Timeinators were Packard and his goons."

"They're not that smart. They chose to be sticker albums," Kurt said.

"But they're winning, Kurt," Daisy said.

"Who the hell is Packard?" Burton asked.

"Tommy's nemesis," Mikey replied.

"Magical bad guy?"

"Oh no, this one is from the real world. A teenage douchebag of the biggest proportions."

"And he's now one of the Timeinators?"

"It's a long story."

"We stopped him before, we can stop him again," Tommy said.

"It might not make a difference. This is Ted's last try. He gets it wrong, and we all plunge to our death," Kurt said.

"We need you to think, Ted," Mikey said.

"Nobody has ever asked me to do that before," Ted replied.

"Clear your mind. No pressure. You screw this up, we're dead."

"To be fair, if we fall, there doesn't seem to be anywhere to land," Burton said.

"Okay, Ted. The *Empire Strikes Back* sticker album. Here goes nothing. We do or die …" Mikey fanned through the pages one last time.

THE sticker album slammed down on top of the plinth. The empty space highlighted with an ethereal glow being hunted down by rampant wildfire.

"No fair," Mikey replied, stepping back from the flames, and almost falling over the edge.

"What happened?" Kurt asked.

"Look at the flames. We're dead. We are so dead."

"What number is it!" Tommy yelled.

"Kiss your asses goodbye."

"Mikey, I swear to God. If you don't tell him the number …" Daisy warned.

"Outta the way." Burton barged Mikey to one side. "Ted, it's fifty-five and fifty-six."

Packard's fire had eaten away eighty percent of the page in no time at all and Ted was yet to utter a word.

With Ted struggling to guess the correct sticker from the earlier rounds, how was he ever going to remember two of them. Like their hopes of survival, the ice planet Hoth melted before their eyes. With seconds remaining, the group shared the same defeated expression.

Then a miracle happened.

"It's on Planet Hoth. The AT-AT attack scene. Rebel troopers are in an ice trench. An explosion erupted to the right-hand side. The scene is called … *Suddenly ... Starfire!*"

As the book burnt to a crisp, the group shared a look, and the floor began to quake.

"Ah shit!" Burton snarled.

Chapter 27

Suddenly ... Starfire!

THE QUAKING continued only as long as it took the plinth to withdraw.

Ted's expected electric shock was replaced by firm pats on the back and the sound of his friends celebrating. He removed the hood and placed it back on the stool. All around him the chasm was endless, only the single pathway remained intact. At the end of the pathway, a sealed, oval doorway materialized. The titanic locking mechanism appeared to need someone as strong as the Hulk to move it.

"That was too close," Burton said, moving cautiously around the plinth.

"That's just Tuesday for us," Kurt joked. "Ted, we owe you, dude."

"I'll take payment in kindness." Ted offered his hand to Daisy.

Rather than ignore him, she hugged him tightly. No words were spoken. The moment felt poignant, as if the line he was previously not allowed to cross had suddenly been erased.

Burton led the group across the chasm, towards the doorway.

"We need some muscle to crank that bad boy," Ted said.

"I got this," Daisy replied, brushing the boys aside.

In a brilliant flash of white lightning, Daisy turned into the most destructive, cybernetic organism the galaxy had ever seen. Her attire, of stylish leather trousers and jacket, was accompanied by smooth sunglasses, supremely slicked back hair and a muscular physique to die for.

"Da Concluder is back," Ted said.

"It's der," said Der Concluder.

"What do you mean der? It's da, da Concluder. Emphasis on the da."

"Not when it's a girl at der wheel. Emphasis on the der."

Rather than start an argument that would lead to him being flattened like a bug, Ted observed with genuine admiration as the Da Concluder's female counterpart used just one hand to crank open the lock and shift the door aside.

Tozer the Voyager offered the teenagers a way out. By passing the test and opening the doorway, they had found it. The portal to the next realm was in touching distance, with the destination only reachable by taking a leap of faith.

"Smoothly done," Burton said to Der Concluder.

As Daisy turned menacingly towards the truck driver, she altered back to her teenage body. "Now do you believe we are *der* real deal."

"Zack Burton never doubted you for a second. Although, this is not the way I was expecting to smuggle you out."

"You've taken us far enough. The portal will lead us to our next destination."

"That's a drop of about twenty feet. That's some leap of faith."

Daisy patted her pocket. She was still in possession of the map but needed everyone to be in proximity for it to work. "Where do we go, boys?"

"Tobias told us the route home. We've crossed the city. We need to cross the wasteland," Mikey said.

"You must mean the Badlands," Burton suggested.

"Sounds ominous," Kurt replied.

"After the city, it's the only logical step."

"Are you sure?" Mikey asked.

"You need to ask yourselves something. When Zack Burton says that you must pass through the Badlands to get yourselves back home, do you trust him."

"Fine, in that case you all need to be in touching distance for this jump to work," Daisy said.

"You know what, I'm coming with you."

"It doesn't work like that, Burton."

"I've been to the Badlands. You'll need help."

"Are you sure?"

"Trust me."

"Thanks, Burton. It's good to have you aboard."

"Don't mention it."

The group huddled together.

"Okay, we step through the opening on my mark." Daisy held up the map and tapped on one of the two remaining clockfaces. "Take us to the Badlands."

THE group's descent through the portal ended abruptly. Nobody but Burton appeared to be lucid enough to notice their surroundings.

The group were in a room with one door, the ground beneath their feet was rumbling, as if travelling in some sort of vehicle.

Burton opened the door and glanced once inside.

"Where are we?" Tommy said, barely able to stand.

"You're going home," Burton said, shoving the kids through the opening one by one.

The teenagers stumbled through the shadows into what felt like a moving room.

Zack Burton stood in the doorway of a moving train carriage. He shone a lit flare inside, revealing at least a dozen other children. All of them chained at the ankles and wrists.

"I'm sorry, kids. This is the only way," he said, as he slammed the door shut and sealed it from the outside.

"Burton!" Tommy yelled, as he pummeled the doorway with his fists.

"Tommy, stop. It's no use," Daisy said.

"Son of a bitch tricked us," Kurt barked.

"Not just us. There are other kids here with us," Mikey said as a sleep agent escaped from the vents, knocking out everybody inside the carriage.

DAY SEVEN

(One jump remaining)

Chapter 28

The Road Warriors

MONTH - DAY HOUR - MIN
JUNE 11 WASTELAND WARRIORS 09:12
REALITY DESTINATION

DAISY DREW'S loathing of hot weather surfaced after an unfortunate sunburn incident at a neighbor's BBQ at the tender age of three. To be thrust into the next step of her journey home with baking hot sand between her toes, had to be the worst possible start to her day.

"Let's all agree. Next time we use the map, we choose our own destination." Tommy's remark, from over her right shoulder, took her by surprise.

She couldn't see his whereabouts due to being in the middle of a moving mob. The crowd moved at a snail's pace. It quickly became apparent why.

The group of around twenty teenagers in chains followed a dirt track towards a shanty encampment. The entrance was flanked by a pair of broken-down school buses, and a group of teenagers, armed with spears and catapults, kept watch from the rooftops. Inside the camp, barricades constructed with piles of tires ringed dozens of makeshift tents.

As the group entered, from all over the camp hundreds of youngsters had been called together by someone using an airhorn.

"This isn't a summer camp I recognize," Ted remarked from somewhere behind.

"Nothing more than a bump in the road," Kurt said from in front.

"That's more than a bump up ahead," Mikey said, from Daisy's left.

It was difficult to see inside the huge, stainless-steel dome at the edge of the encampment. The manic cheers erupting from inside after a chorus of boos had imaginations running wild.

Leading the convoy on horseback, a single, cloaked slave trader lowered his hood.

Tommy was first to recognize Zack Burton. "Traitor," he muttered.

Burton spoke to a group of older teenagers, who had exited what appeared to be the camp's food tent. Zack Burton made no effort to hide the fact that he was trading a bunch of kids he smuggled out of the city. Most of the campmates had been shipped from the mainland. None of them looked older than the group talking to Burton.

"He fooled us all," Tommy blasted.

"Maybe we should call him Lando," Kurt said.

"He did help defeat the Timeinators," Ted added.

"He didn't. He was like Indiana Jones in *Raiders* or the *Lost Ark*," Mikey remarked.

"What do you mean?" Tommy asked.

"Indiana Jones plays no role in the outcome of the story. The Nazis would still have found the Ark, taken it to the island, opened it up, and all died, just like they did."

"He did a bit more than that," Daisy said, although not sure why.

"Like what?"

"Indy saved that chick from the snakes," Kurt added.

"Big deal. If he's not there, she doesn't get caught up in all the drama," Mikey replied.

"Not Indy, I'm talking about Burton. He showed us to the sewers," Daisy said.

"We could've found that ourselves, by using the map."

"Okay, he blew up the trackers that entered his hideout."

"Trackers we could've taken out ourselves."

"Okay, Burton helped us find Tozer."

"No, she found us. He also didn't answer any of the sticker album questions. Der Concluder opened the doorway to the portal. All Burton suggested was that we enter the Badlands. He did nothing, except trick us, drug us and leave us at what I can only imagine is a slave camp."

"Ted's right. All along, Burton wasn't on our side," Mikey added.

"He just sold us out to the dark side. What a total Lando," Kurt added.

Ahead of the new arrivals, a stern looking blonde seventeen-year-old girl, with scraggy, cropped hair, and vine tattoos on each arm, took a bag on offer from Burton and handed it to a kid wearing glasses. He looked no older than ten or eleven.

"He's dumping us. Like garbage in his junk yard," Mikey said.

"Burton, you traitor! We had an agreement," Tommy blasted.

Burton glanced nonchalantly over his shoulder, before raising his hood and riding out of camp.

"What a piece of slime," Mikey called out.

All eyes were on the camp leader, her air of authority clear to see. Wearing a worn navy, purple and black t-shirt, cut off at the sleeves, she gestured for Kurt and Daisy to be led away. Her leather gauntlets matched the armbands tied off around her biceps. Her leather boots were scuffed beyond repair.

"Where are you taking them?" Tommy demanded.

He stepped forward from the line and felt the sharp sting of a cattle prod in his abdomen. As he dropped to his knees, two burly enforcers, with shoulder length hair and wearing juvenile detention style boiler suits, secured a metal collar around his throat.

"What is this?" he gargled, pawing at the brace, unable to shift it.

"We use it to keep unruly dogs in line," one of the enforcers replied, whilst the other dragged Tommy away as he kicked and cursed.

The blonde motioned with her chin, to give the order for collars to be fixed to the other two arrivals. Mikey and Ted chose to let it happen, rather than fight the inevitable losing battle.

"What is this place?" Mikey asked as the collar snapped closed around his throat.

"Campus Christi," she replied with the strongest of Texan accents.

The crowd of kids erupted with a chorus of barks and banging of steel drums. The din was deafening, until she cut it off by raising her hand.

"Campus Christi. A wretched hive of scum and villainy," Ted joked, shortly before he folded in half from a double jab of a cattle prod.

"I'd watch what you say," one of the enforcers said.

Rather than reply, Ted gave thumbs up.

"Know who I am, do you?" the girl asked.

"Is this multiple choice?" Ted joked, only to be prodded for a second time.

"They call me Billie-Jean."

More and more children gathered around the new arrivals, chanting.

Right is right ...
Fair is fair ...
Truth is truth ...

"I always thought Billie-Jean King would be older." Ted remained in a heap on the floor following the aftereffects of being electrocuted for a third time.

The blonde teenager stood over him, with no idea of the reference to the popular tennis player.

"Wait, you're *the* Billie-Jean," he said.

"That's right," she said.

"How is Michael Jackson? And have you seen him lately?" Ted was hit with the cattle prod for a fourth time. "Wait, now I know. You're Billie-Jean Mabel, from Rosewood Falls."

Clearly irritated, Billie-Jean ordered Ted to be taken away to the same tent as Kurt, Tommy, and Daisy.

The girl faced Mikey, giving his attire the once over. "Anything funny to say?"

Mikey had no intention of being prodded, or probed, so he chose the safe option of telling the truth. "I've never said anything funny in my entire life."

"Is the correct answer. You and your friends are here, why?"

"You'd better ask Zack Burton. He was the one who brought us here under false pretenses."

"Kids here are mostly here for a reason. Some are running from something."

"That's not me. I'm running towards something."

"And where might that be?"

"Home." Mikey offered his cuffed wrists. "Now, if you wouldn't mind letting us all go, I'd like to get back on the road."

Billie-Jean laughed. "Your confidence will be your downfall. Five minutes on *the* road you would last."

"I've crossed one before. I'll take my chances."

"Those are some big words."

"I like to think so."

The crowd had grown bigger, their laughter choking any intention Mikey had of debating their rights to appeal.

"Take this one to the branding tent with the others," Billie-Jean ordered.

"You're making a big mistake," Mikey barked.

"We'll see."

MIKEY Drew was dragged away in front of a riotous mob and dumped inside the *branding* tent. Inside, Daisy and his friends' prisoner restraint collars were being activated.

Billie-Jean entered the tent with the bespectacled youngster. Apart from his striking blue irises, the scruffy kid's features were obscured by a year's worth of dirt and unkempt hair. The idea of his blue eyes being contact lenses was highly unlikely considering everybody they had come across so far shared the same iris color.

The kid studied each collar, making sure every light had altered from red to green. Happy that the collars had been activated correctly, he uncuffed each prisoner in turn.

"There are two rules when you are in the Threshold. One. You cross the perimeter when the light on your collar is green, you will lose your head. Two. Cross the active Threshold without a collar, and we're having brain soup for chow," he snarled.

Tommy and his friends knew straightaway the kid was telling the truth. It still left them looking towards the exit, which the kid noticed.

"Before you try and fight your way out of here, I suggest you listen to what Billie-Jean has to say." The kid's gaze lingered uncomfortably on Tommy.

"Are you thirsty?" Billie-Jean motioned to one of the orderlies who activated the collars to hand out some goblets of water.

Tommy batted away the water being offered to him. "You treat us like prisoners, and you expect us to be civil."

"I expect nothing more of you than to drink."

"You can shove that drink up your ass."

The youngster wearing glasses grabbed Tommy by the chin and squeezed, until his tongue was showing. From his pocket he removed a laser scalpel and turned it on. The narrow laser between two pincers buzzed with electricity. "Take that back, or lose your tongue," the kid ordered, moving the scalpel to within an inch of Tommy's tongue.

Tommy tried to speak but couldn't. He nodded feverishly until the kid let go.

"Leave him be, Tobias. He didn't mean rudeness," Billie Jean said.

"Your name is Tobias?" Tommy asked, slightly embarrassed that a kid so young overpowered him.

"What of it?" the kid replied.

Billie-Jean eased Tobias aside. "Tobias, you can leave us now."

The kid left, glancing back once at Tommy, only to flash him the bird.

"He's a real charmer," Ted said. "Have you got any more of those?"

"Hundreds," Billie-Jean replied.

"We really have hit the jackpot."

"A younger brother, Tobias is to me. Your collars are his work. You be more polite to him, or you could lose your heads."

"That kid built exploding collars?" Mikey asked.

"Smarter than he looks, he is. A long time here, like me."

"How long?"

"Long enough to adapt to the environment."

"You mean your blue eyes?"

Billie-Jean nodded; "We forget until new arrivals point it out. A nutrient in the water keeps us young and healthy. Blue eyes are a side effect."

"You should market it. Kids back home would go wild for a drop of blue juice," Ted remarked.

"Sacred the water is to this area."

"Is that why you stay here? For the water," Daisy said.

"We stay, only to protect the springs from those who wish to use it for financial gain."

"Why is it so important to you?"

"A life source it is. A planet's true product. Its protectors we are. And now, so are you."

"You protect water?" Ted said, before laughing.

"That's funny to you."

"It's not, it's just, where we come from, water is everywhere."

"As it is on this planet. But a natural resource, the lifeblood of the planet. That is something that should not be marketed for profit."

"Why do we need collars? It's not like we can go anywhere," Kurt said. "And we're clearly not here to steal anything."

"You wear a collar for your own safety."

"You don't have one," Ted stated.

"That's because I'm not stupid enough to leave the Threshold."

"Are we your prisoners?" Tommy asked.

"Free to roam the camp you are, but curious I am. The usual kids who join us, you don't seem like them."

"We're not," Daisy said. "If Burton would've stuck around long enough, he might have backed us up."

"Enough he told me about you all."

"It was probably bullshit," Kurt remarked. "Big Z promised to lead us to the Badlands. No offence, lady. There isn't anything bad about this place at all."

"There is one thing," Ted said. "The smell! It's worse that the sewer."

"We're probably not even in the Badlands," Tommy said.

Billie-Jean paused on purpose, waiting for him to introduce himself.

"Tommy West," he said.

Billie-Jean shook his hand and felt the spark of a connection. She could tell he felt it, too. The boy had fire in his eyes, a desire that rivalled her own.

"What do we need to do to get your help?" Daisy had noticed the spark and purposely stood in between them to fan the flames before they could ignite into something more serious.

"Earn my trust, first you must," Billie-Jean replied.

"How?"

"Politeness is a start."

"You collared us. That's hardly polite."

"Leave camp without my say so, you cannot. To follow the highway to hell, suicide it will be."

"Isn't that our choice."

"Weapons you have none. Vehicles, gasoline."

"Let me ask you a question," Tommy said. "Are you stuck here?"

"Protect the springs we do."

"Do you have weapons? Any vehicles, gasoline?"

"Why is you interested?"

"Burton brought us here, along with other kids. Despite the collars, you're not giving me the Prison Warden vibe."

"Warden I am not, custodian is all." She studied Tommy from head to toe. It was hard not to notice his determination to leave.

"Forget it, Tommy," Daisy said. "It's impossible to bend the rod of authority once it's imbedded in someone's spine."

Billie-Jean quickly picked up the vibe that the girl in the group and Tommy were an item. She moved closer to Tommy, running her hand through his hair. "A while it's been, since new blood in camp showed some grit."

"Hands off my man, bitch."

Stirring the cauldron of jealousy broke some of Billie-Jean's daily monotony. "Relax, friend. Follow me. Something to show you, I have." Billie-Jean linked arms with Tommy and led the group outside.

"Is she flirting with him?" Ted asked Kurt.

"What do you think?"

"I'm finding it's easier to ask questions. You know how it is. I tend to get a lot of things wrong when I talk. I mean, who can blame Tommy for not lapping it up. She's the hottest thing in this place, and there are twin suns outside."

"Ted, shut the hell up," Daisy barked.

OUTSIDE the branding tent, the residents' excitement over the new arrivals remained. Billie-Jean led Tommy and his friends towards the dome at the edge of the encampment, an entourage of youngsters following them. The crowd passed through a graveyard of rusted car frames varying in models and shapes. Tires, engine parts, wiring, equipment worthy of any repair shop, a mechanic's wildest dream.

The steel cage, constructed of anything from stainless-steel sheets to car doors, and tied together with electrical cord, twine, and metal chains, appeared nothing more than a sand pit style gladiatorial arena.

Tommy and his friends entered through one of two entrances, located at opposite ends. Spectator benches, fixed up to pulleys on the outside, allowed a full view from different heights.

"We call this the Well of Life," Billie-Jean said. "All disputes are settled here."

"I heard cheering earlier," Mikey said.

"Forever quarrelling we are about leaving this place."

"So why don't you?" Tommy asked.

"My oath I swore to my predecessor stands. To protect the water, I will."

"Is the sand to cover up the blood?" Mikey asked, his foot brushing some aside to check.

"Heated matters get sometimes, but blood is never spilt. A peaceful tribe, we are."

"It looks like this arena was pieced together from scrap found in a junk yard," Kurt said.

"You'd be correct."

"Let me guess, Zack Burton sold it to you?" Daisy sniped.

"Donated."

"He doesn't seem the type to give something away for free."

"Burton is not who you think he is."

"I know what he is. He's a slimy, double-crossing, no-good swindler."

"That's enough, Daisy," Tommy said, motioning for calm.

"You've changed your tune. When we got here you called him a traitor."

"An aggressive approach isn't going to get us out of here."

"Right, you'd be," Billie-Jean said. "You have no way out of here, unless I agree."

"The sun must be getting to you, Tommy, if you believe that's true," Daisy snarled.

"I'm thinking with a clear head. Perhaps you should start," Tommy said.

"She won't let us leave no matter what I think. We'll die here."

"Can we talk?" Tommy asked Billie-Jean.

"About?" she replied.

"Our reasons for wanting to leave."

"Yeah, why don't you tell her the story, Tommy," Daisy sniped.

"Fear I do, in the middle of something I have stumbled," Billie-Jean said.

"Right, you'd be, young lady," Daisy snapped.

"She doesn't mean that," Tommy replied.

"Fine, you stay here with your new girlfriend." Daisy marched towards the exit.

The two guards on the door stepped aside, allowing her to leave the arena with her brother, Kurt, and Ted.

"Firey, she is," Billie-Jean remarked.

"Not always. We've just been re-building our relationship," Tommy said.

"Arguing helps?"

"It is a weird situation."

"Life you take too seriously. You're how old?"

"That is something a person should know," Tommy laughed. It felt good to relax, even if for just a few moments.

Amid the laughter, the two of them shared a knowing look, which eventually made Tommy feel like he was cheating somehow.

"Don't mind me asking you, but you are trying to get to where?" Billie-Jean asked.

"Our home. Across the Badlands."

"Wasteland crossing is suicide."

"We need to try. Which is why we need your help."

"Help you, even if you all die in the process?"

"It's a chance we're willing to take."

"Tommy, I'm sorry. The blood of you and your friends, is something I do not wish to have on my hands."

"You have to at least let us try."

"I'm sorry. We spoke openly. All of you seem genuine enough. Burton would not have brought you here if he thought differently."

"I get it. I might not agree with you entirely, and I appreciate your opinion stands when it comes to this place, but Burton was wrong."

"Safe, the camp might not look. Collars, everyone wearing. The safest place you can be right now. Trust me."

"And that's your final answer?"

"It is."

"Lucky for you that nobody sleepwalks here."

"Ha ha. Tobias has the collars set up so they …"

Tobias entered the dome in a hurry, eyeing Tommy with a daggerlike stare.

"Speak of the *devil*," Tommy said.

Tobias handed Billie-Jean a parchment. She opened it briefly to read the contents.

"Arrive when did this?" she asked.

"With Burton," Tobias answered.

"He didn't say anything. Where was it?"

"With the parcel he delivered." Tobias nodded in Tommy's direction. "He left quickly after this idiot started hurling abuse."

"Hey, don't blame me. We were tricked," Tommy said.

"Tricked! More like saved."

"It doesn't feel that way."

"You don't know how lucky you are to have found this place."

"Tobias, enough," Billie-Jean snapped. "A reason Burton left in a hurry. Why, we now know."

"This will change everything, Billie-Jean," Tobias said.

"Are you okay?" Tommy asked Billie-Jean.

"Not really," she replied.

"Billie-Jean, I don't beg for help lightly but …" Tommy grasped her by the hands.

She hesitated before pulling away. "Tommy. Talk no more, we can. Matters going on here, you are not aware of. Leave you now, I will. Your friends are waiting." She smiled awkwardly, as if she wanted to leave in a hurry. "Thank you, for sharing your story with me. Hoping now, you can settle quickly and become part of our family."

"Yeah, help yourself to food and stuff," Tobias added, as he followed her outside the dome.

TOMMY located his friends in the automobile graveyard's only garage. A canopy shaded them from the relentless heat, a divide separating the scrap from a handful of workbenches. Everything a mechanic would need was on hand.

Mikey and Kurt were across the yard, searching for a car that looked roadworthy.

"We've got plenty of cars, parts, and tires. Just a shame we don't know a good mechanic," Ted said as Tommy arrived.

"Find whatever you can," Tommy said.

"Does that mean we can leave?"

"I'm still working on it."

Daisy made herself busy by scrubbing the grime off a pickup truck's windscreen. She seemed irritated and was putting in more effort than she needed to. Tommy purposely sat in the driver's seat so she would need to face him.

"How's that flirting working for you?" she said.

"Can we talk?" he asked.

"If we must."

"And I wasn't flirting."

"Yeah, you were," Ted said, with a wink. "Just really badly."

Daisy jumped down from the tanker and grabbed Ted by the chin. She squeezed until his tongue was poking out. "Ted, you speak another word and I'll get that little nutjob with the laser to cut off your balls and make you eat them."

Ted nodded feverishly and she let go. "Okay, okay. Enough said."

"Now clean." Daisy slapped the scrubber into his hand.

"But I've found a tanker. It's hollow inside. I already checked. It'll be good for transportation."

"Clean, or balls. Your choice." Daisy turned back to Tommy. "Well?"

Tommy climbed down from the pickup. "I'm trying to get us out of here."

Daisy's shoulders sagged. "And you do that by flirting."

"We talked, nothing more. I stopped shy of begging. She said no. The end."

"I'm sensing there's more."

"Fine, I wanted to ask her about my kids."

"Then why didn't you?"

"It's weird. You won't understand."

"Try me."

"Okay. That little nutjob with the laser."

"What about him?"

"His name is Tobias."

"You think he's one of Tobias's weird offspring?"

"No. My son's name was Tobias."

"That doesn't mean anything."

"It's him. I'm telling you. He looked at me like he knew me from somewhere. I know how crazy that sounds because he's never seen me as a teenager."

For the first time since she reappeared in the time machine, Tommy felt he had lost her confidence. She seemed more eager to get them home than she did helping him find his kids.

"Daisy, I know this is hard for you."

"Do you now."

"Yeah."

"Okay, lover boy. You tell me how I'm feeling."

"You're frustrated that I'm concentrating on another girl. When all I am doing is trying to get information."

"Tommy, that's not it at all."

"You're not jealous?"

"Not in the slightest."

"Then why are you acting weird with me?"

"Because, if you find your kids, then what? You go back to your old life? You bring them with us? We don't have time for it. I don't have time for it. We're on borrowed time as it is. Those green clouds overhead?"

"I can just about see them."

"Exactly. We're running on fumes."

"That doesn't help me with my kids."

"Fine. How old was Tobias?"

"I don't know, eleven."

"No, *your* Tobias."

"Four. He was four when he was taken."

"The kid in the tent is older, Tommy."

"I know that. Look, I don't even know how old I am right now. As much as that sounds crazy, it's the truth."

"You're sixteen. Sixteen. So am I. Enough with this. You gotta let go."

"Why would I when I know it's him. He has my son's features, and traits."

"You mean psychotic mannerisms."

"He's even wearing the same type of glasses."

"Fine, say it is him. When we get back to Earth, you're sixteen, he's eleven. You do the math. And what about your other kids? If Tobias is eleven here, then how old are they."

"If Tobias is eleven, Logan would be fourteen. That makes Starbuck and Apollo sixteen."

"Sixteen, your age. How would you explain that to your parents? *Hey, mom and dad. Nice to see you. Oh, while I was vacationing on another planet, you became grandparents. Don't worry about the age difference. It's not as weird as you think. We were just living accelerated lifelines*."

"Why are you acting like this?"

"Because you need to hear it. To show you that you don't belong here. None of us do. It was all make-believe. They're not real. Trust me. It's all due to this game Mikey got us into."

"If you thought so strongly about it, then why offer to help me in the first place?"

"I didn't have a choice. You had your heart set on finding your kids."

"Wouldn't you have?"

"All I wanted to do was find you. Nothing was going to stop that from happening. Not the Wishgiver, not HIM. Not even your kids, as crazy as that sounds right now. What about your wife? You haven't mentioned her once."

"Do I really need to mention my wife."

"It's important. What do you remember?"

"She was, she had …"

"Well?"

"Nothing, okay."

"Was she alive, dead, what?"

"She was alive."

"Did you see her?"

"No."

"No?"

"It was you."

"Fine. Did you see me?"

"I don't know. I can't remember."

"Great."

"What I do know is, I'm looking right at one of the most important people in the world to me."

"One of? You once told me I was the most important." Warm tears streamed down Daisy's cheeks as she finally knew in her heart what she had feared all along. The boy that she loved had been duped for so long, he was starting to pull away from her and there was very little she could do to stop it.

Had searching for him been a mistake?

If there was any feasible way of Tommy being together with his kids, she would have already thought of it. The boy meant everything to her. If the moment came, she would give her life for his.

"Tommy, I wish there was a way for you all to be together," she said, wiping away her tears.

"You should've been honest from the start, Daisy," Tommy replied.

"How can you say that after everything that happened. I didn't want to lose you again."

"You just have."

AFTER Tommy stormed out of the staging area, Daisy slumped against the wall, sobbing.

Mikey's sister and Tommy had quarreled before. Today was different. A coming together so severe, he feared, unless he could douse the flames and get the band back together, the team might not make it back home in one piece.

"I'm sorry," Mikey said.

Daisy looked deflated when she realized it was her brother apologizing, and not Tommy.

"That pleased to see me, huh?"

"I'm sorry, bro. I just …" Daisy cradled her head in her hands.

"I'm not sure what to say."

"I think I said enough for both of us."

"Look, I didn't hear all of it. Just the ending, the middle, and the start."

"Am I wrong to confront him about his kids?"

"No, you're being honest. I'm just not sure a sixteen-year-old with a life worth of fading memories is ready to hear the truth from the girl he loves."

"If not from me, then who should he hear it from?"

"If what he said is true, and somehow his kids are here, then he needs to make the call for himself. He knows he can't take them home. He just didn't want to hear it from you."

"I had to say it, Mikey. He knows they're not his. He told me that. He just wants to help them."

"Then let him."

"You don't understand. It's not that simple."

"I understand more than you realize. You were the mother of his children in his dream state."

"It wasn't me."

"I know it wasn't *you.* It was another Daisy."

"He doesn't remember her. He told me."

"Is that important?"

"I don't know. If they are here, what if he chooses to stay with them?"

"That's his decision. No matter how much we love and need him. If he stays, he stays."

"I felt lost without him, Mikey. I've sacrificed everything. You have no idea how hard it was at home without him, and you. I thought about ending it all. Taking my life. Perhaps then it would all end. Maybe I'd wake up and everything would reset."

Mikey put his arm around his sister. "You were the one who brought us back together. Don't ever forget that. If Tommy makes the decision to leave with us, he will be distraught. You may well need to be the bond that binds us again. If those memories are real, he'll need your love and support, no matter how much he pushes you away."

TOMMY ran until the open wasteland bathed under the planet's twin suns. Branches from the comet's green plasma trail were the only blight on an otherwise perfect, desert horizon.

"I wouldn't take another step if I were you." A teenage boy, with a ponytail, sat atop a sand dune, with his identical twin sister.

Flashing red lights on the threshold perimeter poles a few feet in front, signified the border Tommy had almost unwittingly crossed.

"A few more steps and you would have lost your head," said the girl.

From the beginning to the end, a teenager's first love was as exhilarating as it was heartbreaking. To leave it all behind, all he needed to do was to keep running. Even if it meant losing his head.

"You're one of the new arrivals," the boy said.

"Is it that obvious?" Tommy replied.

"Not unless you're used to sticking out like a sore thumb."

"So would you be, if you'd been what I've been through these last few days."

"You make it sound like you're the only person here who has suffered recently."

The teenage twins shared a skinny, rolled up cigarette. They shared an auburn hair color and comparable features to the collar creator, Tobias.

The desire to run returned, flooding his veins with adrenaline.

"You want a hit?" the girl asked, offering the cigarette.

"No thanks," Tommy said, almost tempted to taste tobacco for the first time.

"It might help you deal with what's bugging you."

"I doubt it. When you get to my age, everyone suffers. Sometimes in silence."

"At your age. You can't be much older than us," the boy stated.

"What have you lost?" the girl asked.

"My family," Tommy said.

"The people you came with?" the boy asked.

"No. They're my friends."

"At least you have some. We only have family in camp. Nobody we can call a friend, except for Billie-Jean. She took us under her wing when we arrived," the girl said. "She does the same for everyone. She'll do the same thing with you guys if you let her."

"No, I'm getting out of here as quickly as I can. If not for this collar, I'd already be gone."

"There is no way to remove it. Not without the key," the boy said.

"I could kidnap that kid Tobias."

"Watch what you say about our brother."

"Your brother?"

"That's right. We come as a four piece."

Grasping at the obvious signs before him, Tommy's legs wobbled, his head starting to spin.

Four siblings.

Twins.

Similar features.

Could it be?

He sat down on the sand dune, trying to take in the possibility that he had found his children. Only by asking their names would he know for certain.

"You're going to tell me next that you have a younger brother called Logan and your names are Starbuck and Apollo," he said.

The twins stood sharply. "Why did you say those names?" the boy asked.

Suddenly, Tommy throat was dry, his foot nervously tapping at the sand. "Erm, just a guess."

"Are you screwing with us?" the boy asked. "Who are you?"

"My name is Tommy."

"And you just happened to guess our names?"

The girl named Starbuck pulled two handmade shanks from her boot and gave one to her brother. "We are not people to be messed with."

"I can see that," Tommy said.

"Do you have a surname, Tommy?" Apollo asked, his raised blade forcing Tommy to retreat towards the Threshold perimeter.

"Lower your blade and I'll tell you." He waited for them to do so, before continuing. "My name is Tommy, Tommy West."

He had nowhere to go, and no need to run. He needed answers, and the two teenagers who could give them to him looked at each other in disbelief.

"I'm going to ask you one question. How you answer depends on whether you are about to lose your head. Why are you using that name?" Apollo asked.

"You mean apart from the fact that my folks named me," Tommy added.

"Don't get cocky, man. One more step backwards and you'll lose your head. It's not a pretty sight, trust me."

Tommy hesitated until Apollo raised his blade. "Okay. I think I'm your dad."

Starbuck dropped her shank as fast as the penny implanting into her memory slot.

"Wait, what?" Apollo said, wondering why his sister was looking so emotional. "You're not buying this BS?"

"Apollo," Tommy said, reaching out for his son.

"Hands off me, creep."

Starbuck gently cupped Tommy's cheek and held his head still. She studied his features, his hair, only for her brother to drag her aside.

Apollo's swift kick to the back of the ankle dropped Tommy to his knees. "You came to the wrong place, man."

"It's me, son. As crazy as it sounds. It's me. I'm your dad. If you don't believe me, then why would I know what you were playing the morning you disappeared? It was Christmas Day. The virtual reality set was playing. All four of you were on the couch. Your mum was playing the mixtape I made her when we were dating as teenagers, over the Bluetooth speakers," Tommy pleaded.

Apollo dropped the shank and stumbled backwards. "How would you know that? I've not thought about that day until this morning."

"Because it's him." Starbuck grabbed Tommy by the hand and helped him stand.

"So, our dad just turns up out of the blue. And he's a teenager. Just like that?"

"Why not, Apollo. Is that so impossible to believe? I told you over breakfast that I just can't shake the feeling that I've been lost, and today I've finally been found. It all makes sense now. It felt like a dream."

"Yep. You're alive, but not living as intended," Tommy added.

"Exactly that. And today, my eyes are wide open."

"I felt the same thing when your mu– … I mean, when I was rescued. I was stuck in an accelerated dream state. Living a life that I thought was real. Only when I truly awoke did I realize one thing."

"That everything that came before was foggy, almost …"

"… fake."

Tommy felt like he'd been stabbed in the heart. He knew straightaway that the kids he had been so eager to find were lost souls. Anything more was just a thread holding him back long enough for his accelerated lifeline to age him rapidly. And when that lifeline was supposed to have ended, he would have been discarded like rotten fruit.

It was Arcadian's way.

Daisy had been right all along.

Nobody mattered.

They were pawns in an endless cycle.

A cycle that needed to be broken.

DAISY releasing Tommy had been the break that was needed.

Before the game, being with Daisy was everything that he ever wanted. That was why she said she sacrificed everything to save him. To take him home, to the real world. The world that mattered more to him than he realized. Rosewood Falls, where his parents and his brother were waiting for him.

How could I have been so naïve?

"This is the way," Tommy said, wiping away tears.

"The way of what?" Apollo snapped.

"How the game is played."

"Now we're in a game, for Christ's sake. Man, you're deluded." Apollo sparked up another rolled-up cigarette.

"Hear me out," Tommy said, snatching the cigarette and stamping it out. "That stuff is bad for you."

"Don't ever do that again. You're not my dad."

"Apollo, sit down and listen to me," Tommy barked, waiting for Apollo to sit.

The kid was taken aback, obviously feeling as if he was being reprimanded by a parent. He sat, but only because his sister forced him to. "You've got two minutes. Talk!" Apollo sniped.

"How did you end up in this place?" Tommy asked.

"I remember it as clearly as if it was this morning. We were walking towards a bright light. When we awoke, someone was already leading us through the gates, like every lost kid that reaches this place."

"You were lost, or taken?"

Apollo glanced briefly at the floor. Perhaps he was starting to believe. "Erm. Help me out here, sis."

"We were taken, but not in the way you think," Starbuck answered.

"It was to keep you safe," Tommy replied.

"It certainly felt that way at the time."

"Are you certain?"

"Yeah."

"As certain as you were yesterday. Or just this morning. When my friends and I arrived at your camp. Is that when it all flooded back to you?"

"Yeah."

"Do you not feel more alive today, than yesterday?"

"Yeah, so, so what if we do. Maybe it's what I put in this cigarette," Apollo said.

"It's not. I can tell you that now."

"Fine. Why do we feel so alive today, genius?"

"We've all been used."

"By whom?"

"By somebody who really needs to pay for putting people, kids if you like, through such turmoil."

"Sounds like an asshole," Starbuck added.

"He's much more than that. Trust me."

"Turmoil. That's a word an adult would use," Apollo added.

"Until a few days ago, I used to be one. Theoretically speaking."

Apollo slumped to the sand, his emotions flying back and forth like a tennis match.

"And a few days ago, that was when your eyes opened wide. Am I right, dad?" Starbuck didn't wait for the answer. She hugged Tommy, unable to hold back her tears.

"I've been searching for you kids ever since," Tommy said.

"And it's been so long, you've de-aged from our dad to a teenager?" Apollo said, standing.

"It's not as easy as that to explain."

"You don't need to explain anything, dad," Starbuck said. "I believe you. Apollo believes you, he's just a stubborn SOB. I guess you knew that anyway. Tobias and Logan will believe us, eventually."

"What about your mom?" Tommy could tell by their expressions that he was about to listen to the words he feared hearing the most, no matter when, where, or whatever dimensional plain they travelled across.

"She never came with us." Someone else unexpectedly held Tommy's hand out of comfort.

Tommy glanced down at a grimy blonde, blue-eyed fourteen-year-old, who seemed to be a lot taller than the last time the two held hands. Back then, Logan was no taller than an adult's knee.

"Logan?" he queried.

"How did you know?" Logan replied, smiling.

"We told him who you were," Starbuck answered quickly, to avoid her brother's likely emotional eruption at the truth.

Tommy clasped at the dagger of destiny piercing his heart. Thoughts of twenty years of his old, happy life were blighted by an unexpected answer. These kids and their mother had been separated when they were taken. At no point had he even considered that a possibility. To live with that for seven years, even if it was a dream state, would be tough for anyone to take, let alone four kids.

"I'm sorry," he said, sincerely.

"Sorry for what?" Apollo barked.

"I thought she would've been with you."

"If everything you've just told us is true and we *awoke* this morning, then she doesn't matter. We didn't know her. We don't know you. We're on our own. Like always."

Tommy hesitated for a few moments. The Daisy from Rosewood Falls was not part of the dream state they all shared, but how could he explain who she really was. Enough information had already been explained. To say nothing would surely be better than stating the obvious.

"So where is she?" Starbuck asked, already dreading the answer.

"Do you know already, is that why you're crying?" Logan asked Starbuck.

"I'm fine, Logan. Just girl things. Remember I told you about those."

"Yeah. Yuck."

"Not yucky. Necessary."

"I thought you were crying because dad had found us." Logan glanced sideways at Tommy, who had no idea how to react.

"You know who he is?" Apollo asked.

"Only because I've been eavesdropping on the entire conversation," Logan added.

"Logan," Starbuck grabbed her brother by the arm and pulled him away from Tommy, "what have I told you about snooping?"

"You told me never to do it. Unless I hear something worth listening to."

"And?"

"This was big news. I mean, I've not thought about dad at all until this morning. It made me feel weird. Am I in trouble, dad?"

"No, son," Tommy said. It felt weird saying it out loud for the first time.

"Are the twins in trouble?"

"No, they're not in trouble either."

"Does Tobias know you're here?"

"No, he doesn't know," Starbuck said.

"Nobody knows," Apollo said, his defenses finally crumbling. "Sorry, Tommy, I mean, dad. Calling you that, with the way you look, sounds weird."

"Despite my appearance, I'm looking at you all through the same eyes. That's not weird. It's life. Your body will change, but it's what's you keep in your heart and your mind that stays with you forever."

"Whatever form of you this is, I believe it is you."

"Finally," Starbuck joked, playfully poking her brother in the ribs.

"I'm happy with that, Apollo. This isn't easy for me either. Thanks, though, for believing in me," Tommy said.

"Can we tell Tobias now?" Logan asked.

"Not yet. Tobias isn't as understanding as we are," Starbuck said.

"Yeah, he's likely to set off dad's collar and ask questions after," Apollo added.

"But wouldn't that kill dad?" Logan asked.

"Exactly. We agree then. Nobody else is told. Not even your friends, Tommy." Apollo looked straight at Logan, who nodded in reply. "Dude, no tell."

"Affirmative, bro. Do you want to hear some other big news?" Logan said.

"What is it?" Tommy asked.

"I heard Billie-Jean talking about getting us out of here."

"Why?" Starbuck said.

"When Zack Burton arrived, he brought news that the wasteland pirate is coming for us. They think he has found a way to cross the threshold, without collars."

"It must have been the letter he brought," Tommy muttered.

"What letter?" Apollo asked.

"I was talking to Billie-Jean. Tobias brought a letter. This must be what Burton warned her about."

"Which means the pirates can walk in here whenever they want," Apollo said.

"When are we leaving?" Starbuck asked.

"She's going to speak to everyone ASAP. Whatever that means," Logan replied.

"It means now."

"That must be why she sent out word for everyone to join her."

"We need to find Billie-Jean, now," Tommy said.

Chapter 29

The Fire of Truth

IN FRONT of a raging fire in the Well of Life dome, Billie-Jean held in her hand Burton's letter. Outside the dome, the beginning of a sandstorm was forcing the campmates to occupy every available space. Be it the sand at their feet, or one of the elevated benches, the campmates eagerly awaited the urgent news.

Wearing hooded cloaks, Tommy entered the dome with Logan, Apollo, and Starbuck. He left them at the perimeter and promised to find them after he had listened to what Billie-Jean had to say. He then made his way through the crowd to the front of the gathering. Daisy, Mikey, Kurt, and Ted had taken position on one of the elevated benches. Despite trying, he was unable to get their attention.

Billie-Jean gave the gathering the once over, and looked to her lieutenants for approval that everyone was now present. Unable to wait any longer, she began to address the crowd.

"To all of you, welcome. The bush, I will not beat around. Concerned, you need to be. The rumors are true."

"*Is the camp still safe?*" a girl shouted out, which led to a volley of abuse and questions.

"No," Billie-Jean yelled, to be heard over the commotion. "Our camp is safe no more." Ignoring the next chorus of questions. She raised her hands to quieten the din. "Abuse and questions help will not." She raised the letter so everyone could see and was unable to hide her concern at its contents. "News reached me not long ago about the wasteland pirates. Coming for us, they are."

"*That means the collars are useless,*" a kid said from the back of the gathering.

"For certain, we know not."

"*Are they going to come here for nothing, Billie-Jean,*" another kid hollered.

The comment was met with derision, forcing someone to whistle loudly. After a few seconds, the arguing stopped. All eyes turned to Mikey Drew, who made his way down from the elevated bench by climbing down a steel chain. He joined Billie-Jean by the fire.

"Billie-Jean's news, you all need to take seriously. If you do not. I guarantee you, you will regret it," Mikey knew the comment would raise even more concern.

Arguments broke out.

Billie-Jean whistled to calm the bickering.

To add to the din, the sandstorm had escalated.

"Enough!" she yelled. "Right, this newbie is. Only one thing, the pirates want. Our water. Take prisoners, they will not. Die, we all will."

"*Do we run?*" one of the younger boys asked from the left side of the arena.

"*No. We fight,*" a girl answered from near the front.

"Fight, we cannot. Weapons, we have none," Billie-Jean said. "Leave the camp, we must. Leave the water behind, we will. Innocent blood will spill on these sands no more."

"There is one way," Mikey said under his breath.

"Which is?" she replied, covering her mouth as she spoke.

"You ever seen the movie Convoy?"

Billie-Jean moved aside, to allow Mikey to take center stage.

"I can help you," Mikey said.

"*Why should we listen to him?*" someone asked.

"Because you have no other choice. My friends and I, we need to get home. To do so, we need to cross the wastelands."

"*You'll die out there,*" a boy said right in front of Mikey.

"And we will die here if we stay," Tommy replied from the front of the crowd. "Isn't it better to burn out, than to fade away? By that, I mean we're willing to take a chance. My friends and I will do all we can to lead you all to safety. And if we fail, we'll go down in a blaze of glory."

Mikey paused until the murmuring ceased. "Not for the first time in our lives, Tommy read my mind. And those of a few rock stars! I've been here a few hours and I've seen enough abandoned vehicles here for us to use."

"*For what?*" someone asked.

"To transport you all and your precious water springs to safety."

"*Why should we follow you?*"

Billie-Jean gestured for the crowd to still.

"Because my friends and I, we're survivors," Ted said, making his way down from the bench the same way as Mikey.

"*Does that make us cannon fodder?*"

"Die here, nobody will," Billie-Jean assured them all, despite not believing it herself.

"*We have no weapons to protect ourselves.*"

"That's a risk we'll need to take," Kurt said, making his way towards his friends.

"*It matters not. Nobody here can drive.*"

"The five of us will drive the vehicles," Daisy said, following Kurt and Ted down from the bench. "We've all done a few hours of driver's ed." Without breaking stride, she joined Tommy and his friends. She squeezed her boyfriend's hand as reassurance.

Tommy leaned over and whispered. "I'm sorry." He hugged her, if only to stop himself from telling her he'd found the children.

"*What planet are you from? Cars need gas!*" someone yelled out from one of the highest benches.

"Zack Burton has gas." Burton lowered his hood as he walked around the campfire, brushing away the sand from his cloak.

"Then I'd think twice about letting rip in front of those open flames," Ted added.

Tommy recognized Burton's voice and whipped round, not knowing whether to hug or punch the truck driver. "Zack Burton."

"The one and only."

"What are you doing back here?"

"Now don't get all sentimental with me. Zack Burton is here for one reason, and one reason only. Gas! The type of gas that will help you kids get home. Not the type that comes out of your alimentary canal."

WHEN the upheaval of Burton's revelation died down, Billie-Jean took back center stage. "Our salvation arrived, just in time," she said.

"What salvation needs to ask you all to do, is gather your belongings as quickly as possible," Burton said.

"*Then what? We pick straws to decide who stays and who goes.*" One of the older boys nearest the front looked less than impressed with Burton's arrival. "*I heard that's how the last ruler decided who lived and who died.*"

The next bout of uproar was cut short by Burton's handheld airhorn. "Billie-Jean is not your ruler. And we have enough vehicles to use," Burton replied.

"He's right. I'm no Max. Never have I ever been," Billie-Jean added. "Max confronted the pirates. Return, Max did not. None of those who joined him returned. Straws, nobody picked. The dangers, the volunteers all knew. Did it hurt, them not returning. Sure. Every day. Today, my heart hurts muchly more. The spilt blood, from all the lost lives since Max left us, I carry, so y'all do not have to. To be safe, we need trust. I trust these newbies, as will you."

"*What about the sandstorm?*"

"It's our cover for now. The pirates won't attack until it clears. And you won't need to do anything. Leave the fighting to us." Burton glanced at his wrist, despite having no watch. "By my calculations, we have a few hours until those pirates get here, and the sandstorm passes us by. That's plenty of time for us to prepare."

"Who's with us?" Billie-Jean asked, raising her fist in the air.

"*Right is right. Fair is fair. Truth is truth,*" the crowd chanted, until the words echoed across the landscape.

Chapter 30

Bracelet Buddies

"I SURE hope you have some magic in those bracelets of yours," Burton said as he entered Billie-Jean's tent. Following him inside were Billie-Jean, Tommy, and his friends. He waited until everyone was inside before he sealed off the entrance from the sandstorm.

"Most folks refer to us as the fellowship of the bling. The only problem is that we lost the bling when you hoodwinked us," Ted said.

"Not one person has ever called us that," Kurt snarled.

"Erm, I think I just did. That's one person."

"Fine, only one person has ever called us that."

"Sorry to interrupt. You're looking for, I think, these." Billie-Jean reached beneath her bunk and removed a small bag that Burton had asked her to keep safe whilst he was away. She handed it to Daisy. "When the time came, Burton thought need these back you might."

Daisy released the pull string to reveal all five of their power bracelets tucked inside. She showed the four boys, handing the first one over to Ted.

"Thank God. I felt naked without my bling," Ted said, snapping his around his wrist.

"What is bling?" Daisy asked.

"It's this," Ted said, pointing at his bracelet. "That's why we're the fellowship of the bling. You know, like in the Lord of the Rings. At Rivendell, they form the fellowship of the ring. I just swapped bling for ring. It's where Frodo, Sam, and Gandalf … why are you looking at me like that?"

"I understood the reference."

"Oh, because you're looking at me a bit weird."

"Only weird, because I actually understood what you were referring to."

"It means you're finally becoming one of us." Mikey smiled at his sister.

"Daisy is a nerd," Kurt said, laughing.

"Never," she said, equipping her bracelet.

"Why would you take them from us?" Mikey asked Burton as he affixed his bracelet.

"You needed to understand that the source of all courage and strength comes from within," Burton said.

"I don't get it, Burton. You drugged us. Dumped us in the desert, and then gave us a life lesson," Ted said.

"I'm not a bad guy," Burton replied.

"You call drugging and kidnapping a good deed of the day."

"Would you have come willingly if I had explained that these kids needed your help? Zack Burton will answer for you. No, you wouldn't have. You would've used your bracelets and left them all behind. I can see you're all upset. Don't blame Zack Burton. If you're blaming anyone, look no further than OCP. They've been taking runaways off the streets for years."

"That's a good thing, isn't it? Keeping kids safe," Kurt asked.

"Safe! Ha. Hardly! This camp might be cut off from the cities, but OCP's research is cloning a workforce, full of juvenile skin jobs. Now don't get old Zack Burton wrong, I am a man of the world and I know money keeps that same world ticking over. But do you know how much you need to pay someone who doesn't need to sleep or eat. Not a dime. And don't get me started on the extracurricular activities. Let me just say it's a sick world out there, and OCP are raking in record profits. Leaving everyone else at the mercy of corrupt law enforcement."

"What do OCP do with the kids after they're cloned?" Daisy asked, fearing already what the answer would be.

"What's left, isn't much. Black market organ donors pay rich bucks after experimentation," Billie-Jean said. "Peaceful abandonment, they call the ones too ill to be donors. Procedures are injections. Painless, or so I've been told. Incinerate the remains they do. Lucky you were, to be found by Burton."

"When you arrived, OCP's stooge, Captain Bryant, he had no idea where you came from," Burton added. "Can you imagine something new on the market?"

"Mega bucks."

"Exactly that, Billie-Jean. That's why April contacted me. She has done so before, and she will do so again."

"Why not be straight with us?" Tommy asked.

"Like you were with your map."

"You can see why we didn't lead with that information."

"In my line of work, Zack Burton needs to be certain before he puts his neck on the line. April was just covering her ass. As were you."

"Tell her that she doesn't need to cover that in future," Ted said.

"Always with a crude remark," Kurt said, digging his friend in the ribs.

"How else do we sort out the ones who need our help from those who work for OCP? Lucky for you guys, Zack Burton believed your story," Burton continued.

"I'm not sure I'd agree it was luck," Daisy said.

"Trust me. Bryant must have been eager as hell to cut you guys open and see what makes you tick. Talking about ticking. We have less than fifteen minutes until those pirates reach us."

"We have just fifteen minutes?" Billie-Jean barked.

Burton held up a handheld device. On the screen were video images of a sandstorm. Driving through it were a fleet of black Porche 911s, motorcycles armed with rocket launchers, and a armada of dune buggies.

"This screen comes in hand with all types of sensors and battery powered cameras. I never leave home without them," he said.

The cameras had been left at specific points on the highway, the last camera being thirty minutes away. Burton had kept track ever since he raided the pirate's camp.

"Why did you tell everyone they had a few hours?" Kurt asked.

"The more time to spare, the less you panic," Burton replied.

"That's not logical," Ted added.

"Okay, I'll admit it. Zack Burton stole from the pirates a gutted gasoline tanker. But it was for a reason. And I might have taken some gas. That was about three hours ago."

"You stole a tanker from the dune pirate?" Tommy asked.

"Where do you think I went when I left you here?"

"We thought you left us here to rot."

"I did leave you. Not to rot, but how else are we supposed to get everyone out of here. That truck is armor plated. I thought we could use the trailer as a passenger hold for the kids."

"Or we can use that to store the water," Daisy said.

"About that," Billie-Jean said sheepishly. "Springs, there are none."

"A truck with no suspension. You're like the worst car thief ever," Ted said.

"She means the water springs, Ted," Kurt added.

"You lied to us?" Daisy sniped.

"Not exactly," Billie-Jean replied.

"Is there water or not?"

"The water spring was a ruse that the older kids use to keep everyone in line," Burton said.

"I thought the water was so potent it turned everyone's pupils blue," Tommy said.

"Lied about that too, I did," Billie-Jean removed her contact lenses and showed them to Tommy.

"Another ruse?"

"Nutrients is a better reason than contact lenses. The lenses keep our eyes moist from the dryness in the air."

When she laughed, Tommy noticed her real eye color was a piercing green.

"Wow. I've never seen green eyes before. You should stop using lenses," Tommy said.

"Hey." Daisy jabbed him in the ribs.

"It was a compliment, nothing more," Tommy said, squeezing Daisy's hand.

"If truth got out about this camp being a safe haven for runaways, everyone would be on edge," Burton added. "The unofficial version of what we're up against. The wasteland pirate is no more than a child catcher. Hunting down strays for OCP. The official line, the pirate leads a phantom army of super elite fighting men whose weapons are the most powerful science can devise. Their mission is to marshal the wasteland. When Max confronted them and never returned, that's when Billie-Jean took over. Ever since, I've been searching for someone to help us get the kids to somewhere safe. I can't do that alone."

"What changed?" Mikey asked.

"You did."

"What Burton means is that stuck here we are no more," Billie-Jean added,

"Is that what the note read?" Tommy asked.

Billie-Jean nodded. "Burton wrote *today is the day.*"

"And you kept us here?"

"The collars kept you here," Burton said. "You're helping everyone escape out of the goodness of your hearts."

"That's the life lesson," Ted said, nodding firmly.

"Exactly. What you all said earlier when you promised to protect these kids, well, it showed me that you are the real deal. Life isn't just about the individual, but the people around you. Don't be blinkered. There's more to life than the road ahead. Sometimes you need to divert to reach the right path."

"Things are getting deep," Mikey said.

"Now we're all on the same wavelength. Shouldn't we be looking into hot wheeling it out of here?" Kurt asked.

"You can use our vehicles, what's left of them," Billie-Jean said.

"I've found pieces all over the wasteland," Burton added. "Some of them have onboard navigator systems. If you can get them to work."

"Leave that to us," Mikey said.

"Drive the truck, who will?" Billie-Jean asked.

"Zack Burton. Need I say more?" Burton said.

"You drive the truck with the kids. Billie-Jean, you ride shotgun. We'll be the protection," Tommy said.

"Now take me to my ride. I'm gonna pimp the ass out of it," Ted said.

"Gross!" Kurt added.

"That came out wrong."

"It normally does when you're involved."

"Before you go anywhere, let's take off those collars," Billie-Jean said.

TED's choice of an eroded, hollowed out Pontiac Trans Am raised a few raised eyebrows from his friends. What they had overlooked was his teenage fascination with the vehicle. He saw beyond the rusted chassis, the lack of interior fittings and the bricks it was mounted on. Potential was key, along with the chance to welcome back an old friend.

By resting his hand on the bonnet, his power bracelet shuttled enough energy through the Trans Am's systems to elevate it into the car of his dreams, the Goodknight 2000. The one-of-a-kind vehicle was the fastest, safest, strongest car on the planet. Smooth to the touch, leather seats, the dashboard resembling Darth Vader's bathroom. The 2000 was fuel efficient and operated entirely by microprocessors, making it virtually impossible for the car to be involved in any type of collision, unless ordered to do so by the driver.

The car's transformation was not the only change he made. Ted paused to admire the reflection in the driver's window.

"Hello again, Mr Goodnight," he said, his scarlet tinted shirt unbuttoned to his navel.

Ted smiled on the inside as he ran his hand through Earth's most radical perm. Never again would he take for granted the golden, muscular physic and the reflexes of the world's most daring driver. Having spent so many teenage years hoping to be as cool as the action hero, he was now once again able to don the tight leather pants that squeaked as he sat in the driver's seat.

Delaying switching on the onboard navigator allowed him the time to hum his favorite theme tune. *Dun da da dun, dun, da da dun, dun, da da dun, dun, dun ...*

As he had experienced before, Michael Goodnight's calmness was the lift that he needed. A boost that relaxed him enough to unleash two thunderous farts. "Two farts! Two furious!"

"*Thankfully, Michael, my odor receptors are offline.*" The car's AI sounded familiar.

"Katt?"

"*The one and only.*"

“You’ve got a lot of nerve showing your face around here, after what you pulled.”

“*If you’re referring to our last mission together, I ejected from the spacecraft for my own safety.*”

“What about my safety?”

“*You are still alive, are you not?*”

“Well, yes.”

“*Would you rather I crashed and burned with you?*”

“Well, no.”

“*Need I say anything else, Michael?*”

“You know what, I can’t stay mad at you. It’s good to hear your voice, Katt.”

“*As it is yours, Michael. Shall I run a diagnostic?*”

“No need. I’m certain breaking wind didn’t do any lasting damage.”

“*That’s not what I was referring to, Michael.*”

“I knew that. Be my guest, Katt. Diagnost away.”

WHEN Kurt spotted the shell of the 1980 Wingho Concordia III, he knew right away that the vehicle could be the tipping point to win the battle against the pirates.

Using his bracelet, he powered up the wreck, transforming it into the prototype, flat wing design that he had seen in the movies. With a Kevlar and fiberglass composite body, Earth’s fastest car, with a five-speed transaxle and high-performance racing wheels, could reach a maximum speed of 325 mph.

He was almost horizontal in the driver’s compartment, behind the tinted windows, when he switched on his onboard navigator system, codenamed Maverick.

“Now we’re talking,” he said.

Due to the car’s power outlay, the navigator’s power core was increasing slowly alongside the turbo boost pressure bar which topped out at 50.

10 ...

Kurt tapped the earpiece communicator Burton had handed out to each of the teenagers. It allowed everyone to listen in. “It looks like my onboard navigator is booting up slowly. While I'm waiting, what enemy numbers are we expecting, Burton?"

Burton was inside the tanker's cab, making sure everything was going to plan. "They're top of the line. I'd say at least fifty vehicles, ranging from dune buggies to motorbikes, all from the Delta Mark four range."

20 ...

"Weapons?" Kurt asked.

"Rocket launchers, twin carbine machine guns. Turbo boosts," Burton replied.

30 ...

"Is that all," Kurt said.

"These guys are the best of the best," Burton added.

"So are we."

40 ...

"Battles are won or lost on quick decisions, Kurt," Burton said.

"That's me screwed," Kurt replied.

50 ...

"Why would you say that?" Burton asked.

"My car's VDU just flashed up, *I feel the need, the need for weed.* The last time I heard a phrase like that was from the cousin of the fastest mouse in all of Mexico."

"Maybe Slowpoke's getting high from all the fumes," Ted said, under the guise of Michael Goodnight.

"My navigator is called Maverick, Ted. Not Slowpoke."

"How did you know it was me?"

"It was a wild guess. And I've got the fastest car here, you'll see."

"Guys, it's not a pissing contest," Daisy said over the comms.

"Yo, Maverick, are you with me?"

"*Hello, senor.*" The car's strong Mexican accent was slow and deliberate, as if carefully picking his words. "*I'm here to assist you.*"

"I don't suppose you've got Speedy locked away next to you?" Kurt asked.

"*I am fast.*"

"No offence, but you don't sound fast."

"*I am as fast as fast can be.*"

"Yeah, you sound ready to haul ass."

"*I feel the need, the need for weed.*"

"Yeah, you've said that already. Any chance I can switch navigators with anyone?"

THE damaged Battle Sled, Mikey had seen once before. It was during their very first journey across the city aboard a state-of-the-art Urban Assault Vehicle. Packard and his goons had used Battle Sleds, a fast, agile vehicle to hunt down the teenagers. With the driver facing forward, a few feet off the ground and supported by the surfboard type chassis, the user's arms would be outstretched, and palms resting atop two circles of light used as controls. Like all Battle Sleds, in the wakes, jetwalls of pure energy vaporized anything organic that touched the wake barriers. It was the ideal machine to take to war.

With his bracelet energy coursing through his veins, Mikey slowly closed his eyes and rested a palm on the sled. By the time he had reopened them, he altered into Jesse Mach-one. A motorcycle cop tasked with a clandestine project named Highway Hawk. The busted chassis had transformed into a sleek black Battle Sled, a knee-high mist adding to the Sled's imperious presence.

"That's some sled," Kurt said from the vehicle alongside.

"And I just turned it into an all-terrain pursuit vehicle. Hyperthrust, vertical lift, a particle beam laser. This sled has everything we need."

"Plus, tight trousers."

"Are you checking me out, dude?"

"No! It's just they're *tight*."

"You think?"

"Any tighter, and you'll be cutting off your circulation."

Wearing a black leather motorcycle outfit, with a white trim, Mikey pulled tight his gloves and sealed them at the wrist with Velcro. Three seals secured his boots.

"It's like the love child of Cyclone and Street Hawk," Ted said over the comms as Mikey equipped his helmet and lowered the visor.

"If only Heather Thomas was here to scratch my back," Kurt said.

"Why would she scratch your back?"

"Because."

"Because what?"

"Unlike you, Ted, I'm trying not to be crude."

As he lay on his front, Mikey's visor switched on to indicate the firing grid, speedometer, energy levels and the name of his onboard female navigator.

"*Good afternoon, I am Cobra, your navigator for this journey. May I ask the name of my user?*"

Cobra's calm tone allowed Mikey a few moments to familiarize himself with the controls. "You can call me Jesse."

"*What are your orders for today, Jesse?*"

"We are going up against bad guys. They're as dangerous as dangerous gets."

"*They're not dangerous. They're the disease, and I am the cure.*"

"Chick's got issues," Ted said over the comms.

"IN a race across the desert, I can think of only one car and driver we need to survive this ordeal." Tommy stood alongside Daisy, Apollo and Logan; their attention focused solely on a battered dune buggy. The vehicle had no wheels, no doors, no headlights. Just an empty shell with two front seats, and enough room in the rear for two passengers.

"I hate to point out the obvious, but your dream machine has no wheels," Apollo said from behind them.

"Ask and you shall receive," Tommy said, resting his hand on the buggy's bonnet.

"We don't have to time to make repairs."

"We have plenty of time. Where's your sister?"

"She's in the tanker, with Tobias."

"Good idea. Probably best to keep him safe."

"Wait. You're not thinking of having these kids in your car," Daisy whispered.

"Why not?"

"Because it's dangerous."

"No more than the tanker."

"I think you need to reconsider."

"This is my call."

"Fine. On your head be it," Daisy said, clearly agitated by his comment. "Who are they again?"

"Just a couple of kids Billie-Jean asked me to keep an eye on."

"Doing her favors now?"

"Perhaps."

"Fine, I'll find my own ride."

She backed away, ready to search for her own car.

"Daisy, wait. I need you," Tommy said.

"Really?" she asked.

"I need you as my navigator."

"You're not using an onboard system like the others," she replied.

"What I've got planned pre-dates any tech. It needs both our power combined."

"You're going old school."

"You better believe it."

Daisy rested her hand on the bonnet. "Then I've got just the bad ass chick from hell you're looking for."

With their powers combined, the dune buggy altered into a supercharged, custom C3 Corvette, with a curvy fiberglass body, and a reptilian paint job. With snake eye headlights, a row of fangs in place of the bumper, and a spiked spine from the tip of the bonnet to the very rear of the boot, the Alligator Car needed just a driver to make the transformation complete.

Tommy's alteration into the sadistic headhunter Tankenstein took the two kids by surprise. The famous Death Race driver's customary black cape was caught up in a non-existent breeze, his disfigured features shielded by a metallic mask painted black and red for effect.

"Was that magic?" Apollo asked.

"Tommy, you're scaring me," Logan said.

Rather than reply, Tommy pointed forcefully to the rear seats. The two kids boarded the car, and watched their dad take his spot in the driver's spot.

"Tommy, are you okay?" Apollo asked.

"He's in the zone. Now button it and let us concentrate. Lives are on the line," Daisy said from the front passenger seat, in her avatar form.

"Who the hell are you? Where did that girl go?"

Daisy had transformed into the tough, worldly mother of the future leader of the human resistance. On her lap, she had a bag full of weapons.

"I'm Sara Connor," she said.

"Why are you here?" Apollo asked.

"I'm here to kill Timeinators," Daisy replied.

The two children glanced at each with some doubt.

"*This is Burton. Time is almost up. It's time to move out.*"

Tommy finally removed his mask. His features were disfigured, as if burnt, his stern glare forcing the kids to sink further into their seats. "Buckle up back there. It's about to get bloody on this highway to hell."

"Isn't that a bit dramatic?" Daisy said, removing an M60 from her weapon's cache.

"Says the badass chick with the M60."

BURTON'S tanker stopped at the edge of the Threshold, his focus on the start of the highway a few hundred feet away. The sandstorm had eased off enough to show the highway was clear, at least for now.

The passenger door opened, startling him. Tobias boarded after having removed the last of the campmates' collars. He dumped the bag full of collars in the space behind the seats.

"And my job is done," Tobias said, folding his arms.

"What are you doing here?" Burton shifted in a panic.

"I want to be up front, with you."

"I need you in the trailer. It's bulletproof. You'll be safe inside."

"I'm staying."

"You're not. The trailer is bulletproof, the cab isn't. Now, back to the trailer before it leaves."

"Fine, fine, fine."

“Hey, don’t be a dick. I’m saving your life.”

“I’m old enough to save myself.”

“Just go, before it’s too late.”

Tobias left the cab and used the affixed cargo netting to reach the top of the trailer.

The tanker Burton had stolen came equipped with weapons. Billie-Jean and her two enforcers in boiler suits wielded the flamethrower mounts at the front, middle and rear. On the sides of the trailer, two orb shaped pods had been mounted, the handlers able to fire out a volley of metal darts from the dart guns.

“Can I help up here?” Tobias asked Billie-Jean.

“The trailer, you should be in it,” she replied.

“I’m a fighter.”

“The fighting is for us older kids.”

“I’m old enough.”

“Old enough to be in the trailer.”

“Babysitting sucks, Billie-Jean.”

“Tobias, listen. Something happens to me today, kids will need someone to lead them. That person is you.”

“And your point is?”

“The point, you can’t lead anyone if you’re dead.”

“Fine, I’ll go babysit and miss out on all the fun. Please don’t die, Billie-Jean,” he said, hugging her.

“I’ll try my best,” she whispered as he descended the cargo netting.

WITH the fate of a camp full of children in their hands, the teenagers’ four vehicles revved their engines as if waiting for the green light to race.

“Do you remember the Cannonballers?” Ted asked.

“More like Wacky Racers,” Daisy replied, whilst wrapping an M60 ammo belt around her forearm.

“Bootleggers! Let’s roll out,” Burton ordered.

Chapter 31

Highway to Hell

THERE WAS a reason the route to salvation had been dubbed the Highway to Hell. Mace Hunter's sadistic Hell Cops policed the road by showing no mercy to those trying to escape OCP's stranglehold. The wreckage from their previous duels still lined the highway as far as the eye could see. Makeshift graves of their fallen colleagues had been marked with a wooden cross, the skeletal remains showing how far back the conflict had lasted.

Billie-Jean had kept the Hell Cops ruthlessness a secret. Another secret had been that more people had tried to escape in the past than she and Burton had let on. Her camp was just one of many. By keeping her kids hidden away inside the trailer, she would hopefully ensure their safety, even if it meant offering her life for theirs.

HUNTER's concentration was super intense, eyeing the convoy crossing the Threshold boundary he had found so difficult to penetrate. Never had these campmates tried such an exodus before.

By stealing his tanker and gasoline, they had given the game away. Perhaps it was on purpose. Or perhaps this would be the final duel. A duel he wanted to win at all costs.

His orders were to bring the Bootleggers back in body bags. He knew very little, only that they had escaped the city and were wanted for studying. The captured campmates would be sent to OCP for experimentation. He cared very little for their outcomes, or for the payment that went with it. The thrill of the chase was reward enough.

Mace Hunter was good-looking, with a perfectly groomed mane of auburn hair. His beard was immaculately trimmed, his combat fatigues looking as expensive as the black Porsche 911 that he parked a quarter of a mile from Campus Christi.

Behind the Porche, the drivers of a line of identical Porsche, and motorbikes equipped with rocket launchers, awaited his orders.

Detaching the CB from its perch, Hunter addressed his unit. "OCP wants the children alive. The Bootleggers total five. That's the number of body bags I have in my possession. Don't disappoint me."

LEADING the convoy, Tankenstein's Alligator Car sat side-by-side with the Goodnight 2000. Protecting the tanker from the rear, Mikey swerved the Highway Hawk across the sand, leaving in his wake the deadly energy barrier.

After leaving the campsite, Kurt's wing shaped car, navigated by Maverick, banked west, in what appeared to be an attempt to lead some of their attackers away.

"That's a good idea, Kurt. Someone on the outside, keeping 'em busy," Burton said.

"That's not what's going on here," Kurt said, midargument with his navigator. "Will you let me drive?"

"*No, senor,*" Maverick replied.

"Do you wanna get us killed?"

"*We will be if I let you drive.*"

"Kurt, what's going on?" Tommy asked, shooting a glance at the car racing into the distance.

"It's a little complicated," Kurt replied.

"Then uncomplicate it."

"We're not on the same wavelength."

"Smoking a joint might help," Ted suggested.

Goodnight's silky tongue almost convinced Kurt to blaze a doobie.

"No! That is a bad idea. Kurt, you chose the car. Fix it," Tommy said.

"I chose the car, not Cheech and Chong," Kurt said.

"Fix it."

"Fine, fine, I'll back off. Go ahead, Maverick. Do your worst."

KEEPING his distance, Hunter had already spotted the sleek Wing pull away from the group and ordered some of his unit to intercept.

"*What about that energy barrier? We can't get anywhere near the tanker while that sled is in play,*" one of the Porsche drivers stated.

"Blow it to hell," he replied.

THE Convoy raced along the dusty highway, with a fleet of black, Porsche 911s on their tail.

From the chasing group, a cluster of motorcycles pursued Kurt. Mini rockets from the launchers mounted either side of the steering column rained down. Explosions rocked the territory; the Wing swerving to avoid the craters in its path.

The rockets were not being used to hit the target, just to slow it down long enough for them to reach kill distance. As the rockets ran out, the drivers switched to the machine guns affixed to the windshield.

"Lucky for us, your reflexes are faster than your dialogue," Kurt said.

"*They miss on purpose,*" Maverick replied as bullets rattled the bulletproof chassis.

"Why would they do that?"

"*I am bulletproof. You are not. You are easier to kill.*"

"Easier to kill!"

"*I crash. The doors open. You are shot twice in the head.*"

"You're a lot smarter than you sound."

"*Fight them off, and we have a chance.*"

"With what, harsh language? I equipped this bulletproof car for speed, not weapons."

Before Kurt could answer, his seat swiveled one eighty, allowing him a full view from the stretched rear window. Hunter's squad of ruthless bikers filled the horizon.

"Great, a front row seat to my imminent death."

The seat shifted forwards a few feet, locking Kurt in place in an alcove just long enough to fit his body inside. Two joysticks rose from the armrests, each of them equipped with a red button. Simultaneously, a pair of laser cannons hidden inside two side panels emerged from above the rear wheel arches, and then secured either side of the window.

"I didn't equip these bad boys," Kurt said.

"*That's my job, not yours.*"

Any slight adjustment with the joysticks brought forth a firing grid on the back window.

"*What are you waiting for?*"

"Instructions would help."

"*Shoot to kill.*"

Kurt shifted the joysticks, locking the firing grid on to the nearest target. He fired without hesitation. The laser bolts took out the first biker. "You know what? That wavelength issue might be okay after all."

AS quickly as Mikey laid down an energy barrier, a volley of rockets took it down.

"I can't hold these cars off forever," he said over comms.

"*We only need to hold them off long enough to reach the flatlands,*" Burton said.

"What's the flatlands?"

"*You'll see.*"

"How far away until that happens?"

"*Five miles.*"

With the energy barrier no longer a concern, Hunter's fleet of Porsche 911s closed in from the rear. With no guidance systems, the rockets blasted craters in the highway ahead, forcing the convoy to weave and dodge at speed.

The dust clouds caused by the bombardment was to shield their next wave of attack - a fleet of dune buggies with mounted grappling hooks perched on a sandbank, ready to intercept the convoy.

"We've got assholes incoming to the east, armed with grappling hooks," Burton warned as the dust clouds cleared.

"Not for long." Tankenstein sneered as he spoke.

"Tommy, we can't let them get those hooks in us. If the tanker stops, this is all over."

"I'll try my best."

"If that happens, you and your friends need to flee."

"No way is that happening. I'm sending some backup. Daisy, are you ready?"

"I thought I was helping you," she replied.

"Protect the tanker with everything at your disposal."

"Okay. Just don't die on me today."

"Would I?"

Holding on to the spiked spine for support, Daisy grabbed the weapons cache and stood on the passenger seat. Tommy slowed the car down long enough to allow the avatar of Sara Connor to board the tanker by using the cargo netting. After she climbed up to the trailer, she took up a position with her M60.

With Daisy safely aboard the tanker, Tommy peeled away from the front of the convoy, towards the dune buggies.

"I hope you know what you're doing," Goodnight said.

"It's about time I showed everyone why I picked a car everyone thought was radical in the 70s," Tankenstein replied.

"Radical isn't a word I'd use for a car designed by a toddler."

"Thanks for the support, Ted."

With the convoy in his wake, Tankenstien increased speed faster than he could count, the landscape whistling past the cockpit in a blur.

"Is that your girlfriend?" Logan asked.

"It is," Tankenstein replied.

"Does she know we're your kids?"

"Hold on, kids," Tankenstein warned as he headed straight for the fleet of dune buggies.

"We can help," Apollo said, brandishing a handgun.

"Where the hell did you get?"

"That tough chick gave us one each for protection."

"Did she now?"

"Yeah, it was quite a motherly thing to do. Don't you think?"

"No, I don't. Who gives kids guns?"

"Well, you were a kid. I mean you are a kid, and you're driving what looks like a killing machine."

"That's true, but if you want to help, keep count."

"Of what?"

"The body count," Logan said, smiling.

"That's my boy," Tankenstein said.

Ahead of him, he could make out the buggies in a flying V formation. The lead buggy refused to slow down, the two vehicles playing a high-speed game of chicken. A moment before impact, Tankenstein shifted the bumper's row of sharp fangs into attack position.

Bam!

Tankenstein's roadkill weaponry sliced through the buggy's chassis. As they continued to rise, the buggy flipped up and over. Erupting in a ball of flame as it crashed down, the driver cried out in pain as he died in the wreckage.

"One," Logan said, a bit too eagerly.

Suddenly, Tankenstein was on the tail of two other buggies. They both had to slow down due to the leader being taken out. He waited for his moment, the chance to make his move, only to be blindsided and almost becoming an alligator sandwich.

He braked hard, the two other buggies scratching chunks of paint off the wingtips as they slammed into each other. Accelerating behind them, he swerved, snatching the left buggy's rear end with the fangs. The driver braked, lost control, and drilled into the side of the other buggy, wiping them both out.

"That's three," Logan added.

Leaving the wrecks in his rear mirror, Tankenstein focused on the remaining seven. They had raced ahead and were now only a few hundred yards away from reaching the highway.

At full speed, he overtook the rear buggy, swerved across its path, and then hit a handbrake turn. The buggy swerved, but not far enough to escape the fangs. The ivory daggers pierced the driver's side, his stomach, and then released, the buggy ending up in a dizzying spin, before tumbling to a stop.

"Six left," Logan bellowed, fist pumping the air.

ACROSS the dunes, Kurt's accuracy with the laser cannons had ended the threat of the motorcycles. Rejoining the highway, the car sped northward. Wreckage of the cars already destroyed by his friends lined the roadside.

"Those laser blasts look like some of Mikey's handywork," he said.

"*Eyes front,*" Maverick ordered.

"Ah, crap. They're all over that tanker. Get us up there."

Reaching the rear of the convoy, which was being hounded by the fleet of Porsche 911s, Kurt noticed the vehicles had bunched up on a twisting road. Soldiers were trying to board the tanker from open sunroofs. Those not burnt by the flamethrowers were being blasted to pieces by Sara Connor's M60.

"MORE assholes inbound," Burton said as a cluster of the sand buggies reached the highway ahead of them.

"Now it's my turn," Goodnight said, increasing speed.

The Goodnight 2000 raced ahead on a collision course with the sand buggies. In single file, none of them were moving aside.

"*With all due respect. You are not possibly considering using me as a weapon,*" Katt said.

"What other weapons do we have, Katt?"

"*Apart from ramming speed? None.*"

"Then you'll have to do."

"*You are crazy, Michael.*"

"They wanna get nuts. Let's get nuts!"

"*If you're going through with this, do you want me to activate the turbo boost?*"

"Turbo boost your ass off, Katt."

Protected by armor plating, the Goodnight 2000 collided with the front vehicle, smashing it to smithereens. The car's booster made sure their follow through took out the next two enemy vehicles, sending debris across the asphalt.

Due to the booster speed, Goodnight was unable to stop the final two vehicles using evasive maneuvers.

"We didn't get them all. Two remain," Goodnight said, reversing through the wreckage as the other two vehicles set off after the tanker.

"*Leave those slimy punks to us*," Cobra said on Mikey's behalf, as Highway Hawk flew by Goodnight in blur, to rejoin the convoy.

"*Your friend's navigator has some genuine psychotic tendencies*," Katt said.

BURTON glanced out the side window a moment before one of the grappling hooks pierced his door and tore it away. A laser blast from Mikey's bike disabled the buggy but not before one of Hunter's men leapt towards the front cab.

The soldier braced the doorframe, grabbed the steering wheel, and pulled.

With the tanker swerving out of control, from his lap, Burton lifted a single cartridge shotgun, and blasted a hole into the assailant's chest. Falling into the road, his body was crushed beneath the wheels.

Before Burton could reload, the other passenger door was ripped off. A girl boarded the cab, wielding a handgun. She wore one of the camp's hooded cloaks they used during sandstorms.

"Who the hell are you?" Burton barked, regaining control of the tanker.

"I'm the person asking you to stop," she replied. "And while you're at it, tell the Bootleggers to surrender."

MACE Hunter had watched from a distance his team being decimated by what his superiors called Bootleggers. It was now time for him to intervene.

He accelerated along the highway, dodging the wreckage. Ahead of him, the tanker was slowing down, as he had planned.

"BURTON. Why are you stopping?" Tankenstein asked as the Alligator Car rejoined the highway.

"It might have something to do with the gun in my face," Burton said, easing the tanker's speed. "Everyone, stand down. It's over."

Mace Hunter's Porsche sped by, the driver giving Tankenstein the finger from the open window.

"Burton, I'm on my way. Hold on, kids," Tankenstein said, shifting up a gear.

"Dad, why is the truck stopping?" Logan asked.

"Someone has pulled a gun on Burton."

"You mean a gun like this," Apollo said, pressing the barrel of his handgun into the back of Tommy's skull. "Now ease down on the accelerator."

"What are you doing?"

"Something I should've done when I first saw you."

Blam!

WITH the two orb dart guns on the side of the tanker destroyed, it allowed four of the Porches to flank the tanker as it slowed down. Armed with handguns, the non-drivers climbed to the top of the trailer with caution.

Acting as the last line of defense and on her last ammo belt, Daisy's avatar, Sara Conner, lifted the M60 from the mount and retreated towards the front of the trailer.

Of the three teenagers using the flamethrowers, only Billie-Jean remained alive. She was still in her mount above the cab, clutching at a stomach wound, her weapon no longer active.

Daisy searched the landscape for help. Mikey's Sled and Kurt's Wing were being escorted by three of Hunter's Porsche Unit. Tommy and Ted's avatars were nowhere to be seen. A sudden tug at her ankle forced her to look down.

It was Billie-Jean.

Daisy knelt by her side. Enough blood ran through the camp leader's fingers to show the severity of the injury. Daisy tore off a strip of cloth from her t-shirt and braced it against the wound.

"You'll be okay," Daisy said.

"You lie good for an outsider," Billie-Jean said, wincing with pain. "If it comes to it, this tanker, blow it to hell."

"I can't. Not with everyone inside."

"It's rigged. Pull the lever. Don't let them win." Billie-Jean slumped back, her body going limp.

"No, no, no. You can't die. Not like this. Not here."

"Freeze," yelled a man from behind.

Daisy glanced over her shoulder at four soldiers, dressed in black fatigues and armed with handguns.

"It's over," the one in front said at the same time the tanker stopped. "Both of you stand."

"It's just me. She's dead."

"Then drop your M60," another man ordered.

Daisy lowered the M60 and stood in surrender. She turned to face them.

"You're almost too pretty to murder," the leader said.

Daisy felt a tug on her ankle. "I'm not the type of girl to spread my legs for just any man, but I'd make an exception today." Daisy opened her legs wide enough for Billie-Jean to open fire with the M60.

The four men were blown to pieces, body parts and blood adding to the paintwork.

"Why did we stop?" Daisy asked Billie-Jean.

"I don't know. Help me up."

With the M60 out of ammunition, Billie-Jean dropped the gun. Daisy helped her to stand, and then used the cargo netting to reach the pavement.

"No matter what happens to me, remember what I said," Billie-Jean said as she slumped by the roadside.

"I'VE stopped. What now?" Burton glanced sideways at his passenger.

"I'm glad you listened, and that I didn't have to kill you," the girl stated, her identity shielded by her hood.

"What now?"

"We wait for *him*."

"Who?"

"You'll find out soon enough. Now, step out onto the pavement and unhook the trailer."

AFTER the collision, the Pontiac Trans Am showed nothing more than a few scratches.

"Are we good, Katt?" Goodnight asked.

"*Better than good, Michael.*"

"That's my girl."

"*Except for the issue ahead us.*"

"What issue?"

"*The tanker has stopped.*"

"Then don't wait for me to say it. Let's get back in the race," Goodnight said, checking his perm in the rearview mirror.

As he did so, he shot a worrying glance over his shoulder. Something approached them fast and showed no sign of slowing down.

"Katt, tell me what that is?" he asked.

MACE Hunter had the Trans Am in his sights and unleashed a volley of laser guided rockets. All of them on a collision course to destroy.

"You collide with my guys. I mess you up," Hunter snarled, as his rockets closed in for the kill.

"*WE have incoming,*" Katt said.

"Haul ass," Goodnight yelled.

The Goodnight 2000 set off, the speedometer reaching 120 mph in a little over three seconds. The first couple of rockets hit the concrete it just vacated; what remained edged nearer, despite the vehicle's increase in speed.

"*Michael, we need a plan,*" Katt said.

"How long until impact?"

"*Fifteen seconds ...*"

"How many of those Porches ahead of us?"

"*Six cars remaining, fourteen seconds ...*"

"What's the distance to reach them, if we use turbos?"

"*Thirteen seconds ...*"

"It's gonna be close. Turbo boost, Katt."

The Trans Am set off just in time to evade the rockets, which continued to track them.

"*Need I remind you, Michael, that the person driving the other car is a homicidal maniac.*"

"I can see that myself, Katt."

"*You need to stop him.*"

"Deal with the rockets first, then we stop the psycho. The question is how."

"*Ten seconds, Michael.*"

AS she altered from Sara Connor back to her teenage self, Daisy witnessed someone under a hood order Burton to unhook the trailer. She couldn't see who it was, and she had no power left to do anything other than wait for the inevitable.

Burton unhooked as instructed and waited for his next set of orders.

"Now, back in the cab and move it up the road," the girl ordered.

"Won't you need them combined?"

"Not when it's being airlifted. And don't get any ideas."

"Aren't you full of surprises."

With the girl alongside him, Burton boarded the cab and moved it ahead about fifty yards.

"DRIVERS, I have a Bootlegger on the run. Follow my co-ordinates, eight seconds to intercept. Don't let him pass," Hunter ordered.

The four Porsche reversed away from the tanker and raced back in Hunter's direction.

"*MICHAEL, we have four cars on an intercept course. Seven seconds until impact,*" Katt warned.

"Damn it. There is no way out for us."

"*I only see one way. Five seconds.*"

"You're right. This time we die together."

"*Four seconds.*"

Katt showed no signs of slowing down even with an overturned vehicle blocking the road. The four Porsche weaved by it wide enough to converge from different directions, and the laser guided rockets the same distance from behind. All of them on a collision course that the Goodnight 2000 could not escape from.

Impact was imminent.

Goodnight braced the dashboard.

"*Two seconds,*" Katt warned.

"Any last thoughts, Katt?" Goodnight glanced behind. The rockets were close enough for him to read the *H.I.M* insignia.

"*Just one,*" she replied.

With his attention elsewhere, Ted failed to notice the Super Turbo Boost symbol on the dashboard lighting up.

As the rockets impacted, an explosion ripped across the highway, the vehicles igniting in a fireball that could be witnessed for miles.

THE explosion lit up the horizon, catching Tommy by surprise.

"What was that?" he said, having reverted to his teenage form. His bracelet retained enough power for the Alligator car to remain intact.

"Hopefully it was one of your friends dying," Logan said, his gun still smoking.

In the back seat, Apollo's dead body was slumped over.

Tommy opened the driver's door and stepped on to the sand.

"Why did you shoot him?" he asked, holding his son's dead body.

"Because I had to."

"But why kill him?"

"Have you not figured it out yet, *dad*?"

HUNTER punched the dashboard in jubilation as he weaved by the raging fireball. "One down. Four to go."

He seemed to care very little about the livelihood of his unit as he parked alongside the trailer. A teenage girl was by the roadside, holding the bloodied body of the person he knew as Billie-Jean. Zack Burton was being held at gunpoint by someone concealing their identity beneath a hood. Two other teenagers were kneeling on the sand, held by what remained of his unit.

"Well, well, well. That was easier than I expected. Now, who dies next?" Hunter said, unclipping a handgun from his holster.

TOMMY'S feelings were as confused as they ever had been. Logan had shot his older brother. It appeared to be to protect his dad from being shot.

"What have I missed?" he asked Logan.

"The most important thing," Logan replied.

HUNTER aimed his gun at Billie-Jean. “You look ready to die. Maybe I should save the bullet and just enjoy the spectacle of you bleeding out.”

“You really are as sadistic as the stories tell,” Burton said.

“Ah, the famous Zack Burton. Someone just as well known, but soon to be dead. You almost made it to safety. Almost.”

“Well, whatever happens now, I will die knowing we took all your people down with us.”

“Almost all of them. I still count four over there. And there’s me. And who do I have to thank for stopping the tanker when all my trained soldiers could not?”

The girl lowered her hood.

“And who might you be?”

“WE’RE not your kids. We never have been,” Logan said, dropping his gun to the sand.

“Say what now?” Tommy stated.

“You didn’t really believe all that? I mean, how would it work? Accelerated lifelines, marriage etc., etc. You’re all still virgins.”

“I know the score. I’ve been listening to it all week.”

“MY real name is not important,” the girl said. “You know what, I guess you can call me Starbuck. What a crude name that is.”

“Why are you helping this creep?” Daisy snarled.

“Because this creep can get me out of here. Unlike you, Burton and soon to be dead Billie-Jean.”

Billie-Jean shifted her gaze. “I don’t know you.”

“That’s right. You don’t.”

“Was she in your camp?” Daisy asked.

“I don’t recognize her,” Billie-Jean replied.

The girl laughed. “Man, it’s so easy to usurp you Horsemen. I arrived when you did, hidden away. Sneaking in, yada, yada.”

"APART from that collar threshold, their security is hardly high tech. When they let you in, the door was wide open. They left it open long enough for Burton to leave camp and the three of us sneaked in unnoticed," Logan said.

"Three of you," Tommy said.

"Yep. Me, Apollo, and Starbuck."

"Timeinators."

"Yep. Doing what we do best. Infiltrate."

"Are you Packard? Cos it's hard to tell you all apart under someone else's skin."

Logan shook his head. "I'm Oggy. Nice to see you again Tommy."

"And I'm guessing that's Skank," Tommy glanced at Apollo.

"He always was the crazy one. And he would've killed you."

"Then why save me?"

"Because I'm tired, Tommy. I'm tired of Packard and this merry-go-round."

PACKARD's Timeinator had used the ultimate disguise. One nobody saw coming.

Tommy's daughter, Starbuck.

"I have to say, this was one hell of a street fight. And you almost made it," he said.

"Let me guess, you're a Timeinator," Mikey stated.

"Welcome to the party, Mikey."

"Timeinator's are assholes," Kurt said.

"Kurt, Mikey, Daisy. Aren't we missing someone? Where is good old Teddy boy? I heard an explosion earlier and he hasn't been seen since."

"I left someone on the highway as roadkill," Hunter said.

Packard laughed.

"Okay, okay, enough with the chatter, young lady," Hunter said. "I don't know who you are but thank you. Now, who is going to open this trailer so I can see the rewards for all my hard work."

"*Your* hard work?" Packard said.

"Yes. My unit. My sacrifice. My reward."

"What about me?"

"What about you? I don't even know you."

"Hey, I want out of here just as much as these Bootleggers do."

"And you shall have your wish. Now, you," and Hunter jabbed his gun in Daisy's direction. "Open up the trailer. The rest of you remain here."

"WHAT about Tobias?" Tommy asked.

"He has no idea who we are," Logan replied.

"But, but …"

"But smut. You assumed. We just went along with it. We've never even met the kid."

"Everything you told me was a lie?"

"What part of infiltrate did you not understand?"

"Daisy was right all along."

"I don't know what she said, but the look on your face is priceless. Now enough talk. It's time to end this charade once and for all." Logan reached inside his trouser pocket and removed one of the threshold collars and a small handheld device.

Tommy backed away. "What are you doing?"

"I need you to do something for me."

BEFORE the convoy had set off, and after speaking to Billie-Jean, Tobias had disobeyed the order to return to the other children. He instead climbed inside the cab through one of the rear windows. Burton was too preoccupied to notice. It was through this same window that he had watched the drama outside unfold.

The girl in the cloak was not a campmate he recognized, and he had no weapons to take her out, or Hunter's remaining drivers.

"Think Tobias, think."

His only real friend, Billie-Jean, was bleeding out. Just thinking about her dying filled him with diabolical ideas about the bag of threshold collars and how to get revenge. Snatching the bag, he gently opened the window and made his way outside.

DAISY moved to the back of the trailer with Hunter. She climbed atop the foot stand and noticed the locking mechanism had not been used for a while.

Billie-Jean had told him that the tanker was rigged, but why?

Why kill all of those she promised to protect?

Was it to keep them away from OCP?

"Are you going to open it? I haven't got all day," Hunter snarled.

"You know what, I'm not your lapdog. If they're your trophies, you claim them." Daisy stepped down and then jogged to the other side of the road.

Hunter ordered two of his drivers to join him at the rear doors, leaving one guarding the prisoners.

BURTON glanced innocently at the cab and noticed the rear window flapping, as if someone had sneaked out of it.

"Tobias. Sneaky kid," he muttered.

"What was that?" Packard said, jabbing the gun in his ribs.

Tobias sneaked all the way behind the only driver guarding Mikey and Kurt. Burton knew what the kid was doing, but also didn't want him to get shot in the process.

"You know what, I've never liked you," Burton said to Packard.

"You don't even know me," Packard replied.

"Exactly. I've known you for, what, five minutes …"

Overhearing the argument, the driver took his eyes off Mikey and Kurt. It allowed Tobias enough time to take the driver down and fix a collar around his neck. He pressed the button to arm it, knowing full well that being outside of the Threshold made the collar a deadly weapon.

As the lights on the collar warned of an imminent detonation, Kurt, Mikey and Tobias ran for cover. The collar exploded, decapitating the driver.

Hearing the commotion, Packard swiveled and fired. The shot missed but he had enough time to re-aim at the fleeing kids. Burton went to snatch the gun, but it was still aimed at Tobias.

The first gunshot snapped Billie-Jean out of her stupor. She needed to look just once at Tobias to know that he was in danger. She struggled to her feet as Burton and the traitorous girl fought for the gun.

A second shot clipped the pavement.

A third shot clipped Burton in the thigh, putting him down.

Packard freed the gun, swiveled towards the fleeing kids, and fired. Billie-Jean jumped in the way, the bullet hitting her midriff, throwing her back to the pavement.

"No, no, no!" Tobias yelled.

FOLLOWING the gunshots, Hunter ordered the two drivers to return to the prisoners. The distraction allowed Daisy enough time to run and hide.

With his reward, the thrill of the chase. Hunter had no interest in what was going on elsewhere. He climbed on the footrest, grabbing the lever to unlock it.

PACKARD strode forwards, using the tanker as a shield as he sought out the teenagers. "Where are you?" he yelled.

Hunter pulled the lever and glanced inside the trailer.

The detonation from the explosives killed him instantly.

Caught up in the blast, Packard's avatar was burnt to a crisp.

A mushroom cloud reached the heavens.

Chapter 32

Where have you been?

MICHAEL GOODNIGHT snapped awake just in time to witness on the dashboard VDU a POV rerun of his car using an upturned dune buggy as a form of ramp. The Goodnight 2000 then punched through a ball of flame, and over the oncoming Porsches, the drivers with no chance to avoid Hunter's laser guided rockets.

"I think whatever luck I had in reserve, I just used up," he said, releasing his seatbelt.

"*It was quite spectacular, Michael.*"

"It looks like the best escape, ever. Just saying. Now let's go find the others, Katt."

The car shifted downwards, as if sinking, dirt, or sand, rising high enough to black out the windows.

"*It would appear that we're sinking, Michael.*"

"Sinking! I now know how Boba felt in the Sarlacc pit."

"*Do you remember when Burton mentioned the flatlands. It would appear we're sinking in them.*"

"Quicksand."

"*Yes. Mr. Burton's plan must have been to force Hunter and his squad from the highway and into the quicksand. Therefore, allowing us to escape unharmed.*"

"You should have told me."

"*Time constraints permitted me to focus solely on our escape from the missiles. Telling you about the quicksand would have been unnecessary, especially if we failed to escape the rockets and died.*"

"I guess living is better than dying. How do we get out of this mess?"

"*There is only one option available.*"

"You better not say swim."

"*No. You must leave me here.*"

"I can't leave you, Katt. Not after everything we've been through."

"*But you must, Michael.*"

"Can't your turbo boost get us out?"

"*I'm afraid the super turbo boost left me with only enough power for one last hurrah.*"

"I hate to break it to you, Katt, but how can I hurrah anything whilst we're sinking."

"*If you can set the pressure adjustment to precisely six hundred pounds, I can get you high enough to escape this plot of sand.*"

"That's it? I just set the pressure and, what, fly out of here?"

"*It would help if you would also open the auto roof.*"

Goodnight pressed the auto roof button. Daylight invaded the driver's compartment as the sunroof peeled backwards. "I'm not sure if you have eyes, Katt, but I can't fly without wings."

"*Look under the seat. There's a parachute.*"

Goodnight grabbed the chute and strapped it to his back. "I've never done this before," he said.

"*There's always a first time for everything. Brace yourself, Michael, it's your turn to leave the sinking ship.*"

Without any further warning, the Goodnight 2000 driver ejection seat fired Michael Goodnight skywards. The parachute opened automatically as he reached a high enough distance.

As he greeted the clouds, Goodnight glanced down to see the Trans Am sinking further into the sand.

"Goodnight, Katt," Ted said as he altered back to his teenage form.

Drifting across the wasteland, he wiped a tear from his cheek as Katt's bonnet opened, signaling a thumbs up, before the Goodnight 2000 was consumed by the quicksand.

TOMMY was alone when he caught up to his friends. They were crowded around the body of Billie-Jean. Tobias was weeping. Ted was nowhere to be seen. Burton had been injured and was being patched up by Daisy.

"You made it, kid," Burton said.

"Barely. Where's Ted?"

The sound of someone yelling forced everyone to look skywards. Ted was strapped to an automated parachute, the guidance control now easing him towards the ground.

"That's something new," Burton said.

"He'll be fine. What happened here?" Tommy said, gesturing to Billie-Jean.

"Billie-Jean saved your friends."

Tommy lowered his head as he came to terms with the news.

"Her sacrifice was for the children," Burton continued.

Daisy yanked hard on the bandage. "Some sacrifice if she rigged the trailer with explosives."

"She did it only in case we got caught by the pirates," Burton said.

"We did get caught."

"Relax."

"Relax! You just blew up a group of kids."

"Daisy, there was nobody inside the trailer."

"When we left, they went in a different direction," Tobias said as he pulled a blanket over Billie-Jean's deceased body.

"We were decoys?" Kurt said.

"More like bait."

"More tricks, Burton?" Daisy said.

"I'm sorry, but it needed to look authentic," Burton said.

"This is turning into a truth tennis match," Mikey said. "First us, then it's back to you. Oh, it's us again. Nope, now it's your turn."

Ted's butt hit the floor with a thud, the parachute smothering him. "Don't try that at home, kids," he said, grimacing. "Now can someone get me out of here, please; this strap is chafing my balls!"

Kurt and Mikey helped their friend escape the entanglement.

"Do we need to ask how you got up there?" Kurt asked.

"I'll save that one for later. Where's Billie-Jean?" Ted asked, and then he noticed Tobias kneeling next to a body covered by a blanket.

"That's also a story for later. Tommy, we need to talk," Daisy said.

"Not now. Later," Tommy replied, squeezing her hand.

"Sorry to butt in on the love parade, but where is the portal from here?" Mikey asked.

Daisy unraveled the map. "A mile further up the highway. There's a tunnel, leading underground. It's right there. The last jump."

"Mikey, Kurt, you guys got a vehicle?" Tommy asked.

"Damn right we have. We have a Porsche," Kurt replied.

"Good. Use it. Ted, Daisy, you're with me. Burton, it's been eventful."

"Stay gold, Tommy boy," Burton said.

"What about Tobias?" Ted asked.

"He'll stay with me."

"Look after him. He'll need a father figure," Tommy stated. "Just not a lying conman, no good swindler."

"You know what old Zack Burton would say at a time like this. That's enough, talk. Haul ass."

Mikey and Kurt boarded their vehicle and set off along the highway.

Ted climbed into the back seat of the Alligator Car and sat in something squishy. "Dude, do I want to know what I'm sitting in?" he asked.

"You're better off not knowing," Tommy replied.

"You want to talk about what happened to those kids?" Daisy asked as she sat in the passenger seat.

"That's a story for later," Tommy said, turning on the engine and setting off along the Highway.

"You think we'll ever see them again?" Tobias asked Burton.

"Who knows, kid," Burton replied. "Maybe, maybe not. Now let's go find the rest of your campmates."

DAY EIGHT

(No jumps remaining)

AFTER JOURNEYING through the final reality portal, Tommy, Ted, Kurt, Mikey, and Daisy found themselves stranded on the cusp of a sand dune overlooking an endless horizon of sand. The vehicles they used were gone, the map showing a blank canvas. The only sign of otherness was a mountain range to the east.

High over the Dune Sea, the comet's tail appeared to be on its way out of the atmosphere, leaving just a few strands of the green haze. Beyond the comet, the familiar image of a Black Hole was flanked by the planet's dual suns. Both events occurring in the same environment, signaled to the teenagers borrowed time had almost run out.

"Am I the only one that thought we almost bought it back there?" Mikey said, coming to terms with their next predicament.

"I used a sand buggy as a ramp to super turbo boost over four Porsches, whilst almost being slotted in the rear by some laser guided missiles. I was like McQueen, in the great escape, vaulting the fence on the motorbike," Ted said.

"Bullshit," Kurt snapped.

"It's true, I have it on video."

"Where is it then?"

"Well, I don't have it with me."

"I'm presuming that was Katt's escape," Tommy said.

"We come as a team."

"But it was all her work."

"And your point is?"

"McQueen also got caught," Kurt said.

"Your points are?"

“It makes no difference. We have no way of reaching the Black Hole,” Daisy added, jabbing a thumb skywards.

“That’s not entirely true. Cobra told me about three old hermits who live beyond the Dune Sea. One of them was a pilot,” Mikey said.

“You had a discussion whilst fighting off a unit of trained killers?”

“It’s not like it sounds, sis. We got to talking and one thing led to another.”

“Did you come together in electric dreams? You know what I mean?” Ted asked.

“We always know what you mean, Ted,” Kurt said.

“Did she have their address? Beyond the Dune Sea is looking a little vast.”

“I didn’t get a chance to ask the question,” Mikey said.

“Then what good does that do us?” Tommy’s remark stung, but his friends did not know why.

“Relax. He didn’t mean to press,” Daisy said.

“I’m sorry, Mikey. I shouldn’t have snapped like that. At least now I know.”

“Know what?” Mikey asked.

“My children aren’t real.”

The Timeinators impersonating two of his children was as raw now as it would ever be.

“You found them?” Daisy asked. “Wait, those two kids in the car.”

Tommy nodded. “They were Timeinators.”

“So was the girl who hijacked the truck.”

“That makes sense. They had a girl with them. To be honest, part of me is thankful that we can finally get out of here and get home.”

“And the other half?” Mikey asked.

“I’m still working on that. At least now I won’t feel bad about leaving someone behind.”

“Have you ever noticed, in every movie or tv show, no matter what genre, there is quicksand. From Falcon’s Crest to Flash Gordon, some sucker almost drowns in it,” Ted said.

“There is no quicksand in Falcon’s Crest,” Kurt replied.

“I swear, in Falcon’s Crest, quicksand is everywhere.”

“Are you thinking straight?”

"Aren't I always."

"That depends." Kurt smirked.

"Then answer me this. Why is Falcon's Crest called a sand opera?"

"It's soap opera, dickhead."

"Are you sure?"

"I'm certain."

"What about Spartacus?" Ted asked.

"It's a sword and sandal movie."

"Does it matter?" Mikey asked.

"Yeah, it matters. All I see is sand ahead. Quicksand behind us. Do you all remember Artax drowning in the quicksand in the Never-Ending Story," Ted said.

Nobody answered.

"I'll take your silence as a yes. That broke my heart."

"That was a swamp, Ted," Tommy added.

"Does that mean it's a swamp opera?"

"No."

"What about swamp thing? Is that a swamp opera?"

"That's a horror movie."

"That's enough!" Daisy roared. "Ted, there is no swamp or sand opera. Okay? Now all of you, look up. A lot of green sky is starting to drastically fade away. Which can only mean we're nearly out of time. Let's get home and then you can mass debate as much as you want about sand, or swamps, or whatever takes your fancy."

"I'll be doing that non-stop, don't you worry," Ted said with a wink.

"That's not the type of mass debating she's referring to, Ted," Kurt added, shaking his head.

"There's another way you can do it?"

"Ted, please stop."

"I mean, normally I just lay on my arm until it goes numb …"

HALF a mile away from the teenagers' location, elderly NASA Captain Dan Hollander sat up in his bunk.

"Vee. Are you awake, buddy?" he asked eagerly, as a nearby radio device crackled with undecipherable activity.

The communication was being broadcast to the tent, having been picked up by the buried sentry scanners scattered around the landscape.

His undernourished frame was a complete contrast to that of his athletic build from his younger years. It meant his bones creaked like rusted cellar doors as he leaned over for the handheld transmitter perched on the wooden stool.

Hollander was certain he overhead human voices. By the time he held the transmitter to his ear, the transmission had ended. Shaking the device did nothing more than loosen something inside of it.

"Tell me I'm not crazy, Vee. Did I hear a human voice, or was I just dreaming again?"

"I heard every word, captain."

Old Vee, a battle scarred, oval shaped robot, rose gingerly from his buried position in the sand outside the cave's entrance. The robot continued to rise, as if using the sand as a soothing bath, its busted frame rattling as he exposed two stabilizing flight legs. Due to the loss of his hover functions, at the end of each leg Vee used two spheres, which had since lost their magnetism, for mobility along the ground.

"Are they friendlies?" Fearing raiders, Hollander tied back his shoulder length grey hair into a ponytail and unholstered his twin blaster from the gun belt hooked above his bunk. The energy bar on it was almost at zero.

"My scan reveals they are teenagers. Three boys, one girl, and one *idiot*."

Halfway down his body, Vee's exterior silver shell struggled to separate. The gap finally parted wide enough to reveal two weary, wide white eyes on a ruddy background. Some of the exterior functions appeared disfigured, a grappling hook hanging loosely from a slot along his chest.

"An idiot?" Hollander asked.

"Yes."

"Are your circuits fried again?"

"My circuits are fine, as they always are. There are three basic types, captain. The girls, the boys, and the idiots. The girls accomplish everything. The boys oppose everything. And the idiots don't say anything worthwhile. After the conversation I've just listened to, he most certainly falls into the latter category."

"Do you think they are from that encampment across the Dune Sea?"

"With the camp being predominantly children, it is the likely scenario."

"Nobody has made it this far in years."

"Twelve years, five months, seventeen days, give or a take a second or two. Not that I'm keeping count of such things, captain."

"Maybe this is our chance to finally get off this planet."

"I sincerely doubt that. They have no spaceship. Neither do we."

"Are your models supposed to be so bleak?"

"No, captain, we just state the obvious to the oblivious."

"Can I state something obvious to you?"

"Be my guest, captain."

"I think someone got out of the wrong side of bed this morning."

"I have no bed, captain. Unless you're referring to the sandpit."

"Relax, old buddy. It was a joke. Now let's go see who's dropped by." On his way out of the tent, Hollander picked up a bulky leather satchel.

SMOKE spiraled from a firepit at the heart of an encampment made up of a ring of worn tents. At the camp's border, consisting of empty toxic waste canisters, two metallic tombstones engraved with the names Kate McCabe and Chuck Pizer could be seen.

From his satchel, Hollander used a pair of worn binoculars to scan the horizon. He stopped when he spotted a group of teenagers heading towards camp.

"Just like you said, OV. A party of five. All humans. No idiots," Hollander said.

"That's still open for discussion," Old Vee replied.

"Can your sensors pick up what they're saying?"

"Unfortunately, yes."

"Well?"

"Do I really need to relay it to you?"

"That's an order, Vee."

"They are discussing mass debating."

"I wish I'd never asked."

"Apparently there are two types. One is a large discussion, the other …"

"No need to state the obvious on this occasion, Vee. Besides, they've seen the fire."

"Shall I ready my lasers?"

"Do they work?"

"Not for three years, two months and …"

Hollander lowered the binoculars. "No, there's no need for weapons. They appear to be unarmed. And we're too old to put up any sort of fight. Let's welcome them."

"Are you sure?"

"No, but what have we got to lose."

TOMMY spotted a small camp had been set up at the base of a mountain scape. The area behind the camp boasted a host of excavated caves, varying in size.

"That has to be the place," he said.

"That's a lot of caves to search," Ted said.

"No need to search. You see that smoke spiral. Look underneath, about ten feet. Do you see that old guy waving at us with the R2D2 rip off?" Kurt asked.

"Don't tell me that's the pilot," Daisy remarked.

"We're doomed," Ted said, shaking sand from his shoe.

"He might be our only hope, Ted," Mikey added, before leading the group to the encampment.

"IT'S not often we have visitors in this part of town," Hollander said, shaking Mikey's hand.

"Twelve years, five months, seventeen days," Old Vee said, as he studied each teenager in turn.

"We covered that already, OV."

"No harm in going over old ground, captain."

"I'm Captain Dan Hollander. This is my droid, OV. Short for Old Vee."

"With all due respect, captain, my identification is Vee, short for vital information necessary centralized. And I'm a rip off of no other droid." Vee glared hard enough at Kurt for his point to sink in.

"OV sounds better," Mikey said, defusing the situation before he introduced each of his friends in turn. "We are looking for a pilot. I'm hoping you're him."

"Nothing like getting straight to the point, kid," Hollander replied.

"If you've experienced anything like the journey we've been on, then you'd understand the need to avoid the small talk," Kurt said.

"I'm a pilot. At least I used to be," Hollander replied.

"I told you, we're doomed," Ted remarked.

"Doom is death, destruction, or any very bad situation that cannot be avoided," Old Vee stated.

"What are you, a talking dictionary?"

"Captain, a warning should be heeded before we take any form of flight with these strangers."

"I know what doom means, OV. I'm old, not an idiot," Hollander said.

"No harm with reminding you before you agree to something you might later regret, captain. And the idiot in our vicinity is still worthy of a debate."

"Behave in front of our guests, OV. Sorry about Vee. He's a little cranky ever since he lost his ability to fly."

"To fly, one needs wings. To glide gracefully, one needs a repair shop. To pilot, one needs a spacecraft."

"I hope that's the spacecraft that will take us there," Tommy said, pointing skywards.

"To the black hole?" Hollander asked.

"We need to fly through it," Ted remarked.

Vee's eyes rotated towards Hollander. "Captain, might I remind you about the girls, the boys, and the …"

Hollander's irritated reaction was enough to cut the droid off. "Kids, every time I look up at that black hole, I expect to spot a guy dressed in red with horns and a pitchfork."

"It's a monster, all right. And so was the monster that almost stopped us coming through it. Or did you forget, captain?"

"How can I forget, OV. You remind me every day."

"You both travelled through the black hole?" Mikey asked Hollander.

"We're not here sightseeing. Don't tell me you came through it?"

"We did."

"How?"

"How and why is a long story. Right now, we need to go back," Tommy replied.

"That's suicide."

"To you, the black hole is a monster. To us, it's a rip in the very fabric of space and time, and it's our way home," Daisy added.

"And time is almost up," Kurt said, glancing at the comet's vapor, which would soon be gone forever.

"Even if we had a vessel capable of flying you through, I'm in no fit shape to pilot it for you," Hollander said.

"What if we could offer up a co-pilot," Tommy said.

"You? You're just a kid!"

"Looks can be deceiving."

"It's irrelevant. We have no spacecraft."

"For the third time, we're doomed," Ted added.

"Did you swallow a bleak pill today, kid?"

"Did you? Look, Hollandaise, do you want off this planet or what?"

"There is no way off this planet. Believe me. My friends died here. We're all going to die here. You might as well get used to the idea."

"Captain, our lives and so many more depend on us getting home. We need to at least try," Daisy added.

"What part of we have no way off this planet do you not understand?"

"There has to be a way," Mikey asked.

"Maybe you can stand on each other's shoulders and reach for the stars. That's about as close as you're going to get."

"You mean there is nothing you can do to help. Not even when the fate of the galaxy is in our hands," Kurt said.

"The galaxy," Hollander laughed.

"It's no joke. Many people have died to bring us this far. We can't give up now. Not when freedom is so close," Mikey said.

"What if I told you we have been battling an interdimensional entity called Arcadian, in a series of games," Tommy said.

"Games?" Hollander snarled. "Ha, now I've heard everything. The suns must have started to erode your nodes."

"Let me at least explain our predicament. Then you can make up your mind if we have fried eggs for brains, or if we might be telling you the truth."

"Don't mention food," Ted said, his belly rumbling with hunger pangs.

"What do you think, OV. Shall we hear them out?" Hollander asked his droid.

"I see no reason not to, captain. They seem genuine enough. If we don't believe them, I can always disintegrate them with my lasers." Two short arm lasers emerged from Old Vee's body. He aimed them at Ted.

"No pressure, Tommy," Ted said, before purposely taking his place behind his friend.

"Okay. Well. Here it is," Tommy said, clearing his throat. "We started by playing games against Arcadian. At first it was a bit of fun. Then it turned sinister. When we thought we had finally defeated him, it turned out that he didn't like that so much. Before we knew it, he turned the tables and cheated us. Ever since, we have been battling for our lives against his minions. We had eight days to reach our destination. That destination is now in the sky overhead. The window to cross through is closing rapidly. To be so close but so out of reach is difficult to take. But I fully understand that if you're unable to help us, then so be it. If we've done all we can, then I can live with that."

"I can't!" Ted yelled. "Look, dude. I've been ejected out of a car. I've had a full cavity search by some warped tracking bug. I've been wrapped in human sized condoms. I've had my brain punctured by some sadistic sphere, with a lance. That's just this week! I seriously didn't go through all of that for a pat on the back and a well done. We have no other options left to us. I want to go home. Now! Help us. Please."

"I hear you, kid," Hollander said.

"I'm sorry for the rant. I just thought you should both know why we're so desperate for help. If you don't believe us, disintegrate away. We have nowhere to go anyway."

Hollander glanced at his droid. The robot's thoughts were whirring so loud the captain could hear them ticking. "What's on your mind, old buddy?"

The droid rolled to a halt in front of Tommy, his lasers aimed at the teenager's midriff. "Arcadian!"

"That's the scumbag we're dealing with," Tommy replied.

"Hmm. If there's one thing I cannot stand, it's a sore loser." Old Vee's lasers returned to their slot in his body. "Let's get you all home."

"Am I talking a different language? *We don't have a spacecraft*," Hollander added.

"What if I had an option for us?"

"Then I'd say your nodes have finally been eroded."

"As always, captain, your wellbeing is at the forefront of my mind, even before my own."

"I know that."

"Then you also know that you are going to die on this planet, unless we can get home."

"Are you going to fly us through one by one?"

"Not exactly. I think it's time to show you why I can no longer fly."

THE group entered the cave system and headed beneath the encampment. Using lit torches from the campfire, they followed the droid until they came upon a large cave, with an open ceiling.

"Why have I never been in here before?" Hollander asked his robotic companion as he stood before a spaceship.

"You sleep a lot, captain," Old Vee replied.

"Were you programmed to annoy me?"

"As I reminded Mr. Pizer on numerous occasions, my models were made to educate you."

"I'm intrigued. Educate away, OV."

"The main body of the vessel is from a Gunstar. A primary space superiority attack craft deployed by the Star League."

"How did you get it down here?"

"I didn't. It was already here."

"Why didn't you tell me?"

"I didn't want to get your hopes up. Not after what happened to Miss. Mcabe and Mr. Pizer. I thought it would be suicide for us to attempt it alone."

"If you don't mind me asking, what happened to them?" Tommy asked.

"Over the years we pieced together our own craft. It was mainly from our wrecked probe ship. Some other pieces of wreckage we found. When it was ready, we picked straws. My friends died on the maiden test flight. Since then, OV and I, we've never discussed trying to leave again," Hollander said.

"Then who left the Gunstar?" Daisy asked.

"Before the main computer crashed, my diagnostic showed that the craft belonged to a Lewis Rogan," Old Vee said. "Lewis was searching for his brother Alex. Alex defeated Xur and the Kodan armada before they had a chance to attack our home planet, Earth. Alex returned to Earth once and was never seen again. Lewis's search brought him here. That was the last entry."

"You're also from Earth?" Ted asked Hollander.

"That's right, kid. We were part of the crew of the research vessel, USS Palomino. After our mission had been completed, we were returning to Earth. We then came across a missing vessel, the USS Cygnet. We boarded the vessel, thinking it was derelict."

"And it wasn't," Daisy added.

"No, we came upon an army. An army led by a madman and his psycho robot."

"We can relate to that," Ted said.

"Our only escape was through the black hole. We've been stuck here ever since."

"Can you pilot this craft?" Mikey asked Hollander.

"Kid, I've known about this spacecraft as long as you have," Hollander replied.

"Is that yes?" Ted asked.

"Vee, what are the craft's specs?"

"The chassis is twenty meters in length and was originally designed as a twin person starfighter," Old Vee replied. "There was room enough for a pilot and a gunner, or navigator. This prototype has been upgraded with greater range and power than the usual attack craft. There was structural damage and corrupted flight controls. To assist, as well as installing other necessary systems, I sacrificed my own flight core to aid the craft's aerodynamics."

"And I thought you were just getting old."

"I may be old on the outside, but in droid years I am relatively fresh off the production line."

"But without your components, are you going to be alright?" Daisy asked.

"Nothing a hammer and a little metal polish can't fix. I also removed all the craft's weapons systems and heavy armor. The Gunstar will now be capable of rapid acceleration and by utilizing the reverse thrusters, abrupt braking. All of which I thought would be of more use to us than weapons."

"Will it fly?" Mikey asked.

"I am yet to try. The only issue thus far is that my initial diagnostic corrupted the onboard computer system. As I searched for a new AI navigation system, my scanners found a downed craft nearby. The system has now been installed."

"That means we can all fly out of here?" Daisy asked, excitedly.

"To answer your question, I don't like it when somebody else pulls my strings. However, on this occasion, I think Knoll will do just fine."

"No way," Tommy said eagerly. "You found Knoll?"

"You sound like you have met her before."

"Does a fart smell?"

"They smell due to the Sulphur in fiber-rich foods. Sulphur is a natural compound that smells like spoiled eggs. Many vegetables are Sulphur-based. If this is causing you flatulence, simply modifying your diet could be enough to reduce it."

"Thanks for, erm, stating the obvious. Yeah. I do know her. We crashed together. Wow, how lucky is that. Have you powered her up?"

"I am yet to power up Knoll or the craft."

"Perhaps now is a good time to try, Vee," Hollander said.

"What if nothing works?"

"All we can do is try," Daisy said.

"Captain Hollander, will you do the honors?"

Hollander boarded the cockpit and sat in the pilot's seat. After a few attempts, the four rear engines rumbled to life.

"Out of the frying pan. Hopefully, not into the fire," Old Vee said to the teenagers.

BY removing the redundant equipment, Kurt, Ted, Mikey, and Daisy were able to occupy the navigator's compartment at the front of the cockpit. Tommy sat behind Hollander's pilot seat, situated towards the middle of the Gunstar.

"Now I know what tinned fish feel like," Mikey said, crammed up against the bulkhead.

"Would you rather stay behind?" Old Vee replied over the internal speaker. The droid had settled into an alcove to Hollander's right.

"You look cozy," Ted said.

"This is necessary, as I will now be integrating with Knoll," Old Vee stated.

"Working together?" Tommy asked.

"The integration will be a full system override, Knoll being the motorcycle and my systems supporting as a sidecar effect."

"What does that mean for you?" Daisy asked.

"Only one of us can pilot the craft. My obsolete systems will aid her but, eventually, I will be overwritten."

"Wait, what?" Hollander disengaged the engines, the craft settling back down to the cavern floor.

"It is the only way, captain."

"No way, Vee. Not after everything we've been through."

"Captain, my priority is the safety of the crew."

"And as captain, it is my job to ensure the safety of my crew. That includes you."

"There is no other way, captain. Ensuring you all return safely home is the most important thing. You know that as well as I do."

"Vee, I …"

"Captain, it's time to hook me up to the mainframe."

Hollander raised the two connectors and inserted them into two visible power sockets located in the droid's sides. As the power coupled with his mainframe, Vee's exterior shell locked down, his two weary eyes closing, his final words sending everyone aboard into a silent prayer for the droid who, despite only knowing the teenagers for a short time, gave everything to ensure they could return safely home.

"As an old war hero once said … down the torpedoes, full speed aheadzzzzzzzz …"

Chapter 33

Event Horizon

IT FELT like years had passed since Knoll's final actions of crashing and burning in a stark desert landscape had left the AI navigator amidst the wreckage of a downed probe ship. In their search for Arcadian, the teenagers knew there was nothing they could do to resurrect the navigator. Leaving the wreckage behind and continuing their journey had been their only option.

Nobody expected to hear her name mentioned again. To do so now left them with the feeling that they were finally going home.

With her power core depleted, and her system in ruins, Knoll's final memory and words were suddenly hauled out of the ether junkyard and hurled upon the crew of the Gunstar.

"*Four teenagerzzzzzzz, one alien life ... f-f ... o ... rmmmmm ...*"

Reignited with what felt like an atomic electric shock, she unleashed a wave of energy across the Gunstar's functions. The engines roared to life as aggressively as a formula one racing engine.

"*Thad! Warning! Four teenagers, one alien lifeform onboard.*"

Every inch of the craft shuddered as if coming apart at the seams.

"*Systems resurrected.*"

Anything with an LED lit up like a firework show on the fourth of July.

"*Full power engaged.*"

The ship's trim glowed with an intense indigo sheen that lit up the cavern, a rapid ascent firing the Gunstar vertically out of the cave as swiftly as a fish being plucked from an ocean.

"Whoa! Whoa! Steady on," Hollander ordered, grabbing the flight control stick, which did nothing more than irritate the navigator.

"*Hands off my stick!*" Knoll barked, and every LED in the inside and exterior flashed red with rage.

"Ease up. We're friends." Hollander sat back, releasing his hold.

The ruddiness eased off, returning to a calm indigo.

Hovering a few hundred feet above the surface, Knoll rotated the Gunstar in a full circle, all the while pondering her whereabouts.

"*Knoll is back in town. Just not a town I recognize.*"

"We need to go through that black hole ASAP," Ted added.

"*I am Knoll, your onboard system navigator. Let me start by saying you will not be going anywhere unless you tell me who you are. And why someone called Vee keeps telling me he is my sidecar on this journey.*"

"Knoll, I'm captain Dan Hollander." Hollander glanced over at Vee.

Old Vee had separated at every join, as if he was being disconnected piece by piece. He was held together by energy beams. His red LEDs gradually being overwhelmed by Knoll's indigo.

"*My sidecar has verified captain Hollander as the pilot.*"

"You are correct." Hollander asked. "Vee sacrificed his systems so that you could come back to life. Now let's get those thrusters burning. Our passengers are on a deadline."

"*Voice recognition does not verify you as my previous master.*"

"Does that matter?"

"*My navigation circuits respond to my master's orders.*"

"I am your new master."

"*That does not compute.*"

"Switch to autopilot?"

"*The Gunstar autopilot is offline.*"

"We're running out of time, Knoll. Burn rubber," Mikey said, craning his neck to see out the front window at the fading comet's tail.

"*No rubber will be burned until my master takes control.*"

"Hello, old friend." Without warning, Tommy had used his power bracelet to alter into a teenage avatar named Thad. The same pilot he had used in their previous encounter had short blonde hair, and a confident demeanor.

"*Thad, is that you?*"

"The one and only."

"*My last recollection is entering the black hole with you and an alien life form.*"

"It's funny you should say that. We kind of need to go back through the black hole again."

"*Go back!*"

"Yeah. What do you say, old friend?"

"*Hell no!*"

"We need you, Knoll."

"*Going through a black hole once is suicide. Twice, is just...*"

"We have no time to argue."

"*Are you so desperate to die?*"

"We've been through worse and we're still here."

"*The last time we flew together, Thad, we crashed.*"

"Only a little."

"*I died.*"

"What's a little death between comrades? I trust you. And besides, you're our only hope."

"*Hope won't stop you from dying this time round.*"

"We won't die. Not with you at the controls."

"*I am not yet compatible with this craft's flight controls. It will take me a few moments to adapt.*"

"We're doomed," Ted said.

"Hollander can take control for you, until you're ready," Tommy said.

"*If this is your wish?*" Knoll asked.

"It is."

"*Order confirmed. Captain, the controls are yours. Everybody, brace yourself. Power at maximum. Engines on. Targeting computer engaged ...*"

"Targeting computer?" Ted asked.

"*How else will we enter the black hole?*"

"It looks hard to miss, Knoll."

"*Vee is knowledgeable of such things. We need to enter the black hole at the exact point you exited.*"

"Why?"

"*Because any misjudgment could be fatal. Do you always ask so many questions?*"

"It's always a good idea to have all the facts, before one put his life on the line."

"Knoll, do you have the exact co-ordinates?" Hollander asked.

"*Yes, they are still in my database,*" Knoll replied.

"Good, then lock them down."

"*Confirmed. Targeting engaged. You can track our route using the heads-up display.*"

On the cockpit window, the heads-up display showed their destination in a small red square. The distance was marked next to it.

"Everybody hold-on. We're starting our attack run," Hollander said.

"Did he say attack run?" Ted remarked.

"Dude thinks he's hunting down an exhaust port," Kurt added.

SPEED. Power. A lightweight craft. The Gunstar's rapid ascent towards the planet's atmosphere went by in a superfast blur.

The first warning Captain Dan Hollander had that something was wrong was when a power surge erupted beneath the Gunstar's dashboard. A sheet of electrical flames coursed through the equipment as if had been doused in aviation fuel and lit with a match.

"Stupid question. Is a console supposed to light up like that?" Tommy asked, cowering behind the pilot's seat.

"Only if we're being shot at." Hollander released his hold on the joystick controls. A second sheet of electric flames swept across the dash, forcing him to brace his seat as the Gunstar dipped towards the planet. "Knoll, check the scanners for enemy craft."

"*I have spotted one unknown craft, closing fast,*" Knoll replied.

"And it's close enough to shoot at us?"

"*No. That was a grounded ion cannon. Capable of disrupting electronic systems.*"

"For a moment I thought it was your fiery charm."

"The craft has been trailing us since take off. It's about to leave the atmosphere."

"And you didn't think to warn us?"

"Nobody asked."

"Thad, or whatever your name is, I can't fly this ship if we keep getting shot at. And I can't do anything if Knoll is refusing to update me with critical information."

"I am doing my best, captain."

One more blast from the ion cannon sent forth across the electronics another wave of flame.

"Great. Now the engines are offline," Hollander bemoaned.

"Indeed. Rebooting systems."

"Knoll, you said one craft?" Tommy asked.

"Yes, and it's closing fast."

"Can we escape?"

"Possibly. The ion cannon is recharging as fast as my reboot. It will be close."

"It must be a Timeinator," Tommy said as the Gunstar's electronics shutdown briefly.

"They come in threes," Ted said.

"That means nothing to me," Hollander said.

"Why is there only one of them, Tommy?"

"It makes perfect sense, Ted. In the desert, I was held at gunpoint by Apollo," Tommy said.

"Who's that?"

"My son. I mean, Skank. Logan shot him."

"Logan?"

"My other son. No, I mean Oggy."

"Is there a point to this?" Hollander asked.

"Oggy shot Skank. Terminating him forever. Oggy then asked me to equip an exploding collar because he couldn't self-terminate."

"So how did he die?" Daisy asked.

"He asked me to switch it on."

"Gross!"

"Knoll?"

"Yes, Thad."

"What are we looking at threat wise?"

"*The Timeinator's Interceptor is a customized attack fighter, armed with chin-mounted twin lasers. Its fast, agile. We are faster, but if we receive too many direct hits, we will be done for.*"

"It's Packard."

"Who is Packard?" Hollander asked.

"The short story, he's an asshole."

"*Need I remind you that our Gunstar is unarmed,*" Knoll added.

"Thanks for stating the obvious," Hollander said, wondering if that was Knoll or Vee's view on proceedings.

"Why don't we use our powers?" Ted suggested.

"In space," Kurt replied.

"No way," Mikey added.

"Screw that," Daisy said.

A volley of laser blasts clattered into the Gunstar.

"Then we outrun him. Knoll, how long until full reboot?" Tommy asked.

"*All done, Thad!*"

The systems rebooted just in time for Hollander to regain control, and to narrowly escape another shot from the ion cannon.

"Hold on to your britches," Hollander said as he engaged full power.

THE Interceptor swooped in, the two craft clashing wing to wing.

It took not one, not two, but three shunts to knock the Gunstar off course. Packard banked in a wide arc, throwing all he had to intercept.

Out in front, and in the faster ship, Hollander knew it was now or never to return home.

Packard's change in direction forced him wide, but not wide enough. He engaged his blasters, rattling the Gunstar's hull, blowing out one of the four engines.

Hollander felt the engine going. "Knoll, switch engine four's power to the other three engines. Max them out, we need to stabilize our ascent."

"*Power swapped. Look out!*"

The Interceptor's blasters pounded the hull.

With one Gunstar engine out of commission, Packard's Interceptor managed to keep pace.

Inside the cockpit, his weapon's system had the fleeing spacecraft in its sights. More direct hits clattered the hull, engine two erupting in flames.

The explosion rocked the Gunstar, but not enough to divert it from the route along the final stretch.

The co-ordinates appeared on Hollander's heads-up display.

10000 m

"All power to our working engines. Hold on tight. We're re-entering the event horizon," Hollander warned as the Gunstar was plucked by a torrent of gravity swells and tossed around like a leaf in a whirlpool.

8100 m

After entering the event horizon Packard's weapon's systems started to falter. Wasting energy with his wayward laser blasts meant he had to release control.

"Ion control. Focus all power on my craft," he ordered.

"*Are you sure, sir?*"

"Do it!"

Eight days' worth of anger, regret, and frustration left him with one final chance to stop the teenagers. Switching full power to his engines, he banked the Interceptor towards the Gunstar.

6900 m

Packard knew full well that any chance he had to escape Arcadian's phantom zone was culminating in a suicide attack. Only by destroying the teenagers could he return home.

4473 m

Dead or alive. It was now or never for Packard.

2892 m

"*CAPTAIN! The Interceptor has locked on to us,*" Knoll's warning came through too late.

Before Hollander could react, the two craft collided. The captain's head struck the dashboard, knocking him out cold.

Wrapped in a deadly embrace of twisted metal, the two craft spiraled towards the center of the black hole.

985 m

Moving the unconscious pilot to the floor, Tommy took over the controls as Thad. A volley of blasts from the ion cannon clattered both craft, disrupting the electronics.

"The controls are dead," Tommy said.

"*That was two more ion blasts, Thad.*"

"Can we still make it?"

"*Yes, but you're close to passing out.*"

"Knoll, it's on you now. Take us home."

"*You got it, Thad. Rerouting power to the heads-up display. Wish me luck.*"

225 m

"*Almost there,*" Knoll continued, unaware that the G-Forces had just knocked out the passengers on both craft.

Still locked in a death spin, the two craft entered the black hole, a world of silence and damnation awaiting them.

DESTINATION REACHED

Within what felt like a few seconds, the combined wreckage of the two craft burst through a heavy cloud front. Caught up in a snowstorm, they were being hurled directly towards a frozen landscape.

"*Captain Hollander, wake up,*" Knoll ordered.

The pilot was lifeless. A piece of shrapnel from the Interceptor's wing buried in his chest, pinning him to the bulkhead, killing him instantly.

"*Thad?*"

Unable to control the craft, Knoll was helpless to deviate from their course. The horizon of snow and ice approached rapidly.

"*Switching power from heads-up to crew diagnostic.*"

By reading the passengers' vital signs, Knoll knew none of the teenagers were able to assist.

"*How can the same thing happen to the same gal, tw–*"

The Gunstar and Interceptor collided with the ice shelf. Smoke and flames erupted, sending a signal to anybody nearby of the crash landing.

Inside the craft, Knoll's systems began to shut down.

"*Five teenagers, three alien life ... f-f ... o ... rmmmmm ...one deceased humannnnn ...*"

"*Five teenagerzzzzz, three alien life ... f-f ... oo...zzzt ... ptt ...*"

"*Five teenagerrrrrzzzzzzzz, three aliennnnnnnnn ...*"

"*Five teenagerzzzzzzzzzzzzzzzzzzzzzzzzzzzzz ...*"

"*zzzzzzzzzzzzzzzt...*"

"*...*"

HOME, SWEET HOME

Chapter 34

The Thingamajig

Three Days Later
USSR Geological Research Station
Antarctica,
Winter, 1982

"PROSYPAYSKA K CHERTU (Wake the hell up)!"

A powerful slap across Tommy's cheek snapped him back to reality. He was roped to a wooden chair in a break room, furnished with a few tables and chairs, an old television set, and a breakfast counter. Alongside his friends, Kurt, Mikey, Ted, and Daisy, were three people he didn't recognize.

A rugged man, with a scar on his right cheek, wore a grubby pilot's uniform. He stood in front of a ping pong table whilst wielding a flamethrower. He seemed to be the one in charge. The other two consisted of a Grizzly Adams reboot; all brawn, reeking of sweat and tobacco. And a woman, who kept to the shadows.

"Why do I keep getting punched in the head?" Tommy said, his wrists bound behind his back.

"You must have one of those faces," Mikey said.

"You should've ducked," Ted added.

"Tikhiy (quiet)," the rugged man said.

"What dialect is that?" Tommy asked.

"I think it's Cantonese," Ted replied.

"Do they look Cantonese?" Kurt blasted.

"It doesn't mean they can't speak the native lingo."

"How many people do you know that can speak Cantonese?"

"Counting everyone I've met, including the people in this room. One."

"He's not speaking Cantonese, Ted," Daisy added.

"How do you know for sure?"

"Because he's Russian," Mikey added. "I recognize the dialect from Rocky 4."

The pilot spoke to Grizzly, who took it in turns to slip a small hearing aide in each of the teenagers' right ears.

"Can you understand now?" the pilot asked.

The teenagers nodded in reply.

"Who are you?" Tommy asked.

"Koloff. I fly helicopter." The pilot made every effort to keep the flamethrower near enough for the teenagers to feel the heat from the lit flame.

"Where are we?" Mikey asked.

"Russian Geological Research Station."

"Are we home?" Kurt asked.

"I ask question. Not you," Koloff stated. "You talk of Rocky 4. Rocky 3 only release in July."

"Wait. What year is this?" Daisy asked.

"You don't know the year?"

"Would I have asked the question if I knew the answer?"

Koloff paused intentionally before answering. "1982."

"Don't take this the wrong way, but Earth, 1982?" Ted asked.

"Of course, Earth. Are you high?"

"We are home, just not the right year," Tommy said.

"Man, this reality jumping is frazzling my nodes," Kurt remarked.

"The cold might be freezing my nads, but if my calculations are correct, Rocky 4 wasn't released until 1985. That means three years until its release," Ted added.

"Thanks for pointing out the obvious, Ted."

Kurt and Koloff stared at each other for a few seconds before Koloff turned the flamethrower in the teenager's direction. "What is reality jumping?"

"Just a joke, Ivan. The Soviet flag printed on your sleeve is a dead giveaway." Kurt grinned.

Koloff glanced briefly at his sleeve and then shrugged.

"And spoiler alert. Drago loses in the end," Ted added.

"Everyone loses to Rocky. The man's invincible," Kurt replied.

"Not everyone. Apollo won the first one."

"Only on the scorecards. Heart and soul went to Rocky."

"Clubber Lang beat Rocky," Koloff added.

"Only because Mickey died," Ted pointed out.

"You can't win a fight with heart and soul," Kurt said.

"Course you can. Roadrunner, Tweety Pie, Bugs Bunny. It's what makes them unique."

"Enough talk." Koloff kicked over Kurt's chair.

The chair toppled back, the teenager landing on his bound wrists. "Dude, that hurt," Kurt blasted.

"Good. You want to make any more jokes at the expense of the motherland?" Koloff increased the fuel outlay on his flamethrower and aimed the nozzle at Kurt.

"Wait! Wait! How are we supposed to react? We've just woken up bound to these chairs and you're threatening us with a flamethrower," Tommy said, shuffling in his chair in front of his downed friend. "And are these binds necessary?"

"They for safety."

"For ours or yours?"

"Both," said the American woman from the behind them. She stepped out of the shadows, her wrists also bound.

"As can see, you not ze first Yankies to arrive. One person, okay. Two more rescue from burning US Research Facility. Perhaps coincidence. Then you are discovered. All of you Americans. You sense paranoia, yes. It is like an invasion."

"Hardly an invasion, but that would explain your love affair with a flamethrower," Ted blurted.

"Perhaps someone else can explain better, yes."

The rangy brunette was moved to a chair by Grizzly. Her bruised face implied she had come out the other side of a brutal fight.

"Jesus, lady. I'd hate to see the other person," Daisy said.

"What makes you think it was a human?" the brunette replied.

"Another American," Mikey said.

"She might also be a Cantonese spy," Ted added.

"She's not Cantonese, Ted. Or a spy," Kurt blurted.

"Good. Perhaps she can explain where we are. Why we're tied up. And where the John is, because I really need to pee."

"I agree. American friend, explain extraordinary situation." Koloff aimed his flamethrower in her direction. "I need to understand, in order to make correct decision."

"What decision is that?" Tommy asked.

"Whether to burn you all alive."

"Out of one shit pit and straight into another," Kurt remarked.

"Story of my life," Ted added.

The American, in her mid-twenties, appeared calm, despite the immediate threat to their lives. "My name is Kate Floyd. I am a Paleontologist and the sole survivor of an alien encounter at a Swedish Research Station. It's one of three in the area. US, Swedish, and the Russian equivalent is where we are now. A few days ago, my colleagues at the Swedish camp discovered a source of transmission. As we investigated, we uncovered a frozen alien life form, buried not far from a downed spacecraft.

"We transported the specimen back to our encampment. Shortly after, my employer, Sander Halverson, asked me to take blood and tissue samples. Whilst studying the results, I added human blood and discovered that the alien DNA started to imitate the human cells."

"At what point did you think tampering with alien DNA was a good idea?" Mikey asked.

"Are you an expert on such things?"

"I've experimented with DNA."

"You don't look old enough to even understand the term."

"And yet we're both bound to these chairs. Go figure."

"Let her speak, Mikey," Daisy said. "Sorry about my brother. Please, continue."

"To answer his initial question. I realized tampering with DNA was not a good idea around the same time all hell broke loose. Shortly after the study, the alien life form thawed from the ice and escaped. A few members of the team were killed as we tried to recapture it. Much to our horror, the alien tried to morph with our Huskies. It was a grotesque meld of bones, flesh, teeth, mandibles, and tentacles. Nobody could quite believe it, and yet all the team wanted to do was capture it for further study.

"I took it upon myself to try and kill this thing outright. Before I knew it, the DNA had already taken over other members of the team. Nobody could be trusted, not even after we discovered that the alien could assimilate every part of the human anatomy. We started to take precautions, but it was too late.

"An American helicopter pilot and I, we managed to track the alien down and corner it. It had altered into the last surviving campmate. We had no choice but to kill it. As we headed back to our snow transport, I realized the pilot's personality had changed drastically. We were split up only for a few minutes. He even helped me burn the other campmate's remains. I had no choice but to turn the flamethrower on him. Then I was found by the Russians. I've been in quarantine ever since."

"What about the two others Koloff mentioned, rescued from the US Research Station?" Tommy asked.

"I believe they arrived yesterday, barely alive. There was an explosion at their camp. You could see it from miles away. They're in the med bay as we speak. I wasn't privy to what they said if anything, or what happened, but I can guess they somehow discovered the same spacecraft as us."

"One question bother me. Who start transmission?" Koloff asked. "Our routine patrol of ze area picked up signal transmitting. Distress call, yes?"

Nobody answered.

"I will repeat. Who start transmission?" Koloff moved the flamethrower towards a downed Kurt.

"Not us," Daisy said. "How could it be anything to do with us. We've been here, how long?"

"You tell me."

"The first thing I remember is waking up after being slapped across the cheek," Tommy said.

"If not you start transmission, this very bad. Swedes' find alien. They all die. US survivors make no sense before passing out. Only evidence we find on them is a tape recording."

"You never told me about that. Have you played it back?" Floyd asked.

"Net (no)."

"Don't you think you should."

"Net (no)."

"It might be important."

"Okay, but if it is Elvis Pressley, my flamethrower will be used."

"I don't remember Elvis singing that song," Ted remarked.

Koloff removed a tape recorder from a shelf, played the cassette and turned up the volume.

I'm gonna hide this tape when I'm finished. If none of us make it, at least there'll be some sort of record. Storm has been hitting us hard now for forty-eight hours. We still have little to go on. It could be anybody, or anything. Nobody trusts anybody now. Nothing else we can do. Just wait to see if it lets us go, or takes over, just like it did at the Swedish site. RJ MacGready. Helicopter pilot. US outpost ...

Koloff turned off the recording and faced Floyd. "Answer me this. If you kill alien dead, how did it reach Americans?"

"How should I know? I thought everyone was dead, except for me. Unless it was one of the dogs," Floyd replied.

"How exactly did we end up at your camp?" Mikey asked Koloff.

"Like American woman. Snow transport. On the border of camp. You just appear, out of thin air. Alarms go off. Wake entire team. We rush out with dogs. You are all asleep. My colleagues wanted to burn all involved, move along to new dawn. We live, you die. Roll on three years, Rocky fight again. Russia wins. We all happy."

"Only happy until your guy gets his ass handed to him by the Italian Stallion," Kurt snarled.

"Wait. Wait. What did the transmission sound like?" Ted asked.

"What does that matter?" Mikey snapped.

"Hear me out. We need to make sure it's not our spacecraft that crashed."

"So you arrive in spacecraft?" Koloff asked.

"Maybe, maybe not."

"Yes or no."

"Maybe it was yes and no. It's a bit hard to explain. What did the transmission sound like?"

"Like transmission."

"I get that. But what noise did it make. You know, bleep, bleep, buzz, buzz. What?"

"No, like child computer game."

"That's what the Swede's radio operator reported before they tracked down the source," Floyd added. "I didn't believe it at first. Not until I heard it for myself."

Ted glanced at his friends and then back at Koloff. "You mean like an arcade machine?"

"Yes, like arcade. Space invaders, Pac Man."

"Anything else?"

Koloff glanced over at Grizzly. "We heard a woman."

"You mean Floyd?" Tommy asked.

"Not her. The woman said five teenagers, three alien lifeforms, one deceased human. Then transmission changed to arcade noise, yes."

Tommy and his friends shared a look.

"We think arcade signal triggered when survivor exited craft," Koloff added.

"Survivor. You mean us?" Daisy said.

"Not you. Another."

"The one the Swede's found?" Floyd asked.

Koloff's slow intake of breath implied otherwise.

"Let me get this straight. The Swedes found one. The Americans clearly discovered one. Now you say there is another survivor." Floyd glanced worryingly at the teenagers.

"That makes three, as in three alien lifeforms," Tommy said, not believing how gullible he had been. "Oggy lied to me. He said Timeinators can't self-terminate. They only stop hunting you when a Timeinator kills another Timeinator."

"But you said Oggy shot Skank," Ted said.

"He did. Which makes it even more sinister."

"If they all got through, maybe they were on Packard's ship," Mikey said.

"No, he wouldn't have them all in the same place. Not unless … wait a minute. Before I passed out, we were hit by two ion blasts. What if they weren't blasts, but some way for them to travel with us. Like attaching to the Gunstar."

"This is all fascinating, but can someone help me up, please," Kurt asked.

"Where is this mystery survivor now?" Mikey asked.

"In segregation. We find maps at US camp. On the way back with two US campmates, we overhear the arcade transmission. It leads us back to the same crash site. We find survivor buried in ice," Koloff added.

"And you thought it was a good idea to pick up a passenger?" Daisy asked.

"We were curious."

"That alien called out to you," Floyd said.

"We discover on our own."

"Only because it wanted you to find it."

"We need to see it," Tommy said.

"Net (no)," Koloff said.

"You don't know what you're dealing with," Daisy said.

"Survivor incapacitated in dense ice."

"So was ours, until it escaped," Floyd stated.

"It will not escape until we get out in one piece. Great discovery for Mother Russia."

"Listen to me," Floyd barked. "This is a carbon copy of what happened to the Swedes. And I'm guessing the US camp wasn't far off what is about to happen here."

"And what is that?" Grizzly growled from his perch across the room.

"I'm guessing a creek full of shit is about to be poured all over us," Ted said.

"You need to kill that thing, before it gets loose," Tommy added.

"He's right. Burn it. Destroy it. Just do it now," Floyd added.

"We need not your instruction. Russians always make right decision. Now you reveal where *IT* come from. No more cryptic words. Truth, now, or I will burn you all," Koloff said, raising the flamethrower.

"It is an underling of an interdimensional pain in the ass," Ted replied.

"Not helpful."

"It's the truth."

"You need to kill it, now," Tommy added.

"If it was on your spaceship, maybe it is like you. Like silly boy, who talk too much." Koloff jabbed the flamethrower towards Ted.

"We're not with it, you have to believe us," Ted stated.

"Then why travel in spacecraft together?"

"It's too long a story," Tommy added.

"You come across *IT* before?"

"We have. Did you not understand my interdimensional pain in the ass comment," Ted added.

"What is *IT* called?"

"It's a Timeinator," Daisy said.

"And if we're right, it can assimilate anything it wants to," Kurt bemoaned, still lying on his side.

"Tell me this. The spacecraft crash in glacier. Swedes rush in, blow up ice to get to it. They do so, without any thought of safety, or for environment. IT felt threatened, so run away. Maybe you are the bad guys here."

"It didn't run away. Like the other two, it was looking for someone to assimilate," Tommy said.

"Why not just escape?"

"It needs to kill us all and stop us from getting home," Daisy said.

"And to end a game once and for all," Mikey said, whilst looking defeated at the same time.

"Our game is like the never ever ending story," Ted added.

"Enough words." Koloff shifted the ping pong table and emptied an envelope full of photos on the tabletop. "This morning we excavate from ice. Within the hour we will discover what *IT* is."

"You can't let that happen. It can mimic anything," Daisy said.

"In Russia, we deal with things better than the rest of the world."

A deafening alarm rang out, the teenagers wishing they could cover their ears. Koloff ordered Grizzly to leave the room. He returned within thirty seconds, reporting that the alien had thawed and escaped the ice.

"It's out, isn't it?" Floyd said.

"I could have told you that was going to happen," Ted added.

"Cut us loose," Tommy ordered. "We can help you."

Unsure if releasing them all would be a good idea, Koloff decided to keep the teenagers bound and cut only Floyd's binds.

"Koloff," she said. "If these kids are correct and they know what that thing is, then we need their expertise."

"They only children," Koloff replied.

"Children that have come across this thing before."

"And lived to tell the tale," Ted added with a firm nod.

Despite her protests, Koloff led Floyd and Grizzly out of the room, leaving the teenagers unguarded.

"This went to shit quickly," Mikey said.

"I still need to pee," added Ted.

"Do it in your pants," Daisy snarled.

"Can someone please help me up from the floor?" Kurt said.

AS expected, Koloff and his team encountered an empty ice cocoon in the storage area. The room was occupied by the rest of his research team. The humanoid outline left in the ice matched the same outline in the shack's wall.

"Arm yourselves and split to pairs," he ordered. "Find this thing. Quickly."

Three pairs left the shack, leaving Floyd alone with Koloff and Grizzly.

"The longer the thing is out there, the more time it has to assimilate," Floyd warned.

"And what if it changed already?" Grizzly asked.

"Koloff, it's time. We need all the help we can get. They clearly know more than we do. Now stop pretending to not know me and cut those kids loose."

IN the med bay, the high pitch alarm snapped Jack MacGready awake. The American pilot rocked up, scratching his thick beard. One of his campmates was on the next bed. He reached across, grabbing his friend's wrist to check his pulse.

"Still with us, Childers," he said.

The black American rocked his head to the side. "Looks like neither of us was exposed to that thing after all."

"Lucky for you, I was too cold to shoot your ass."

"Snap. Where are we, Mac?"

"I don't know, but that alarm is doing shit for my headache."

MacGready staggered to the alarm and slammed his palm against it. It stopped, so he opened the doorway and glanced into the hallway. Two burly men, armed with axes, sprinted along the corridor. Rather than confront them, he closed the door.

"Was that an axe?" Childers asked.

"It was two."

"Are you thinking what I'm thinking?"

"Out of the frying pan, into the fire. Come on, let's go find someone who can tell us what we've stumbled into."

"RELEASE them."

Following Koloff's order Grizzly cut the teenagers' binds.

"Where are our bracelets?" Mikey asked Koloff.

"We take nothing off you," Koloff replied.

"Perhaps they're in the snow mobile," Kurt said, still on his back on the floor. "I'd go check if someone could get me off this damn floor."

Grizzly reached down with one hand and hoisted Kurt upright.

"Thanks, dude," Kurt said as his binds were released.

"Where did it go?" Tommy asked.

"Somewhere in camp," Koloff replied. "My men are searching for it."

"How many campmates?" Floyd asked.

"We have twelve overall. Twenty, if we include everyone in this room and the two Americans."

"And it could be anyone of us."

"We can help. But without our bracelets, we are defenseless," Mikey stated.

"We went through the black hole. Maybe nothing came through with us but our clothes," Ted replied.

"You came through a black hole?" Koloff asked.

"I said it was a long story," Tommy replied.

"If two of the three that came through with us are out of commission, it's just us, and him," Kurt said.

"Maybe this is our final stand. We either defeat him, or he assimilates with a polar bear and rips our heads off and shits down our throats," Ted said, to astonished looks from everyone in the room. "Sorry, I wasn't supposed to say that out loud."

"What weapons do you have, Koloff?" Floyd asked.

"A couple of flamethrowers. A few handguns. Will that be enough?" Koloff replied.

"I doubt it. One of these things managed to wipe out the Swedes in less than twenty-four hours."

An explosion erupted across the camp.

"And the ball is rolling," Ted said.

A communication could be heard over the walkie talkie handsets Koloff had distributed to each of his search teams.

"*Koloff ...*"

Koloff swiped the walkie talkie from his belt clip. "Koloff here."

"*This is Igor. Detonation complete.*"

"Is it sealed?"

"*Wait. The teams are checking. Smoke is clearing.*"

"Well?"

"*Yes, it's sealed. Mission accomp– ... wait, he's here.*"

Koloff turned down the walkie talkie due to the gunfire at the other end of the line. "Igor. Status?"

"*He sees us. Run! Ru–*"

The call cut off amid a terrifying scream.

"Igor, come in."

"Sounds like Igor and his posse is very much dead, my Russian friend," said a voice from the doorway.

MacGready entered the room with Childers, both men armed with fire axes.

"The Americans are finally awake," Koloff snarled.

"Barely." MacGready glanced loosely at each person in turn, until he stopped at Floyd. "Are you the teacher for this high school day trip?"

"That's funny," Floyd said, turning her back on him.

"Koloff, what did Igor mean when he said he's already here?" Daisy asked.

"Nothing. He was ... flustered," Koloff said.

"People tend to speak the truth when their life is about to end," Tommy said.

Floyd, MacGready, Childers, and Koloff shared a look. It was clear to the teenagers that the adults in the room were holding something back.

"Is it just me, or did the atmosphere suddenly turn cold in here," Ted said.

"You're not wrong," Childers said, brandishing the fire axe in a threatening manner.

"Lower the axe," Floyd ordered. "It's time we told them the truth."

"More truth. That's just what we need," Kurt said sarcastically.

"Are you sure?" Koloff said.

"They seem genuine enough," MacGready added.

"You've been in their presence about thirty seconds. How can you tell?" Floyd asked.

"It's my job to root out and dispose of the garbage. And these kids, they don't smell like garbage."

"Maybe these are the ones we've been waiting for," Childers said.

"There's only one way to find out," Floyd replied, facing the teenagers.

"I don't like where this is going," Tommy added.

"You might change your mind when you listen to what we have to say. Please be open minded. And no stupid remarks. Okay?"

The teenagers shared a moment to take onboard the comment and then nodded in unison.

"What you won't know is that our three camps are part of a bigger organization. Tasked with guarding what these three invaders you brought here are searching for. Until they arrived, our existence had been a peaceful time. We were hidden from *HIM.* No encounters. No deaths. No incidents. Just snow and frostbite."

"You're all in on this?" Kurt asked.

"Three camps separate. All guarding the same cave," Koloff added.

"What's in the cave?" Daisy asked.

"I think it's a portal of some kind," MacGready said.

"How do you know that, and I don't?" Childers asked.

"Orders came from up high."

"And you didn't think that was important information for me to have?"

"The orders were to keep it under wraps."

"And the Timeinator we brought here is now trying to reach it," Daisy said.

"Nail on head you hit," Koloff replied.

"They were looking for a way out of their realm and we brought them right to your doorstep," Mikey said.

"No offence, bro. But they crashed into us, and we entered the black hole. We could've ended up anywhere," Daisy added.

"But we're here. Where we need to be. And we need to rectify our mistake right away," Tommy said.

"Mistake already resolved. Cave was sealed by detonation," Koloff added.

"Your friend said he was moving the rocks aside. In my experience, this thing won't let a few boulders stand in its way," Kurt added.

"You'll need weapons," Floyd said.

"You made that sound like we're on our own," Ted added.

"This is your fight. Not ours," MacGready said.

"We're just kids."

"That's not stopped us before, Ted," Mikey added. "How did the Swede's stop it?"

"Fire, guns, it matters not what we used. That thing kept surviving," Floyd said. "If there is someone to assimilate, it will do so until there is nobody left."

"You can add blood samples to that list. Although it did tell us who was infected," Childers added.

"None of that will work. The five of us need to confront it face to face," Tommy said.

"The five of us it is then. And I have a suitcase full of harsh language on the backburner," Kurt said.

"Harsh language," Ted remarked.

"We don't have our bracelets. What else can we use?"

"We use this." Daisy held up the floppy disk that McLeod had given to her on the OCP rooftop right before he died.

"You play it at chess," Koloff stated.

"Where did you get that?" Tommy asked.

"From McLeod right before he …" Daisy handed over the disk to Floyd.

"What's on it?" Floyd asked.

"I don't exactly know for certain. I just know that now is the right time to use it."

"That's some assumption, sis," Mikey said.

"You couldn't have picked better timing," Floyd said, switching on a computer. "We set this system up earlier today."

The VDU came to life, details of the system startup flashing up on the screen. Floyd inserted the floppy disk in the driver. It took only a short while for the program to boot up. The title flashed up on the screen.

T.O.B.I.A.S

"How am I not surprised. Dude gets everywhere," Ted said.

MANKIND'S LAST STAND BEFORE EXTINCTION

"Exactly how bleak was this McLeod dude?" Kurt asked Daisy.

"I have no idea what this is," she replied. "His only instruction, you'll know when to use it."

"Hello time, hello place," Ted remarked.

"There's more," Floyd said, pointing at the screen.

T.O.B.I.A.S
CREATED TO STOP THE ADVANCEMENT OF
H.I.M

"Him, as in Arcadian," Kurt said out loud.

"There's a prompt," Floyd added.

COMPUTER MAINFRAME ONLINE ...

TOBIAS: HOW CAN I HELP?

GUEST: HI, I'M KATE FLOYD.

T: HOW CAN I HELP, KATE FLOYD?

G: WE HAVE A PROBLEM.

T: DEFINE PROBLEM.

Floyd glanced over at the teenager. "You called that thing a Timeinator. Is that right?"

"Yep," Daisy added.

G: HOW CAN YOU STOP A TIMEINATOR FROM REACHING THE PORTAL?

T: ...

T: ...

"I think we broke it," Ted said.

T: YOU CAN SLOW IT DOWN. IT IS IMPOSSIBLE TO STOP.

G: IT WILL KEEP GOING.

T: YES. UNLESS THEIR MISSION IS OVER. THEN IT WILL STOP.

"If I've told you all once, I've told you all a million times. We're doomed," Ted added.

G: THERE MUST BE SOMETHING WE CAN DO.

T: YOU COULD CONFRONT IT FACE TO FACE. WEAPONS ARE ADVISED.

G: WILL WE SURVIVE?

T: PROBABILITY THAT ONE OR MORE TEAM MEMBERS MAY BE ASSASSINATED BY TIMEINATOR – 75%.

G: IF THE TIMEINATOR REACHES THE PORTAL, WHAT WILL HAPPEN?

T: PROJECTION - IF INTRUDER ORGANISM REACHES CIVILIZED AREAS ...
ENTIRE WORLD POPULATION DECEASED 27,000 HOURS FROM FIRST CONTACT ...

"That's three years," Floyd said.

"Then we have no choice. We either kill it, or we die trying," Tommy said.

"Where is this cave?" Mikey asked.

"A mile north of here. You will need coats, and the use of a snow mobile," Koloff said.

"Coats," Ted remarked.

"We're in Antarctica, dude," Kurt said.

"How was I supposed to know that? We've been inside the entire time."

"Just remember one thing," MacGready said. "Whoever has the control, has the power."

"Thanks, dude, some spiritual guidance will certainly stop that thing from breaking all of my limbs and using my flaccid remains to mop up my friends' blood," Ted said.

"Here." Koloff handed Daisy the keys to a snowmobile.

"Good luck," Childers added.

"Take some torches from the vehicle. Just in case the generator is offline," MacGready said.

"Great, we can teach it Morse code and bore it to death," Ted remarked.

"Good luck to all of you," Floyd stated as she handed over thick winter coats as they exited the room.

"After all this time I never thought he would make it this far," Childers said.

"It was bound to happen sooner or later. His branches are many. Too many for anyone to control forever," Floyd added.

"And our fate is in the hands of a few kids," MacGready added.

"We're dead. Drink?" Koloff said, offering around a full bottle of Vodka to the others.

Chapter 35

This is the end, my jealous friend.

THE SNOW mobile came to an abrupt halt on the verge of an ice wall, overlooking a crater spanning a few hundred meters wide and with an excavation at its center.

To reach the crater, the Russians had used climbing equipment to descend a treacherous slope. Smoke still lingered along a roped off trail leading to the excavation. Ice and snow crumbled from the explosions the Russians had used to try and seal off the site.

After exiting the vehicle, the teenagers made their way down the slope.

"I could really do with my bracelet right now," Mikey said.

"I could really do with a dump," Ted remarked.

"Whatever happened to our bracelets?" Daisy asked.

"Maybe we can't use them here," Kurt said.

"Yeah, our powers work on the other side of a black hole, but they don't stretch as far as the Arctic," Ted replied.

"It's Antarctica."

"Same thing."

"Since when."

"Since they're both cold. The only difference, one is at the bottom of the planet, the other at the top."

"You make no sense, ever."

"Guys, where we are doesn't matter. It's just us against him," Tommy added.

"It," Ted added.

"What?"

"You said 'him', not It."

"What does that matter?"

"Nothing, I'm just biding my time and building up the courage to abseil into another black abyss."

"Let me check it out first," Tommy said.

"Are you sure?" Daisy asked.

"He's right. There's no point in all of us dying," Ted said.

"Maybe we should just throw Ted down there. When his screams stop, we'll have an idea how deep it is," Mikey said jokingly grabbing his friend by the arm.

"And waste all that wit and humor. No, I'll go. Stand back." Tommy stood on the edge of the opening, and used a rope already secured to rappel down to the floor eighty feet beneath the surface.

When he reached the bottom, he switched on his torch and waved it from side to side. Wiring along the cavern walls was connected to some futuristic looking equipment. A generator was nearby. He switched it on, releasing a flood of illumination across the cave from rows of dynamic spotlights.

"About time," said the Timeinator.

Tommy swiveled on his heels, expecting to be set upon. What he didn't expect was to see a familiar face from his childhood.

"PACKARD?"

"Surprise!"

Packard Walsh was slumped against the cavern wall, in a pool of his own blood. It was the first time Tommy had laid eyes upon the teenager in what felt like decades.

"I guess you're not so invincible after all," Tommy said.

"I can't disagree with that."

"Did we do that to you?"

"Unfortunately, no. When I thawed from the ice. I realized I had a little friend for company." Packard rocked to the side to reveal a wound, inflicted by what appeared to be debris from the crash in the ice.

"And the bullet wounds?"

"In your world, my master's protection isn't the best."

"Our world used to be yours."

"Not since I followed him."

"You mean Arcadian?"

"That's a good name. He likes it."

"I've heard. Nice trick with my kids."

"Ha, you liked that one. Some of my best work to date. I really didn't think you'd be dumb enough to board the good ship gullible. Your face was a classic. It was a polaroid moment. *My kids, I found my kids*. What a dork."

"That was cruel."

"That's the name of the game."

"What about Oggy? You put him up to shooting Skank?"

"No, that was his idea. This isn't wrestling, Tommy. We don't just turn heel and change allegiances at will. You're the enemy. End of."

"And yet we escaped you time after time, or did you forget that."

"You haven't escaped anything, yet."

"We will. We always come out on top. No matter the odds."

"You know what. You should change your geeky club's name to Mystery Inc. No, that's been used. What about Fluky Sink! That sounds about right."

"Why is that?"

"Well, you have been lucky every step of the way. And because you pesky kids are always scuttling my plans."

"Resilience surfaces when your life is threatened," Daisy said from behind Tommy.

"And here's the girlfriend. Dampknee, is it?"

"Daisy."

"What the hell are you doing here?" Kurt snarled.

"And here's Scrappy Don't. I thought it was about time you found out who was been trying to kill you all this time."

"You suck as a Timeinator," Ted said.

"And here's Saggy, the comic relief."

"Let me guess. Oggy and Skank were the other two intruders?" Mikey asked.

"And finally, Mikey Dooby Dickhead," Packard said.

"Why am I Scooby?"

"I guess that's better than Velma," Ted said, not in the least bit reassuringly.

"Why did you come back?" Tommy asked.

"I was floating around in the phantom zone. Not alive, not dead, just bored. I now know how Zod felt. Then I was offered a way back in, as the servant of H.I.M. I was sent to kill you all, the only ones who had broken through. And to make matters worse, you stole his map."

"And you're still following orders. But why? We have returned home. The game is over for you," Mikey said.

"You are not home yet. There is one more doorway to enter."

The teenagers shared a puzzled look.

"Don't tell me you haven't seen it. Must I do everything for you?"

Despite not having the energy to do so, Packard pointed at the wall to their right. A circular doorway had been marked in the cavern wall with the same design used on the map they had been using since Tommy stole it from the Wishgiver.

"Your final step home," Packard said.

"You're just letting us go," Ted remarked.

"Do I look in any fit state to stop you, Saggy."

"Then why come here?" Daisy asked.

"Because I wanted to win. I wanted to beat you."

"Instead, you will die here and remain his slave," Tommy added.

"Let's speed up the inevitable, shall we?" Kurt snarled, raising a fire axe overhead.

Mikey grabbed his friend by the wrists before he could swing the axe.

"Where did you get that?" Ted asked.

"Topside. Considering what he did to the Russians, I thought we might need it," Kurt added.

"Kill me if you wish, Scrappy, or don't. See what I did there?" Packard added.

"Call me that again and you might just get your wish."

"Do it. Go ahead. Miss out entirely on seeing the bigger picture."

"I don't see any pictures," Ted remarked.

"You are slaves to your own masters."

"We have no masters," Mikey asked.

"Are you sure? The human masters have made slaves of you all."

"This guy isn't making any sense," Ted added.

"What do you expect? He's bleeding out, his mind has gone gaga," Kurt replied.

"Let's rip off this mask and ask the dude underneath instead."

"If only that were true," Packard added.

"Where are these masters?" Tommy asked.

Packard pointed upwards.

"Dude, that's the sky," Ted added.

"Saggy, its time you buttoned it and let the adults talk. Tommy, there is more to this situation than meets the eye. You have all felt it since the start. Something isn't quite right."

"Yeah, it's called being screwed over into playing a game," Mikey replied.

"A game some might call it. A war, others would say."

"What war?"

"Two sides who will stop at nothing until one is victorious."

"You mean us versus Arcadian," Kurt said.

"Arcadian, Mr. Nobody, HIM. They'll all the same entity."

"And the other side?" Tommy asked.

"You mean the side of the righteous. Hardly the good guys. To keep you all in line, they made sure one of their own has been with you all along. And now that person has come here with you. They are very close. So close."

"But there are only six of us in this cave," Ted said, after double checking the numbers.

"Is this a good time to point out that Packard might be referring to himself," Mikey said.

"Not me, Dooby," Packard added.

"I'm more partial to Fred, not that that matters."

"Enough with the jokes. Listen to me, take notice. Someone is lying to you all. They have been listening to your every word. Following every action, no matter how insignificant. All the while, with one goal."

"Which is?" Tommy asked, standing over Packard.

"Control," Mikey said sternly.

"Whover has the control, has the power," Ted said, referring to MacGready's warning before they left camp.

"Wise words, for once," Packard said, shifting his body to try and slow the blood flow.

"If they're so close, why don't they just show themselves?" Daisy asked.

"I wouldn't. Not unless I was going to gloat about it. That's just me, though. No, this person was with you when you entered this realm via the video store."

"We didn't start the game until a few days after," Mikey said.

"Are you sure? How far back can you remember?"

"Everything he's saying is a lie," Daisy said. "It's what he's programmed to do."

"Do I look like a Timeinator right now, Badknee?"

"It's Daisy!"

"The insider was with you when you took to the stars and entered the black hole. And then through every adventure you have taken since, assisting you to reach this exact point in time."

The teenagers looked at each other in turn. Teenage paranoia of the highest level had set in quicker than fast drying cement.

"You mean like a spy," Kurt said, eyeing his friends.

"They are near enough to weave their own narrative. To lead those gullible enough into a path they do not understand," Packard said, with a wink.

"That's me screwed," Ted remarked.

"One of you will soon realize how important you are. Someone in this cave has the power to stop all of this. Someone else has the power to lead you all to safety. The rest are just here as cannon fodder."

"He's screwing with us," Daisy said.

"She's right. It's trying to divide us. It's what Timeinators do. They infiltrate and eliminate," Mikey said.

"All I am doing is being honest with you," Packard said.

"That's a first," Tommy added.

"Believe what you will. You are all a part of this never-ending war. Only by revealing the truth will you all eventually be set free." Packard reached behind him for a concealed Star Trek phaser. He held it up, showing the ammo count as six particle beams.

"Does honesty always come fully loaded?" Mikey asked.

"This isn't for me to use. It's time for us all to choose where we stand."

"In that state you won't be standing at all," Ted remarked.

"Since when were you in the *us* category," Mikey added.

"Choose what?" Daisy asked.

"Isn't it obvious? The phaser has six shots, one for each of us," Tommy said.

"I thought the phaser appropriate, rather than a six shooter. I know how geeks get a boner over sci-fi memorabilia. And it's not set to stun, before you ask. Only by using kill shots will you be able to escape," Packard said, almost grinning.

"This is funny to you?"

"No. Me being so close to escaping Arcadian's hold and bleeding to death is not humorous. It sucks balls, big time. However, watching your tight bond break at the very last moment is hilarious. I just wish I had a polaroid right now to capture the looks on your faces. Oh, there is one more thing. The portal home will only open when you have eliminated the narrator. Maybe I should've led with that little chestnut." Packard purposely tossed the phaser into the middle of the group. "Happy hunting, Horsemen."

"We choose to do nothing," Daisy said.

"Then you will die here." Packard pointed to the ceiling. The entrance was now sealed.

"That's a harsh reality," Tommy remarked.

"He's lying," Mikey said.

"No, he's bleeding. Look at your feet," Ted said, pointing at the floor covered in claret.

"I ain't got time to bleed. Now choose before the countdown reaches 666," Packard said.

"What timer?" Mikey asked.

"The one on the wall behind you."

A huge digital clock, affixed to the cavern wall with masking tape, had already started to count from 00:00. Blood oozed from two cannisters attached to the clock face and down the wall, leaving an increasing claret puddle spilling across the cavern floor.

"When the blood runs out, it's game over. I guess none of you remember Ferris Bueller's warning," Packard added.

"I don't remember a bleeding clock in Bueller's bedroom," Ted said.

"I know what he means. Life moves fast. If you don't stop and look around occasionally, you could miss something," Daisy said.

"I have to admit, I didn't expect Darknee Drew to know that one." Packard clapped and grimaced at the same time.

0:59

The extreme paranoia had already reached the breaking point, testing their brotherly bond to the limit.

01:23

Packard's comments fueled the furnace, eager eyes falling on the phaser that would surely severe their friendship bonds forever.

01:58

The Wild West standoff ended when Kurt snatched the weapon from the floor. "Screw this. If we're about to die anyway. I'd rather die fighting." Kurt aimed the phaser at the rest of the group.

"Kurt, think about what you're doing," Tommy said.

"I am. Packard said we can only leave here by eliminating the one who has been tricking us. I'm starting to think that might be you, Tommy."

"You're trusting Packard over me."

"Is there a reason not to?"

02:23

"We don't even know if someone is tricking us. He might have just fed us a load of horseshit."

"I don't think so, Tommy. One of us is a traitor. I can feel it in my bones."

"If it's in your bones, maybe it's you," Ted stated.

02:51

"Before you pull that trigger, you better be certain Packard's right," Mikey said.

"Oh, I'm certain all right. I'm certain of one thing," Kurt replied.

"Which is?" Daisy asked.

"It's not him," Kurt said, firing a particle beam into Packard's forehead.

03:33

Packard slumped backwards, the body vanishing in a bright flash before the back of his skull had even hit the deck.

"That's one way to eliminate the competition," Ted remarked. "And the door is still shut."

"Sorry, dude," Kurt said, firing a beam in Ted's chest.

Ted crumpled to the floor. He glanced up, heartbroken that his best friend had shot him, before he vanished in an identical flash of light.

04:11

"What the hell are you doing?" Daisy barked, snatching the phaser from Kurt before he could turn it on anybody else.

"No way is it Ted," Kurt said imperiously. "He's been a pain in the ass since birth. He's no traitor. No way."

"Which is something a traitor would say," Mikey added.

"The door is still shut, guys," Tommy stated.

"Meaning it wasn't Ted or Packard," Daisy added, turning the phaser on Kurt.

04:47

"Go ahead, Daisy. Take your best shot. I've got nothing to hide," Kurt said.

"Daisy, wait." Tommy blocked her path to Kurt.

"Why? We have four shots left. Four of us. And time is running out. You do the math."

Without pausing, Daisy pushed Tommy aside and fired a shot at Kurt. By the time he realized he'd been shot, his body had vanished.

05:35

"What the hell, sis," Mikey said.

"He lost the plot. He was going nuts. Shooting everybody and stuff," Daisy replied.

"And you did what, shake hands?"

"I eliminated the competition."

Daisy blasted Mikey in the chest. His body vanished, the doorway remaining sealed.

05:59

"You just shot your brother," Tommy said, backing away.

"I know. And the doorway is still shut."

"I can't believe it's one of us."

"Believe it, Tommy."

Daisy flipped a glance at the shot counter. Two live beams remained.

Tommy flashed a look at the digital clock. "We have less than a minute."

06:13

"There is only one way we're getting out of here," Daisy said.

"I'm not shooting you," Tommy replied.

"I'm not asking you to."

Daisy turned the phaser on herself, Tommy snatched it away before she could fire.

"We're not going out this way," he said.

06:29

"Tommy, we have thirty seconds left. Shoot me."

"I won't."

"Pull the trigger now, or everything we've fought for will be for nothing."

Tommy raised the phaser and hesitated. He couldn't let himself believe Daisy was a traitor. At the same time, he couldn't be sure that he wasn't one either. Once before Mr. Nobody had tricked him into signing a deal. Was that deal still in place?

Had he been tricked again?

Was he certain his own actions were not being manipulated?

Had Daisy been honest from the start?

Was she the same girl he fell in love with?

He glanced at the timer.

06:43

"Remember when I said I gave my life to save yours. I meant it. Now end this, once and for all," Daisy ordered.

"I can't," he replied, his hand wavering as he aimed the phaser ahead.

"Just do it," she shot a look at the clock. "Shoot me! End this!"

06:58

Tommy was about to lose his entire world in the blink of an eye.

The weight of the decision twisted his gut in knots.

He backed away, with the phaser pressed firmly against his temple.

06:65

"Tommy. Wait. It's …"

"I love you, Daisy Drew," he said, pulling the trigger.

EPILOGUE

Day of the Dead

TOMMY WEST awoke with what he felt like chronic whiplash all over his body. Unable to move, due to the restraints around his ankles and wrists, he felt suffocated, and instantly panicked.

He had no visual sensations, fueling his claustrophobia. The more he struggled, the more his cranium throbbed, his temples pulsating as if on fire from a prolonged neurological procedure.

A muffled sound went off. It sounded like an alarm, but he was unable to hear it clearly due to the headset he was wearing. He barely had time to contemplate his surroundings before the headset's visor lifted, the vapor around him gradually retracting to reveal he was in a coffin and locked behind a glass window.

The window slotted in an alcove to his left allowed him to breath normally. At the same time, the coffin rose vertically.

The ankle and wrist restraints released next, allowing him to push his body from the cushioned stasis pod, and he stepped awkwardly onto the floor. To avoid falling, he held on to the pod, his eyes adjusting to what appeared to be a room, pristine and uncomfortably white.

The more his eyes returned to normality, the more he feared he had reached heaven's waiting room with its white walls and floor, and an unblemished ceiling with customary air vents. A solitary, spiky plant in a flowerpot was the only diversion from the white love affair.

On the side of his stasis pod, a screen blinked on and off with what looked like the Trans Am reality jump circuits. One glance at the details sent a wave of dread through Tommy's gut.

MONTH - DAY YEAR HOUR - MIN
6 - 6 6 - 6 6 - 6
DESTINATION

He slammed his palm against the screen to clear the numbers.

MONTH - DAY YEAR HOUR - MIN
9 - 9 9 - 9 9 - 9
DESTINATION

One more strike seemed to return it to the correct date and time.

MONTH - DAY	**YEAR**	**HOUR - MIN**
***DEC* 27**	**1999**	**21:47**

DESTINATION

The wave of uncertainty gave way to a memory of a date, a time when the world's population believed the end of the millennium would bring the imminent arrival of doomsday.

"The end of days," he muttered, not believing it for a second.

Preferring to waste no more time, he tiptoed cautiously to the doorway and tried to come to terms with learning to walk again on a cold, tiled floor.

The immaculate, carpeted corridor outside came with just one exit, leading to a foyer, where the décor's colorless romance continued.

Fronted by windows, the foyer's vacant reception desk, chairs and computers had gathered enough dust to make him realize that the area had been untouched for a long time.

Tommy was more preoccupied with exiting the building, by using the revolving door, than the T.O.B.I.A.S logo printed on the wall leading to a first-floor mezzanine overlooking reception.

Night-time was a welcome distraction from the blandness of the building he just exited. At first glance he appeared to be in an empty city street, full of tall Wall Street type buildings. There were no people, no traffic, no noise. Just an extravagance of Christmas decorations lining a lengthy avenue leading to what could've easily been the Washington Monument.

He recognized nothing and yet couldn't shake the feeling that he'd seen it all before.

When a line of black SUVs headed his way from the direction of the monument his heart skipped a beat. The convoy stopped about thirty feet away, blocking the end of the street in a roadblock maneuver. There was something written on the side of each vehicle.

T.O.B.I.A.S

MANKIND'S LAST STAND BEFORE EXTINCTION

"You're right, Ted. Dude gets everywhere," Tommy muttered.

A line of typically dressed secret service looking agents exited each vehicle, all of them wearing sunglasses and armed with firearms. After blindfolding Tommy, they escorted him to the middle vehicle.

"Where are you taking me?" Tommy asked as he was manhandled.

"To safety," the nearest agent replied.

"Safety from what?"

Tommy was ducked beneath the door frame and shunted across the rear passenger seat.

As if answering his question, pressure could be felt building beneath the pavement. As the world around them started to tremble with fear, manhole covers lining the street rattled in their slots.

The pressure grew more intense, reaching a deafening crescendo that fired shrapnel from the manhole covers across the city. Detonations shelled out debris and dust clouds.

The SUVs took off as a swarm of winged demons escaped from the manholes, each one more terrifying in appearance than the one before it.

Tommy pushed up his blindfold and looked skywards after overhearing a message coming from a fleet of blimps overhead.

'A thousand years has ended.
The Dark Angel is loose from his prison.
You have reached your End of Days.
Prepare to meet H.I.M ...'

Tommy held his head in hands. "Did I just hear that right? Now there's a dark angel. When will this nightmare end?"

"The end. There is just one end," a man said in the next seat. "No more games. No more nightmares. This is the real world. This *is* the end of days."

Tommy glanced to the man sitting to his right. "Who the hell are you?"

"I'm your guardian angel."

"Since when?"

"Since you started working for Tobias. Welcome home, Tommy."

TO BE DA CONCLUDED ...

ABOUT THE AUTHOR

We would love to say Paul is a Hollywood actor, but where's the fun in that? This Paul Rudd is a self-proclaimed geek, in every sense of the word. Without even realizing, Paul's passion for writing started when he first watched Jaws at an age far too young to print, so writing about this awesome specimen seemed an obvious route for him to start the ball rolling.

From Megalodons, to Wild West zombies, to supernatural warfare, back to Megalodons, to a tribute to his friends in the short story – Satan's Band – followed by an Apocalyptic battle for survival in London, and the mysterious Ningen species, Paul has covered many genres but never had he travelled back to his youth, in the 1980's, when every day was an adventure. That changed when he wrote Bootleggers, a mammoth read, which took him back to his childhood.

Paul also shares responsibility of his own publishing house – Ravenous Roadkill – with his good friend Reggie Jones, who also has some wonderful books to his name, as well as being co-authors of The Chronicles of Supernatural Warfare – Part One.

Most of Paul's books can also be found in audio format, check them out on Audible.co.uk and Audible.com. OR check out Facebook and Twitter for Paul's latest news…

Facebook - https://www.facebook.com/theauthorpaulrudd
Twitter - https://twitter.com/Sharcwriter

Other Books by Paul Rudd

PAUL RUDD
SHARC
BOOK 1
PAUL RUDD
SHARC
BAIT
BOOK 2

SHARK
SPAWN
PAUL RUDD
PAUL
RUDD
NINGEN

PAUL
RUDD
BOOTLEGGERS
BOOTLEGGERS
SAYS
TOMMY WEST KURT CONNORS MIKEY DREW THEODORE LOGAN

Printed in Great Britain
by Amazon

38075091R00264